The Disenchantment

—

The Disenchantment

Celia Bell

—

First published in Great Britain in 2023 by
SERPENT'S TAIL
an imprint of Profile Books Ltd
29 Cloth Fair
London EC1A 7JQ
www.serpentstail.com

1 3 5 7 9 10 8 6 4 2

Typeset in Tramuntana Text by MacGuru Ltd
Designed by Nicky Barneby @ Barneby Ltd

Printed and bound in Great Britain by Clays Ltd, Elcograf S.p.A.

A CIP catalogue record for this book is available from the British Library.

ISBN 978 1 78816 992 9
eISBN 978 1 78283 957 6

To V. & W.
without whom this book might not have been written

Pour la propriété des moeurs, le poète doit considerer qu'il ne faut jamais introduire sans nécessité absolut, ni un fille vaillante, ni une femme savant, ni un valet judicieux. Car encore ces parties se recontrent quelquefois en ce sexe et dans ce métier, il est néanmoins veritable qu'il y a peu de Sapphos, encore aussi peu d'Amazons.

Jules de La Mesnardière, *La Poétique*, 1640

I

—

The Stone Bride

Chapter One

———

It was the first sitting. The portrait was conventional, and yet Alain Lavoie was nervous as, with his brush and palette, he attempted to turn the chaos of life into ordered forms of light and shadow. Hôtel Cardonnoy was a grand house, and it bristled with servants – a Swiss guard at the main gate, two lackeys in gold braid standing watch outside the door of the room in which Lavoie now worked. When he had arrived he'd half expected the guard to see his shabby rented carriage and turn him back at the gate. Now the baronne's lady's maid kept watch on a stool with a copy of *Le Mercure galant* open on her lap. She mouthed the words as she read, sounding them out silently. Some noblewomen had their girls read aloud while he painted, to make the time pass more quickly. Marie Catherine la Jumelle, Baronne de Cardonnoy, was not one of these. She stood silent and straight as a sword in the centre of the room, looking into the light with an expression of sweet contemplation – the face of a woman, Lavoie thought, who was imagining her own beauty from the outside.

For himself, Lavoie was attempting not to show how the wealth of the room discomforted him. It always happened like that at the beginning of a new sitting – he'd spend an hour worrying over whether his subjects would notice the worn collar on his silk coat, before his work had the opportunity to speak for itself. It was difficult to feel self-assured in a room with so much gilding on the furniture, even though Lavoie had painted the baron himself six months ago.

The baronne's right hand rested lightly on her young son's shoulder. Her daughter stood at her left side. The children were perhaps six and nine, and both had reached the point of the sitting where they had begun to fidget. Lavoie disliked painting children. They didn't know how to stand still, and the children of the rich were often little monsters, raised permissively by servants and then summoned to pose for hours with parents who were unpredictable strangers.

Only the baronne, her children and the fresh beam of light they stood in appeared on the canvas. Behind them he had outlined the shadow of a heavy column, and beyond that, the first strokes of manicured woodland, as if Madame de Cardonnoy and her children stood in a Roman ruin growing back into the gentlest kind of wildness, with no breeze to stir the confection of lace flounces on Madame's full skirt or mud to dirty the children's shoes. Lavoie could see the scene in his mind, superimposed on the room, although the canvas showed only a few bare lines over the blue field of *imprimatura*. The scent of Madame de Cardonnoy's perfume, which floated through the room and mingled with the sharp smell of his paints, might have been blowing off the imaginary arbour.

He would soften the light around her face and draw it through the expertly arranged fawn-coloured curls on her head, returning to her some of the glow that she would have had as a young girl. Now, in her early thirties, she was still lovely, in a slightly creased, pensive way that Lavoie would have liked to paint. But the baron would be happier if Lavoie made her look like a teenaged shepherdess. She might even appreciate that too, if she was sensible to flattery.

He had blocked in Madame de Cardonnoy's face, the shell-shape of her hand resting on the boy's shoulder. The blue *imprimatura* reflected through the layer of colour like the glimpse of a vein showing through skin. The boy, a blond child with a bit of a rat face, was twisting back and forth, wringing his mouth into stretched-out shapes like wet washing. The girl, older and more able to keep still, shot a look at her brother that was half condescension and half envy. She was dressed like a fashion doll, in imitation of her mother, the green ribbons on her cream skirt clearly chosen to match the grass-coloured silk of her mother's gown. One of her hands kept

4

digging surreptitiously behind her in her skirt, where something must have itched. She never put the hand back in the same place, once she was done scratching – sometimes she folded her arms neatly in front of her, and sometimes she made a fist in the fabric of her dress. Lavoie decided that he would paint the arm tucked demurely behind her back.

The part of his mind that wasn't occupied with the canvas was doing sums in his head, comparing the cost of the little girl's dress to that of his own silk jacket, which he wore only on professional visits and spent his Sundays washing the paint stains out of. Did the Cardonnoy girl have six dresses like the one she was wearing, or had this one been ordered specially for the painting? Surely her mother, who came from a bourgeois family and had married a baron, must have come with an enormous dowry. Beauty didn't mean much for that kind of marriage. Lavoie had heard that it was her financier father's money that had purchased this hôtel.

The boy was now rocking from his toes to his heels, bending at the waist as if he was being pulled back and forth on a string.

'Please, if you could keep him still, Madame,' Lavoie murmured.

'Nicolas, hush. Stand straight.'

Lavoie had expected her to pinch the child's ear to enforce the command. The most unruly and spoilt children, he found, often lived in fear of their mother. A nursemaid would allow them to gallop around the nursery and break their toys, but the lady of the house still expected them to be polite and presentable before her friends. '*Look how gallant he is,*' they might say of a little boy. '*Come now, darling, bow and kiss the comtesse's hand!*' And if the child didn't behave, he'd be slapped, to teach him manners. It wasn't that Lavoie had never been slapped during the years of his apprentice-ship, but the way these fine ladies lost their polished mannerisms the instant a child disobeyed unsettled him.

So it surprised him when she smiled at her son and patted his hair with her hand. No part of her, except her hand and the wrist attached to it, moved – it was like watching a puppet's hand, pulled smoothly through the air on a string.

'If you like,' she said, 'I'll tell you a story to make the time pass faster. But you must stand perfectly still.'

The boy sighed at this, and the girl straightened up and folded her hands neatly in front of her, her face turning eagerly back towards her mother.

'Can we have the one about the girl under the peapod, Maman?' she asked, and the corner of Madame de Cardonnoy's mouth turned up. Her expression had been so poised that Lavoie had not realised that her polished smile did not reach her eyes. Now it did, and he saw the difference.

'Don't forget to look at Monsieur Lavoie, Sophie,' the baronne said. 'The story I'm going to tell you is one that you haven't heard before, but my mother told it to me.'

'Are there ogres in it?' the boy asked.

'Of course there are.' Madame de Cardonnoy raised her eyes to Lavoie and gave him another of those secret smiles. 'That is, if you don't mind listening to a children's story, Monsieur Lavoie.'

'Of course not,' he said. He returned the baronne's smile only belatedly, and with a feeling approaching dread. Occasionally he painted some wrinkled Parisian lady with grandchildren who expected him to entertain her by flirting. The baronne was not in that category. If he offended her, her servants would throw him out onto the street and he'd lose his commission.

'Good.' Madame de Cardonnoy's hand moved, just slightly, caressing her son's shoulder. The boy held himself quietly. The lady's maid was fidgeting with the pages of her book. Lavoie dabbed his brush in shadow and began sketching in the features of the son's expectant face while he was, for the moment, holding still.

'Once, in a place far from Paris,' she began, 'there was a travelling man, who, having wandered far and wide, came to a village that stood in the shadow of a great, dark wood. He had nothing more than the clothes on his back and a bag of tools, and he was tired and hungry.'

She held herself almost supernaturally still as she spoke. At the beginning of the sitting, Lavoie had assumed that her composure was the result of dullness or lethargy, but now she seemed to be animated by some emotion that she kept in check only through great self-control. Even her expression barely changed, and when she paused for emphasis, only her eyes moved, gliding from the point on the far wall where they'd been fixed to Lavoie himself, as if silently appraising him. The effect was of a woman trapped inside

6

a sculpture, only her living eyes betraying that she was about to step down from her pedestal.

'But when he walked into the town square,' Madame de Cardonnoy went on, 'he found that the people drew back from him and barred their doors. There were no young women in the streets and no young men, but only sad and fearful old people, hurrying from doorstep to doorstep as if they feared to let the sun touch them. Finally the travelling man caught an old woman by the arm and asked her what made the village people so unfriendly to a stranger, and she told him that the village was under the rule of an ogre who lived deep in the wood.'

If he had been painting the portrait according to his own designs, and not according to custom, Lavoie would have liked to show the way the boy's head tilted upwards to watch his mother speak, his mouth hanging slightly open, as if he could look through her face and into the scene that she was describing. Instead, he outlined his face half from memory, looking straight out from the canvas.

'When the moon was new,' Marie Catherine continued, 'the ogre would ride out of the forest on a horse whose hooves struck fire from the earth, and when he came to the village he would demand a young woman for his bride. These wives never lived long, for the ogre's thirst for blood was such that on his very wedding night he would devour them, and soon after he would ride out again, to take another bride by force. Now there were few girls left in the village, and the remaining villagers kept their daughters under lock and key. The old woman could only advise that the travelling man continue on and seek his fortune somewhere else.'

Nicolas was leaning back against his mother's legs now. She put her hand on the back of his head and gently turned his face until he was once more watching Lavoie. Her daughter had remained surprisingly still since the story's beginning. Even the murdered wives didn't seem to frighten her.

'But,' Madame de Cardonnoy said, 'the travelling man refused to go. "Perhaps I can help more than you know," he said, and then he asked the woman for a large block of white stone and some water to drink, and when she brought him these things, in some bemusement, he took a chisel from his belt and began to chip away at the stone, humming all the while. For seven days he stood thus in the town square, and the townspeople peered at him fearfully from their windows, and some brought him bread and meat to eat when he was famished. And at the end of seven days, what had emerged from the block of stone was a statue of a woman so life-like that it seemed the breeze was blowing the finest hairs away from her cheek, and her eyes of white stone were overflowing with real tears.'

The earlier impression that Lavoie had had of Madame de Card-onnoy as a speaking statue had been so distinct that for a moment he felt as if she had been looking into his thoughts. He left the boy's face with his brush and tried to get an impression of her eyes, the way the sun fell over her forehead and pulled a veil of light over her hair.

'The sculptor – I think we shall call him that, instead of the trav-elling man – held out his hand, and the stone statue took it and let him help her down off the pedestal. For although she was stone, she lived.'

Lavoie raised an eyebrow at her. It was the first slip in his painstakingly correct manners, and Madame de Cardonnoy had to suppress a laugh. He was still a young man, perhaps not quite thirty, and it was clear that he found the portrait a little boring. She thought it had only just occurred to him that she might have chosen the subject of the tale to flatter him, as well as to entertain the children.

'"Look," said the sculptor to the villagers. "I have made you a woman to give to the ogre. Send her to him and he will be satis-fied, for she is made of cold stone and cannot be harmed by his appetites."'

A shiver passed through the children. Nicolas, hungry as he was for stories about ogres and dragons, was easily frightened.

'The villagers were afraid,' she said, 'for none of them had ever seen such magic, but for the first time they felt some hope in the face of their fate, and so they dressed the stone woman in a gown of red silk – the best that any of them had, the best their daughters had left behind – and they combed and plaited her white stone hair, and put slippers on her feet, and then the oldest of the men took her by the hand and led her to the forest's edge, where he thanked her and left her in the shadow of the trees.'

Now she had reached the part of the story that she hadn't yet invented. She watched the painter, whose gaze was focused carefully on his canvas, and she went on.

'The stone woman had been silent as they dressed her, and she was silent still. For a moment she hesitated beneath the trees, but she knew the purpose for which she had been made, and so she gathered her skirts up in one hand and took the first steps into the forest. The woods were dark, although it was bright day outside, and silent, as if even the birds of the wood feared to nest in the shadow of the ogre's house.'

She paused for a moment to catch her breath and collect her thoughts.

'But what happened next?' asked Nicolas.

Sophie shifted restlessly against her other side. Madame de Cardonnoy could feel her own back beginning to ache with the effort of maintaining her posture, but it was no worse than dancing at a ball or attending the court. One of her stays poked into the soft skin under her arm.

'She walked among the trees,' Madame de Cardonnoy said, 'until she came upon a path through the forest that had been carved by some creature's enormous footsteps, and on the path were the bones and the rusted sword of a man who must also have tried, in his own way, to end the ogre's reign.'

Nicolas swayed on his feet and sucked in his breath. Sophie, older and more sure that stories, as a rule, ended happily, let out a little sigh that rocked her shoulders up and down. Madame de Cardonnoy found herself glancing conspiratorially at the painter, whose lips were pressed together in concentration. He blushed when he looked up from his work and saw her watching him back, as he'd been watching her. She smiled.

'Was she afraid then?' he asked. He'd lost his tone of professional solicitousness.

It was funny how quickly inclination could move her towards someone. Monsieur Lavoie had seemed unremarkable when he arrived, with his easel and paintbox under his arm, but his obvious curiosity for the end of the tale charmed her and made the sharp lines of his face more appealing. There was something birdlike about the way his hands flew and pecked at the canvas.

'No,' said Madame de Cardonnoy. 'She wasn't afraid. For her heart, too, was made of stone, so that both fear and pity were beyond her.'

'I think many would call that a dangerous gift for a woman,' said Lavoie.

'The stone bride followed the path deep into the woods. She had walked for some time when she came to a gate, on which a gnarled face guarded the keyhole. Beyond the gate was a garden and a great house, but although the leaves of the trees shone silver, and the gate was made of the purest gold, all of this beauty was spoiled, because the fountains and the meandering streams of the garden flowed with red blood instead of water, and the roses bloomed black under its influence and gave shelter to only bats and wasps, where there should have been songbirds and hard-working honeybees.'

Outside, a fast-moving cloud was passing over the sun, or else she had lost track of the time, despite her sore feet and the ache starting in her back. The children were fidgeting again, and Sophie's shoulders slumped dejectedly. At nine, she was old enough to wear stays, like her mother, but she hadn't yet learned to ignore her discomfort. Madame de Cardonnoy could hear the fussy huffs of her breath as she leaned against her mother's side for support.

The room was growing dim. Madame de Cardonnoy took a breath.

'At that moment the stone woman heard footsteps behind her, so heavy that they shook the earth, and a shadow fell over the gate. Slowly she turned and, dropping into her lowest curtsey, she murmured, "Good evening, husband." For the ogre had come home for the evening.'

She let go of Nicolas's shoulder. Stepping forward, out of the tableau, was like crossing an invisible threshold. She noticed for the first time that there was a trickle of cold sweat running down her back, as if she had lived the story and not just told it.

'And there, I think, we should stop. Monsieur Lavoie, I'm certain you're losing your light.'

'A little, Madame,' he admitted. He was already packing his brushes into their box. The children slouched like dolls where she'd left them. Nicolas whined softly that he wanted to hear what the ogre looked like.

'Will you finish the story tonight, Maman?' Sophie asked.

'Of course, darling.' Madame de Cardonnoy turned to her lady's maid. 'Will you take them up to the nursery, Jeanne?'

The light in the room now was dim and golden, and the smell of the paints seemed to have intensified. Sharp, like freshly mown hay, and even, Madame de Cardonnoy thought for a moment, the rank smell of the sizing in the canvas. Jeanne herded the children away.

'I hope you weren't too bored by the story, Monsieur Lavoie. You know one must find some way of keeping the children quiet.'

'Of course not, Madame,' said Lavoie, wiping his hands down with a cloth and turpentine. 'I was fascinated. You're lucky to have such an inheritance of stories from your mother.'

Madame de Cardonnoy smiled and gently shook her head.

'On the contrary, I'm afraid. My mother wasn't the type to tell stories. I make them up myself.'

'Is that a secret, Madame? You gave your mother the credit when you began.' The painter had stored his paints away neatly in his box. The easel he moved near to the wall, where it would stand, to avoid smudging the paint as it dried. The canvas showed a series of blurry forms coming into being – the green shadows of Madame de Cardonnoy's dress, ribbons and lace just a vague suggestion of shadow. Her face he had worked more completely, and she saw herself younger, pink and pale, as if she was looking into a smudged mirror. He'd painted her with her lips a little parted, as if in the moment before she was about to speak.

'They're just children's stories,' Madame de Cardonnoy said. 'Mother Goose tales. There's nothing to take credit for.'

Lavoie bowed.

'Still, I'd like to hear the end of that one, some day.'

There was a wistful tone in his voice. Madame de Cardonnoy held out her hand.

'Perhaps at the next sitting,' she said, and then she called the Swiss guard to see the painter out.

A carriage had overturned near the Church of Saint-Sulpice. Lavoie, walking on foot from Hôtel Cardonnoy in the brisk wind, heard the squeals of the horses first, and then the sound of a woman cursing, calling, *Foutu, jaufort, fils de putain*. The overturned carriage, a rented fiacre, had collided with some nobleman's gilded coach, and now the poor scabby horses lay tangled in their traces, crying as they tried to free themselves and regain their feet. The woman who was cursing like a fishwife was still trapped inside the fiacre and was trying to prise the door wide enough that she could crawl out through the half-frozen mud. She flopped out into the street like an eel, her curls in disarray. Half the street had stopped to watch, and the others skated uneasily around the gathering crowd, on their way to some other business. Lavoie stopped too.

One would have thought the woman was a countess if it hadn't been for the cheap rented carriage and the way she cursed. Could one render it in paint, he wondered, the way her doll-like exterior creased and revealed the history of the woman beneath it: the bourgeois wife, or the shopkeeper dressed above her station, or the whore? The second, gilded carriage had a cracked wheel and a doughy face pressed against its glass window, watching the scene intently. The gold-braided coachman jumped down from his post and walked to where the driver of the fiacre was trading insults with the woman who had been his passenger as he tried to untangle his horses. The fiacre's driver was pulling one struggling horse by its hoof and trying to dodge the flailing morass of the other legs long enough to unbuckle the harness. He didn't see the other coachman's whip until the uniformed lackey had already raised his arm over his head, and then the woman who'd been his passenger screamed at him to watch his back, and he half turned, sneering, and the whip caught him across the shoulder and chin and knocked him back into the horses' legs.

The servant didn't seem to care whether he hit man or horses. They were churning together in a froth of mud, and then the fiacre's driver found his hands and knees and crawled ratlike out of the nest of hooves, the blows of the whip still raining down on his head and the hands that protected his face. The lackey's face was twisted with rage, as if he imagined he could avenge every insult he had ever received on the body of this coachman, if he could only beat him until he was one with the dirt.

Lavoie had the strange feeling that he had turned into nothing more than a giant eyeball. It happened sometimes when he was painting, this feeling of a being a screen onto which the world was projected, in all its terrible colours. He could not move, although he saw the blood on the coachman's face and the way the crowd was murmuring – those who stood on the fringes dispersing and hurrying away, while the rest tightened in a knot around the carriages, blocking the road and knotting their hands into fists, the smell of horse shit and blood hanging over the street like an evil fog. The churned mud itself looked like a palette slick with badly mixed paint.

The woman passenger was now cursing both coachman and lackey interchangeably, and finally she darted between them and shoved the lackey, who spun with a snarl and snapped the whip at her face. She flinched, but then in the instant after the flinch she had stepped still closer to him, so near that he could have reached out with his gloved hand and slapped her.

'You're brave, aren't you? Hit me then!' she cried, so angrily that Lavoie could see the teeth shining wetly in her mouth. She gestured at the gathering crowd. Other carriages had stopped now, their coachmen jumping down to see what commotion was blocking the road. 'Fils de putain, do you think that no one here will come help me?'

'That's enough.' The door of the gilded carriage had cracked open, and from it came a man's voice and one extended hand. The passenger waved to his servant, and the lackey slumped, as if a string that suspended him had been cut, and slouched back towards the carriage. His gold braid was spattered with mud, like the rest of the road. Lavoie turned and walked away before the servant reached his master.

But the scene stayed with him, superimposed on the road as he walked, displacing the hanging signs, the women selling vegetables from window stalls, all the noise and movement of the city. He was sweating, even in the half chill of the February thaw. He saw the nobleman's hand extended languorously from his coach, beckoning, and somehow the image recalled another – the marriage of the ogre, as Madame de Cardonnoy had told it, the brides abducted in the night and the woman made of stone, with her cold heart and hands. It seemed like a darker tale, now, than when he had first heard it, not really a tale for children, and yet it fascinated him. As the baron's wife, Lavoie could admit, had fascinated him.

Didn't her story reveal something about her own marriage? Perhaps it seemed that way only because he wished to believe that she had told him a secret. Lavoie didn't know if it had been a slip in her self-control or just a game that she was playing with him. And he wasn't sure if the guilt that he felt came from his attraction – a woman above his station, the wife of a man who had hired him – or from the fact that he had stood by while the lackey beat the fiacre's driver and, until the woman turned to the crowd for help, it had never occurred to him to intervene.

There had been no reason for him to make it his business.

He could have hailed a rented carriage and taken it back to his home, but he instead he walked a long way, until the cold bit him through his coat and made him shiver. He wanted to forget the carriage driver and Madame de Cardonnoy and think instead of his work hanging in that fine hall, in the salons of Paris, in the palace at the Tuileries itself, lit by the glitter of a crystal chandelier. On the boulevard he passed one of the new shops that sold coffee and sweets, and he lingered outside the window in a cloud of the bittersweet smell. His ears stung from the cold.

The city would wash the image of the lackey and the whip from his eyes. A seamstress dressed in grey grisette was stitching ruffles onto a hem in a shop window, her dress of cheap cloth cut in a startlingly elegant silhouette, so that she was herself the advertisement for her skills. He bought a packet of hot chestnuts from a man on the street corner, more for the scent and to keep his hands warm than because he was hungry. When he looked upwards, the street signs formed a barricade against the winter sky, a jumble of giant-sized household paraphernalia suspended from the face of each building – boots and fish and loaves of bread, cart wheels and wigs and hands brandishing pistols. All clanking on their hinges when a breeze passed the rooftops. Paris, conglomeration of senseless objects, where the gutters flooded when it rained and carried diamonds and old fish alike in their current.

As the sun began to set, Lavoie was shivering and had thought better of his impulsive decision to walk, but he was nearly home, and the fiacre that he had tried to hail did not stop for him. He could feel the shape of the frozen cobbles through the soles of his boots.

When he arrived on his street, the signal bell that sounded the arrival of the lamplighter was ringing. The lanterns crawled down the walls on their pulleys and then rose up again, a candle burning steady inside each glass cage. Those men and women out on the street stopped to watch, and Lavoie stopped with them, while the busiest souls bustled past the waiting bodies in their hurry to get wherever they had to be. A young woman in a white bonnet leaned out of an upper window and watched the shadows cast by the rising flames stretch and recede below her. Her face was coloured warm and ruddy by the candlelight, and her bonnet was tinged with the deep blue of the sky overhead, in which there was, as yet, not a single cloud.

Madame de Cardonnoy had planned to meet Victoire at the Hôtel de Bourgogne after dinner. They had not met for a week, and nervousness and excitement dampened her appetite as she ate alone in her room before the play. The baron was away at Versailles. Jeanne had folded up the white cloth that held her toilette, so that she could dine off her table. She had specified nothing for dinner, and the cook had sent up a dish of stewed leeks flavoured with milk and lemon peel and a dish of baked sole. He often skimped when her husband was away, and she thought the bread had gone stale. She could feel the meeting with Victoire hanging over her, making her sick with anticipation.

In winter the sun set early. Jeanne helped her into her evening clothes – silk stockings with little Chinese figures hand-painted on them, and a blue silk mantua that swirled loosely around her body, clinging at the waist and gaping at the chest to show the barest hint of her shift. The sleeves billowed out at the arms and buttoned tightly at her wrists with gold buttons. She had Jeanne pin up her skirt, so that a flash of the painted stockings would show when she stepped out of the carriage, or when she climbed the stairs of the theatre. Finally she took a pinch of argentine and threw it up in the air, so that it fell in a glimmering snow over her hair and tinted her brown curls silver. Jeanne dusted the excess powder off her mantua with a handkerchief.

There was a delight in the clothes that she never stopped feeling. She judged herself a little for her vanity. Whatever Victoire loved in her, it wasn't the slenderness of her waist – not after years of child-bearing. Jeanne laced and buttoned her and pulled and tucked the fabric of her skirt so that it would fall in the most flattering way, and Marie Catherine caught a glimpse of her own face and neck in the mirror on the wall and felt as if she had never been so fully herself. The baron would have disapproved of the mantua, if she'd worn it to dine with him – of the loose, billowing fabric and the glimpse of white lace that peeked through the neckline. '*Is that what I paid your couturière so much money for?*' he'd say. '*You look like you're going to bed.*'

And his tone of voice would have suggested exactly what he meant by that.

His imaginary words rang in her head as Anne, the children's nursemaid, brought Sophie and Nicolas down to kiss her goodnight before bed. Marie Catherine pulled her skirt a little higher and spun, so that they could see the dancing figures on her stockings.

'It's like you're wearing a painting,' said Nicolas. There was something envious in his voice as Anne picked him up to carry him away to the nursery. 'I'd like to have ones like that when I'm old.'

She sent Jeanne out to call the carriage around and put on her cloak. She shouldn't have called the children down to see her off, when she was dressed for her lover. But she found she didn't care. The anticipation blunted the guilt, as if she'd drunk too much wine and the spirit was rushing through her, pulling her off her feet.

She had married the baron young. He had been her father's choice, but she hadn't rejected him, although he was twice her age, thirty to her fifteen. They had met in Madame de Fontet's salon, when she had been a gawky girl with big feet who stumbled over witty conversation and blushed when men looked at her. Of course she had been flattered when Monsieur de Cardonnoy paid her court. She remembered her deep embarrassment at her mother's accent, when she went calling on her arm. Marie Catherine's father had been a financier, who made his fortune from the salt tax and then purchased the title that would ensure his daughter's advancement, the convent education that made her speak as finely as any lady of the court and the dowry that would let her marry a man with an older, more noble name. Her father had planned and studied to live his life in the court – his manners were as polished as any other nobleman's. But her mother, despite her lovely hair and her eye for clothes, spoke like a shopkeeper, and wrote letters in a crabbed hand full of eccentric spellings. Marie Catherine had seen ladies laugh behind their hands when she spoke. Her father sometimes laughed to her face.

'You can dress a pig in silk,' he'd say, 'but you can't teach it to speak French.'

Her marriage to the Baron de Cardonnoy had seemed like triumph. Her father had wanted it ardently – more, almost, than any of the other honours to which he had risen. Marie Catherine was his only living child. The baron was older than she was, but he was not an old man, and he had been kind to her, at first. Was still kind, by some standards. Madame de Cardonnoy knew women who lived in their husbands' houses like prisoners of their servants, afraid to ask for even a glass of water.

Jeanne was waiting for her by the carriage, in a purple cast-off dress that had once belonged to Marie Catherine herself. The street lamps were lit for the evening. Marie Catherine settled into her seat and leaned into the glass window of the carriage, as close as she could without mussing the curls on her forehead, listening to the cries of coachmen fighting for the right of way, the rattle of the wheels on stone. Two girls in fine dresses stood on a street corner and attempted to negotiate with the greasy-looking driver of a public fiacre.

When she was a new bride, they had ridden to Versailles, when it was still only a hunting lodge and the construction of the palace was just beginning. They had danced in the gardens through the night alongside the rest of the court and lain down to sleep in the hay in all their finery and woken up dew-wet and danced again, as if they were under a spell. The king had styled the ball 'Les Plaisirs de l'Île Enchantée'. She had seen the king dancing with his mistress while the queen rested and drank the fennel-scented rossoly that the servants were passing around in glasses that fluted outwards like the shape of a woman's breast, and it had seemed that the whole world and all of those brightly dressed dancers spun around the royal body, the way the earth spins around the sun. She had danced with the baron, she had gone home smelling like hay and the sweat of strange women, the taste of brandy and coriander lying thick and sour on the back of her throat. Then for a brief few days the fear of the married life stretching out before her had warmed into something sweeter, and she had thought that she might step out of her mother's world through a window and live in that enchanted island for ever, if only she could bring herself to take her husband's hand and pull him close.

Marie Catherine had done her father's bidding. During their courtship she had found the baron gracious, gentle with her, reserved and formal in the way that a gentleman was expected to be when he admired a lady. After the wedding he seemed to have decided that he had won as much of her affection as he required. She no longer found him gentle on the night of their marriage, when he took off her gown and looked at her body. She was close enough to him, for the first time, to discover that he had a rotten tooth in the back of his mouth that made his breath smell foul. At Versailles she had thought she might find it within herself to love him, in spite of all this, but, in the end, she did not.

The smell of the river rose up and wrapped the coach in a heavy cloud of dampness and sewage as the carriage crossed the Pont Neuf. She spied a few bedraggled white swans bedding down for the night under the bridge, their feathers gleaming in the darkness. The king had imported them to beautify the city a few years before, but now their white feathers were grey with mud, and it was said that he hated to see them.

Jeanne pulled out a handkerchief and held it across her nose, shifting ostentatiously on the cushion next to Marie Catherine. She was a country girl, and seemed always to be trying to convey her experience of the world, and her comfort in her hand-me-down clothes, by the great delicacy of her manners.

The summer after Marie Catherine's marriage, the Baron de Cardonnoy had torn down his family's decrepit hôtel and purchased the new Hôtel Cardonnoy in Saint-Germain-des-Prés with the money from his young bride's dowry. While the house was under construction they had travelled by coach in June to the Cardonnoy estate, to set his family's affairs in order there and to plan for Marie Catherine's lying-in, for by the spring she was pregnant.

The baby was stillborn. It would take four years and three miscarriages before she conceived Sophie – who was, alas, a girl, when the baron needed a male heir. By then all the devotion she had tried to cultivate for her husband had faded. She would have paid a king's ransom out of the Cardonnoy coffers to never have had to sit across from him at dinner again. She slept in her own room at Hôtel Cardonnoy now, and she locked her door before she went to bed.

At twenty-two, pregnant again after Sophie with another child that she'd miscarry, she'd gone to her father and begged him to do something – anything – to free her, although she had known that the request would injure his sense of self more deeply than anything she had ever asked of him. To see her unhappy had always caused him pain. He had advised her to meekness and to prayer, to soften her husband's heart. Instead she had hardened her own. Perhaps she simply didn't love as some women did. She could not mend her defect. She was cold.

So Marie Catherine had quietly believed for years that she had been made with something lacking, and any spark of inclination that she might feel for a man in company was a short-lived thing that fizzled out after the first imaginary movement of love. Then she had met Victoire de Conti, had laughed with her in Madame de Fontet's salon and sat beside her in a coach, travelling through the city at night with only the hems of their skirts touching, and wondered what force had swept the veil off the city and pulled her heart into her mouth.

She didn't love as some women did.

When they reached the rue Mauconseil there was a crowd outside the theatre. The coachman jumped down from his seat, handed the reins to a man standing by and elbowed a way through the waiting patrons so that Madame de Cardonnoy and Jeanne could walk up the steps. It was freezing again. A few lacy flakes of snow drifted down over the crowd and melted on hats and gloves. A pair of itinerant coffee-sellers in white aprons had set up shop near the entrance, and the smell of their drink drifted over the crowd.

The Comédiens du Roi were performing a play they called *The Fortune-Teller, or The False Enchantments*. She had heard that the Lieutenant General of Police, Gabriel de la Reynie, had written part of it, and every night since the arrest of the Maréchal de Luxembourg and the flight of the Comtesse de Soissons there had been a crowd of hundreds outside the theatre, waiting in vain to get inside and steal a morsel of fact or fiction from the theatre's table. For both the maréchal, famous as he was on the battlefield, and the comtesse, although she had once been intimate with the king himself, were rumoured to have consorted with witches and dabbled in poison and black magic.

What people whispered was that some lords and ladies had been so anxious to lay hands on the money of their husbands and wives, sisters, brothers and even parents that they had resorted to poison to speed up the delivery of their inheritances. Rumour had it, also, that there were a great many men and women at the court who were biting their nails, waiting for the summons to appear before the Lieutenant General of Police at the Châtelet. Madame de Cardonnoy herself, though she had never frequented fortune-tellers, had gone to the same gatherings as the maréchal, where sometimes, as night fell and the lamps were lit, someone would usher in a magician who claimed to be able to divine a man's deepest wish by casting a little ball of wax in the fire. It was the kind of blasphemy that made ladies laugh and – she would have said, not so long ago – hurt no one.

Inside, the theatre was just as crowded. As Marie Catherine made her way to her box, greeting friends, leaning close to the Marquise de Courtanvaux, the Comtesse de Combois, she felt impatient. None of it mattered except Victoire, who might already be sitting in her box, expecting her. They were discussing the Princesse de Tingry, sister-in-law to the disgraced Maréchal de Luxembourg, who, they said, had been questioned so viciously about her brother-in-law's involvement in black magic that she had left her audience at the Chambre Ardente in tears. They said she'd been accused of incest.

Marie Catherine turned away. She knew the princesse, though not well, and she had heard this story already.

There was only one face that she wanted to see in the crowd.

She couldn't really feel sorrow for Mademoiselle de Tingry, not when she had Victoire's name on her tongue as she wandered through the bright gowns and brocade jackets. But her box, when she reached it, was empty. A heavy pendulum swung through her, from shoulders to pelvis. Maybe Victoire had been delayed at Versailles. She knew that her face was calm and showed nothing of her anger. A distant part of her was impressed by her own self-control.

The play was a limp curtain fluttering over the stage, the actors mincing through their jokes while the crowd shifted in their seats, laughing the laughter of the fearful, waiting for the play to explain the mystery of the sorcery, of the poisons that rumour placed in every cup. Which it could not do. Finally Marie Catherine put her head in her hands and let the weight of her hair bend her neck forward as if she were praying. When the curtain drew closed for the intermission, and still Victoire had not arrived, Marie Catherine felt fear drawing around her like a cold draught creeping under the curtain of her box. It was not like Victoire to leave her waiting with no explanation. She shouldn't be angry. Victoire's family was as noble as that of the Princesse de Tingry. But that might not protect her, not now.

After the intermission she sent Jeanne out to watch the hall from the door to her box. She would have left early, but she still hoped Victoire might appear. And if something had happened, wouldn't the gossip in the aisles have been about Victoire de Conti?

Two years ago they had met by chance at the Hôtel Bourgogne, on a night something like this. They had been the kind of acquaintances who might kiss each other on the cheek at Madame de Fontet's salon, but the younger girl would never have sat next to Marie Catherine long enough to really see her. And then Victoire had slipped into the Cardonnoy box during an intermission, laid the edge of her fan on Marie Catherine's neck, just beneath her jaw, and spoke in the voice of a highwayman. 'Excuse me, Madame, I'm fleeing a rude suitor. May I hide with you?' And, giggling, she'd crawled in her rose-coloured silk to Marie Catherine's knees, ducking her head as if she really were desperate to escape, the unfurling scent of her perfume betraying her hiding spot. Marie Catherine knew the girl who'd barged in on her was a cousin of the king, a Princess of the Blood, rich as Hades, with a wit that a man could cut himself on. The offhand way she broke the rules of etiquette was thrilling. She hadn't even brought her maid into the box behind her. For a moment Marie Catherine had almost climbed down on the floor with her. Instead she threw her skirt over the girl's head and kept a breathless lookout, in case the errant suitor barged in.

'Forgive me for not introducing myself,' the girl said, once they had waited long enough that each was sure the coast was clear. 'I'm Mademoiselle de Conti.'

'I know who you are.'

And later that night, drinking coffee very late at Victoire's hôtel, with her heart still beating in her temples from the sudden feeling of adventure, Marie Catherine asked, 'Do you know when we first met? It wasn't in Madame de Fontet's salon. I don't think you'll remember, it was so long ago. Do you remember, when the palace at Versailles was first being constructed, that party the king held there? The guests came and slept in the hay. I was fifteen. And I remember a little girl with black hair who'd begged her mother to let her come, and although she was much too young, she was wearing a ballgown made to measure and was dancing with the highest lords of the land. A Princess of the Blood. You were the star of the ball, Mademoiselle de Conti. Until you stole a glass of spirits and had to be put to bed, sick, in the hay.'

Victoire looked startled. Now that Marie Catherine knew her better, she'd learned how much she hated to appear ridiculous. But she recovered and said, with the same air of the bandit as when she'd barged into the opera box, 'Wouldn't you know, the brandy erased even my memory of you?'

And she had leaned so close in the candlelight that Marie Catherine had jumped to her feet in fright and gone to look out of the window into the darkness. So close that it had seemed she knew the secret that Marie Catherine could not have spoken, even to herself. She could not have explained why she felt as she did – not motherly, not like a friend or a sister, but as if she had set the sleeve of her dress alight and the fire was consuming her, but without pain.

That was the first night, almost two years ago now. Tonight she left the theatre alone, with little memory of the play. Victoire had sent no message to explain her absence, and Marie Catherine's fear was freezing back into anger.

You told me you would come and you did not come, she wrote by candlelight, much later, when she was dressed in her nightgown and she could hear the sound of Jeanne's sleeping breath from the alcove off her bedroom. *What kept you?* She folded the letter and sealed it. Then she thought better of it, broke the seal, opened the letter and tore it into pieces.

The next morning she woke, groggy and half rested, to the sound of a carriage in the courtyard below. It was late morning – the light coming through her window was as yellow as lemon peel. Her room smelled of candle smoke and her own sweat. She turned over under her blankets and listened to the stable boys calling to each other as they unhitched the horses.

The baron had returned from Versailles.

Chapter Two

——

Imagine an ogre. So Madame de Cardonnoy thought to herself, sitting across from the baron at the dinner table. Surely he has long yellow fangs and warts over his eyes. Surely the grime under his fingernails stinks of blood. Surely he looms over the table, the enormous strength of his shoulders struggling to fit into the delicate gilded chair, his gut as broad as six men, each eye a soup tureen in which unknown fish might swim.

Smack, crunch – one bite and those teeth will swallow you up.

In fact her husband was an ordinary man as he sat across the table from her and served himself poached fish. His hair was beginning to go silver, his forehead was lined with the cares of his station. The fact that he had dripped a bit of butter sauce on the collar of his coat should not have moved her to rage.

Sometimes at the table she tried to imagine that the man across from her was only an ageing stranger, who had not yet disappointed her in any way. Sometimes she imagined that he was Victoire, in a dress with lace-trimmed sleeves. She could hold whole conversations that way with her imaginary dining companions, while she pretended to listen to the baron's complaints.

'And how was your stay at the court?' she asked him, her eyes fixed demurely on her plate. The first stalks of hothouse asparagus had just begun to appear in the kitchen at Hôtel Cardonnoy – or so the cook would have had her believe. Her husband, who paid the cook's wages, if only irregularly, was the one member of the household who he felt bound to impress. Marie Catherine and the children could have eaten cabbage and brown bread when the baron was away, and her husband would have commended the cook for his thriftiness. That the money that had paid the servants and purchased the house and saved the Cardonnoy estates outside Paris from falling into the hands of the previous baron's creditors had all come from Marie Catherine's inheritance did not entitle her to set the menu in her husband's home.

The baron chewed his fish and swallowed. 'The court thrives, other than the plague of poisoners that La Reynie is rooting out.'

Marie Catherine impaled a green spear on her fork and swirled it around in the smear of yellow sauce on her plate. She took tiny bites, from the spear-end down the stalk.

Poison was on her husband's mind recently, since the Maréchal de Luxembourg's arrest. Many of those accused had been a part of Marie Catherine's social circle, like the Princesse de Tingry, and she could see the way the baron's eyes narrowed as he watched her eat.

The thought turned Marie Catherine's stomach from her dinner. It was impossible to know exactly what evidence would be brought against the accused. People filled the gaps with rumour. That the fortune-tellers who supplied the poison had tested it on invalids, in the guise of distributing charity. That they made their potions using arsenic and the corpses of murdered infants. That they could treat a bouquet of flowers so that the recipient fell in hopeless love, or wash a shirt in poisoned water so that its wearer would break out in sores, then die.

'One wonders,' said the baron, 'how parliament will consider the cases when their own wives and daughters are on trial. Go lightly on one of these women and every lady in Paris will follow her example!'

'How terrible,' murmured Marie Catherine, cutting a piece of fowl into little bites with her fork. All that food laid out on the table – the bird, the fish, the soup, the asparagus. Marie Catherine had her suspicions of why, exactly, the cook might object so strongly to her requests about the menu. The rumours circulating in Paris might be enough to make one believe that every unhappy woman was merely one friendly kitchen servant away from poisoning her husband. She suspected that the baron feared what she might do, if left in charge of the household.

The court talked of poisons from Italy that could be sprinkled on a pair of gloves or painted onto the pages of a book, whose effect counterfeited every kind of natural illness, or left no trace at all. One woman named Madame de Poulaillon, it was said, had administered an ointment to her husband's body that had mimicked the effects of syphilis, and had reproached him for infidelity as she administered her deadly treatment.

Near the time of Madame de Poulaillon's arrest, the baron had been struck down with a fever that left in him bed for days, gasping and vomiting and fighting the doctor who came to treat him. Afterwards he had dismissed the cook, the children's previous nursemaid and the lackey who had been on the best terms with Madame de Cardonnoy, and had ordered the rest of the servants that his wife was not to pour her own wine from the decanter or go into his rooms unless he was present. He had never allowed her much control over the household, but now any influence she tried to exert roused him to suspicion. *Are you waiting for me to die?* he had asked her, the last time they had argued. *You'll be waiting a long time!*

'Surely,' Marie Catherine said now, 'some of these rumours of poison are founded on air.'

The baron grimaced.

'It's what happens when you give women control of the government,' he said. 'First their influence makes the court itself grow soft and feminine, and then – this.'

Marie Catherine nibbled a bite of fowl, found it cold, pushed her plate away. Her husband's valet looked up from where he stood at the door, murmuring with the lackey.

'I'm unwell,' she said. 'Remove this plate, please. And tell the cook the meal came cold.'

'Sit down,' said the baron, when she began to stand.

She sat. The lackey came and took her plate away.

'I don't like that dress,' her husband said. 'How much did you pay for it?'

'I'm sorry it doesn't please you.'

'Do you know how many expenses I have at court, while you fritter away your income on dresses and perfumes?'

'Very many, I'm sure.' The baron coveted a set of apartments in the new palace at Versailles, but was reduced to staying with a cousin during the time he spent there. The rooms were cramped and windowless and smelled like the contents of the chamberpot under the bed. Marie Catherine imagined him burrowed in there, festering.

'May I go?' She thought she knew the answer, but she smiled sweetly.

'No.'

The baron seemed content to sit in silence, contemplating her. She drank her wine in gulps, feeling the drink dry and bitter on her tongue. She tilted her head back for the last drop, her eyes on the ceiling draped with cobwebby shadows, pretending that she couldn't see the baron across from her at all.

'Pour me another glass,' she said, and held her hand out to the lackey.

'She's had enough,' the baron said. 'Take her cup away.'

There was never any point in arguing. She put her hands in her lap and stared down at them, as if what she felt was gratitude, or humility.

She went up to the nursery to see the children. The baron was still at the table, drinking wine and eating pastry. Perhaps if he was in a good mood he'd go out, and take his valet with him. If he was in an overly good mood, he might insist that she accompany him. Those nights were endurable as long as they stayed out, among the distractions of society, where she could talk with whoever she pleased. But when they returned home, the baron would want to follow her to her bedroom, or he would accuse her of flirting, ask her who among the company she had preferred to him, whether she knew that she should save her smiles for her husband.

It was true that she rarely smiled at him. She had once told him, during an argument, that he rarely gave her reason to.

The children were dressed in their nightclothes already and were eating from a selection of the same dishes that the cook had sent to their parents. Marie Catherine had entered the room in the middle of a stream of complaints from Nicolas about how much he hated asparagus, how it made his mouth feel slimy and smelled like urine. His nursemaid, Anne, was standing by his chair and resolutely eating the offending stalks off his plate, her back to the nursery door. She jumped when Marie Catherine entered her field of vision.

'Maman,' said Sophie, 'Nicolas won't stop talking about pee!' Her little nose was wrinkled up in indignation, and she had a shiny ring of grease around her mouth.

'Eat one stalk of asparagus, Nicolas,' said Madame de Cardonnoy. 'It's a delicacy. The cook's made it specially because your father's home. Sophie, use your napkin.'

'I won't eat it, it's disgusting,' said Nicolas, pitching his voice to a horsefly whine.

'I'm so sorry, Madame,' said Anne. The girl was hovering behind her and curtseying. When Marie Catherine turned to wave her away, she saw that Anne's face was rather red.

'Have they been behaving badly?'

'No, Madame, they're very good.'

It was impossible to get a straight answer out of Anne about anything. Marie Catherine suspected that her previous employer must have spent a great deal of time slapping the confidence out of her.

'You can have your dinner in the kitchen, if you like. I'll put them to bed.'

Anne nodded, then stayed in the room tidying the children's toys and shoes away and tucking in the corners on the rumpled beds. Sophie had a sheaf of papers by her elbow on which she appeared to have been practising her penmanship. When Marie Catherine lifted it out of the range of her daughter's dirty spoon and passed it to Anne, she saw that Sophie had copied the same lines over and over, with increasingly elaborate flourishes. Nicolas had a rank of tin soldiers lined up as if they were about to launch an attack on the shadowy cave under his bed frame.

The disorder was comforting. It made Marie Catherine forget that her husband was waiting downstairs and that Victoire had not written to her since the night of the play.

'You know,' she said to Nicolas, 'when I made a mess in my room and refused to eat my dinner as a little girl, my nursemaid used to threaten to take me to the night market and sell me to the witches there.'

Unlike the story about her mother's tales, this one was true. Her nursemaid had been a village girl named Manon, whose main way of getting the young Marie Catherine to bed early was to invent bizarre and elaborate stories about the things the market witches liked to do to young girls. It had never worked well. Marie Catherine would devour the stories and then beg Manon to sleep in the bed with her, to ward off nightmares. Often she'd wake up to find that Manon had left on some secret errand, and the bed was empty.

Nicolas eyed her warily. 'Would the witches eat you?'

'That depends,' said Marie Catherine. 'They turn some children into chickens or pigs, and put them in their soup. But the most wicked little children they raise to be witches themselves. They'll make you eat newts' eyes and drink warm blood for your dinner, and as you grow up you'll grow warts and learn to speak to the devil.'

'Ugh, eyes!' said Sophie, as if she'd been forced to eat thousands of them. Nicolas took two grudging bites of his asparagus and then stared at his plate with a look of deep betrayal. Anne bundled away the last of the dirty linen, then slipped out of the door with a curtsey.

'Will you finish the story from yesterday?' Sophie asked, sitting up straighter in her seat and dabbing at her mouth with her napkin.

Marie Catherine smiled. 'Tell me where I left off.'

'What does a newt look like?' asked Nicolas, who was still studying his own plate with distrust. Sometimes Marie Catherine found herself surprised by his questions. Had Sophie been so wary when she was six? She couldn't remember.

Sophie rolled her eyes at her brother. 'The stone lady had reached the ogre's palace.'

'Of course, thank you.'

She pulled up a chair at the children's table and sat in it, closing her eyes, picturing the stone bride facing her husband at dinner across a grisly table. The room she was imagining, she realised, was like a vaster, more shadowy reflection of the house at her father's summer estate. Even the dining table, enormous and richly carved as she pictured it, was like the table she had hidden under as a girl, playing hide-and-seek by herself while her nursemaid Manon sneaked off to the kitchen or to the town. A vast river of polished wood in which she could see the faintest impression of her own reflection. Her mother had never been there in those days, had been busy dressing and doing accounts and cultivating the women who laughed at her behind her back, and so many of Marie Catherine's memories of her childhood were of wandering through empty rooms and turning them into new worlds, making friends with the inanimate tables and chairs and vases, and with servants who mostly ignored her.

Now, she sometimes wondered if her mother had been equally lonely in those years. Marie Catherine was ashamed when she thought of how, even as a little girl, she had corrected her speech and taken her father's part whenever they quarrelled. She had thought that her mother cared for nothing but money and clothes, but perhaps she had simply looked at her child, destined for the convent school, and known that her daughter would grow up a stranger to her.

It was odd, the extent to which her father's house outside Paris lived on in her mind. However she described the castles that her princes and princesses wandered through, the many-jewelled mosaic floors and richly tapestried walls, always the hallways took the same long-ago twists and turns as that childhood summer house, and the passage leading to the princess's bedchamber was superimposed over the corridor outside her mother's room. It was as if there was only one house that survived in her mind, and all other castles were merely a reflection of it, and inside it she was still a child, wandering the same halls, seeing in every shadow the same ogres that she now summoned to life with the sound of her voice.

'Do you know what an ogre looks like, children?' she asked. 'He was as much bigger than a man as your father is taller than you, and his skin was as thick and rough as the hide of a rhinoceros in the Orient. He was naked to the waist, and in his shoulders and broad back were embedded the remnants of arrows and broken swords from his many battles, which he wore instead of armour, to show how indestructible he was. He sat astride his great horse, and this made him taller still. From the horse's mouth came clouds of fog, and its hooves struck sparks from the path.'

'What's a rhinoceros?' asked Nicolas.

'It's like a bear, but with big horns,' said Sophie. 'What did the stone woman do?'

'Wash your faces and get into bed,' said Marie Catherine, 'and I'll tell you.'

She helped Sophie with her dress, as if she were the girl's nurse-maid, and Nicolas with the buttons of his shirt. Sophie was old enough to comb and plait her own hair, and young enough for her face to show her pride in her own adultness.

'No sooner had the stone bride curtseyed than the ogre grasped her by the wrist and pulled her up on his horse in front of him. Now the stone bride was newly made, and knew nothing of the world besides what her creator had told her, but on seeing the ogre for the first time, her cold heart felt some disappointment. As he carried her through the gates to his palace, she wished, just for a moment, that she might leave and go back out into the sunlight.'

The door creaked.

'Anne?' said Marie Catherine, turning. 'If you would – oh.'

It was the baron, standing in the door of the nursery.

'Papa!' Nicolas jumped up and stood barefoot by his bed, but his shyness overcame him before he could go to his father.

'Bonsoir, Papa,' said Sophie. 'Did you have a long trip from Versailles?' It must have been the first time the baron had looked in on them, since his return.

'I see your mother's playing nursemaid tonight,' he said. 'A bedtime story?'

It was true that her husband's eyes sometimes softened when he looked at the faces of his children. He would not have been pleased if he had seen them quarrelling over dinner, but now he smiled and stepped into the room, and put his hand on Nicolas's head. When Nicolas looked up at him, one might have said that they had the same eyes. Marie Catherine held her breath. Sometimes she wished that she could sever the relationship between her husband and his children. He spent enough of his life away, after all. Let them be hers alone, and the baron only a stranger that Nicolas might address, faltering, as *Monsieur*.

'Have you ever seen an ogre?' asked Nicolas, and his tone of voice was an exact imitation of the way Marie Catherine herself had resumed her tale.

'What's this about ogres? Tell me.' He leaned down and ruffled Nicolas's hair.

'There's an ogre, and he eats his wives. And he's big like a rhinoceros.'

'You forgot the stone woman,' Sophie said primly. She was always a little cautious around her father, who might appear from Versailles with ribbons and stories of the ladies there, but who didn't tolerate her misbehaviour the way her mother or Anne might. It was Nicolas, his only son, who the baron loved best.

The baron straightened up, his expression dissolving into a scowl. 'I wish you would stop telling them this wet-nurse nonsense. They should be at prayers.'

'It's a fairy story.'

'I think we've had enough of those tonight. Children, your mother is needed downstairs.' He held his hand out, pointing at the door. Marie Catherine stood. 'To bed.'

'They need someone to see them to sleep.'

'Call the nursemaid,' said the baron. 'She's idle enough.'

'Do as your father says, children,' said Marie Catherine. 'To bed.'

Outside the room, she turned away from the baron and refused to catch his eye, although he put his hand on her shoulder and guided her down the stairs. She'd expected him to say more about the tale, but he didn't break the silence. She had been afraid that this might be a night when he would follow her into her bedroom, reproaching her with how often she refused her marital duty, but he left her at the door and continued downstairs, shouting for his valet to bring out the brandy. It was early yet for bed, but she bit her tongue and let Jeanne wrap her hair in taffeta, to prevent it from tangling while she slept.

She was near tears when she lay down. The children had been a refuge from the loneliest years of her marriage, and she found her husband's interference with them unbearable. She had suffered in begetting and bearing them, she had suffered through the bloody terror of the miscarriages. She had earned the right to tell them whatever stories she wanted.

They had put Sophie out to nurse as an infant, with a peasant woman near Cardonnoy. Lying in the birthing bed, Marie Catherine had heard Sophie cry and felt as though there was a glass pane between her and her daughter. The bloodletting that the doctor had advised to speed the labour had exhausted her, and the sound of her daughter's voice was a worm of pain burrowing back up into her pelvis and then receding away into unknown hallways. The servant who carried her daughter away had reached the wet nurse's house on the day after Sophie's baptism, and during all that time the only nourishment that had passed the baby's lips had been a little water on a twist of wet rag.

Perhaps she lacked motherly love – the child's absence had been easy at first. The milk in her breasts quickly dried up, and then the baron was back in her bed, trying to conceive a son. In the year and a half that Sophie stayed with the wet nurse at Cardonnoy, Marie Catherine lost another child, pre-term, whose jellied limbs did not prevent the doctor determining that this baby, too, was a girl. More than anything, she had feared the next pregnancy. It had taken her five years of miscarriages to bear Sophie. She was a wife who gave birth to dead girls, and it seemed that Sophie was no different, an infant who had dissolved into blood without ever being held by her mother.

When the wet nurse came to the house with her own boy on one hip and Sophie on the other, and passed her off into the arms of her father, Sophie had recoiled from his touch as if he had been a giant come to devour her. When the peasant woman curtseyed and took her leave, the girl reached after her and wailed, twisting her pink ribbon of mouth into a Medusa scream, until her eyelids were red and raw and her wispy tow hair was dark with sweat. She had struck Marie Catherine in the face with a tiny fist when her mother took her from the baron's arms, and when Marie Catherine had tried to pin her arms more firmly by her sides and keep her from flailing, she had squirmed and cried with redoubled force, so that Marie Catherine had looked into her swollen face and wondered what she could have done to create a creature that hated her so much.

She had heard other women speak of the bond a child had with its wet nurse, the sorrow it felt at parting from her. She had not imagined that she would be presented, after so many months, with this half-formed being to whom her touch was repugnant. The girl spoke in only fragments – *no* and *please* and *dark*. She called the wet nurse *Maman*.

33

That night Marie Catherine had gone to her daughter's room with a candle and stood in the doorway. The nursemaid was sleeping in the alcove. The child was face down on her bed with her face pressed flat into the linen sheets. She looked like a doll dropped in the mud. Marie Catherine had stayed there for some time before she realised that the child was not asleep. Slowly the girl had turned her head so that a single open eye glinted at Marie Catherine. Her first impulse had been to flee from that look, as she would have stepped back from the edge of a long fall into darkness. Instead she had stood, feeling skewered by the alienness of the child's glassy eye, trying to imagine the immense darkness of the room from her perspective, and how she, standing in the shadows, must look like the wicked fairy from a story. She crossed the room to the bed and put her hand on the girl's hot back, and the child snuffled and blew a bubble of snot into her pillow.

'I'm going to tell you a story to help you sleep,' Marie Catherine had said. 'It's one my mother told me. It's about a kind peasant woman who found a baby as small as her littlest finger lying under the shadow of a vine of peas in midsummer and brought her home to her cottage to raise as her own, not knowing where the little girl had come from. She didn't have any milk to give her, so she spoon-fed the child a little mash of brown bread and watered wine ...'

It was not the first story she had invented. She had told stories to keep herself company in the long afternoons when her nursemaid had left her alone in her parents' house and she wandered through the nursery too lonely to play with her dolls; and at night in bed at her convent school to frighten the other girls; and in salons surrounded by women who laughed and made suggestions. But it was, she felt, the most fragile story, a thread thrown across the chasm that separated her and the child, until the bridge was strong enough to walk on, and the strange, soft, angry creature that the woman from Cardonnoy had brought to her had turned into her daughter.

The painter's letter arrived with a messenger the next morning. Marie Catherine, uneasy at the sound of the baron's laughter downstairs, had woken up more than once in the night, hearing the early cocks crow in the courtyard. She slept in and, when she woke, the letter was on her dressing table:

Madame,

I hope you can forgive this intrusion on your time. Since I last came to paint your portrait, I find myself continually absorbed in your story of the stone woman. I expect that by the time you next sit for me, your children will know the end of their story and whether it resolves itself happily or not, but I remain in suspense to the first enchantment of the tale. I pray, if you have a moment to spare for such a frivolous concern, write to me and tell me how it ends.

Your faithful servant,

Alain Lavoie

At first she had thought the letter was from Victoire, and her heart had fallen when she broke the seal. But after a moment the letter gave her a cool satisfaction. She had her own admirers, whatever the girl was busy with.

Monsieur Lavoie,

May the enclosed papers satisfy your curiosity. I'm afraid it is only the part of the story you have already heard, and was revised somewhat hastily, so that I must ask you to forgive any errors in the writing. As to the adventure's final end, I must leave you in suspense. But wait until the next sitting, or pay me a visit at Hôtel Cardonnoy without your paints, and I will tell you everything that has happened to our stone bride.

Yours, et cetera,

Marie Catherine de Cardonnoy

In fact she had taken a little bit more care with the writing than her letter suggested. She recopied the first version she'd written, corrected the words that she always forgot how to spell, made sure her handwriting was neat. It was pleasant work. She hummed as she wrote. In the past days she'd paused in front of the unfinished portrait in the salon and felt, briefly, as if she was standing before a mirror that reflected her image back just a little brighter than she felt she was. The painter hadn't wanted to like her, she thought. But he had.

Victoire had still sent no message explaining her absence from the theatre two nights before. Marie Catherine told herself that if anything had happened to her, she would have heard. The baron would have brought news back from the court. Or some mutual friend would have called on her, hoping for gossip. But then, what kept her? While it hurt Marie Catherine's pride to write and ask where Victoire had been, she could feel her resolve wavering. And so when the stranger appeared in her courtyard, she took him at first for a messenger carrying news and her heart leaped in relief.

Marie Catherine had taken her time at her toilette after answering the painter's letter, sponging her face and neck with orange-blossom water from rue de l'Arbre Sec and then patting her nose with an iris-scented powder puff, painting her lips and cheeks with rouge, refreshing the silver dusting of argentine in her hair. She fussed with her face until she heard the baron's carriage pulling out of the courtyard, and then she relaxed on her stool as if a knotted thread inside her had been cut. He'd be gone at least until dinner, and quite probably later than that. Marie Catherine called Jeanne to help her put on her dress.

It was as Jeanne was doing up her laces that a commotion erupted in the courtyard – chickens squawked, the Swiss guard called out a greeting, and a horse whinnied hysterically over the calls of the stable boys. For a moment Marie Catherine thought that the baron had changed his mind and returned early, but there was no sound of carriage wheels. When she pulled away from Jeanne and peered out of the window, she saw a single rider, tall and slim, his face invisible under an ostrich-plumed hat as he dismounted and dashed indoors. He was no man that she recognised.

'Jeanne,' she said, 'go and see—'

But there was already a commotion of servants on the stairs, a lackey calling indignantly, and then the door to the bedroom burst open and the young man tumbled through it, taking huge long-legged steps like a deer surprised in a wood by hunters, until he was close enough that he could have reached out and put his arm around Madame de Cardonnoy's waist, or brushed her face with the plumes of his hat. Her visitor sank down on one knee, so close that his boot rested on the hem of Marie Catherine's dress and tugged at her skirt when she stumbled back, and, gallantly removing his hat, revealed himself to be no man at all, but Victoire Rose de Bourbon, Mademoiselle de Conti, her cheeks flushed with exertion and a few grains of argentine still clinging to her dark hair. She took Madame de Cardonnoy's hand and kissed the inside of her wrist.

Marie Catherine felt relief, like cool water, with lust running through it.

'Good morning, Madame,' Victoire said.

'What are you *wearing*?' Marie Catherine had pulled her hand back instinctively, but she couldn't repress a giddy laugh. 'I was terrified you were some gentleman.'

'Don't you like it?' Victoire stood up and spun around, as if she were showing off the floating skirts of a new gown. 'I had to go to a tailor, and he almost refused to make it for me.'

The sleeves of her coat were embroidered in the same shade of red as the feathers in her hat, fastened with a row of gold buttons. She had always been tall, her figure straight up and down, and with her sharp-nosed, aquiline face, the layers of her white shirt and her red-heeled rider's shoes, she looked remarkably like a clean-shaven young man – except for the way that she twisted a loose curl around her finger and watched Marie Catherine through her eyelashes, coquettishly.

'I didn't even recognise you,' said Marie Catherine. She was rubbing her wrist where Victoire had kissed it, as if her mouth might have left a mark. Who knew what the baron would say when he discovered that her friend was running around Paris cross-dressed. Victoire's family might be too ancient and eccentric to care what scandals she caused, but Marie Catherine's husband would probably bar her from Hôtel Cardonnoy.

'If I'd been ready a little sooner, I might have met you at the theatre two nights ago and seen which ladies recognised me,' Victoire said, laughing.

Marie Catherine turned away to toy with a pot of rouge on her table, embarrassed by the memory of how frightened she'd been when Victoire missed the play.

'I hope you weren't too preoccupied, since you didn't bother to tell me you weren't coming,' she said.

'Don't be angry with me.' Victoire caught her hand and leaned against the table, standing close enough that Marie Catherine was suddenly conscious of Jeanne's eyes on her, although her maid had stepped back nervously into the alcove where she slept. She put her hand on Victoire's shoulder and pushed her backwards, gently, by a half step. The girl blinked, glanced at Jeanne and then smiled, brilliantly.

'I'm in disgrace at court. I would have come immediately, but there's a very influential person who's angry with me, and I had to pacify her because I was afraid I'd be banished from Versailles entirely if I didn't.'

'What have you done now?' Marie Catherine raised her hands in exasperation. Victoire's wildness always filled her with a mixture of pleasure and envy. Sometimes she felt as if she were in the position of the girl's mother or her governess, constantly trying to restrain her more destructive impulses, and uncertain whether what she really wanted was the power to rein Victoire in or the freedom to run wild with her. Having neither was exhilarating and miserable, like riding a headstrong horse bareback and without a bridle.

It had been that way from the first moment they'd kissed, on a Saturday like this, late in the evening, at Madame de Fontet's salon. Marie Catherine had been talking about the land of the Amazons in *Artamène*, a novel she'd loved as a girl, about the country ringed by an impassable desert so that no man would ever look for it – how did the women find it? How did anyone know? They were alone in an alcove, it was summer, the rest of the guests were watching a man perform sleight-of-hand tricks in front of the great fire. Their corner was in a kind of grey half dusk, because neither Victoire nor Marie Catherine had wanted to get up and light a lamp. Suddenly Victoire had leaned forward and kissed her on the mouth. As if it were the natural response to what she had been saying.

Downstairs there had been a sound like an explosion and an outcry from the assembled ladies and gentlemen. Just as suddenly as she'd first kissed her, Victoire had stood up and fled the room.

Now she took off her feathered hat and bowed again, playing herself up as the gentleman. 'I'll tell you what I've been doing when your coachman brings the carriage round. I want to go to the Bois de Boulogne. And it's Saturday. We can visit Madame de Fontet.'

'Jeanne,' said Marie Catherine, 'I think we'll take our promenade alone. We'll call back at the house if we need you.'

'Yes, Madame,' said the maid. Her hands finished tying Madame de Cardonnoy's laces in quick, discreet silence, and when that was done, she dusted the baronne's face with powder and held the door open for her to leave.

In the corridor Victoire looked up and down the hallway to make sure no servants were coming up the stairs or waiting in a doorway, then put her hand on the small of Madame de Cardonnoy's back, pulled her close and kissed her, so that the thrill of danger ran between their lips. It was only a moment before they had jumped apart, and then Marie Catherine ran ahead down the stairs, with the feeling that a thousand eyes had opened up across her skin, multiplying her senses, so that she experienced every sight and sensation in the familiar hallway as if newly born.

Chapter Three

———

'Tell me what you've done,' said Madame de Cardonnoy in the carriage. Victoire was still acting half as the gentleman, lifting Marie Catherine's slipper up with the toe of her riding shoes as they sat side by side in the carriage, but she giggled and brandished her hat when Marie Catherine asked her questions.

'It was stupid of me,' said Mademoiselle de Conti. 'Don't be angry with me.'

Marie Catherine felt a familiar combination of admiration and helplessness. Victoire was eight years younger. Her grandmother, Madame de Chevreuse, had been a famous intriguer, a conspirator, a rebel of the Fronde that had nearly unseated the king at the start of his reign. Her father, a Prince of the Blood, had been imprisoned in the same rebellion's aftermath, and, it was said, had gone mad, fallen in love with his own sister and attempted to take his life. He had died young, leaving Victoire's mother to manage the affairs of his heirs. These were the kinds of stories that Marie Catherine's father had told her at the dinner table, to prepare her for the world that she would one day join. Victoire had been born to that world. She did as she pleased. At twenty-one she had refused all suitors, a defiance in which her mother supported her, happy enough not to break up the family fortune to fund a dowry for a younger girl. Victoire had commissioned a portrait of herself in which she posed as an Amazon, with a golden breastplate and spear. She liked women better than men, and spoke so freely about their virtues that Marie Catherine sometimes found herself wanting to cover the girl's mouth to keep her heart from spilling out of it, as much for her own safety as for Victoire's.

'Tell me,' said Marie Catherine.

'I wrote a poem,' Victoire replied. 'It was only a joke! But I gave it to another of de Montespan's ladies, and she gave it to Madame de Thianges, who is a little viper, and *she* gave it to Athénaïs herself.'

Athénaïs de Montespan was the king's official mistress, a woman who wielded as much influence at court as the queen herself, if not more.

'I imagine there was something in the contents of the poem that upset the king's mistress?' Marie Catherine asked.

Victoire rolled her neck back and looked at the carriage ceiling, in a loose-boned way that made her look younger than she was, or more wild, as if she really were a young man who had just ridden back from some adventure. Although Victoire was not exactly a beauty, with her unruly dark hair and her beaky nose, she had a halo around her that broke hearts.

'It was only a love poem!' She blushed. 'Nothing serious – really – I only thought that the lady I showed it to would take it as a joke. But it was quite clearly addressed to a woman, so I had to convince Madame de Montespan that the poem was only intended for a piece of drama I was writing. For a *male* hero, naturally. And then I had to stay and mollify her by losing at cards all night, when I'd meant to ride back to Paris!'

'That sounds like an expensive apology,' said Marie Catherine. Athénaïs de Montespan was a notorious gambler.

'It was. I'm going to murder Madame de Thianges.' Victoire sighed and tugged at her shirt cuffs.

The carriage rocked around a corner, and Marie Catherine had to brace herself to keep from sliding off her seat. Victoire reached out and gripped her elbow. Outside, someone was cursing. Marie Catherine shook off the girl's hand.

'And which lady did you give the poem to?' she asked, and Victoire sighed and leaned her head against Marie Catherine's shoulder, turning so that her eyelashes brushed Marie Catherine's neck when she blinked and the plume in her hat tickled her forehead. She was always leaning in for a kiss, always so quick to touch, and so easy to touch in return. Marie Catherine could have leaned into her, but she wasn't feeling forgiving. Instead she brushed the feather out of her face and, when it sprang back up, flipped the hat off Victoire's head. It landed upside down on the floor of the carriage, and Victoire sat up and pulled away from her with a needy sigh. Her discomfort pleased Marie Catherine more than she wanted to admit.

'It was no one, really,' Victoire said. 'Just an idea I had. But I've brought you a copy to read, if you want it.' She straightened up and reached into the breast of her coat and drew out a folded letter.

'I prefer not to receive love poems second-hand,' Marie Catherine said.

Victoire took the letter back with an expression that said she'd apologised as much as she planned to. Marie Catherine pulled the shade on her carriage window open and peered out through the glass at the city. They were near the Bois de Boulogne, a popular promenade, and a row of other carriages – grand coaches gilded with the crest of the house they belonged to, or cheap rented fiacres – were blocking the traffic ahead of them. The church bells were tolling the half hour.

The inside of Marie Catherine's head also felt like a ringing bell, vibrating with suppressed desire. The worst part of her heart wanted to punish Victoire for having disappointed her, for her carelessness in making her wait at the theatre two nights ago, and for the regard she might have shown another woman. But the more she held the girl at arm's length, the more the air in the carriage seemed cold and the less she felt the triumph of her own anger.

Slowly the carriage crept forward. She watched a man pasting flyers on a wall, moving methodically with his brush and bucket while the pedestrians hurried past him. The glass pane gradually warmed against her skin, and the pulse beating in her ears slowed down.

'I'm sorry,' she said to Victoire. 'I'm not angry.'

'Yes, you are.'

It was true that she had kept silent for too long.

'I gave it to Mademoiselle de Tavanne,' Victoire said at last. 'Not because I'm infatuated with her, but because I believed she was one of us. Mistakenly.'

'That was a risk,' said Marie Catherine.

'I *take* risks, Marie. You've never known the loneliness of believing that you're the only woman who—'

'I know what it means to be lonely, Victoire,' she said snappishly.

'But not what it means to love another woman knowing that she'll never love you back, and to believe that you're the only woman in the world who is made that way.'

Marie Catherine could feel herself flushing. It was true that she had not spent her girlhood encased in the prison of her own difference. As Victoire had. She had heard enough stories of Victoire's childhood. How at eight she had attached herself to her nursemaid, and given the older girl a betrothal ring from her mother's box and been switched for stealing, and had wept and waited at the window when the girl was sent away. How in her days at convent school she had crept out, disobedient, and wandered the cold gardens in the evening, avoiding the moment when the other girls would strip down to their shifts, and comb their hair, and go to bed, fearing that someone would see how her heart leaped into her mouth and would know that she was a monster.

Victoire laughed off all of this loneliness as she was telling it, but Marie Catherine's heart ached for her in those moments. Victoire would not hide. Everything that she was remained hidden in plain sight, as if neither law nor custom could touch her. Still, Marie Catherine thought that her comparison was unfair. That her own nature was to feel more than she showed did not mean that she had not felt the loneliness or the terror of her own desire.

After that first kiss at Madame de Fontet's, Marie Catherine had intended to stay away from the salon for a while. She doubted she would miss the excuse to dress in her best clothes and admire herself coldly in the mirror, or the glittering light of the chandeliers in the evening, or the flattering astrologers or the charming men and women who she could so easily imagine laughing at her behind their hands, as they'd once laughed at her mother. There was nothing there for her, she thought, except bitterness – she was jealous of Victoire's freedom, and that was the reason why she'd felt so strange when Victoire had kissed her. It had been the jealousy and the surprise of it, because who could have thought of such a thing. She'd stay away for a month, she wouldn't speak to Victoire, everything that had happened would blow away with the passage of time. At the end of the week she wrote Victoire a note asking whether she would like to go with her to visit her perfumer on rue des Gravilliers before Madame de Fontet's gathering, and then that morning she sent Jeanne running out of the house because she was out of argentine and the pomade for her hair had dried out, so that when Victoire came she was still in déshabillé, in her shift and stays, with her hair loose down her back. Of course one could receive a lady friend that way. It was a mark of intimacy, and Victoire needn't have known the calculations that had gone into getting the maidservant out of the room.

'Will you close the door?' she'd said, and Victoire had jumped up from where she was perched on the edge of Marie Catherine's bed and closed it. And crossed the room to where Marie Catherine was sitting at her dressing table, with her shift tucked up so that the ribbons holding up her stockings peeked out from under its lace hem.

'What do you think you're doing?'

Victoire had stopped.

'I understand you're not married yet, Victoire, and perhaps you're more innocent than many of the girls at court, but I can't imagine what you were thinking last week at Madame de Fontet's salon. If anyone had seen what you did that day, you'd have lost your good name, and I think I'd have been blamed as much as you.'

She was speaking very calmly and precisely, despite the feeling of pressure that was building up in her throat, as if there were a wave of something rising up inside her that was going to end by pushing her entirely out of her own body. Whatever court game this was, she couldn't play it. She was so focused on the words that she couldn't look at Victoire. When she did look up, she saw that the girl was standing very still in the middle of the room, one hand pressed over her mouth.

'Forgive me,' Victoire said. 'I thought you felt as I did.' She took a step back towards the door, and for a moment it was clear that she was going to leave and they wouldn't see each other again after that, but the wave that Marie Catherine had felt rising through her finally crested and, without having made any decision to do so, she jumped up from her chair and intercepted Victoire at the door. For a moment Victoire stood there, within arm's reach, looking surprised, and then Marie Catherine stepped in towards her and ran her hands up from Victoire's waist, feeling the movement of her stays under the silk as she gasped.

She was burning with what felt at first like anger – she, Marie Catherine, who had always been cold, who was the master of her own passions, who had turned the resentment she felt against her husband into a surface of stone. How could Victoire – unmarried, headstrong, without responsibilities – how could she play on her feelings this way? How could she ask Marie Catherine what she felt? She expected Victoire to flinch when she put a hand on the back of her neck. Instead she brought her hands up to Marie Catherine's face and kissed her back, and held her there, when she would have pulled away.

Marie Catherine had never taken a lover. She had had only her husband. Sometimes she had imagined what it might be like if she had been a man and had married the girl she'd been, or a different girl – how she might have won her wife over. Now she was halfway between that daydream and something she'd never thought of, and she didn't have to think about what she wanted to do with her hands or her mouth. Victoire's hair smelled like irises, softly metallic. She pulled up the hem of Marie Catherine's shift. The down on her neck prickled with goosebumps. Victoire, she thought, had done this before, and the thought made her both jealous and grateful. She let herself fall backwards onto the bed, pulling Victoire with her. She'd sent Jeanne away. She hadn't known. And, also, she'd known.

Now, in the carriage, she took Victoire's hand again and ran her fingers over the seam where her nails joined her skin. Victoire's skin was soft, her nails shaped into clean ovals, but she chewed the thumbnail sometimes, when she was lost in thought, and so that one was rough. Her knuckles were redder than the rest of her hand, and green veins patterned her fingers like lacework on the creamy silk of her skin. Marie Catherine brought the hand to her lips and kissed it, the way she might have done if she were the one playing the gentleman.

What must it be like, to wear those clothes so easily, to climb the stairs in her coat with as much freedom as if she had been a man? She couldn't imagine it – the gesture that Victoire performed naturally was a parody on Marie Catherine's lips. Perhaps it was the effect not only of Victoire's social station, but of having a heart that was always spilling over with a flood of feeling. Victoire no sooner desired a thing than she was transformed.

'You know I love you best.' Victoire clenched her hand on Marie Catherine's until the knuckles turned white. A blush was making the tip of her nose red.

'It's all right,' Marie Catherine said, at last. 'Try to send me a note with a servant next time you're stuck at cards.'

She leaned forward and kissed Victoire, her nails finding the soft skin behind the girl's ear, tracing a hieroglyph that she knew she liked, inhaling the slight sourness of her breath. Victoire, nimble in her gentleman's clothes, swung her leg across Marie Catherine's lap and sat straddling her.

'And what else, Madame?' Victoire asked her.

'And I love you,' Marie Catherine said.

The carriage jerked forward, the suspension bouncing, and outside the coachman called out to someone passing in his way. Marie Catherine pulled the curtain across the carriage window and the inside of the box fell into a cool twilight, as if they were in some bower deep in the forest.

She made a fist in Victoire's hair and pulled her head back, not gently, so that she could kiss her neck, where the skin was as soft as a pair of new gloves. Always the fear rose up at these moments – of discovery, of damnation. What passed between them was something for which the only name she had ever heard spoken aloud was ugly. Victoire pulled back against the grip on her hair, straining to kiss her, inhaling her breath in the moment before the kiss. She was reaching through a gauze of fear and shame to touch her, as if they were both children wandering in a wood at night, holding hands to scare away the wolves and the witches. They kissed. Victoire kicked her hat away and began undoing the buttons of her own shirt.

Jeanne found the painter waiting for her in the courtyard outside the kitchen. The lackey, Arnaud, had warned her on her way down the stairs, with a swatting gesture in the direction of her buttocks. She'd had a chamberpot in her hands and, when she'd jumped away, Madame's morning piss had nearly slopped over onto her skirt. She didn't want to go and meet the painter with the pot in her hands, so she'd thrown its contents out on the midden behind the kitchen and then left it sitting on the doorstep. Agnès the chambermaid could put it back.

Now the stab of irritation she'd felt with Arnaud swelled into a tight, searing band across her forehead when she saw Lavoie's nonchalant silhouette, his back turned, admiring the stables. He looked like someone's prize hunting dog, begging at the table – sleek and long and hopeful. She hadn't eaten breakfast and she wanted nothing to do with him.

'Bonjour, Monsieur,' she said, when she was close enough to have put her hand on his shoulder. He jumped at the sound of her voice. 'If you are looking for Madame, I am afraid that she is not here.'

Although she had been born on a farm outside Paris, Jeanne could, when she desired to, speak a French as icily correct as that of any young marquise. She had recognised the same schooling in Lavoie, in the combination of stiffness and gallantry in his manners. He was good at hiding the fear that someone would see through his handsome face and polished voice, the fine cloth of his good coat, and make him out for what he was. Now she held her back a little straighter than normal, and her chin a little higher. There was nothing in her bearing that anyone could have pointed to as definitively rude, but she saw from the way the painter stepped back a pace that he realised she did not want to speak to him.

'I hope I'm not intruding,' he said, with a smile and a slight bow. 'I had the day free, and I thought I'd come back and see you.'

'You're too kind, Monsieur.'

'Your mistress suggested that if she wasn't too busy, she might finish her tale.'

Jeanne was good at reading people. It was indispensable, in her profession. The painter did not care at all if he saw her. His interest was in her mistress, and he hoped that charming Jeanne might open a path to Madame de Cardonnoy. He was not the first man to have had that idea, which was common to a number of gentlemen who rarely seemed to understand that their mere attention was not the infinite flattery they supposed it to be.

'I was about to eat my meal,' she said.

'By all means. I'm at your service.'

He held out his hand to her as if she were a lady at a dance, and she reluctantly took it and let him lead her into the steam and smoke of the kitchen. One of the kitchen boys was plucking a pheasant for the baron's dinner, and handfuls of feathers drifted across the floor like blown snow and stuck wherever the cooking grease had dried without being properly scrubbed. The whole cavernous room smelled of hot oil, fresh bread and fresh blood.

Lavoie's manners were wrong here, but he kept up the game even as Jeanne called to the cook to give her something to eat. The painter bowed to the other servants, led her on his arm, found her a chair at the table and pulled it out so that she could sit. It was a little bit mocking, but his disdain seemed to be directed at the custom itself, and not at her. He brought her a plate with cold chicken from last night's dinner, a wedge of cheese and a cupful of bay-scented broth. She ate with her fingers.

'Do you mind if I sketch you?' Lavoie asked.

'What, like this?' There was a smear of soft cheese stuck to her finger that she would have liked to lick off, but she couldn't do that and still play the lady. She pointed at the chicken bone on her plate. 'It's hardly a fit subject for a portrait.'

But Lavoie had already produced a sheaf of paper and a little nub of charcoal from his bag. His hands moved quickly over the paper. Jeanne put her hands in her lap, trying to surreptitiously wipe her fingers on the inside of her sleeves.

'No, just sit naturally. It's a sketch, you don't need to pose.'

'I don't want you to draw me with a chicken bone in my mouth.' As if she'd like to see herself with a greasy mouth and fingers red from washing.

Lavoie smiled. 'If you don't like it, I'll tear it up.'

Jeanne sniffed. 'How gallant of you.'

Lavoie concentrated on his paper, with only the occasional sharp-eyed glance up at her. Albert, one of the two kitchen boys, whooped that Jeanne was having her portrait done, and his companion, Philippe, scuttled out of the pantry with a bunch of greenery in his fist and peered over Lavoie's shoulder. The cook was rolling out pastry and did not look up.

'Tell me about yourself,' said Lavoie. 'Is your family in Paris?'

Jeanne shook her head. 'I grew up in the country. My mother had a sister in service and too many mouths to feed, so when I was fourteen they sent me to my aunt.'

Lavoie nodded, distractedly. 'How many brothers and sisters?'

'Seven, last I counted.' Her mother had cried when she fell pregnant with the youngest, when Jeanne was twelve. Jeanne found now that she was worrying the hem of her sleeve between her fingers, finding a place where the ruffled seam had started to unravel and caressing the rough edge with her fingertips. The question had called up a memory, filled with abrupt shame, of her first placement in a household, where she'd discovered with incredible relief that she could steal down to the kitchen and eat bread whenever she wanted, without worrying that it would be missed, or that she was taking food from a little brother's or sister's mouth. She'd never eaten choux pastry or jam made with white sugar or veal before, but the cook had been generous and there was always something left over from the master's table. It had taken only six months in service before her breasts had filled out and her skirts hung several inches too short on her new frame. 'Why don't you tell me about *your* family.'

'The job of a portraitist is to make his subject comfortable. To open him up, so that he can perceive his character and translate it to the page.'

'I thought his job was to flatter the rich with their own images.'

'That, too.'

'Perhaps we ought to change professions,' Jeanne suggested. She'd let a touch of acid creep into her voice.

'Yes, come here and chop this parsley,' called Philippe from his post at the other end of the table.

Lavoie shrugged and gave her a green-eyed look. 'I doubt I'd make a good cook. I can mix paint, but I wouldn't eat it.'

'A valet perhaps,' said Jeanne. 'Since you're used to flattery. Monsieur le Baron has kept his man for a long time, but I could find you a comte who needs a new valet every six months or so.'

49

She had expected this to goad him, but he merely frowned and held the paper out in front of him, looking from her to the page.

'Look.' He offered the picture to her.

Jeanne took it and held it by the very edge of the paper, afraid the grease on her hands would mark the drawing. It was a quick sketch, with her hair smoking away around her head in a soft drift of shade. But she was surprised at how he'd drawn her expression – her face half shadowed, as if she'd been disturbed in the contemplation of some secret. An angry look almost, but her eyes and the cast of her mouth seemed more beautiful than she would have expected from the glances she'd stolen in the little square mirror that hung over Madame's dressing table, her figure fuller and more elegant. All the folds of the baronne's cast-off dress fell beautifully across her lap, like a statue's.

'You've made me look quite fierce,' she said.

'You don't like it?' Lavoie made a ripping gesture.

She held the paper out in front of her with two hands, and for a moment he looked so doubtful that she almost did tear it in half, just to shock him. But her nerve failed the moment after she'd tested the paper. She set it down on the table.

'So you are pleased.' Lavoie's smile was wider than she'd seen it before, more genuine. He liked to see his work liked. She put her hand down flat on top of the drawing.

'Careful, you'll smudge it.' He leaned over, fussily, and pulled her hand away from the table. She heard Philippe snort, and she drew her hand back.

'May I keep this?'

'Of course, it's yours.'

'I really don't know when Madame will return. The baron came back from Versailles last night.' Jeanne paused. She'd been charmed by the drawing, but she still knew why he was here. 'She often stays away, as much as she can, when he's here.'

'How unfortunate,' said Lavoie. His tone was equivocal. He might almost have been expressing genuine disappointment in an unhappy marriage. Jeanne stood up from her chair, and he offered her his arm again.

'She goes to Madame de Fontet's ruelle most Saturdays. She said she would come back for me today, but she's visiting with a lady friend and she might forget.' Jeanne might have told the painter he was wasting his time, but no amount of flattery could have induced her to explain the situation with Mademoiselle de Conti.

They left the kitchen and walked back through the courtyard. Jeanne held the drawing by her side, fingering the edges of the paper.

Lavoie smiled. 'I'm afraid I don't have an entrance to Hôtel Fontet.'

Jeanne couldn't help but sigh. 'Some men would pay money for this kind of information, you know.'

Lavoie looked affronted, although he ought to have known that a lady's maid was a valuable ally, if you wanted to be close to the lady. Perhaps he guessed that Madame had another lover and would have nothing to do with him, however much he bribed her maid. 'Are you going to send me your bill?'

'I'm beyond your means, Monsieur.' Jeanne laughed. 'Consider it an act of charity.'

They'd crossed the courtyard. Lavoie stood with his hands in his pockets, looking at the ground. The lace on his cuffs was a little shabby. He probably *couldn't* afford her kind of help.

'You really don't know anyone?' Jeanne waved the sheet with the drawing at him. 'And to think that everyone at Hôtel Fontet is missing the fun of having their portrait taken.'

'I'm sure they have no shortage of talent.'

The sky was grey, and the thick clouds hung very low overhead. Jeanne wasn't sure whether to invite him into the salon or not. The other servants would laugh, to see Jeanne entertaining this man as if she were the mistress of the house. Arnaud already lost no opportunity to point out when she acted above her station.

'I've been there, accompanying Madame. I haven't seen anyone do what you did.' She was holding the drawing close by her hips, almost hidden in the gentle wave of her skirt. She peeked at it, surreptitiously, and saw the painter smile. 'Everyone likes games. And everyone likes to know how others are looking at them.'

A finger of cold touched her nose, and when she looked up, the snow was falling in fat, sticky caterpillars. They settled on the painter's hair and stayed a while before melting.

'Ah, look, snow,' he said.

'Yes.'

Lavoie drew her a little closer by his hold on her arm, so that she felt her elbow pressed into his ribs and the warmth of his body through his coat. A snowflake touched her forehead and slid in a droplet down her cheek. She held out her free hand and watched more snow fall into it.

'I suppose I'd still need an introduction,' the painter said.

Jeanne sighed and took her arm back.

'You're such a man. You act a little bit gallant, and then you expect me to do absolutely everything for you.'

Lavoie covered his face with his hand and laughed. Jeanne turned back to look at the façade of Hôtel Cardonnoy. The weak sunlight caught the windowpanes and reflected it back, so that they looked like polished teeth exposed in a smile.

In Madame de Fontet's salon, Mademoiselle de Conti and her scandalous outfit were the centre of attention. She had entered Hôtel Fontet like a general announcing a victory, and circled the room exchanging absurd gallantries with men and women alike. At the moment she was down on one knee before Madame de Fontet, offering a very flattering description of her beauty and wit. The saucer of coffee that she'd just taken from a servant's hand was in danger of spilling all over the sleeve of her red coat. Madame de Fontet was laughing in delight, and her expression filled Marie Catherine with conflicting emotions – jealousy for Victoire's attention and the kind of near-despair that came from having got away with something. She felt as if Victoire's mouth must have left an indelible mark on her skin. It was astonishing that no one else saw it. She'd got out of the carriage with her hair all mussed up on the side and had had to fabricate a story on the doorstep of Hôtel Fontet – the sickness of her maid, the cancellation of her hairdresser, the terrible jostling of the carriage, which had knocked her head right against the door: could she possibly borrow Madame's servant girl and retreat to her cabinet to fix it?

Her hair had turned out quite nicely, although she'd been tempted to linger in Madame de Fontet's cabinet, as if she could get back to that moment of joy in the carriage when she and

Victoire were alone. The coffee, served in a gilded cup the size of a walnut, was too bitter. Marie Catherine preferred hers sugared, although Madame de Fontet insisted that this was not the way to take it. She found the side table on which the servants had laid out a selection of pastries, and scooped a handful of candied nuts onto her saucer to nibble between sips. Then she drifted back towards the silk couches where Victoire was paying court. She had moved from admiring Madame de Fontet herself to admiring her newest treasure – a table whose surface was a slab of green porphyry, its surface polished so highly that the guests could see their reflections in its green crystals. The base was a profusion of carved nymphs and fauns, gilded gold.

Flatterer, Marie Catherine thought, affectionately. She enjoyed seeing Victoire admired too much to be upset that she'd left her and rushed into the crowd. But her memory was still lingering in the carriage. Marie Catherine had kissed Victoire's neck down to her breasts, both of them swimming in the froth of Marie Catherine's skirts, hiked to her waist. The skirt had seemed to have a life of its own. It was like being caught in a capsizing boat. It made her laugh helplessly, the way the fabric kept spilling up over her shoulders and down to the carriage floor, as she tried to kick free of it, the ribbons that held up her stockings untied and swimming away from her like eels. She had felt the gooseflesh rising across Victoire's skin as if it were her own skin, her own heart beating, her own face buried in her lover's hair, the same moment of release – and now Victoire seemed as alien and unknowable as rain. Why didn't she feel the fear that Marie Catherine felt, that anyone in this room might look at her and see that a careless kiss had left a mark on her neck, or that she'd dipped her ungloved fingers somewhere forbidden?

'Truly, you're incomparable,' Madame de Fontet was saying. 'We'll send you over to the young men at court, and you can instruct them.'

The lackey who served the coffee was dressed as an Armenian, in an elaborately embroidered caftan and a fur hat, under which one could see his ears sweating. The toasted scent of the drink and a sour human smell hung in his wake. He appeared to be about sixteen, was very tall, and handsome in the girlish way of young men.

At the end of the pink silk couch nearest Marie Catherine was a wizened old woman with a strand of pearls across her chest, and skin like old crinkled paper that settled under her eyes in bruised rings. Marie Catherine leaned close and touched her shoulder.

'May I get you anything, my dear?'

'I beg your pardon?' Madeleine de Scudéry, who had been known to her friends of a former generation as Sappho, the wisest of women, was deaf in one ear, although Marie Catherine had trouble remembering which one. She pointed at the coffee cup, then the candied almonds.

'Would you like me to bring you a sweet?'

Mademoiselle de Scudéry stood halfway up, only to subside back onto the couch into the rolling hills and rivers of her dress with a sigh. 'I'm afraid I can't hear you, Madame.'

'Oh, don't worry.' Marie Catherine sat down next to her, feeling her face flushing. In her youth she'd met Mademoiselle de Scudéry, not then quite so old, once or twice, and had barely been able to stammer more than a sentence or two about her great love and appreciation for her books. Every time they met now, she felt herself becoming almost equally tongue-tied. Mademoiselle de Scudéry ran her own ruelle, from her house in the Marais, and although it was not as fashionable as the gatherings of Madame de Fontet, Marie Catherine had always wanted to be invited. Recently she had begun trying to win the old woman over, but she was never certain if Mademoiselle de Scudéry remembered her from one week to the next, or if she thought she was subject to an entire parade of identical female flatterers who'd read *Artamène* and *Clelie* and wanted to sit down beside her and tell her about the passages they'd memorised as girls. About how she had read and reread the story of Sappho herself, who had extracted a promise from her lover that he would never ask her to marry him, for marriage was little more than slavery for women. How, reading, she had felt that she was looking through a window and into a different possible world.

At Madame de Fontet's, Mademoiselle de Scudéry often appeared with a companion, a Monsieur Pellisson, some twenty years younger than her and a one-time royal historian. With his unhandsome, jowly face and stolid manner, he made a strange pair with the old woman who had once been famed for her wit and invention, but he paid her such careful attention that Marie Catherine couldn't help but like him. Today, however, she did not see him.

'Let's have a game!' Madame de Fontet clapped her hands together, and her voice rang out over the room. 'In honour of our Mademoiselle de Conti, who has so recently transformed herself into *Monsieur* de Conti, we'll play the game of metamorphoses!'

'Madame de Cardonnoy,' said Victoire, bowing, 'will you start? Your stories are the best.' Their eyes met across the room.

'If she's the best, then she ought to go last, otherwise no one else will want to go after her,' said Monsieur de Crésny, one hand on the back of the sofa on which Marie Catherine sat with Mademoiselle de Scudéry.

'When you introduce me like that, I'm afraid I can only disappoint you,' said Madame de Cardonnoy. 'I just tell the stories I heard from my mother.'

There was a little rustle of laughter around the room. Her apology about her mother was a well-known and threadbare fiction.

'Nonsense, darling,' said Madame de Fontet. 'Everyone knows you're entirely unique.'

Marie Catherine smiled and raised her gilded coffee cup to hide the smile that betrayed her pleasure in the compliment. There had been a time, before the birth of her children, or even after, when she would have been terrified to speak at one of these gatherings, and many of the guests would have looked down on her for her father's birth. It always pleased her, even now, to see them draw close around her, praise her tales and the way she told them.

A little crowd had formed around the chair. Marie Catherine recognised Monsieur Perrault, the secretary of the Académie des Inscriptions et Belles-Lettres, with his young niece, Mademoiselle L'Héritier, who, teenaged and shy, hung in her uncle's shadow with an expression of furious concentration and said very little.

'Will you give me an object?' Marie Catherine asked. The game began with a choice selected by the audience. Afterwards the storyteller's wit would supply the tale.

'Tell us,' said Monsieur Perrault, 'of the buttons on Mademoiselle de Conti's coat.'

Madame de Cardonnoy took a small sip of her coffee and held it in her mouth before swallowing. The bitterness scorched her throat. She was conscious of Mademoiselle de Scudéry shifting in her seat, searching out her voice with her good ear.

'There was once,' she began loudly, the warmth of the coffee still in her mouth, 'a fertile kingdom with a broad river running through it. In this land lived seven brothers, alike as acorns that have fallen from the same oak tree. Although they were not of distinguished birth, they were strong and fearless, and their bravery covered them with the gold of glory.'

The trick of the game was to tell a story whose character would show some clever correspondence with the object chosen by the audience. A glittering diamond might become a woman who was beautiful, but hard and unfeeling; a silver serving spoon a generous lord who shared his gifts with everyone he knew.

'It happened that when they were away at war, a great calamity struck the land. An enormous water serpent, its tail as thick as a tree and its fangs like two long spears, came into the river and laid waste to the land around it. Every day for seven days it rose up from the water and killed any who happened by – farmer or traveller or humble wife washing her linen at the river's edge. Soon the people of the valley were afraid to go out and tend the fields or do their daily work. The crops fell to ruin, and the serpent crept up to the very doors of the houses and painted the fields red with blood.'

Monsieur de Crésny hummed appreciatively. So the red fabric of the coat might become a field stained with blood, the opening at its front a wide river. Marie Catherine took a sip of her coffee, to disguise her need to think, and let her thoughts run in the creases of Victoire's coat, as if they were high grasses in which she could stumble back on her lost path. Funny that she should have made the body in whose arms she felt safest into the site of a massacre.

'The seven brothers had also one sister, who despite her age and her sex was clever and brave.' Now she was looking at Victoire and speaking only to her. 'She knew that, if her brothers heard of the beast that ravaged their home, they would return at once to kill it and avenge the deaths of their neighbours. And so, under cover of darkness, she put on her travelling cloak and went boldly through the bloody fields to the river. The trees cast terrible shadows in the twilight, each looking like the approaching serpent, and every step that she took left her soft slippers warm and wet with blood.'

'This story's rather gruesome, Madame,' Victoire protested. 'You'll convince me that you don't like my outfit.'

'A fairy tale need not always apply the rules of bienséance,' said Monsieur Perrault. 'It's only the theatre that forbids blood to be spilled.'

Marie Catherine smiled sweetly. Was it so wrong to tease Victoire? It was true she felt something like jealousy, that she wore those clothes so easily. That her rank permitted her eccentricities. But although Marie Catherine, the financier's daughter, would have been met with silence if she had worn that outfit, only she knew the body under the clothes.

'She had reached the bridge over the river before the serpent found her. Its head rose up like a spear from the water, and she could see its mouth opening like a dark cave before her. The brothers' sister feared then that her cause was lost, but, keeping her back straight, she curtseyed and said, "Bonsoir, Monsieur le Serpent."'

'Brave girl!' Madame de Fontet applauded.

Madame de Cardonnoy smiled. 'And the serpent, who was unused to being addressed with such respect, asked her whether she was not afraid for her life, alone as she was. "Not even a little," said the girl. "For while I know that you are strong and terrible, I confess that you are too beautiful to provoke my fear. May I stay awhile and talk with you?"'

She paused again, but now it was not to discover what she ought to say, but to see the effect her story had on the room. Victoire looked up at her, no longer annoyed. The clever heroine made up for the jibe about her coat's colour. Even Mademoiselle de Scudéry was listening.

'At her words,' Madame de Cardonnoy continued, 'the snake approached her more closely and looped its enormous body around her waist. "And now are you afraid, Mademoiselle?"'

She tapped her coffee cup with one fingernail.

'"Not at all," the girl said. "Though you feel me shiver, I confess it is only because the river water has wet my cloak through."'

The servant in the Armenian robe hovered around the edges of the group, pouring coffee into each tiny cup, unasked.

'"Well then," said the snake, "if you are so curious, would you travel with me to my kingdom, which is far away at the bottom of the sea? There you will find many strange wonders, which must surely fill you with delight, if even the sight of my face, which I know to be terrible, cannot move you to fear."'

Here she paused, smiled, took a sip from her cup and, when she had finished drinking, resumed her tale at a different point.

'When the seven brothers returned from battle, the serpent was gone and so was their sister, and the wheat in the fields grew red from all the blood that had been spilled there. No one could tell them what had happened that night their sister left their cottage and went to face the serpent all alone, but each brother held out hope in his heart that either there would come a day when she would return, or else, if she was dead, the serpent who had devoured her would reappear so that the brothers might have their revenge. Each chose a post along the river and, with one foot on the left bank and one on the right, they wait there still, protecting their kingdom, and waiting for news of she who is gone.'

She gestured at Victoire.

'As you can see, they would be waiting there still, if not for their metamorphosis.'

'Very clever,' said Madame de Fontet, reaching out to adjust the drape of her skirts. 'But whatever happened to the serpent and the brave sister?'

'Oh, that's another story!' said Madame de Cardonnoy, laughing. 'Shall we say that, in her travels with the beast, she tricked it into devouring its own tail, and now it is knotted around itself, much like Mademoiselle de Conti's belt?' She glanced sidelong at Mademoiselle de Scudéry and found that the face of Paris's Sappho was creased into a smile.

'Now you've skipped the best part of the adventure,' said Monsieur de Crésny. 'We'll have to drag it out of you!'

'I'm afraid you're unfamiliar with my mother's stories, Monsieur,' said Madame de Cardonnoy. 'I must stop somewhere or we'll be here until midnight, and no one else will get a chance to play the game.'

'You ought to choose the next object,' said Monsieur Perrault, steepling his hands under his chin with an air of high solemnity.

'Who will go next?' said Victoire.

'Marie-Jeanne,' said Monsieur Perrault, drawing his niece forward by her arm, 'will you try?'

The girl shook her head. 'Oh no, I can't.'

Madame de Fontet cast a dismissive look at the girl. 'Why don't you tell one yourself, Monsieur Perrault?'

Shyness won no favours in Madame de Fontet's household. But Marie Catherine felt her sympathy unexpectedly contract for Mademoiselle L'Héritier's sake, as she saw the girl step back and turn away to conceal her dismay. She had wanted, clearly, to be coaxed into speaking, and she must have felt she'd lost her chance to impress the company.

'I'm sure Mademoiselle L'Héritier has a story to tell,' Marie Catherine said. 'You'll find it's not so difficult, once you start.'

'All right,' the girl mumbled, and then she pulled her spine straighter and seemed to find her voice. 'Will you choose the thing I'm to describe?'

'Why don't you tell us the story of the ring on your uncle's right hand?'

Monsieur Perrault extended his hand so that his niece could look more closely at the ring. Mademoiselle L'Héritier pored over it as if she was reading his fortune.

'Well,' she said, huffing out a short, nervous breath, 'once there was a woman with blue eyes who had no suitors ...'

Later the servant boy in the Armenian robe circled and poured coffee again, along with stronger spirits. There was populo, smelling of lemon and musk, and the drink made with carnations, cinnamon and vanilla that gallants called the water of Venus. The gathering had quieted, and now the guests stood spread out in little knots in various rooms, murmuring in pairs by a harpsichord or breaking out into laughter in the twilight illumination of a window. At one time this would have been the height of the gathering, when guests began to gamble, and Madame de Fontet might summon a magician to tell fortunes in the fire.

Now fortune-telling was dangerous, and the company was more subdued. Marie Catherine was beginning to feel the effect of the coffee, a high humming in her temples and a stiffness in her shoulders, as if her body was a thread in a dress that had caught on something and now pulled the fabric of the entire garment askew. She set her cup on the porphyry table and brushed down her skirt to stand.

Madame de Fontet had led a small group into her bedroom, where they were playing cards around the polished dressing table. The lackey at the door was eating a pastry, his gold braid dotted with crumbs. Victoire threw down her cards in defeat and laughed, her hair loose on her shoulders, as if she'd entirely forgotten about her humiliation at cards in the aftermath of the scandalous poem. The whole group was framed in the doorway like a scene in a miniature painting, the kind that one might keep in a locket and look at, privately, in moments of quiet. Marie Catherine stood in the doorway for a moment, waiting for them to see her, until Monsieur de Crésny glanced up and caught her eye.

'I think I'll be going, my dear,' she said, with a little bow towards Madame de Fontet.

'Oh, that's too bad.' She tossed a card triumphantly into the centre of the table, then laid down her hand. 'I was hoping we could convince you to play a round with us.'

'I'm afraid Monsieur de Cardonnoy will have my head if I lose.'

'Oh, my horse is at your hôtel,' said Victoire. 'Will you wait until I've finished this round?'

'I'll be downstairs.'

Marie Catherine stood by a window and watched the red sky fading over the gardens and the adjacent roofs of grand houses, like the dye leaching out of a bolt of new silk. A hand touched her arm.

'I enjoyed your story.' It was Mademoiselle de Scudéry, the incomparable Sappho. Her smile creased her face.

'I feel I owe you a thousand stories, for the books of yours I loved as a girl.' The words tripped off her tongue without her having to puzzle over them, and too loudly, but that was all right. Mademoiselle de Scudéry was hard of hearing.

'They're out of fashion now.' Sappho spread her hands, as if to ask, *What can you do?* 'I'm afraid the little gathering at my house is also not so fashionable these days, but you would be welcome there.'

'Thank you,' Marie Catherine said. 'Thank you very much.'

'Do you have other stories?'

'Only small ones. Fairy stories.'

'Bring one to tell. Monsieur Perrault collects them.'

'I will.'

Victoire stepped into the room, the last light of the sun and new-lit candles reflecting together in her eyes and off the glazed china of her teeth. Her hair floated like a dark cloud against her red coat.

'I hope to see you soon,' Marie Catherine said and, impulsively, she raised the novelist's hand to her lips and kissed her bony fingers. Her skin felt like the very softest old leather and smelled like pastry.

Mademoiselle de Scudéry laughed.

In her excitement, she nearly kissed Victoire before the carriage had pulled safely out of Madame de Fontet's courtyard.

'She invited me! Now I think I can die happy.'

The carriage wheels sounded on the cobbled streets like the rhythmic crack of an axe.

Chapter Four

———

Where the baron spent all of his nights in Paris, Marie Catherine did not know. Perhaps he was gambling. Perhaps he had a dancer from the ballet installed in a room somewhere under a false married name. She didn't care. She loved the house when she and the children were its only occupants. Some nights she still woke up from a dream in which he crawled in beside her and pulled up her shift, a memory of all those nights he'd spent trying to conceive a son. Awake, she would lie still in the bed until her pulse quieted, listening to the night noises of the house and breathing the cool reassurance that he was elsewhere, spending her money or losing it at cards, or inflicting himself on some other woman who was at least getting paid for it. She was alone and she was lucky.

This night she wasn't lucky. She always locked her door before bed, but the baron had a key to every lock in the house. He came in late, his wig set lopsided on his head, his sweat smelling sourly of wine. He shook her awake, grabbed at her breasts. She curled up like a beetle on her side and buried her face in the feather pillow. Closed her eyes while he shook her. He gave up after a little while – she was balled up as tightly as a piece of twine wound around itself, and she knew he wouldn't go so far as to prise her hands off the pillow or get in between her legs unless she showed some sign of giving in.

'Salope,' he said, and slammed the door behind him.

From her bed, Marie Catherine could hear Jeanne's unsteady breathing from the alcove where she slept. She didn't want to acknowledge that the servant girl was awake. She was stiff with anger. Her hands wouldn't unclench from the doughy mound of the pillow.

A minor quarrel. By the morning, everyone except she herself would have forgotten it, and perhaps the baron would be off to Versailles to curry favour at court. She imagined, in detail, the sound of the carriage wheels announcing his departure, but as much as she summoned up the breath of the horses or the coachman's call from the night noises of the house, Jeanne's breathing kept intruding on her thoughts, reminding her of the witness to her humiliation. The cocks were crowing in the road before she drifted back down into something resembling sleep.

The next morning she let Jeanne dress her without speaking. The servant girl offered one word about the cold weather and then met silence with silence, her eyes focused only on her hands as she laced and tied Marie Catherine's dress, bracing one hand on her mistress's shoulder as she adjusted a sleeve, then pulling the fabric of her bodice out and away from her waist before she laced it tight. Jeanne untied the taffeta wrap that protected Madame de Cardonnoy's curls while she slept and combed out her hair until it hung straight down her back like a peasant woman's shawl.

Marie Catherine felt her touch like an insect walking over her skin. She wished the servant girl would leave her alone. She wanted to get back in bed and pull the covers over her head, or else leave the house and buy a new dress, a new table like the one that Madame de Fontet had, a Chinese vase, a jar of powder, a dozen orange trees to line the courtyard, a hunting horse – anything that would remind her that the money was hers, even if her person was not.

Instead she had an appointment with her hairdresser, and her hair needed to be combed.

She called the children in while the hairdresser, Monsieur Paget, was fixing her hair. Paget was a small, broad man with a pot-belly and powdery, gentle hands, and he smiled at the children and offered his compliments as if he was admiring an elegant new statue or a pretty piece of pastry. Marie Catherine called Sophie to her side and had her read aloud. The past week her tutor had caught her in the salon, reading from her parents' edition of Villon, but when Marie Catherine gave her the book now, she took it eagerly but stuttered over the spelling.

'La – royne blanche comme ung lys,' she sounded out slowly, 'qui chantoit à voix de sereine.'

'How marvellously she's doing,' said Paget approvingly. He was in the midst of working powder through Madame de Cardonnoy's pomaded hair, running handfuls of powder down its length and then combing them through until each strand shone.

'Slow down and read the whole word before you say it aloud, Sophie,' said Marie Catherine, and her daughter huffed out a frustrated breath and continued shakily.

'Et Jehanne, la bonne Lorraine, qu'Anglois bruslerent à Rouen, où sont-ils, Vierge souveraine? Mais où sont les neiges d'antan!'

'*Brûlèrent*,' corrected Marie Catherine. 'You don't need to pronounce every letter in the word.'

Sophie sighed and dropped the book on the floor. 'Why doesn't he just spell it the way it's pronounced then?'

Paget chuckled. 'The little lady's going to be a wit one day, Madame.'

He lifted the whole length of Madame de Cardonnoy's hair away from her, holding it out to admire the way it reflected the light. It was as heavy as a woollen cloak.

'Maybe,' said Marie Catherine. 'But can you tell me who Jehanne is?'

Sophie paused.

'She doesn't know!' Nicolas exclaimed.

'She will, if she thinks about it. Today we'd say *Jeanne*.'

'Oh,' said Sophie, 'like Jeanne!' The maid jumped a little. 'Or Jeanne d'Arc.'

'Very good,' said Madame de Cardonnoy. Paget, finished with his comb, was beginning to roll the upper layers of her hair around a padded woollen form, rolling and pinning until her hair rose at the back of her head like a chest of drawers. She eyed his work in the small mirror over her table, approvingly, as he began to secure the hair in place with short plaits and her set of pearl-headed pins, pulling the hair tight so that the skin at the back of her neck felt stretched.

64

'Jeanne, are you named after Jeanne d'Arc?' Sophie's eyes were bright with the excitement of discovery. Jeanne hummed.

'I don't know if my mother was thinking of her when she named me,' she said cautiously.

The baron appeared in the doorway, flanked by his valet.

'You.' He pointed at Paget. 'Get out.'

The children inched closer together, uneasily, like two burrs stuck to each other. Paget paused midway through a bow. Madame de Cardonnoy kept her neck straight and searched in the mirror until she found the baron's eyes. His expression was furious.

'My hair isn't finished,' she said.

The baron gestured to his valet, Henri, who came and took Paget by the arm. The hairdresser fumbled to pack his combs and ribbons back into the open travelling case on Marie Catherine's toilette cloth while the valet tugged at his elbow.

'What's the point of this?' said Marie Catherine. 'What can possibly be this urgent? I'm going to look *ridiculous* – my hair is a mess!' She could hear her voice rising in pitch as Paget's case slipped out of his hands and the hastily packed contents rolled out over the floor. Jeanne joined him on her knees to stuff his tools back inside, but the baron had finally left his post in the doorway and, with the heel of his boot, he kicked the case across the room and then seized Paget's other arm.

Jeanne scrambled back. The hairdresser had resisted the baron's valet, but when the baron himself gripped him, Paget bowed his head and hurried out of the room, snatching up the handle of the open case, which bounced against his leg as he jogged.

Marie Catherine looked at herself in the mirror, where her hair hung lankly around her ears instead of curling in ringlets, as it should. She snatched a pin that was pricking her from the back of her neck, felt the plaits loosen, then followed her husband and his valet as they hustled Paget away. Her hair fell down over her shoulders with the woollen form still attached.

She couldn't quite manage to be properly angry, the way she would have been if the baron had insulted her dress or ordered her to stay at home instead of going to the ballet. It was as if the stupid scene was happening on a stage at the theatre, and she was a spectator puzzled by the husband's inexplicable behaviour.

'How dare you treat my hairdresser like this!' she called from the top of the stairs, hurrying down.

The baron's tall back didn't turn. The three of them made a little row like a peak of mountains trailing off into a pass – Paget's diminutive form wedged between the baron and his valet. The hairdresser glanced back at her fearfully.

'Do you think I'm just a slave in your household and I have to obey your every whim? Take your hands off him, he's done nothing to offend you!'

The baron did release Paget, and for a moment Marie Catherine felt a surge of triumph as she stood halfway down the grand staircase. Then he turned back towards her and charged up the steps, with his chin tucked into his chest like a ram defending its pasture. Somehow the ridiculousness of the situation had blinded her to his fury. She stumbled backwards on the stairs and, when he reached out for her, she bent over the polished balustrade and screamed before he had even knotted his fist in the sleeve of her dress.

'Do you think I'm going to let you put horns on me in my own house?' he shouted. 'Who was the man who came to see you yesterday?'

Marie Catherine's slipper slid off her foot, and the baron wrenched her arm so painfully that she struggled to keep her balance on the steps. Below, she could see Monsieur Paget casting sad glances back her way as her husband's valet hurried him out of the hall. A flock of servants had dropped their work when she'd screamed, and now their heads peeped through doorways like little birds. Above, Nicolas stood frozen and tearful in the centre of the hallway, until Jeanne hurried out and picked him up and rushed him back into her bedroom.

'I don't know what you're talking about!' Marie Catherine said, trying to keep her voice steady and honest, although her heart was banging against the tendons of her throat as if it were a small animal trying to escape through her mouth. 'I've never deceived you. Never!'

'My man saw you kiss him in the hallway! Did you think no one looks up at those windows?'

He raised his hand to hit her, and she shoved him down the stairs.

He only stumbled and slid a few steps down, catching himself against the wall, but it was enough time for her to hike up her skirts and kick off her remaining slipper and run back up the stairs as if death were behind her. The baron did not, customarily, hit her. But kissing another man in the hallway of his house was more provocation than even she customarily gave him.

She ran to her bedroom and slammed the door behind her before he could wedge his shoulder into the gap. As she fumbled with the key in the lock, she heard him step back and then take three running footsteps that would have sent the door flying into her face, if she hadn't leaned against it to brace herself for the impact. The whole wooden panel shook with the force of his charge. She turned the key, shot the bolt home and stepped back. The baron pounded angrily on the door.

Jeanne had crowded the children into the corner behind the bed. Both of them were red-eyed and pale, like little ghosts. Sophie broke away from the maid and ran out to hug her mother's skirts. Marie Catherine heard the baron's pounding cease. And then, again, the three steps back across the hall and the resounding impact of his weight against the locked door. She heard the wooden panels crunch. The bolt rattled in its lock like a gunshot. The baron made a pained noise outside the door, then there was another resounding crash that split a yellow edge of wood where the hinges fastened to the wall.

Madame de Cardonnoy pushed Sophie behind her. She was at her toilette table and fumbling for something that she might use as a weapon – a glass bottle of perfume, the book of Villon's poetry, her powder, the bundle of ribbons that she'd pulled out of her half-dressed hair – nothing, in short, absolutely nothing that would help her. The baron threw himself against the door again. She was crying, little choked-off sobs with her right hand pressed over her mouth.

She took her hand away from her face and clenched her fists in her skirts. Then, once she'd made herself straighten up instead of cowering, she put a hand between Sophie's shoulder blades and pushed her back towards Jeanne. She shook her hair out as best she could, raining down pins that landed with a half-dozen soft thuds on the carpet.

Another *crack*, and then two wide running steps echoed through the hallway. *Crack.* Marie Catherine put her hand up to her throat to hold her pulse in and backed away from the door.

Crack. The lock broke. The baron sent the remains of the door flying open.

'Have you gone completely insane?' she cried. She was pleased to hear that her voice shook only a little, although she'd taken an involuntary step backwards into her table when the door swung wide.

The baron strode across the room towards her, no longer concerned to run. He knew he had her cornered.

'Are you trying to make yourself a laughing stock with your ridiculous jealousy?' she went on, crossing her arms over her chest. 'How can you expect to control your household when you can't even control yourself? Look at that door!'

She pointed. The baron grabbed at her wrist and she stepped back again, grasping at the wall behind her until her hands found the curling carved leaves of the windowsill.

'You have the key in your desk.' Her voice was trembling very badly now. 'And yet you broke down a door *in your own house*, and terrified your children, because you were too possessed by rage to go down the hallway and get it. Look at it! Look at *yourself!* You should be humiliated. I'm a woman and I have more restraint than you.'

Her voice broke into a sob on the last sentence. She could see herself in the little mirror over her table, red-faced and weeping, her hair a disastrous witch's broomstick. Not self-restrained at all.

But the baron paused. He didn't turn back to the door, but he looked at the children cowering with Jeanne, who had clamped her hand over Nicolas's mouth to keep him quiet. The baron twisted back to look at the door, and his face flushed unpleasantly.

'You have no idea how ridiculous you look,' Marie Catherine told him. His hesitation had given her strength, and her voice now gained volume. She pushed herself away from the window, as if she wasn't afraid to step nearer to him, as if her eyes weren't still stinging with tears. 'In front of your children. In front of your servants. Oh, you've done great work for your good name today. And over a complete misunderstanding. I have *always* been faithful to you.'

As she said it, there was a moment when the clarity of her voice convinced her, and she believed it herself. The baron's head snapped back towards her, and she knew she had gone too far. But he caught himself just before he would have raised his hand and stood, very angry and very still.

'Do you think,' he said. Then paused and drew a breath.

Marie Catherine pulled herself up straight, as if she were preparing for a royal audience. She couldn't look afraid.

'Do you think,' the baron repeated, once he'd calmed his breathing, 'that you can still put me off with your lies? I know what Arnaud says he saw through that window, and I will find out who he was and punish you both.'

He'd lowered his voice, but his hands were shaking. Marie Catherine could see his nostrils flare and crease as he huffed out each breath.

'You'd best prepare your things. I'll send you somewhere you can't continue to shame yourself and your family.' He walked over to her desk, wrenched out the drawer in which she kept her papers and tucked the whole drawer-frame under his arm, trailing letters and bits of old ink-stained quill.

She reached out to save them, reflexively, and then she let her hand drop.

With that, the baron turned on his heel and walked out of the room. She could hear him down the hallway, calling for his valet. Marie Catherine braced herself against the baseboard of her bed, then gasped and let herself sink down onto the floor. The muscles in her legs were jumping as if she'd been thrown from the back of a powerful horse. She felt the children's arms around her neck, the porridgy smell of Nicolas's breath on her face, and closed her eyes.

When she had enough strength to open them again, she pushed the two little bodies back, gently.

'Take them up to the nursery,' she said to Jeanne. 'Tell Anne to keep them there for the rest of the day. Then come back here. There's more for you to do.'

'Yes, Madame,' said Jeanne. The children were both crying, Nicolas with his face screwed up, and Sophie numbly and almost silently.

'Go with Jeanne,' said Marie Catherine, as Nicolas held out his arms to her disconsolately in the broken doorway. 'I'll visit you this evening, and everything will be all right again.'

She had a sudden moment of nausea as Jeanne led them away down the hall. She put a hand over her mouth and tasted bile, and for a moment she thought she would sink down onto her knees on the floor and be unable to do anything at all, as if her husband's presence down the hall, behind his closed and doubtless locked door, to which she had no key, was enough to sap her strength entirely. She steadied herself against the wall until the moment passed.

She met Anne, the children's nursemaid, coming up the stairs. She looked distressed to see Marie Catherine. She must have heard the fight.

'Anne.' Marie Catherine didn't bother trying to disguise the way her hands were trembling. 'Jeanne has the children in the nursery. Will you get me a cup of milk from the kitchen before you go to them? I feel—'

She closed her eyes and drew several slow breaths.

'Of course.' The stairs creaked under Anne's descending footsteps.

Marie Catherine waited in her broken bedroom until the nursemaid returned. She kept her pen and her inkpot with the toiletries on top of her table, and not in the drawer that her husband had wrenched out of her desk. Looking at the hole, resting her fingers on the ledge where the drawer would have rested, she hoped that he would find nothing incriminating in it.

But she was not sure that it would matter what he found. If he wanted to send her away, to have her imprisoned in some convent far from Paris, it would be enough to put forth the evidence that she was cold, that she had an evil tongue, that she neglected her marital duties, that he had proof of her infidelity furnished by his servants. He would easily obtain the lettre de cachet that would authorise her imprisonment.

Anne returned with the milk in a gold-rimmed teacup.

'Thank you,' Marie Catherine said and took a long sip. It slid unctuously down her throat. 'Now go and see to the children.'

The nursemaid left, and Marie Catherine sat down at her desk and put a clean leaf of paper in front of her. The milk she put by her right hand, and then she dipped her pen in it and wrote:

Dearest V.,

I don't know how to write this letter, and I cannot put any of the usual honorifics before it. Some servants observed you entering the hôtel in your new clothes and have told my husband the whole story. They take you for a gentleman. I've denied everything, but he is determined to discover your identity. He says he'll get a lettre de cachet to lock me away in a convent somewhere, and I don't know what I can do to escape.

For God's sake, do what you can to protect yourself.

Yours always,

M.C.

When she had finished, she waved the sheet before her until the damp writing on it had dried down and become invisible. Then she replaced the teacup with her inkwell and wrote another message over the first one:

Mademoiselle de Conti,

My congratulations, again, on your costume yesterday. I cannot express my delight in your company, and I hope we may meet soon at the ballet or at the place Royale.

Kindly read this message in the manner to which you and I have become accustomed, with my warmest regards,

Madame de Cardonnoy

If the paper was held over a fire, the first message would reappear as the milk darkened from the heat. It was a trick she'd used as a schoolgirl to pass secret letters to her friends. If Marie Catherine had kept all of her correspondence, the baron might have found other such messages among her letters. But, once revealed, the hidden message was plain for all to see, and so every letter from Victoire that instructed her to read it *in the manner to which you and I have become accustomed* was a letter that ended its life in the fire.

By the time she had signed her name to the false message, Jeanne had returned.

'I need to you take this to Mademoiselle de Conti at the place Royale. Wait to leave until the baron and his valet aren't watching the front gate, and don't let anyone take it out of your hands except Mademoiselle de Conti herself.'

For a moment, Marie Catherine saw a shadow of some emotion – anger, frustration, fear – pass over the servant girl's face. Then she smoothed it down again into her customary calm.

Jeanne certainly knew who the mysterious visitor had been. But she hadn't said anything in front of the baron, and Marie Catherine hoped that she wouldn't betray her now.

'Here's the carriage fare for a fiacre. Be careful.'

'Yes, Madame,' said Jeanne.

Lavoie heard the rapping on his door from his studio on the second floor and returned to himself with a sigh. He had been daydreaming as he mixed his paints for the next day, letting the grindstone and the bright smear of pigment upon it become a sort of portal into a painting that he hadn't made yet, a world of pure colour. Orpiment, called the king of poisons by those who wanted to kill rats or other men, made the purest yellow, the colour of canary feathers, of soft buttercups blooming in a field, of the jaundiced skin of an old man's cheek. A colour he might have wanted to lick off the tip of a paintbrush, but, when ingested, it caused headache, vomiting, convulsions, death. One had to keep it away from the pigments containing verdigris or it discoloured and became ugly. So too there was green earth from Verona, pale-blue bice pigmented with finely ground cobalt glass, candleblack, blue ash, bruise-coloured Roman vitriol. He prepared his colours and they left a stain on his vision, floated up to the pure canvas of the opposite wall and composed themselves into scenes.

He could step out of his body and into pure fantasy, but often, too, what he saw when he looked into space were the brushstrokes that made up the scene, the way that one could manipulate light and colour so that the picture – myth or battle or portrait or landscape – would be transfigured by the brush and would appear to the viewer as only those scenes most coloured by memory and emotion ever did in real life. These perfect imagined paintings were beyond the skill of his hands, but he painted them internally, and they filled him with the confidence that one day, before he grew old and his fingers began to tremble, he would paint them on canvas. Some day, when he had the money and the fame to paint exactly what he wanted to.

The knocking tapered off and then began again, fiercer and more prolonged. He levered himself out of his chair with a groan for his sore feet – he had gone from appointment to appointment today, and his knees ached from standing still in front of a canvas. The anxious visitor, he feared, was Pierre Maçon, his neighbour, who had taken it into his head that the rank and unpleasant smell that pervaded Maçon's own house was the smell of the sizing that Lavoie used to prepare his canvases.

Lavoie could not have truthfully denied that he prepared the sizing in his own back garden, that the smell was disagreeable, that it did occasionally leak out onto the street and linger there – but over the course of Maçon's increasingly outraged visits he had found himself less and less inclined to be conciliatory. He went downstairs already preparing a barb in response to Maçon's inevitable complaint. Perhaps, if Monsieur Maçon disliked the smell of his own house so much, he ought to ask his wife to bathe more often. Perhaps his servant ought to check the larder for dead rats. Perhaps the offensive smell was emanating from Monsieur Maçon himself. Perhaps Monsieur Maçon ought to let other men practise their professions in peace, and anyway, Lavoie hadn't prepared any sizing this week, so his neighbours really couldn't have anything to complain about.

He was surprised to open the door – a quip already making its way up his throat to the tip of his tongue – only to find not his meddlesome neighbour, but the Baron de Cardonnoy and two lackeys. Lavoie attempted to disguise his astonishment with a deep bow.

'Monsieur de Cardonnoy,' he said, holding the door wide, 'come in, please.'

The baron nodded and gestured his servants in before him. They came through the doorway shoulder to shoulder, so that the door was pushed out of Lavoie's hands and he had to step back to let them past. He was flushed from the surprise of the visit and the embarrassment of having worked himself up into a sweltering irritation over his self-righteous neighbour, only to find, at his door, a loyal patron. He recognised one of the lackeys from his visit to Madame de Cardonnoy's maid – the Swiss guard who stood at the door, although he couldn't remember his name. They'd exchanged a joke and a smile at the gate when he left, but now the other man stood in his entranceway like a block of wood and gave no sign that he recognised Lavoie.

'May I ask what brings you here so late in the evening, Monsieur?' asked Lavoie, once the baron had stepped through the doorway after his men. Lavoie circled around the Swiss guard and closed the door behind them, shutting out the twilight and the dull glow of the street lanterns. When he turned round, the baron had his back to him and was appraising the walls and ceiling of Lavoie's house as if he intended to buy it. His servants formed an ominous flanking guard on either side of the nobleman, and they regarded Lavoie without affection. The candle that Lavoie held cast flickering shadows on the ceiling. Its light didn't reach the corners of the room.

The embarrassment he had felt on opening his door to Monsieur de Cardonnoy intensified ominously. He had the distinct feeling that he was about to lose his portrait commission, and perhaps without payment for the work he'd already done.

'You visited my wife,' said the baron, to the stairs that led up to Lavoie's workshop.

'Monsieur, I did not,' Lavoie replied.

It took him only a moment to realise that his dismay at the question had betrayed him.

The baron's face, when he turned, was stern but composed. Although Lavoie's thoughts were racing, he couldn't help but see how he might have used that face for some biblical scene – Moses delivering the tablets, Abraham sacrificing his son. The inappropriateness of the thought wrung his face into a grimace.

'You came to my house yesterday in the afternoon. So I am informed by my guard.' The baron gestured to the Swiss. 'And you sent this.'

The baron reached inside his coat and pulled out a folded letter.

Lavoie did not need to study the signature to know that it must be the note that he had sent Madame de Cardonnoy after the first sitting. He tried to steady his breathing. Little pins and needles were running up his limbs.

'Monsieur, I am deeply sorry if I've behaved with any impropriety. I thought—' He didn't know what he'd been thinking. He bowed instead, deeply.

The baron let out a short exhalation that widened his nostrils and revealed, for a moment, the anger that lay underneath his controlled exterior. Lavoie spent a great deal of his time observing the subtleties of expression in the human face. He did not like the baron's expression. Surely he could not be so angry over one visit to his home, during which his wife had not even been present. Over one letter. But there was something there, beneath the surface of the baron's skin, that troubled him more than Lavoie's visit could possibly have done, and Lavoie knew the nobility well enough to realise that he would be expected to bear this anger, even though he was not the one who had caused it.

'My household,' said the baron, 'is beyond reproach, and my wife will no longer receive correspondence from a puffed-up little painter with ideas beyond his station.' He crossed the room and stood at the door. The knot of Lavoie's fear loosened enough to let him find his tongue again.

'Monsieur le Baron,' he stammered, 'I assure you I never meant to cause you any kind of offence—'

'I'm not interested in your lies,' the baron spat. 'I know my wife would not fall so low as to consort with *you*, but that doesn't excuse your presumption. Caspar, Henri, I will be waiting in my carriage. Wash your hands before you join me.'

He opened the door and went out, leaving Lavoie alone with the two lackeys.

Lavoie held up his hands as the men stepped towards him.

'Caspar,' he said, remembering now the Swiss guard's name. 'Don't do this.'

The Swiss shook his head, as if Lavoie's voice was a gnat crawling in the sweat at his hairline.

'I've done nothing to offend you, and nothing to offend your master,' Lavoie continued. He had tried to back towards the door, but the other lackey, Henri, moved faster than him, and he found himself instead edged in the direction of the pantry, with the front door and the stairs both blocked by the baron's men. He was clutching at his candlestick, stupidly. 'You cannot believe that this is justice,' he said.

And then Henri took three brisk, cautious steps towards him, trying to herd him up against the wall where he wouldn't be able to turn or flee, and Lavoie despaired of diplomacy, dropped his candle and swung a fist at the servant's head. The lackey raised his arm to protect his face, and Lavoie's hand met the bone in his elbow with a crack that sent a jolt of pain up his wrist. The candle rolled across the floor and went out. The blow had turned his back to the Swiss, who lunged at him and wrapped his arms around Lavoie's waist, pinning his other arm to his side and nearly lifting him off his feet, while Lavoie strained to brace himself or hook the Swiss's ankle with one of his own and wrench him off-balance as the sudden darkness pressed in around him.

The other lackey did not waste time hesitating, and the impact of knees and fists in Lavoie's chest and on his face was horribly disorienting, as if he had wandered out into the surf of the ocean and fallen, unable to swim and brutalised by the waves until he was uncertain even of which way was up, whether the air was above him or below, whether his desperate breaths would drown him or give him a few more moments of life. He hid his face with his free arm, trying to protect himself. In the dark, he was unable to judge where the other lackey was with enough certainty to think about hitting him back. Lavoie threw his weight back against the Swiss guard who held him and, falling himself, his balance disrupted by pain, managed to send him careening into the balustrade. But the blow that shook the Swiss sent Lavoie stumbling to his knees, where the other lackey kicked him in the ribs over and over again as he tried to get up. Soon the Swiss joined him, casually, the way a pair of little boys might kick around a stick or an old stone, out of boredom.

Lavoie felt himself turning into a kind of small, tortured animal. The world receded to a very small circle of floor at the level of his eyes, and his goal was only to crawl across it, laboriously, as if making for some imaginary safe burrow at the other end of the hall, while the lackeys tried to cave in his ribs and send his head bouncing into the lower stairs. The burrow did not exist. He curled into a ball around his soft stomach, and put his hands over his head.

Eventually they decided that he had had enough and they left him alone.

Chapter Five

———

As a little girl at her Ursuline convent school, Madame de Cardonnoy had once stolen a piece of money from one of the nuns who taught her. It had been a few sous, enough to buy a ribbon or a sweet bun. She couldn't think why she had done it, except that she knew it was wicked, and the wickedness had added its own spice to the deed. And that the sister in question had ridiculed her the week before and sentenced her to scrub the floor as a punishment – for what offence she didn't remember, although she knew that first she had been made to bow down and kiss the muddy shoes of the girl she'd wronged. She'd crawled around on her knees with the bucket, the spoilt child who had never held a scrubbing brush or knelt except at her prayers, feeling the dampness of the floor creeping up through her skirt, and she'd had, perhaps for the first time, the distinct impression of a divine watcher above her, who could see through the back of her head to the hard knot of unrepentant anger lodged there.

When they'd caught her with the coin, the sisters had informed her that the penalty for theft was hanging. They'd bundled her up into a laundry basket and then suspended the basket from the ceiling of the chapel. She was nine years old and the basket swung perilously every time she moved or tried to peer over the edge. When she looked up, she could see the cobwebs hanging above her. She could have touched them, if the basket's rocking hadn't frightened her too much to stand.

Below her, the nuns lined the other girls up with candles and marched them back and forth, chanting funeral orations, until a strange heaviness descended on her body and she wondered whether she was not actually a spirit watching them from above, waiting for judgement. The image of Christ on the cross was below her now, but she still felt its heaven-turned eyes on her. *The holy ghost*, she'd thought with a shiver. *The holy ghost*. With a child's understanding of the words. The guilt over the stolen coin pricked like a pin stuck in her bodice, pinching every time she moved and the basket swung. She was still breathing, but she felt death's presence all around her.

Finally one of the youngest girls, marching under the basket, had looked up white-faced and tearful and called up, 'Are you dead?' Marie Catherine had caught her breath. The room spun dizzily around her as her spirit descended back into her body. Her hands and feet tingled. She'd leaned over the side of the basket and watched the room spin.

'Not yet,' she'd called down.

And, she'd discovered, touching her hands to her face, that it was true.

'Chéri, you're lying on my sewing,' she said to Nicolas. She had to prise his shoulder up with one hand to pull the creased fabric out from underneath him. The child was snuggled into her like an infant, his arms around the softest part of her waist, his face buried in her stomach. She'd come up to the nursery after the baron had stormed out of the house, passing her broken door without speaking to her. With her, in a pile on Nicolas's bed, she had one of her linen shifts, a purse of money and a small pile of her jewellery. A porcelain cup full of lukewarm coffee sat on the table by the bed. She had forgotten that it was there. As the daylight faded outside the nursery window, she unpicked hems, threaded her needle and stitched a hidden fortune of rubies, white pearls, smiling emeralds, gold louis and moon-coloured silver écus into the seams of her underclothes.

If her husband planned to send her to some convent, away from Paris and her children, she had decided, she would make it as difficult as possible for him to keep her there.

The children had been sombre and tearful since she had come up to sit with them and sent Anne away. Nicolas had launched himself at her when she sat down on his bed and refused to be unglued from her side. Sophie, more contained, turned to her lessons and sat at her little table reading her prayer book with the expression on her face of one who is afraid to confront the problem facing her by questioning it too closely. She looked strangely adult, with her back straight and her chin tucked down in reflection. At Sophie's age, Marie Catherine had already been at convent school, her father determined to secure her the lady's education that her mother could not provide her. Her daughter's quiet prayer reminded her of herself, of the little ways the convent girls found to mother each other, while the nuns treated them, mostly, like diminutive ladies or like a particularly wilful and unreliable breed of farm animal.

She had not wanted Sophie to be sent away to school. She had taught her to read herself, with so much complaining on Sophie's part that Marie Catherine had lost her temper and slapped her hand more than once, when the girl had tried to get up and run around or slither under the table like a snake. She had been filled with guilt afterwards, remembering how when she was a girl her own mother had slapped her and ordered the nursemaid to take away her dinner, for what had seemed then like the smallest infractions. Even with the guilt, it had taken her a long time to stop – she could not seem to control her temper, and she wondered also if her tenderness towards Sophie was a different kind of sin, which would make her undisciplined and spoiled.

Now that Nicolas was old enough for lessons, a tutor taught both children their sums, their letters and prayers and a bit of Latin, but this was only at Madame de Cardonnoy's insistence. If the baron sent Marie Catherine away, then it was likely that Sophie, too, would be shipped off to the Ursulines.

If only she had controlled her passion for Victoire – but it was now too late for that.

'Would you like me to finish the story I began the other day?' she asked the children finally. She was afraid that if she didn't find something to distract herself, she'd cry in front of them.

Sophie sighed over her prayer book and shook her head.

'No, it's too scary. Tell us a nice story.'

Marie Catherine put her sewing aside for a moment and ran her hands through Nicolas's hair, combing it up into a rooster's crest and then stroking it flat again. Sophie's eyes followed her movement, as if she too would have liked to put away her prayer book and lie down beside her mother.

'Are you frightened too, Nicolas?'

He whined into her skirts. 'Are you going to go away?'

'For a little while, if your father commands it. But I'll come back.' She took a ruby ring out of the stack of her jewellery and began stitching it into the folded hem of her shift – a plait of small stitches around the golden band, to hold it in place – and then she folded the hem back over to conceal the jewels.

'I know the story's frightening,' she said. 'Sometimes things occur in life that are also frightening, and we don't have the choice to turn away from them. The day may come when you need to be brave in earnest, and the story gives you the chance to practise that virtue.' Marie Catherine swallowed. She had dried her eyes before she came up to see the children, but she knew that Sophie at least was old enough to see that she'd been crying.

Sophie sniffed. 'Tell us if it ends happily first. Before you tell the rest of it.'

Marie Catherine held out her hand, and her daughter left the table and curled up by her side next to Nicolas. Between the two of them, it was like sitting before a dying fire, the soft heat of their bodies seeping through her clothes.

'Yes, darling, the story ends happily. There's no reason to be frightened, because everything turns out all right in the end.'

Sophie nodded, and Nicolas looked up at her solemnly. Marie Catherine took up her dress again and, as Sophie touched the hem and found the hidden jewels, she rethreaded her needle and resumed the tale.

'Where did I leave off? The stone bride lived with the ogre in his palace, and for a while the village in the shade of the forest knew peace. The ogre's other wives had wept and begged him to release them, but the stone woman showed neither fear nor any other emotion, and the ogre, for the first time in his life, was fascinated by another creature. At first he admired her for her coldness, for she neither shied away from his touch nor attempted to flee the palace. She had no fear of the ogre, for, being stone, she was invulnerable to harm.'

'Couldn't something crush a stone, though?' said Nicolas.

'I suppose so,' said Marie Catherine, pausing to rethread her needle, 'but it would be very difficult.' Marie Catherine felt Sophie squirm impatiently beside her. She hurried on, before Nicolas could ask her to explain what might happen if she dropped a heavier stone on the stone woman, or stabbed her with a very, very sharp sword.

'Soon, however, the ogre began to feel that something was missing in order to make his marriage happy. He still had, in the first place, an inordinate hunger for blood, which his wife's stony kisses could not satisfy. So, as the weeks passed, he began again to ride out into the forest to hunt, where he would take any unfortunate soul that he came upon and carry him back to his palace for a gruesome meal.'

'You said it wasn't going to be too scary,' said Sophie.

'It's all right.' Marie Catherine put her shift down and reached out for her daughter's hand. 'I promise it all ends happily.'

Saying that it would end happily was as easy as laughing off one of her stories in the salon. *My mother's tales, not mine.* If her mother had never told stories, then she'd simply invent a different mother. Her voice remained steady, and telling the tale allowed her hands to work at the seams of her shift without having to think too clearly about what she was doing. But although she had regained her calm, there was something in her heart that set her against the happy ending that she had promised Sophie. If her childhood nursemaid had been telling it, the ogre might, at the end, have been transformed into a prince. But she would not give them that ending.

'As the ogre spent more and more time at the hunt, returning each evening to his wife's indifferent greeting, he began to feel more and more dissatisfied. Surely, beneath his bride's stone flesh, there should be a woman who loved him and missed him. So he tried to impress his bride, and performed feats of strength for her. He tore down trees in the garden, he juggled great boulders, he shot an arrow from his bow so precisely that he cut a fly in two.'

Marie Catherine paused her sewing to stretch her fingers, which had cramped around the needle.

'When the stone woman merely smiled her disinterested smile and thanked him, then lapsed back into her customary silence, he began to accuse her of treachery, saying that she was hard and unfeeling. And when he left for the hunt he locked her in her chambers, so that she could see no one – as if any creature would have come to that palace of blood.'

Suddenly the anger in her own voice surprised her. The hairs on her arms were standing on end. She was saying more than she should.

'Maybe Sophie's right and we should tell a different story. Would you like that?'

Sophie shook her head. 'You promised it would have a happy ending! If you stop now, we'll know that it doesn't.'

'It's not that, my darling. I just haven't made up the ending yet. I could tell the story about the little girl in the peapod. You love that story.'

'But I already know that one,' said Sophie.

'Nicolas? What do you want?'

Nicolas had buried his head deep in Marie Catherine's side, his hand clutching her skirt. She had, she knew, made the story too bloody. He would be frightened.

'Shall I tell a different story, my love?'

His ribs rose and fell as he thought about it.

'No. I want the story Sophie wants. I'm not scared.'

'All right then.' Outside the window, the dusk was lengthening into full darkness. The light had become dim enough that Marie Catherine could barely see her own stitches. She got up from between the children and lit a pair of candles.

'Sophie, why don't you fetch your needle and help me with my sewing?'

Sophie did as she'd been asked to and came and sat back down beside Marie Catherine, curling her legs up to her chest like a cat.

'Maman, why are we ...' Sophie's voice trailed off as she concentrated on threading her needle, her eyebrows furrowed.

'I'll tell you later, Sophie,' Marie Catherine said. 'For now, help and keep this secret, and don't tell Anne or anyone else.'

Sophie nodded, slowly, and tied off her thread.

'So,' Marie Catherine began again, 'the stone bride and the ogre might have continued that way for ever, if the ogre had not been so set on winning his wife's affection. He killed a hundred songbirds and made her a cape of their feathers. He took the knucklebones of all the men he'd killed and strung them into a grisly necklace. But the stone bride remained unmoved. The ogre mounted his horse and rode throughout his lands, and everywhere he went the birdsong fell quiet and the villagers hid away inside, and if he caught some unfortunate out on foot far from shelter, then that man went down on his knees and declared himself the ogre's most loyal servant, and pleaded with him to be allowed to return to his family. Only the ogre's stone wife greeted him with indifference.'

'Tell us what happened next,' said Sophie. 'It can't go on like that for ever. Tell us how it ends.'

Marie Catherine picked a purse of coins up from the table and began stitching them one by one into shift's side seam and, as her hands worked, she continued.

'Finally the ogre, jealous and miserable, decided on a plan. He would invite the men from his lands to his forest palace and there, before his wife, he would hold a contest of strength. For surely if his wife was not impressed with him, it must be because she had not seen how superior he was to all other men.'

She remembered the coffee cup on the side table, reached for it to take a sip, grimaced when she realised that it had long ago gone cold. The drink left the inside of her mouth feeling unpleasantly coated, as if she had swallowed a spoonful of raw flour.

Jeanne, as far as she knew, had not returned, and neither had her husband. The task of sewing, of spinning out the tale, kept her from thinking about where either might be. She cleared her throat and continued the tale.

'But the truth was that there were few strong men left in the village, for those who were brave had already taken up their swords against the ogre's rule and been defeated, or else they had left to seek their fortune in some other, happier place. And so the file of men who the ogre chased and harried to his great hall on the day of the tournament were old grandfathers, long past their best days, with stiff backs and swollen knees, and young boys carrying their brothers' rusted swords. There was not a single one of them who might have made a formidable enemy.'

'Where did the ones who left go?' asked Nicolas.

'I don't know,' said Marie Catherine. 'Maybe they came to Paris.'

Sophie, on her other side, was putting tiny stitches into the seams of the shift, holding the fabric so close to her nose that it fluttered when she exhaled.

'Nevertheless, the ogre was determined. As his wife watched from her dais, he allowed the old men to break their swords on his iron skin, and then he roared and felled them with a swipe of his long nails. Some fled, and some begged for mercy. Only one boy, perhaps fifteen, raised his bent sword and advanced on the ogre. He was the fairest child of the village, and so beloved by his parents that they had kept him, for most of his life, locked away in a cellar, lest his spirit should lead him to take up arms against the ogre and fall as his brothers had fallen. His confinement had left him as fair and delicate as a girl, so that, facing the ogre, he was like a single straight stalk of wheat standing tall before a rampaging boar. He knew that his sword would not pierce the ogre's flesh, but nevertheless he wanted to die bravely.'

'What would happen if ...' Nicolas began, and Sophie let out an exasperated sigh and dropped her sewing into her lap.

'Maman, does he have to interrupt *everything*? Can't you just listen?'

Nicolas burrowed deeper into the coverlet beside her. He'd been crying quietly into her skirt, at intervals, sometimes cheering up as the story took hold. Now he was sobbing again.

'Sophie,' she said softly. 'Both of you. Listen. As the stone bride watched the battle, sitting above the bloodshed in her dress of red silk, she saw the boy's bravery in the face of fear, and for the first time she was moved. Not by her husband's fearsome strength, but by the bravery that can only come with weakness. With a blow from the back of his hand, the ogre knocked down the boy, and as, gloating, he prepared to deliver the killing blow, the stone bride's heart beat for the first time and she cried out, "Stop!"'

'The ogre paused. "What is it, wife? Surely you don't wish to save this wretch?"

'The stone bride stood up, her expression, for the first time, betraying an emotion other than indifference. "Husband," she said, "you bore me. You have boasted so much of your strength, but all I see is a child crushing ants."

"'And so it must be," said the ogre, "for who could stand against me? My footsteps are like an earthquake that knocks strong men to the ground. My breath is a storm sent from the fires of hell. If no man can defeat me, would you have me beat down the mountains? Shall I drink the rivers dry, or turn the seas to fire? What will satisfy you, you ungrateful wife?"'

Marie Catherine was looking at the needlework in her own hands, but she felt Sophie reach across her lap to squeeze Nicolas's hand. She'd put down her own sewing. Marie Catherine could not have scolded her for it.

"'You need not boast so much about your strength," said the stone woman. "I am not even sure that you are stronger than me, and I am only a woman, even if I am made of stone."'

"'What nonsense you talk," said the ogre, enraged. "Do you not live in my house? Do you not do as I bid? Can you uproot a tree with your hands, as I can, or kill a man with the flick of your nail? So what business have you to say that *you* are stronger than I am?"'

Marie Catherine winced. She'd let her attention wander from her sewing and the needle had pierced the base of her thumb, below her thimble. She blotted the drop of blood that welled up there on the shift's hem.

"'But, husband," said the stone bride, "this is easy to put to the test. Come here, and I will put my hand in your mouth. And if, when you bite down, the stone breaks, we will agree for the rest of time that you are the stronger. But if you cannot break what I am made of, then perhaps you will admit that I have bested you."'

Marie Catherine wasn't sure if it was she who was holding her breath or the children. She had given them a story that was too much for them, and now she must tell her way out of it. Whether it ended happily or not.

'The ogre,' she said, 'was furious, and wasted no time in taking his wife's hand and biting down with all his strength. Soon there was the screech of iron teeth on stone, but his wife's hand did not give way. He chewed and gnashed his teeth until his jaw ached, but to no avail. He might have given up then, if he had not been so angry and humiliated. But just as he might have surrendered, the stone woman laughed gaily. It was the first time he had ever heard her laugh. And so angry was the ogre at the sound that he found a new reserve of strength and bit down once more, and the stone bride's hand snapped off in his teeth.'

Outside, it was beginning to rain. A cascade of droplets spilled over the moulded laurel leaves that framed the window and drummed against the glass panes. When Marie Catherine looked up, she couldn't see how hard the rain was coming down, but she saw her own reflection in the glass, cradling the children in the circle of candlelight, as if it was something that had happened a long time ago, as if a door had blown open somewhere in the house and given her a chance vision of something as fragile and impossible as the stone woman of her story. She took a breath to go on speaking, glancing up occasionally to meet the too-knowing eyes of her reflection in the window.

'But that was not the end. For the stone bride did not feel pain. She went on laughing. And the ogre, in his rage, had bitten down so forcefully that her severed hand stuck in his throat and he began to choke on it. Though his skin was so thick that no sword could wound him, still, like all creatures, he needed to breathe, and a little piece of white stone lodged in his throat was enough, in the end, to lay him low.'

'So she rescued the boy from the village?' Sophie asked hopefully.

'Yes, she rescued him.'

'Was she all right without her hand?'

'Sometimes she missed it, but—' Marie Catherine began, and then the sound of carriage wheels on the wet flags of the court-yard carried up to the nursery window, along with a servant's voice shouting. A feeling of resignation fell over her like a cold blanket of snow, but infinitely colder. She bit off the end of her thread and bundled up the shift into which she'd been sewing her gold, the fabric heavier for its secret treasure.

'I have to go downstairs now,' she told the children. 'Try to fall asleep.'

Both started to plead with her, but she left the room and closed the door, a candle in one hand, the underdress folded into a ball on her hip. Her head was throbbing with the need to hide away the shift before she crossed the baron's path.

Running footsteps sounded on the stairs below her. Whoever was coming up must be taking them two at a time, and a servant had no reason to hurry that way unless the baron had been in a rage when he returned. Unless it was the baron himself coming up. She pressed herself against the wall by reflex as the approaching figure entered the circle of her candlelight and cast a witch's shadow down the hallway.

It was Henri, her husband's valet, his hair plastered down to his head by the rain. The race up to the nursery had left him panting. His gold-braided coat gave off the smell of wet wool. He leaned against the wall, trying to catch his breath, staring at her as if she was the monster, then he wiped the rain from his face with his hand and croaked out, 'Murder!'

'What?' Marie Catherine raised her candle to look at his face. He had a bloody streak from his nose to his chin.

'Murder, Madame,' he said again, and she realised that the redness of his eyes was from tears. His hands were also bloody, and looked black in the candlelight.

'Where's Jeanne?' She was pressing the petticoat up to her mouth. If her maid had been caught – or had there been enough in her letters to incriminate her? The panic was like a white light that obliterated rational thought. Henri had now stepped closer to her.

'He came at us in the street. The street light was broken – it was too dark to see. I was on the seat with the coachman, with Caspar riding behind. He threw down a torch in front of the horses, they nearly bolted. It was all we could do to keep them from overturning the carriage.'

Henri was stuttering, shaking. She could see the tears streaming down his face.

'No.'

She dropped the petticoat and ran down the stairs, her footsteps hammering on the steps and inside her head. The candle in her hand guttered and nearly blew out behind its mirrored glass shield. On the second floor, silence and emptiness.

Henri staggered down the stairs behind her, calling now, 'Madame, do not go down there!' – a sound like the call of an owl.

On the ground floor the servants pressed out of the hallway, she saw Jeanne in the crowd, through the doorway there was the carriage with all its gold trim gleaming in the rain, the horses spattered with mud from hoof to chest, and she pushed aside the cook and one of the chambermaids, calling, 'Out of my way!' Until the circle of servants drew back with a gasp and left her there before the body, the rain wetting down her hair. Through the open door of the coach she could see how the velvet inside was all dark with blood. She found herself staring into those stains, because on the ground was the corpse, the baron, his eyes open, his throat – the bullet had gone through his cravat and left what was under it looking like mangled meat. His eyes were open and she thought that they stared at her.

'You can't—' She couldn't catch her breath. It was the nausea of looking at the body. 'You can't leave him lying out in the mud like that.'

She went down on her knees. It was easy to cry. There were a thousand images racing through her head – his open eyes, the bloody carriage, Jeanne's face among the servants, her letters, Henri's shadow, the baron's dead and open eyes, again – and they all poured out of her as if she were vomiting them up onto the corpse. The wet ground soaked up through her dress. Harder than crying, infinitely harder, was the moment when she put her head down on his bloody chest and embraced him. The corpse was still warm. The blood soaked into her hair, and its butcher-shop smell filled up the space behind her eyes. There was a moment when she saw, on the back of her eyelids, the rack of ribs, the haunches, the whole body undressed and sectioned like a dead pig. The servants were prising her up off the ground, and she let her body hang limp and heavy as a bolt of uncut cloth.

'Madame, you must go inside. You can't help him.'

'Where are the children? Don't let them come down. Someone go and keep them away from the window.'

There was blood all down the front of her dress and on her hands. She'd wash it off, with Jeanne's help, staring at the darkened window of her bedroom as the servants went to find the police, to lift the body out of the mud and lay it out on a sheet on a long table downstairs, where it lay like the centrepiece of the grisliest feast. The smell of blood seemed to fill the house, and she couldn't help but imagine that the thing on the table might sit up and cry out with its mangled throat, and point at her, although the masked man had disappeared into the night on horseback, and Marie Catherine had not fired the gun.

II

—

Sorceresses

Chapter Six

———

To the right of the columned entrance to the Church of Saint-Sulpice stood a statue of Moses, the holy tablets balanced in his right hand, a long sword held before him in his left, its shadow falling over his alcove like the shape of a cross. Sometimes when she had recently done something that provoked her to guilt, Marie Catherine would feel the eyes of the image of Christ on the cross hung high in the arches overlooking the nave, but as she knelt beneath her veil of black crepe and listened to her husband's funeral oration, her conscience drifted outwards, towards the image of Moses, and she felt the shadow of the sword on her neck.

In the Lady Chapel, off the nave, there was a third statue, depicting the Virgin, her mantle wrapped around the child on her hip. She had been cast from old silverware donated by parishioners, and her look was sweet and sad and forgiving, as if she knew that she had been made of cast-offs. She was humble and ready to embrace high and low alike. Our Lady of the Old Tableware, the parishioners called her, laughingly.

Together, the three statues formed the vertices of a kind of triangular net that seemed to be wrapped around Marie Catherine as she knelt and prayed. Christ offered repentance, Moses the sword, and Mary some kind regard that she could not name. Each tugged at her. She prayed, and tried to weep. She had wept the night of the baron's death. That morning, after Jeanne had dressed her in her mourning clothes, she'd climbed back into bed and cried again, dreading the funeral and the moment when she would have to face the other mourners. It would have been good, in the eyes of the public, for her to weep now, but she couldn't. She dropped her eyes from the silhouette of the priest in the pulpit and focused on her hands, clasped before her.

The north end of the cathedral was under construction, a project of expansion that had been under way for some years already, as the funds from parishioners ebbed and flowed. The night outside stole its fingers into the chapel, despite the candles lit in honour of her husband. A cold draught picked at the edges of Madame de Cardonnoy's veil and sneaked up her sleeves and down her collar. Her skin was all gooseflesh, a kind of shiver that was half from cold and half from the feeling of being a profane creature impinging on the sacred. Her mourning dress was the one she had worn to her father's funeral, hastily refashioned by her seamstress, and the many yards of black wool pinched at her bust and rasped at her throat. Beside her, Sophie and Nicolas knelt in their own black clothes, fidgeting and poking each other occasionally.

Repent, said the image of Christ and, as if she were a child again, she answered, *I do.*

Atone, said Moses and, again, she wrung her fingers together, insistently. *I will.*

And Mary, away in the chapel, looked on in silence.

The nuns of her girlhood had been quite descriptive about the torments of hell, so that sometimes, when she lay in bed at night, Marie Catherine had kept herself awake with the image of the convent building and the ground beneath it, the earth only the thinnest rind over an infinite sphere of fire, like the skin of a lemon – a layer that, at the end of the world, would be peeled away by the hand of God to expose the bitter fruit. If she had to get up at night to use the chamberpot she'd lie frozen in bed for a long time, then find herself tiptoeing softly from one bare board in the dormitory to the next, as if the sound of her steps might wake the vast burning thing that she knew slept under her feet, inattentive for now.

The image came back to her as she knelt, mixed up with the regards of the saints and the memory of her husband's bloody body as they dressed and prepared it for the coffin. When the funeral was over and the burial procession had begun, she stepped softly, pushing the children in front of her, her shoes descending on the steps of Saint-Sulpice with only the softest whisper, and she felt, again, the depths of the earth beneath her, as if she was balancing over a long fall. Her crepe mourning veil cast the receding silhouette of the church into shadow.

It had been Victoire.

She knew it, although she wished not to know. *I take risks,* Victoire had said, about that foolish letter. She had no fear of discovery. But even a Princess of the Blood must resign herself to living by the laws that governed the world. She had paid a servant, perhaps, to stand out in that rainy night. There were men who would do such things.

And Madame de Cardonnoy had sent the letter.

If only she had known.

But even now she barely believed that Victoire would be capable of it. For all her rebelliousness, she was still so young. She lived in her mother's house. It was she, Marie Catherine, who had imagined, with an attention that was almost like love, the day she would stand by her husband's grave and see him in the ground. She felt that the baron's death was a spectre that she had coughed up from her own body, that she had infected Victoire with it, by dreaming of it.

The walk to the graveyard was not long, but the moving circle of candles about her seemed to make the time stretch and shiver like a guttering flame. She felt Nicolas press against the sweeping circle of her skirts, cold and afraid of the ring of darkness that pressed around the mourning party. It had been Victoire. The ground's chill seeped up through her shoes and numbed her toes. She should never have sent the letter. She should have known that Victoire would try to save her. Her husband's cousin, the Marquis de Favrier, walked behind her, dressed in his own mantle of mourning, its hood drawn over his face so that she couldn't see his expression. It was her crime, too, although she had neither paid the murderer nor held the gun. She reached for the children's hands and clasped them in her gloves.

They put him in the ground, with songs.

She was still cold long after the burial, when the coachmen had brought the mourners' carriages around in the street, and each relative and friend who had walked behind the baron's body had climbed once more into a coach, their lackeys running before them through the night or clinging behind the carriage, casting long shadows in the street lights. It was late. The children, up long past their bedtime, were tired and crying. She made Nicolas a nest in her thicket of black skirts, drew the mantle over him and said, 'Go to sleep, the guard will carry you up to bed.'

Sophie, too, was pale and yawning, but she wouldn't lie down next to her brother. She kept touching her little gloved hands to her face, sniffling into the soft leather. Jeanne, next to her, pushed her hands with the tear-stained gloves gently back into her lap and put her handkerchief between her fingers, and Sophie sat still and looked at the white linen square without using it.

Madame de Cardonnoy leaned her own head back against the carriage seat and closed her eyes. The ride back to Hôtel Cardonnoy was short. When they arrived, she was nearly asleep herself.

The next morning she was exhausted by the time she'd finished dressing. Jeanne laced up her stays, unwrapped the cloth that covered her hair while she slept, rearranged the curls that had fallen into disarray. She left the mantle until last. Soon the visitors would begin arriving, offering condolences. Marie Catherine was glad there was no breach in etiquette in receiving them in bed. She lay back once her sleeves were fastened, drew the long veil over her face, closed her eyes and watched the morning light make shadows on her eyelids.

Two workmen had been summoned on the day of the funeral to set the broken door to her bedroom back in its frame. Now all appeared normal, except that there was a pale edge of new wood showing in the doorframe, where the hinges had given way.

Earlier than she had thought possible there was a knock on the door, and the lackey announced that Madame de Cardonnoy had a guest waiting downstairs.

'Who is it?' said Jeanne. Marie Catherine opened her eyes. A guest who had not been admitted to her bedroom must be unknown in the house. Or else unwelcome.

'Monsieur de la Reynie, Madame.' Henri's gaze, as he spoke, looked through Jeanne to Madame de Cardonnoy.

Marie Catherine brushed off her skirts and sat up. The Lieutenant General of Police would have been a laughing stock if he were not so dangerous. He was a man who had come from nothing and had made his career on his wife's fortune. Now he had the ear of the king himself. In Paris he had made himself reviled for the ferocity with which he had pursued allegations of poison among the court, which everyone agreed must have been born of jealousy. Madame de Fontet said that he was out for blood, like a hound that sniffs out the slightest lingering trace of sin and then worries it with his teeth. Another woman, the Duchesse de Bouillon, had admitted to the Chambre Ardente that she had dealt with the devil and that he had worn the face of Monsieur de la Reynie.

'Tell him I'll see him,' she said. She leaned on Jeanne's arm to get up.

In the flesh, La Reynie was a tall man whose height was accentuated by the bramble-bush of curls that framed his head and fell as far as his shoulders. He was about fifty, his fleshy jaw had thickened with age, he wore a close-trimmed moustache that adhered to his lip like a stripe of paint. He looked something like a bear that had just stood up on its hind legs and turned into a man. He wore a sombre look that seemed almost theatrical, as if his frown had worn grooves in the slack skin of his cheeks.

He did not look like the devil. This made Marie Catherine no happier.

He bowed deeply when she entered the salon. The bow cast his hair over his forehead.

'Forgive me for interrupting you on this day, Madame,' he said.

The winter light was coming through the shrouded window like an army of silver arrows. The draperies in the salon and her own bedroom had been replaced with black cloth, cut hastily before the funeral, like the white-ribboned mantle that Marie Catherine herself wore, whose skirts looped back into a long train that dragged on the ground. Under her widow's veil, she wore a tight white cap held in place on her forehead with a band of Cyprus crepe, which trapped her hair against her forehead and made her sweat. She had already put in the order for the servants' new uniforms, for every member of the household must be dressed in black while they mourned. The baron's portrait, which overlooked the room, was festooned in black garlands.

'Surely you don't need to apologise,' she said to La Reynie. 'Have you caught my husband's murderer?' Her voice sounded clipped to her own ears.

'You saw your husband's body brought in, did you not, Madame? I'd like to ask you some questions about the night he died.' His tone, in response to her rudeness, had become almost obsequious, which frightened her.

'You haven't found his killer yet, have you?'

Marie Catherine pressed her hands into her black skirts, then released them. She tried to breathe and let her consciousness float up and out of the crown of her skull, the way she did when she was telling a story, when the words came without her having to think about them. She must not alienate this man.

She was disgusted with herself, with the way that terror, in this slow, quiet, light-filled room of her house, made her want to lie down on the floor and surrender and say, *Forgive me, Monsieur, I am the wickedest of women.* As if he were God himself and commanded the fires of hell, not merely the torturers at the Châtelet. How quickly he made her fear for her own life.

'Can you tell me what happened?' La Reynie had stepped a little towards her where she stood at the window, and when she summoned the courage to look at him, she found that he had looked away from her, towards the portrait of the baron that hung on the wall. The consciousness of her need to impress him made it almost impossible to read his expression. It was like trying to read whether a soul had been damned or saved from a death mask.

What did she know of him? He was said to be envious and vindictive, but those he struck were almost always those who had fallen into disfavour with the king: the general who had lost one battle too many, the comtesse who had gossiped about the king's love affairs, the little fortune-tellers who advised women about their lovers and men about their wealth.

She pressed her gloved hand against the windowpane. A scrim of fog formed around her palm. La Reynie was still looking at the baron's portrait while he waited for Marie Catherine to tell him her tale. Perhaps she could make herself into someone who needed to be saved. A good wife, who had given all her father's wealth to advance her husband. A jewel innocent of the court, who loved God and the king. They said that La Reynie had written that play, *The Fortune-Teller*. Perhaps he'd appreciate a little drama.

'I was with my children that night,' she said. 'My husband's valet came to fetch me. He said that the lanterns on the corner had been broken, or had gone out, and so it was fully dark when my husband's carriage was returning. The murderer threw down a torch in the road that caused the horses to take fright, then opened the carriage door and shot my husband.'

She took a breath, took her hand away from the window and held it to her throat. The fabric of her glove had grown cold. The veil obscured her peripheral vision just enough that she couldn't tell whether La Reynie had moved, without turning her head to look at him.

'There were three men with him – with my husband, that is. The coachman, his valet Henri, and the Swiss who guards our door. Usually he did not take the Swiss when he went out.'

She had sat down with each of them, the morning after the death. Caspar had been sombre and terse in his replies, the coachman bewildered. It was Henri who had sobbed his way through his story, looking at her with eyes that said quite clearly that he believed his master's death was her doing. He had loved the baron.

Partway through the conversation she had realised that a little of her husband's blood was still clotted in her hair and she had recoiled.

'Both the Swiss and the valet were riding clinging to the back of the carriage,' she told La Reynie. 'When the coachman lost control of the horses, they jumped down to help him. My husband's valet told me that he did not see the man come out of the shadows or open the carriage door until he heard the sound of the gun. My husband must have supposed that it was one of his own servants opening the door to help him out.'

Her voice didn't tremble, which might count for her or against her. Perhaps La Reynie was the sort of man who considered obvious displays of grief to be a kind of detestable play-acting.

'Could the valet describe him?'

'Not well,' Marie Catherine said. A meeting between Henri and this man was something she needed to avoid at all costs. 'He wore a hat and a cloth over his face, and his clothes were so wet with rain that my husband's man couldn't tell their colour. He'd half pulled the body out of the carriage, and Henri thought he was looking for a purse or for his jewels, but when he saw there were three men coming for him, he took fright and ran away. He'd hidden his horse in the alley, where the servants throw the household refuse. He escaped.'

Henri, she knew, had not actually believed that the man was a thief. He had spat out his description of the murderer pawing through the baron's clothes as if it were spoilt milk.

La Reynie paced back and forth at the edge of her chaise longue, reaching one end, tapping the scrollwork, and then brushing his hair out of his face and turning and pacing back again. It was a strange habit that made it seem as if he had forgotten that Marie Catherine could see him, despite her veil. She wondered if he fidgeted like that when he had to appear before the parliament, or when he was in conference with the king. Did it mean anything that he felt no need to dissemble before her? Despite the flightiness of his gestures, he had the expression of a man who was thinking furiously, who would have liked to summon a clerk to his side to write down her testimony. She turned her back on the window and watched him, pressing her shoulders slightly against the cold glass.

'And was anything missing from the body? His purse? Or rings?'

Marie Catherine shook her head. 'No. I don't know. Perhaps a ring. I don't remember what he was wearing when he went out.' She hoped her distraction seemed like grief. She saw that La Reynie's eyes had flicked again to the portrait of the baron that hung on the wall, as if checking his painted hands for baubles.

'If he was merely a brigand, we might catch him by finding where he sold the jewels he took. If he took any.'

'And what could he be, except a brigand?' If only Victoire's hired man had had the presence of mind to steal from him, she might have let the police spend the rest of her life searching pawn shops for his missing jewels.

La Reynie's head twitched, almost imperceptibly. Madame de Cardonnoy felt that he might have heard her thoughts.

'One cannot be too careful in the pursuit of justice, Madame. Do you know of anyone who might have held a grudge against the baron?'

'I do not.'

'I'd like to question the servants, if you will give me permission.'

'They will tell you what I have already told you.' She didn't think he would have asked her that if her husband were alive. His word would have been trustworthy. His eyes kept meeting the painted eyes of the baron's portrait.

'I'm sure. But sometimes servants ...' He trailed off, spread his hands gently. 'It helps to be certain.'

'If I were you,' said Marie Catherine icily, feeling the cold of her voice in her hands, 'I would not be at the house of a new widow asking to question her domestics. I would be sending my men to search for news of who had seen the murderer loitering under a broken lantern, waiting to waylay some nobleman's carriage.'

She feared this was not an argument that she could win. But if La Reynie did question the servants, he could not avoid hearing the story of the argument that she and the baron had had on the day of his death. Perhaps he would also hear that her maid had been absent, and that she had carried a message that Madame de Cardonnoy had not entrusted to the men who usually ran such errands. Perhaps Henri would tell him what she knew he suspected.

'Of course, Madame,' said La Reynie, with another of his deep bows, as if she had said something reasonable. 'And if I were in your place, I am certain I would answer to the best of my ability the questions put to me to find my husband's murderer.' He turned his back on her and began to walk towards the door.

She couldn't let him leave thinking she was untrustworthy. She had a moment of inspiration.

'My husband's servants were loyal. They did not conspire to kill him.'

La Reynie paused by the door. 'Of course. I should not have suggested it. I will only disturb you when I have more news.'

'Wait,' Marie Catherine called, stretching out her arm. Gratitude – that he believed, or pretended to believe, her poor excuse – made her feel faint. La Reynie turned back to her, and she crossed the arm over her chest and took a breath. He tapped his foot. A heavy cloth seemed to have settled over the room. Whatever she said next might lose his trust, or win it. She edged along the wall until she was standing below the baron's portrait, touching the frame with her hand as if to draw strength from it.

'I don't want you to talk about this with your men,' she said. 'It is embarrassing to me.'

La Reynie was silent. She picked at a loose thread in the hem of her sleeve.

'My husband considered it wise not to share too much of his affairs with his wife. I could not blame him for it. I was very young when I married him, you understand, and at court men often approach other men's wives in order to win favour or influence over them.'

'Go on, Madame,' said La Reynie, when she paused.

'As far as I know, my husband had no enemies. But he spent a great deal of his time at Versailles, in the Marquis de Favrier's apartment. And when he was in Paris he did not always sleep at Hôtel Cardonnoy. I don't know what kept him away. His father loved to gamble, and lost a fortune that way, and while my husband condemned it, I know he played cards at Versailles to win him friends.'

La Reynie nodded. His frown had softened a little. It was obvious that he liked hearing this kind of thing, in the same way the gossips liked it. And perhaps he also liked that she had been sharp with him and was now throwing herself on his mercy.

'He had debts?'

'I would believe more readily that other men owed him,' she said.

'And was he loving, apart from his absences?'

'He was distant.' Marie Catherine looked away, so that her forehead almost touched the baron's painted foot in its frame. 'I tried to consider that my cross to bear, but I was not always as forgiving as a good wife should be.'

She let the sentence hang in the air for a long time, afraid to look up into La Reynie's eyes, in case she saw in them the beginning of suspicion.

She did not know who had killed her husband, she told herself now. She must believe it so. Questions crowded around her, speaking in La Reynie's own soft, polite voice. *Did you kill your husband, Madame, or did you do it with help? And what was the subject of the argument you had on the day of his death? Are you sure? Where did you hide the pistol? What was your lover's name?*

Finally she looked up. He was looking at her now. It must make a pretty picture. She inclined her head towards the portrait's frame, again, as if she were going to kiss it.

'I want justice for my husband, Monsieur. But not at the expense of his good name and his family's honour. I will go through his papers myself, and anything that might help I will bring to you. But I believe that he was a good man, and if, God forbid, he was involved in anything disreputable, I would not want to see his children humiliated by what came to light.'

La Reynie nodded.

'And you think that the man who killed him might also have the power to ruin his good name?'

Marie Catherine met his eyes. The lieutenant general seemed discomfited by this. As she spoke, he looked away.

'I think that, because of your diligence, the Maréchal de Luxembourg is imprisoned in Vincennes for black magic – when only a month ago the entire court would have called him a great general and a hero – along with those ladies whose reputations will be forever smeared by charges of poison and adultery. I know little of such things, except what other women say, and so I could not tell you whether I think that all of this wickedness is true. But I know that two years ago such things were not even whispered of, and now I am afraid of what I might discover about my own husband if I look at him too closely. Can you forgive me for that?'

The Lieutenant General of Police bowed to her.

'Of course, Madame. On hearing these charges of poison in such high places, one feels as if the ground has opened up. But you understand that I have to do my duty.'

Marie Catherine risked a small smile. He spoke so courteously that she could almost forget how his demeanour had changed when she let him know that she understood he had power over her.

'It has not made you well liked at court, I'm afraid, if my

103

husband's words are anything to go by.' If only he would believe that the baron had been one of those wits who likened him to the devil, fearing to have their own faults uncovered.

La Reynie frowned at her.

'I hope I haven't offended you,' she said. 'I'm afraid I was not expecting a gentleman.'

The frown softened, just slightly. She held her breath. La Reynie bowed.

'Then I am sorry that my reputation preceded me,' he said. 'You are right. Though you are gracious enough to call me diligent, there are those who see in my work not duty, but envy and cruelty. I will send my men to ask if anyone saw your murderer that night. Perhaps after that I will ask again whether I may question your servants.'

'Thank you,' Marie Catherine said.

When he had gone, she sank down onto the chaise and felt the floor rock beneath her as she lay there, her veil twisted uncomfortably over her arm. Her neck was running with sweat under the widow's cap, and her legs had gone strangely numb.

How safe, she wondered, had the Comtesse de Soissons felt, the night before the king issued the order for her arrest as a poisoner? Falling out of her life would be as easy as stepping into the shadow of a passing cloud. La Reynie only had to see the darkness touch her and she would become expendable again. The knowledge kept her limp on the chaise like a discarded dress, as if her bones and nerves had melted out of her mourning clothes and left her awareness of the cloth. For a long time she watched the panel of light cast by the window as it crept backwards across the floor. Finally she closed her eyes and fell into a wingless rushing half dream. She woke when Jeanne and Anne brought the children down in their black clothes and white stockings to see her, and their sticky, warm, living hands touched her face and pressed her own chilly hands, encased in their gloves. She looked up into Jeanne's eyes, and the maid sighed and turned her face away towards the black-draped window.

'You have visitors bringing condolences, Madame,' Jeanne said. 'Will you receive them?'

*

She was allowed to lie on the bed while they milled around her, propped up on a pillow that Jeanne rearranged and plumped up underneath her when she shifted. The black crepe veil trailed limply across the coverlet to the floor. Madame de Fontet, sitting by her, held her hand for a while, and then the Comtesse de Combois took her place, and she could hear the hum of voices in the hallway, Jeanne deciding who should come through the doorway to her room, depending on her own whims. Everything was arranged so that Marie Catherine had only to lie back like a doll, listlessly, raising a hand to acknowledge the men and women who came and sat beside her or peered in at the door. The lackeys came in and out, bringing sweets for the guests to eat.

The enforced stillness, however, quickly became oppressive and exhausting. It felt as if she too had been buried and the mourning dress and veil were growing into her skin. Alone, she had wanted to lie down on the floor itself, and now that her well-wishers had arrived, she wanted nothing but to jump up, hike up her skirts and run out into the cold, bright streets.

It was a long time before Victoire arrived. She was dressed as a woman today, with twilight-blue ribbons in her hair and in the trim of her dress. She came to the bedside and, instead of sitting on the tufted stool pulled up close by Marie Catherine's right hand, she knelt on the floor in a froth of skirts and pressed her forehead into the trailing edge of the black veil. Her eyes were very red from crying. In the doorway, a marquise whispered to her companion that Mademoiselle de Conti's flair for the dramatic was truly too much. No one shed tears like that for the husband of a friend.

Marie Catherine could see the blue veins through the skin of her eyelids and gloss of a tear on one cheek. Her bedside was crowded with well-wishers, so she could say nothing to Victoire. She said nothing. She turned her face away and closed her eyes and allowed the Comtesse de Combois to dab a little oil of jasmine on her temples with her handkerchief.

'Are you feeling faint, darling?' said the comtesse.

The air was contracting around her like a vice. Soon she would cry. She could feel the pressure of it behind her eyes, but it was a very cold, angry kind of sorrow. How many hours before they left? Victoire went out and then came in again, pressed a glass of brandy into her limp hand. Every time the girl moved, Marie Catherine felt her presence as if they were connected by a noose that tightened, the more they struggled with it. She had become a block of weeping ice. She heard the women in the room talking, but couldn't follow their conversation. The light was starting to fade.

'Can we bring you your supper, Madame?' The servant Arnaud was in the doorway.

'I'm not hungry.'

'We'll leave you to your prayers, my dear,' said Madame de Fontet. This, Marie Catherine knew, was a polite excuse, designed to allow her to eat if she wished. To dine in front of her guests would look heartless.

'Thank you.'

Victoire did not leave. That the room was now empty made it no easier to look at her.

'Jeanne, you may go downstairs for your own dinner. There's no reason you should fast as well.'

Jeanne curtseyed and left. Marie Catherine and Victoire sat for a few moments in silence. Jeanne had gone away without lighting the lamps. So Victoire's hair blended into the growing shadows, and only her face was a pale smear in the grey twilight. She put her head in her hands and her face disappeared.

'Marie,' she said, her face still buried, 'I have such a confession for you ...'

'Spare me the fucking play-acting, please. And close the door.' The curse turned to ash in her mouth, although she had not spoken above a whisper. It was her mother who had spoken that way, when she was angry. Marie Catherine had learned young that she must never talk like a servant.

Victoire was looking at her with her eyes full of tears, her mouth pressed into a thin line. Her head had snapped up when Marie Catherine spoke, as if Marie Catherine had struck her. She rose and went to the door, and closed it very slowly.

'This isn't play-acting, Madame,' she said when she had turned round. 'I know I should never have done what I did. But I acted to save you. After discovering us, he would have killed us both, and no one in Paris would have blamed him.'

'So you ran out and found an assassin to kill my husband?'

Madame de Cardonnoy asked. 'Who did you hire? The police are already looking for him, and Monsieur de la Reynie does not believe he was only after my husband's jewels. Do you trust this man not to betray you?'

'I hired no one,' Victoire said. 'I held the gun myself.'

'The servants saw a man.' She realised how stupid she sounded as soon as she'd closed her mouth. So, too, the servants had seen a man when Victoire had come to Hôtel Cardonnoy in her red coat.

Victoire laughed, quietly. Then she covered her mouth as if she were horrified at the sound that had escaped from it. 'So did you. I had only to dress as one.'

'Oh God.'

Every time she had re-created her husband's death she had managed to avoid thinking that Victoire might have opened the carriage door herself. It was impossible to imagine that bloody body and the girl she loved together – a curtain must separate them, hiding one from the other. When Victoire had first sat down next to her bed, Marie Catherine had blamed her: for her eyes that were red with tears, the paleness of her face, the stunned attitude of grief for a thing she could not have seen, a man whose death she had only imagined, although she must, without doubt, have ordered it. Now something terrible was moving over her face. She doubled up in her blue dress, she clasped her hands over her mouth as if to contain the noise that came out of her mouth, a dog's howl. Marie Catherine leaped up and crossed the room and took the girl's face between her hands.

'Quiet,' she whispered, 'quiet, the servants will hear.' She was shaking.

'Any gentleman with any honour would have done the same,' Victoire choked out. Then she clasped her hands over her mouth as she was trying to force the words back in.

'Quiet,' whispered Marie Catherine, and Victoire shook her head and whimpered. She didn't seem to be breathing or, rather, she was drawing in short, choking breaths and with each exhale she seemed to be about to scream. It felt as if her panic was contagious. Marie Catherine pushed her away, and then she drew her hand back and slapped her.

There was a strange intimacy in the slap, as if it were one more secret they shared, or as if, in the moment Victoire jumped back from her, her mouth open, Marie Catherine could glimpse some secret self that the girl had never shown her.

Victoire raised her hand as if she was going to hit her back, and Marie Catherine embraced her. Despite the pressure of Victoire's silk skirts against her own, she felt that she was holding the straight body of a young man.

Victoire must have felt herself a hero, and then, the moment she pulled the trigger, she must have realised that this time she had made a mistake she couldn't undo. Marie Catherine could see her, riding through the night in her gallant coat, to save them both from her husband. And if she had been a man, the law would still have condemned her, but the world would have regarded her with a grudging admiration, because who hadn't dreamed of rescuing a lover from catastrophe, even at the cost of his own life?

Victoire's hands, braced against Marie Catherine's shoulders, were cold, and the rest of her body was tense and breathing warmth through her dress, so that Marie Catherine remembered fucking her in the carriage, every kiss they had stolen in her box at the theatre, every time she had sent the servants away and recklessly pulled her down onto the bed that she'd thrown her husband out of. How could she have believed it possible they wouldn't be caught?

As she breathed in Victoire's scent, part of her wanted to surrender and let herself be swept away by the gallantry of it, as if she were the princess in a tale, rescued at the last minute from a monster. If she was damned, then let her be damned.

But there were Nicolas and Sophie, who she had to protect. Perhaps it was too late for her to die for love.

'I'm going to confess,' said Victoire. 'I just wanted to speak with you first.'

'What are you talking about?' said Marie Catherine. 'The Lieutenant General of Police was just in my house, and you're going to confess to him?'

'I have a plan.' She was speaking quickly, as if she hoped to get the words out before she had to weep again. She kept stopping to take enormous gulps of air. 'I acted hastily before, because I was in a panic when your maid brought me the letter. But I promise you,

I will be the only one to bear the consequences of this. I swear to you. And you'll be free to live in peace without him.'

'If you confess and are condemned, they'll want to make certain the confession is a full one,' said Marie Catherine. 'And what are you going to say when Monsieur de la Reynie asks you *why* you killed him?'

'I'm going to tell him that the baron was my lover, and I was furious when he tossed me aside.'

'The whole of Paris society knows that you're my friend, they'll hardly believe that you were in love with my husband.'

Victoire shook her head. Her silhouette moved like a shadow across the window, away from the door where Marie Catherine still stood. 'They will. They already say that any of the ladies at court would kill each other to sleep with the king. That Madame de Montespan poisoned Mademoiselle de Fontanges when his attention turned her way. And Madame de Montespan may wish the queen were dead every day of her life, but she still pretends to be friends when they ride in a carriage together. If I tell the chamber that I begged the baron to poison you and marry me, and he refused, so I killed him, they'll wail over the falseness of women, but they won't doubt my word, because it's only what they already believe.'

It was true that people whispered that Madame de Montespan, the king's mistress, had murdered her rivals. But they said it, most often, with a laugh, not quite believing. Victoire turned away and lit the lamp by Marie Catherine's bedside, bringing her face and her shining eyes out of the dimness.

Marie Catherine snorted. 'I doubt they'll consider my husband as great a prize as the king.'

'They'll consider him enough of one, as long as the story is scandalous.'

'Oh yes.' Marie Catherine's voice had risen without her noticing it. 'Here is this grey-haired baron, they'll say, with his famous stinking breath, and of course he's managed to seduce Mademoiselle de Conti, who is so far above his station, and who, so recently, would accept *no* man for her own!'

'God damn you, Marie, what do you want me to do? I'll die before I let the blame fall on you.' Victoire, also, was no longer whispering. She tossed her head back as if she were on a stage, and the gesture made her look very young. Just the girl who'd rested her head on Marie Catherine's knee and listened to stories about wicked fairies and the land of the Amazons.

'I didn't ask you to save me,' Marie Catherine said.

'What else could I have done?' Victoire asked. 'Should I have sat by while he imprisoned you in some workhouse for disobedient wives?'

'Wait. Hush.' There'd been a sound from outside the room. Marie Catherine opened the door a crack. Henri was coming up the stairs with a candle. She closed the door as quietly as she could. Henri's footsteps travelled down the hallway.

'I wanted to give you your freedom,' Victoire whispered.

'I had grown used to being without it.' Every nerve in her body was still listening for movement in the house. She was so tightly wound that when Victoire flinched, she flinched with her.

'I know,' said Victoire. 'I hated him for that. You bore it so silently, but you could barely bring yourself to say his name.'

And that was true, although it hardly mattered now.

'It's not too late. I'll take the blame.' Victoire was taking deep, slow breaths, visibly trying to master herself.

The house was quiet. Victoire's hands were fisted in her skirt. Finally she turned away, towards the window.

'I don't regret his death,' she said. 'Sometimes I would see him at court, and all I could think about was how much I hated him, for the power he had over you. I wished him dead. But now that I've done it—'

She looked at her hands, as if she were trying to trace the shape of something she couldn't see.

'I waited so long, it was as if I were in a kind of dream,' she said. 'The rain began after I broke the glass on the street lamp, and the night was so dark that I could barely see the crests on the carriages as they passed. It was only afterwards – he was so close when I shot him, he was wearing fine gloves and they were all soaked through with blood, where he'd clutched his chest, I was holding him with my hand on his shoulder – he started forward as if he thought I was there to help him. I only wanted to save you. Do you understand?'

Marie Catherine bit the inside of her lip, picturing the bloody gloves laid over the face of her husband's corpse, like an evil death mask. She wanted to shove the image away and, for a moment, Victoire with it.

'Did you think I would agree to a plan in which you also died?' she said instead.

Her voice was tight. She looked past Victoire to her reflection, which hovered in the windowpane, distorted by the faint ripples in the glass, so that it looked as if she was moving through a world of dark water that pressed in and threatened to extinguish her flame.

'I murdered him. That burden's on my soul.'

'I forgive you.'

She said it as if she were a priest who had the power to offer absolution. And, for a moment, she felt that she did, as if the words had lit a candle flame inside her mouth that burned with the light of her love. She did not, would never, believe that flame was the flame of hell. Not if every confessor in France lined up to tell her that she was damned.

'We could flee together, like the Comtesse de Soissons and Madame d'Alluye did when she was accused of poison,' Victoire said quietly.

'The Comtesse de Soissons's children are grown.'

'Then what do you intend to do?'

'I don't know.'

It was true that when the comtesse had received the news that she was to be arrested, and made up her mind to flee, her closest friend had climbed into the carriage with her and ridden out of France by her side. Marie Catherine had never heard any whisper that there was anything more than friendship between them – two ladies in their middle age, the comtesse, who everyone called The Snipe for her long nose and sharp-edged looks, and Madame d'Alluye, who had been famous for her beauty in her youth and was still – and yet she let herself imagine it for a moment. Riding out into the unknown night.

How could she not have seen it? It was clear that Victoire thought it must be obvious. But even when she had heard that Madame d'Alluye had fled with the comtesse, Marie Catherine had thought only of friendship, or that Madame d'Alluye feared herself implicated in the same crimes.

When Marie Catherine told stories, Nicolas wanted tales of

princes, but the ones that Sophie loved best were always the ones where the heroine, the princess or the peasant girl, or the fairy in disguise or the girl who was only as tall as a mouse had to leave home, fleeing an ugly marriage, a wicked stepmother, a hungry monster. Always they were forced out, the girls, and returned home only through their own cleverness and bravery, to the shock of their old parents, who had long ago called off the search parties and given them up for dead. There was something in the story of Madame de Soissons's flight that recalled these tales, except that she had set off not as a girl but as a woman, abandoning her grown children, her husband, her house and her land, at a point in her life when the tale might usually have ended, as if the force of her desire to save herself could turn back time and flip the world upside down.

The magic carriage hung in the air before her, so close that Marie Catherine thought she could touch it, if only she stretched out her hand. Victoire left the window and tiptoed to her on quiet feet, touched her cheek with her fingertips.

'No,' Marie Catherine said. 'I won't leave the children.' The image dissolved in the air. She wondered if Victoire had felt it, too.

'Then what will we do?' Victoire asked. She had slipped a hand under the widow's veil, and her fingers were laced through Marie Catherine's hair at the base of her neck.

Marie Catherine leaned in and kissed her again. She felt Victoire's breath in her ribs and on her lips, and her touch still felt like a haven from the world. Her imagination had shaken her: the carriage, the night, Madame de Soissons with her unbeautiful face and Madame d'Alluye sitting side by side, sharing, maybe – only maybe – the same bond that she and Victoire shared. The power of the story that no one had ever told. There was sweat running down her back.

'We'll keep them at bay,' she said.

Victoire looked at her. 'And how?'

'We're going to tell Monsieur de la Reynie a story,' Marie Catherine said. 'A story he can believe. He wants witches and murder and poisoning, doesn't he? We will give him that, and then we'll give him a helpless widow, so that he can be a hero, for once.'

She would believe it if she said it aloud. Didn't they say she told such stories, the kind that could be believed?

'How, Marie?' Victoire's hand tightened on the back of her neck, and Marie Catherine put her own hand in the girl's hair, so they were mirrors of each other, as if in a soldiers' pact.

'We're going to find another murderer,' Marie Catherine whispered, close to her lips. 'Someone else to take the blame.'

'An innocent?' Victoire shook her head, a tiny movement that filled Marie Catherine's whole field of vision. She'd never lose her gallantry.

'I don't know yet.' But she wanted to live. She felt as if she could move any mountain with her wish. 'If any cloud falls over us, it will mean death. Can you do it, Victoire?'

'Can *you*?' Victoire drew back from her a little, and Marie Catherine wanted to follow her, to lean forehead to forehead until it felt as if they were inhabiting the same flesh. 'I don't know if I can.'

'I will find a way,' she said. 'I will.'

Chapter Seven

——

Light entered the room without him seeing it. The world had contracted to a band of hot steel that lay across his eyelids, the colour of red ochre, bruise-red, a wound cut deep into the body of the earth. In his half sleep, he felt the ground moving under him, like a running horse, each galloping step jarring his bones a little, recalling him to the places where he'd been bruised.

'Monsieur,' said a voice that tilted up his head, and water ran down from his lips and made him cough, without soothing the burning thirst that had wrapped its hands around his throat.

'Who has done this, though?' And then there were pacing footsteps that kept him maddeningly half awake, when what he wanted was only to float down into oblivion and remember nothing of the blows or the moment when they had found him in his house and carried him out into the cold of the street. The cessation of pain seemed like a dream from some other man's life. He turned on the bed. His body had forgotten how to move under his own will. He sank down into the cavern at the back of his skull. He heard the intruding voices mumbling in the hallway. He slept.

When Lavoie woke, the light from the window was a slice of lemon peel lying across the floor, and he was in a bed that wasn't his own. He tried to raise his hand to wipe the sleep out of his eyes, and a tearing pain crawled down his shoulder as far as the base of his spine.

He saw his own muscles as he might draw them. Sisyphus losing his grasp on his boulder, Laocoön struggling against the serpents as they dragged him into the sea. He imagined nothing, and the lack was like a white sheet thrown across his brain.

His throat produced a croaking sound. Steps pattered down the hall, and then the door creaked open.

'Thank the Lord, you've woken.' It was Berthe, Monsieur Maçon's maidservant, who earned a few extra sous by making Lavoie's bed and cleaning his studio. Her dress was splashed down the front with washing-up water, and tendrils of hair were frizzing out from under her bonnet. So he must be in Monsieur Maçon's house. She bent over him and smoothed out his blanket, a gentle touch that still made him aware of new sore places on his flesh. 'I was the one who found you, this morning, when I came to bring the milk. You were so cold that I thought at first they'd killed you.'

Lavoie's fingers twitched, involuntarily. *They* – yes, he remembered, and the memory came with a feeling of humiliation that fell sickeningly down his throat and settled in his stomach like rancid milk. He turned his head away from Berthe, looked across the yellow-white ripples of the linen on Monsieur Maçon's bed, finding the pockets of blue in the shadows, the hidden secrets of colour that he had spent his life training himself to see.

'Water,' he said. His face seemed to have swollen up into a mask – his lips mumbled and cracked against each other.

'Of course.' She hurried away.

It had not occurred to him yet to try to sit up or stand – his body, painful, felt like a heavy chest or some other piece of furniture. The light from the window filtered through the leaves of the dwarf plum tree that Madame Maçon grew in her windowbox, casting a dappled pattern on the blankets. He closed his eyes. He was still trying not to remember.

'Here now, drink up.' Berthe's footsteps crossed the floor, followed by an echo.

'Good Lord, we thought you were dead.' Maçon's wife.

Lavoie opened his eyes in slits and saw her standing behind Berthe, her baby cradled against her shoulder, as the maid leaned over him and applied her cup of water to his lips. He drank. The water ran down the sides of his mouth and pooled in the crease of his neck. The two women standing over him were haloed in light,

Berthe plump and rosy, Madame Maçon still a little blanched from her most recent lying-in.

He had to piss. He was dying of thirst. He heaved himself up on one elbow, feeling as if long iron pins were being driven in at each of his joints.

'No, no, you must rest.' Madame Maçon shook his pillow out and then put her hand on his shoulder to push him back down, as if he were a small child. The warmth of her hand felt nauseating on his skin – he remembered the baron's lackeys – and besides that, the pressure of her hand hurt him. And he realised for the first time, seeing his swollen hands poking out from the cuffs of his shirt, how ruined he must look.

'I have to—' He gestured.

'Oh. Berthe, help him stand.' Madame Maçon turned smartly around and left the room, while Berthe was still pulling back the bedcovers.

'Go. I'll do it myself.' He struggled until he was sitting up, his face burning.

Berthe clicked her tongue against her teeth. 'You'll make a mess.'

She had her arm wrapped around his shoulders, her fingers tucked into his armpit, as if he was an aged grandfather.

'Leave me be!' He pushed at her shoulder, his hand slipping accidentally down almost to her breast. He took in a deep breath. 'Please. I'll manage.'

Berthe shook her head. 'As you wish.'

After she'd gone out, Lavoie realised too late that he should have asked for her help with retrieving the pot from under the bed. He tried holding the bedpost to steady himself as he bent, but his fingers were painfully swollen, and it was difficult to grip either the post or the handle of the chamberpot. Eventually he went down on his knees, and although he could reach the pot from that position, he couldn't stand once he'd got down. He lay curled sideways on the floor, gazing under the bed at the cracks in the boards, the occasional dead fly rising up into his vision all out of proportion, looking as large as a horse killed on a battlefield. He closed his eyes and touched his swollen face with the tips of his fingers, feeling the grotesque mask that the baron's men had made of him. One of them had stomped on his hand while he was on the floor. How would he hold his brushes?

Berthe rapped on the door. 'Monsieur Lavoie?'

He dried his eyes hastily on the sleeve of his shirt. 'Leave me be!'

Her footsteps hesitated outside the door, then paced up and down. Lavoie heaved himself up onto all fours, but rising onto two feet was an impossibility. He tried it, fell back painfully onto his knees, remembered the baron's lackeys standing over him. If only they'd killed him, he'd have given anything to escape this humiliation. Finally, desperate, he wormed his cock free and pissed crouching over the pot like a dog, seeing himself, the whole time, as if he were an eyeball suspended somewhere at the apex of the ceiling, loathing his ridiculousness.

Finished, he crawled away from the evidence and propped himself up at the foot of the bed, determined to rest until he was able to pull himself back into it.

Berthe's pacing footsteps paused, then the door burst open. She paused on the threshold, apparently taken aback to see him sitting upright and not in a puddle of his own excrement that she would have to clean up.

'There, now.' She clicked her tongue against her teeth. 'That's all right, isn't it?'

Her tone of voice was of the sort he could imagine her using on Monsieur Maçon's infant. He turned his face away from her as she lifted him under the arms and heaved him back into bed, with her strong, red-knuckled peasant woman's grip. Madame Maçon's face peeked around the corner before she entered the room, checking, no doubt, to see that he was fully clothed. She must have put the baby down in the other room. Lavoie's head was spinning with motion. He found it hard to follow what Madame Maçon was saying.

'And once my husband's here, you must tell him the whole story. We've told the police, but naturally they have no idea what sort of ruffian they ought to look for. I've asked about the street, but no one saw anything other than a nobleman's carriage, just after the lamps were lit, and of course you have such customers ...' She smiled, hesitantly, a merchant woman's combination of awe and nervousness at the nobility, at the thought that Lavoie himself, though he lived beside her in the same street, might find his ears abraded by the roughness of her accent.

He was astounded by her civility. He knew Monsieur Maçon despised him, thought him a dandy and a snob, who made the whole street stink with the smell of treated canvas and spent his Sundays washing the paint stains out of the lace trim on his sleeves instead of going to church. For his own part, Lavoie had judged Maçon and his wife to be provincial, with their windowsill pots full of carrots and parsley, the hutch of rabbits that Madame Maçon kept in her kitchen and butchered herself. And yet here he was in the man's own bed, being tended by his wife, while neither would have supposed that it was Lavoie's noble customer who had left him beaten and bloody, for an infraction that had happened only in the privacy of his mind. The thought might have moved him to gratitude, but instead, exhausted as he was, he felt ashamed.

'I don't want the police,' he said.

'But why not?'

He closed his eyes. 'It doesn't matter. I won't have them.'

Madame Maçon huffed out a little sigh. Berthe had returned with a basin of water and was wiping his face with a cloth. The cool water was dragging him down into the waves of an unhappy sleep. He turned his face away from her cloth and tried to rally himself awake.

'You should tell us what your quarrel was. I'm sure it isn't so hard to explain.'

He seemed to have drifted back into Madame Maçon's speech after some time. He was having trouble following the thread of her conversation, but as he tried to shake off his exhaustion, he became more and more aware of the pity written on her face.

'You're thinking of your business, no doubt,' she went on, 'but surely it can't be right to let such a man get away with this?'

Slowly the realisation came over him that, for all her careful stepping around the issue of the noble carriage parked in his street, she did not truly think he had been beaten by common thieves intent on making off with his paintings or avenging a public-house slight.

'What did you tell the police?' he asked, struggling up on one elbow. The movement wrenched him from neck to hip and he found himself gasping.

Madame Maçon shook her head. 'My husband made the report. No one knew whose seal was on the carriage, and so he named no names.'

'Devil take him – he couldn't have waited until I was awake?' Lavoie's breath hissed out between his clenched teeth. It wasn't even the knowledge that his reputation was going to be ruined, that no one of the baron's stature would ever buy another of his paintings. The shame went, somehow, deeper than that.

Madame Maçon stiffened on the bed. 'Devil take *you* if you talk about my husband that way in his own house.'

Lavoie turned his face away from her. In the next room the baby began to cry, and Madame Maçon got up and went to see to it, with a huffing breath that suggested she felt there was nothing she could do about the problem of Lavoie. Berthe came in soon after she'd gone, carrying a tin plate covered with a cloth.

'I expect you're hungry,' she said. 'The meal's not ready, but there's bread and ham and butter.'

Lavoie swung his feet creakily off the bed. The movement hurt, but standing, although dizzying, was tolerable as long as there was some wall or table within arm's length to lean on and he didn't have to bend down for anything.

'I think I've imposed on Monsieur Maçon enough,' he said. 'I'll go back to my own house.'

Berthe put her plate down on the rumpled sheets and shook her head sadly.

'You're not well enough, Monsieur,' she said. 'You'll never get up those steps to your studio, and I'll be carrying you back here, come evening.'

He had groped his way to the door.

'Will you get me my shoes?' he asked.

'There's no bread in your house, either,' Berthe continued. 'You may as well eat this here.'

'I'd rather be in my own home. If you don't mind, I'd like my shoes.'

Berthe went down on her knees and retrieved them from under the bed. When she came up, she was wearing a look like someone humouring a spoilt child.

'Shall I help you with them?'

'Thank you.' He was grateful to have been spared the ordeal of bending over.

'Your coat now, that's wet. It was all covered in mud and blood. There was nothing to do but soak it.'

'I'll manage.'

'You do as you please, but I've got to tell Madame Maçon you're leaving.'

Once he'd made his shaky way down the hallway to the front door, Lavoie was confronted by the full fear of going out into the street. There was no mirror in Monsieur Maçon's house, and his studio had only a distorting one of beaten metal – silvered glass being a luxury that was beyond his means. But he had the inescapable sense that there was something monstrous in the bruises on his face. He was afraid of stepping outside and seeing his neighbours stare.

'You're going?' Madame Maçon had stepped into the hallway, rocking her baby up and down against her shoulder. He'd seen her hold one of her rabbits that same way.

'Yes, thank you.' Lavoie felt himself drawing his head into the protection of his shoulders, turning away from her. 'For your help. You've been kind.'

'You should stay a little longer.' Her wan face was creased in sympathy. 'My husband will be home in the evening.'

'Thank you, no. He can visit me at home, if he wants.'

'I'll send Berthe over with a meal then. You'll not want to go to the traiteur.'

'Thank you.' He made a little abortive bow, clipped by the pain of the movement and his need to brace himself against the door with one arm. Then he turned away from her and scrabbled at the door handle and pushed himself outside.

The air in the street was cold, the sky overcast, and he was in his shirt and no coat. He had a moment of fleeting gratitude for the fact that he had been wearing his second-best coat when the baron's men came calling, and not the one that he wore when clients sat for him, which was made of silk brocade and had lace trim on the sleeves and would have cost a small fortune to replace if he'd ruined it by bleeding on it.

The street was quiet, but he thought he felt the eyes of the grocer on him, that the man selling a tray of baked apples turned to follow him. Who else had seen the baron's carriage? He pulled his shirt collar up around his face and groped his way shakily the few steps to his front door, which was unlocked.

Inside, it was still cold. He poked the embers of the fire in the grate until they sparked a little, and rolled a log off the wood pile and onto the flames using the poker and the tip of his shoe. He sank into his chair and ached.

There was no one watching over him and nothing, now, to distract him or to pull his mind back from the night on the floor, the way he'd lain there, stunned, long after the baron's men left his house, watching the shadows move on the stairs and seeing, at times, some enormous beast skulking in and out of them, painted the colour of the inside of his eyelids, waiting for him to try to move. Finally he'd had the sense that he had got up and walked to the top of the stairs and was watching his dead body from the landing, without much passion for it. He had the same feeling now – he sat with his head lolling bonelessly against the back of the chair, and his mind got up and kicked his lump of a body where it sat, and found a pen and paper in his writing desk upstairs and began a brief, clinical letter:

This is to recount that, on the 18th of February, the Baron de Cardonnoy came to my house with two lackeys and, having forced his way in, accosted me with suspicions about the honour of his wife, whose portrait he had previously engaged me to paint. That, on his departure, his servants stayed and beat me until I was half dead. There being no just cause for this offence, I demand – *demand?* he wondered. *Entreat? Request?* – I request that the full force of the law be brought to bear on the lackeys who abused me.

His dream self put the pen down and sealed the letter. In the chair, his battered hand twitched. He could not stand yet. The letter might easily damn his reputation, for what man would hire a portrait painter who might be too free with his wife? Lavoie barely cared. The world of paint was too far away, and in his house every colour was muddy with pain. Neither the light nor the shadows made a place where his eyes could rest.

He wanted to take from the baron some measure of what the baron had taken from him. Make him twist as the public discussed whether his wife's infidelity was real or a product of his own jealous imagination. Make the law pursue the lackeys who did his bidding. It could not possibly be enough, and yet.

Lavoie recited the letter over in his head. *Demand?* he wondered. *Request?* He knew that, when he could stand again, he would write it.

Elsewhere in Paris, a man was walking the streets in a red coat. He began his tour in the Church of Saint-Sulpice, where he went down the nave without regarding either the Virgin or the statue of Moses that guarded the door. A phantom entirely, he raced down the steps and through the mud-clogged streets to the graveyard, undisturbed by street lights, hanging signs or merrymakers out late, their carriage wheels rattling over the cobblestones, going from theatre to opera to cards and waking the working folk with their passage. The mud they splattered in their wake did not touch him. A close observer, had there been one, might have seen that his red coat was stained already, and with blood.

Reaching the churchyard, the walker removed his hat at the newly turned grave. He waited for some time there, but no one joined him, and he left no offering.

When the moon had risen yellow over the city, he walked on past the graveyard. He had lost his horse, which was flesh and blood, while he was only a phantom, animated by the power of his clothes, his long dark hair floating like an obscuring cloud around his face, which could not rightly be called either a man's or a woman's. In another life, some poor would-be dandy might have fished his coat out of a second-hand bundle and scrubbed the blood out of it. But now the coat summoned up its own ghost to inhabit it, and it was this man who went walking by night. Down the rue Saint-Germain, around the corner, into the alley where a rag woman picked over the household rubbish, looking for scraps to sell to the paper mill. She alone jumped when she saw him, and crossed herself.

He passed through the gates of the Hôtel Cardonnoy, without being stopped or seen by the drowsy Swiss guard.

Once within the gate, he pressed his face against the leaded glass windows, gazing first at the empty salon hung in black drapery, the servants coming and going in the hall. Then, flying with the lightness of a being made of cloth and secrecy, he climbed upwards and left his fingerprints on the windowpanes of the baron's locked study, then edged along the scrollwork on the window ledge to look in at the baronne's window, where the lamps were lit and two women sat talking on the bed.

It was true that he resembled Mademoiselle de Conti, the way a brother resembles a sister. He had her dark cloud of hair, the snakish line of her jaw. But pick any two strangers out on the streets of Paris and they may look alike, by pure coincidence. Mademoiselle de Conti peered out of the window, as if she was aware of being watched, and the spectre in his borrowed coat stepped back, over the window ledge, and fell to the ground unharmed.

'I feel like someone's watching,' said Victoire. 'Will you check the hallway?'

Madame de Cardonnoy got up and cracked open the door, peering into the shadow of the lamps. The hall was empty.

'I'm sorry,' said Victoire. 'I've brought all of this upon you.'

It was the first time Marie Catherine had ever seen Victoire ashamed.

'Don't be sorry,' said Madame de Cardonnoy. 'We do have to be careful.'

'You must wish you'd never known me.'

'No.' She took a deep breath. 'I don't.'

Outside, the man in the coat leaped over the wall in one bound and then set out, like any ordinary night-walker, through the streets of Saint-Germain-des-Prés. By night the street was quiet, except for the rumbling of carriage wheels, which muffled the sound of his footsteps. He skirted the bright halo of the street light and hurried past a pair of young women walking the street arm in arm, whispering to passing men. One of them reached out to touch him, pulled at the solid sleeve of his jacket and then drew back when he passed on without looking at her.

'I can't go to confession,' Victoire said.

Marie Catherine sat up on the bed. She had been watching the shadows flicker in the moulded leaves that crowned the door, and now she reached out and ran her fingers through a curl that was escaping from the elaborate pins and netting that held Victoire's hair in place. Victoire, sitting on a stool by the bed, leaned her head against the coverlet.

'I suppose not,' said Marie Catherine. 'I haven't been in a long time.'

When had the last time been? Sometime after she had met Victoire at Madame de Fontet's, after that first night alone at the theatre. She'd worn silk the colour of myrtle leaves, with argentine casting a silver gleam over her dark hair. They had joked together, casually, at first, forehead to forehead, and before they had ever kissed, Marie Catherine had knelt in front of the grille of the confessional and, burning with the possessive desire of a girl faced with a new and lifelike doll, had confessed to the sin of envy. *There is another woman, and I envy her because she is more beautiful than I am, younger than I am, wittier and more free in company, more admired, more daring, whose family's age and stature allow her a licence that I do not have.* She had known, even then, that envy alone couldn't explain the jealousy that she held close to her breast, and that seemed to inflate inside her when the girl sent her a note after a night at the ballet, or caught her eye across a room and smiled. If she had looked at a man that way, Marie Catherine would quickly have recognised it for an inclination. As it was, she felt like a child kneeling before the secret and magical body of a doll, asking her to speak to her, move, smile. To open her painted-on mouth and speak.

If someone had asked her what it was she longed for, she would not have been able to answer.

'Do you still love me?' Victoire's eyes were fixed on the design on the rug.

'I do.' And this, still, was true, despite the image of the baron's corpse that had made her recoil. She wanted to kiss Victoire, to pull her up onto the bed and fix the image of the spiral of her ear, the slightly crookedness of her teeth and her outstretched arms forever in place there. It was the same beast that had seized her by the throat and insisted that she would live – they would both live – whatever the cost. For a moment she imagined taking back what she'd said before, calling a carriage, leaving the children, as if she could have betrayed or abandoned anything at all in exchange for their escape.

'It's late,' she said instead, still feeling the pulse beating in her throat from the vividness of her imagination, of her desire. Could they live in a furnished room somewhere in Spain or Belgium, in an apartment paid for with their jewellery, alone, without regard for the law? Could she take the children with her, carry Nicolas out to the carriage with Sophie sleepily stumbling behind? Instead she said, 'You ought to go. Jeanne will be done with her supper soon.'

'She carried that letter,' Victoire said. 'Do you think she suspects?'

'I don't know what she thinks.'

'I gave her some money when she brought it. But she's loyal, isn't she?'

Marie Catherine shook her head. 'I hope so.'

She touched Victoire's eyelids with her fingertips, feeling the spider's web of her eyelashes when she blinked.

'I'm going to look through the baron's papers. I hope there will be something there that helps.'

'I can ask at court if there was anyone who hated him. I think he had a fortune-teller he went to. Someone will know.'

'Maybe. But ask carefully.'

Victoire nodded, her mouth pursed as if she was sucking on something bitter.

'I should go.'

Stay, she wanted to say. Instead she caught Victoire's wrist at the door and kissed her mouth and then her hand. She didn't know the next time she'd dare to get into the carriage with her, or send Jeanne away on some imaginary errand so that she could throw off her mantua, keeping one eye always half on the door. Already the time they spent together had been hasty, secret, always cut short.

'Here, let me fix your hair.' Marie Catherine pulled a curl back into its place.

She walked Victoire as far as the stairs, and then some invisible barrier prevented her from following farther, down into the entranceway where two servants sat sullenly, Victoire's coachman with his coat half buttoned, playing cards with Caspar who guarded the gate, slapping the cards down, spitting into a vase. Marie Catherine touched Victoire's littlest finger on the landing, felt a spark zip through her, as on cold days when the handle of a door, or a pen, or the hands of a servant all give off their own quick shock. And then Mademoiselle de Conti slipped down the stairs as if floating on the blowing kite of her dress.

Elsewhere in the city the assassin's ghost was running as if pursued. The blood on his coat had dried now, but his hair was wild, and his face was like a face trapped under ice, straining to break through and back into the air. Still, few passers-by watched him for more than a glance. A party of theatre-goers in fancy dress, headed by a lantern man who lit their way, drew back from him in fright, as if he'd come to cut their purse strings and their throats. In the courtyard of Hôtel Cardonnoy, Mademoiselle de Conti's carriage pulled out and into the street, attended by lackeys.

Victoire felt for a moment as if she were a knot being pulled tightly in every direction, and then as if she were the sword slicing through the knot. She saw the sword clearly – it hung in her mind, a more potent image than the pistol she had used, which lay wrapped in a handkerchief and hidden deep in a locked drawer in her cabinet. She was the knife that cut through the quiet of the night. She felt her dress and the stays of her corset as a tight sheath enclosing a blade.

I should have been a man, she told the darkness. Perhaps a man would not have been afraid. She should have been the queen Semiramis, riding into battle with her long hair falling free over her armour; an Amazon with a bow and a leopard skin; Jeanne d'Arc with her hair cut short. She should have been her own grandmother, Madame de Chevreuse, plotting against the king, exiled, triumphant, dressed as a warrior and leading the rebel troops towards Paris, dressed as Diana and leading a captive stag by a halter. She could have been any of them. She felt she was all at once, ancestor and archetype and patron saint. In the next moment she was a stupid girl with bloodstained hands, again.

I should have been born a man.

She crossed her double's ghost at the Pont Saint-Michel and, looking out of the window of her carriage, she recognised him for her own bad angel. Then he was one more anonymous figure in the night, and Victoire could not have said whether his escaping silhouette was her true self or only the shadow of her crime, alive so long as she went unpunished. After her carriage had crossed the bridge, he stripped off his jacket and then the rest of his clothes.

Naked, no one could have told whether he was male or female. The night clothed him thoroughly. He dropped the bloody bundle of cloth over the edge of the bridge and, as the current teased it apart and tugged it beneath the surface of the water, he stepped up onto the railing and dissolved into the air.

Chapter Eight

———

When the letter came on the day after the funeral, Jeanne assumed at first that it contained a note for Madame, expressing sympathy, and then, when Henri dogged her footsteps and said that the boy insisted that it be left with *Jeanne Durand, the servant girl, no other*, she assumed it was some further secret message passed between her mistress and Mademoiselle de Conti. The realisation sent a wolfish shiver up her spine, and she almost asked Henri to tell the messenger boy to leave Paris and drown in a ditch, but she knew very well that she had carried a note on the night of Monsieur's death, whose contents she had not read, and that Mademoiselle de Conti, on receiving the message, had clasped it to her chest and then given Jeanne a silver écu for her trouble, which was worth a good percentage of her yearly salary. She carried the coin inside her bodice, against her chest, and, like the letter, it involved her inextricably in the secrecy of the household and incriminated her. She knew, from listening to the baron's valet talk in the kitchen, and to the men and women at Madame's salon, that a servant who carried papers for his master was not innocent of the master's crimes. The Maréchal de Luxembourg, for instance, long before his arrest, had suggested far and wide that Monsieur de la Reynie ought to question his secretary, who, he claimed, was the real author of a satanic paper signed with the maréchal's name.

But the écu was too big a sum of money to throw away, and she hadn't realised when she carried the paper that the baron would be dead by the next morning. She had thought it simply told Victoire that she was suspected of the kinds of crimes Jeanne knew she had been committing with the baronne and should prepare to run away. Now, slipping away from Madame's bedroom full of guests and walking to the courtyard through Hôtel Cardonnoy's black draperies, Jeanne felt herself becoming queasy, the hallway seeming to stretch the way it did sometimes in her dreams, like a piece of cheesecloth pulled tight enough to rip.

The boy was about twelve and had a rash of red pimples on his chin. He smelled like he'd been knocked into the mud recently. He was not in servant's livery, and Caspar the Swiss had stopped him outside the main gate and wouldn't let him in. He had the look of a boy who'd complained too vigorously about the Swiss's decision and had had his ears boxed. One of the pimples was bleeding. A visiting coachman – the Comtesse de Combois's, from the coat of arms emblazoned on the coach door – sneered at him, and then at Jeanne.

'You should tell your lovers to deliver their letters in better packaging,' Caspar said, when Jeanne was close enough to hear him. She shrugged. They were always like that, Caspar and Arnaud. They egged each other on.

'Are you Jeanne Durand, the servant girl?' The boy's voice was a reedy squeak.

She held out her hand for the letter.

'She says it's urgent. She says you're to come as soon as you can get away.' The folded letter appeared in his hand and he gestured with it.

'Who sent you?' Jeanne asked. She reached for the paper, and the boy twitched it away and danced into the street.

'I don't know her name.' He twisted his hands behind his back and shook his head slyly. Jeanne grabbed his collar and found it greasy. She pinched his ear.

'Give me that. And tell me who.'

He stopped trying to hold the letter out of her reach and went limp in her grasp.

'The woman with the mark right here.' He pointed at his left temple.

Jeanne bit her lip, let him go, wiped her hands on her skirt.

'You should give me some charity, Mademoiselle. I came a long way.'

'I'll send the kitchen boy out with some food.' She was already turning away. Caspar snorted.

'I want *money*, not food,' he called after her, and then she heard him kick a stone into the street and huff, and curse her and servants everywhere.

It was impossible to find somewhere private to open the letter. Jeanne ended up hidden at the far end of the stable, smelling the heap of food scraps in the back alley, the horseflesh and hay that always carried with it the shadow of a childhood memory. The woman with the mark on her face was Laure La Chapelle, and although she had helped Jeanne learn her letters, her spelling was now much worse than Jeanne's own and the letter was written in a cramped hand, the words wandering down the page in crooked lines as if they were looking for a way to escape off it:

Dear Jeanne,

You must help me. The police have come for Maman. La Voisin or one of her old companions must have given them her name. I was in the road when they took her away in the morning, and so frightened that I pretended not to know her, God help me, although I feared the police would recognise me at once. I dare not go back to the house, in case they come for me. None of the neighbours will stand with me, or say that I am not a witch. I am in a room in the house run by a Madame Camille, near rue de la Clef, but I spent all the money I had to pay the landlady, and I am nearly ready to sell the dress off my own back.

God knows, Jeanne, though I am not innocent before the law, I am innocent in his eyes. I still believe that.

My mother helped you once. I hope you haven't forgotten either her or me.

Laure

When she was done reading, Jeanne tore the letter into pieces, which she deposited in a muddy corner and kicked straw over. A moment later she wished she hadn't. She imagined a stable boy forking aside the rotting hay and finding the letter, piecing it together until he found Jeanne's name in proximity with the name La Voisin, the notorious poisoner. With Laure La Chapelle's. That the stable boy could not read made no difference to the vividness with which the scene presented itself.

Laure was a few years older than Jeanne, but she was so small and thin she might easily have passed for younger. The hair on her head was as pale as a baby's, and clung flat to her skull like cobwebs. Her face would have been plain, but it was marred by a red mark that began on her left temple and spread in long, blotchy fingers as far as her upper eyelid, which was perpetually as red and soft as a tulip petal. People stared at her in the street, and in her mother's smoky sitting room she would sometimes roll her eyes back in her head and speak in a whispering voice, as if she were communing with the spirits.

She read cards, and palms as well. The strangeness of her face made it easy to believe that she could see the future.

She had been close to the circle of fortune-tellers who were now rotting in the cells of Vincennes and the Châtelet, accused of selling poisons and black magic to the lords and ladies at court. The witches. La Bosse. La Filastre. La Voisin. La Chapelle.

And her mother was the woman to whom Jeanne owed her life.

Jeanne had been fourteen when she left her family, riding into Paris on the back of a neighbour's wagon with the address of her aunt memorised, and a request that the aunt should find work for Jeanne because there was nothing for her on the farm. The aunt had sighed and wrapped her fingers around Jeanne's skinny arms and found her a place as a chambermaid in a parliamentarian's house, with instructions not to open her mouth too much, lest anyone hear how badly she spoke French.

The position had seemed, at first, too good to be true, with the endless supply of food in the kitchens, the fine accents of the staff, the ladies in their lovely dresses who came and went. The crisp maid's uniform was the nicest thing Jeanne had ever worn. By the time she turned fifteen, good food had made her shoot up like a sapling, and the uniform was too tight on her shoulders and too short at her ankles. A few months later it was too tight again, this time over her belly. She'd missed four months of bleeding, which was enough time for her to have realised that the master's valet was not going to marry her and, moreover, that he thought she was a little imbecile. Jeanne could not have disputed his opinion. She was a farmer's daughter, and while she knew nothing about love, she should have known better than to let him bed her. She took a little bit of rat poison mixed with wine, hoping to miscarry, and was sick for days, which didn't kill her or the baby, but did provide an opportunity for the lady of the house to discover the pregnancy and send her packing.

Her aunt wouldn't have her. She went back to the parliamentarian's hôtel, to try and plead with the valet one more time, and the cook, with whom she'd been on good terms, gave her a meal, and a pallet in the larder to lie down on, and in the evening, after the household had eaten, he took her to La Chapelle's house.

'Can you help this child?' he'd asked, while Jeanne stood in the doorway with her hands crossed over her stomach. She'd cried during the entire walk, and her eyes still stung.

And Laure's mother, her greying hair hidden under a respectable veil, still dressed in black mourning clothes in honour of a husband no one on her street had ever laid eyes upon, took Jeanne into a private room and had her pull up her skirt and, when she came out, she shook the cook's hand and said, 'Yes, I can.'

So the cook left, and Jeanne stayed.

When the thing was done, La Chapelle had given the fetus – which didn't even look human, was only a knot of hardened blood, a creature that Jeanne could not have imagined would have caused her so much pain – to Laure, and then she had made the sign of the cross over it and touched it with holy water, and wrapped it up in a clean cloth to be buried. A baptism. La Chapelle communed with her own particular set of angels, which insisted in no uncertain terms that children born before term were not doomed to hell.

'With God, everything is forgiven,' she'd said, once she'd finished the ritual. There were tears in her eyes. The clyster sat in a bloody bowl on the floor. 'Your child is in heaven.'

Jeanne had been sick for a long time after the abortion. For a day she could stand and help in the kitchen, though weakly, bleeding and cramping a little as if she had been menstruating, but then a fever crawled up her spine and she dreamed, over and over, about hell, until La Chapelle called for a priest. When, at last, the fever broke and she returned from delirium, Jeanne found that La Chapelle had supplemented the last rites performed by the priest with a charm of her own, for under Jeanne's pillow there was a communion wafer tied up in ribbon, on which had been written the word *AGLA*.

'Now that you're awake, you must eat it,' La Chapelle told her, 'and its power will protect you.'

Anyone else would have said it was treason against God. Selling the consecrated host was a mortal sin. But the light was bright in La Chapelle's bedroom, and for days Jeanne had lain in La Chapelle's own bed, while the abortionist slept beside her like a parent and sat up in the middle of night to stroke her forehead when she cried, fearing that God no longer loved her, and that when she died her soul would descend to hell. Jeanne opened her mouth and took the wafer on her tongue, and La Chapelle's daughter, Laure, gave her a pewter cup full of milk to wash it down.

Jeanne stayed in the house for a month, recovered, cooked meals, hid when noblemen and women came to the house in fine carriages to have Laure tell their fortunes, learned her letters, paced up and down the kitchen garden arm in arm with La Chapelle and her daughter while the two of them corrected her accent and her grammar. Until she could talk like a lady and sound out most of the words in La Chapelle's Bible, if haltingly.

'Maman needs people who can send her gossip from the court and the salons,' said Laure, as they walked in the garden between rows of cabbage. 'It makes my fortune-telling much easier.'

'You mean the spirits don't speak to you?' Jeanne said. She'd grown less innocent, but it was a slow transformation. Laure laughed at her. Jeanne had found her marked face frightening at first, but she didn't look so ugly when she laughed.

'They speak when they want to,' Laure said, turning serious. 'Through dreams, mostly. But most people don't really want to hear their future. They just want to hear that their plans will succeed.'

'Can you tell me mine?' said Jeanne.

Laure took her palm and squinted at it.

'You're going to make your fortune,' she said with a smile. 'And you're going to die old and happy and rich.'

'Will I get married?'

'No.' Laure answered without pausing to consider.

Jeanne nodded. 'Good.'

They looked at each other and laughed. The next week a friend of La Chapelle's came and took Jeanne to Hôtel Cardonnoy, where the baron liked to consult a fortune-teller before undertaking business dealings, and the baron's wife needed a new lady's maid. When Jeanne came to Paris, she had been known as Jeanne Gagnier. Now she called herself Jeanne Durand. Her family did not know where she was. Jeanne Gagnier, for all anyone knew, was a prostitute working the worst streets with her baby at her breast, or she was a pauper, or she had died in childbirth.

The farmer's daughter had learned to listen, and keep her own counsel, and when the servants gossiped about what the high folk were doing, or the women in Madame's salon discussed their affairs, she wrote down what they said and sent the letter to La Chapelle. With, always, her gratitude.

The knowledge of the letter made her feel queasy all day, as she attended the funeral guests, standing guard at Madame de Cardonnoy's door and listening to the hushed conversations of the mourners, the men and women who gossiped on the stairs. She could not sneak away. She realised only after two or three hours had passed that she had forgotten to send one of the kitchen maids out with food for the urchin who'd carried the message, and she thought first of the ruckus he might have raised, and only second that he must have waited and been hungry. She bit her lip. She was disgusted with her own cowardice. Because hadn't Laure and her mother done things for which they knew the sentence was death, over and over – the abortions, the good-luck charms, the fortune-telling – done them for money, yes, but also for Jeanne, a destitute stranger. Laure had never reproached her with the trouble or danger that Jeanne had put her to, nor had her mother worried that Jeanne's body might call the police down on them, when it had seemed she was near death. She had called the priest. She had given her the magic wafer. But Jeanne had listened in Madame's salons and heard of the net closing around the other sorceresses and selfishly hoped that it would spare La Chapelle. Now she was afraid to sneak away for half a day, in case it caught her, too.

Her feet ached from rushing after visitors. The écu in her bodice chafed her skin. She kept moving it from its place inside her stays to her pocket, then back again. Finally all of the guests left, except for Mademoiselle de Conti, and Jeanne went down to the kitchen for her supper and took it away to a far corner where no one was talking about the baron's death, and ate soup and hot bread, feeling as if the food was going down into a deep hole inside her, as if she could make her ingratitude be silent by stuffing its face.

'Look at Jeanne, all on her own,' Arnaud called from the servants' common table. 'Cheer up, Mademoiselle Durand, you'll find a new mistress if Monsieur de la Reynie arrests ours.'

Henri, the baron's valet, punched him in the shoulder.

'Be quiet,' Jeanne snapped. 'She's grieving.' But she swallowed. Usually Henri and Arnaud tried to outdo each other in disgusting behaviour. If Henri didn't want Jeanne to hear them joke about Madame's guilt, then he must think Jeanne was guilty too. God in heaven, but she should have broken the seal on the letter she'd given Mademoiselle de Conti. She was damned from every side.

'I hope she's paying you well for your loyalty, sweet Jeanne,' said Arnaud.

Madame did not call for her supper that night. Perhaps grief killed her appetite, where it whetted Jeanne's. Grief, or fear. At another time Jeanne would have tried to eavesdrop on whatever her mistress was saying to Mademoiselle de Conti alone in her room, but tonight she couldn't be bothered. She sat by the servants' fire with Anne, and the nursemaid put her arm around Jeanne's shoulders. Jeanne wasn't sure if they were friends, exactly – she wouldn't have confided in the nursemaid, and she suspected that, like the other servants, Anne thought Jeanne put on airs – but Anne was gentle and she seemed to sense Jeanne's unhappiness. They waited like that until Madame called for her.

After Mademoiselle de Conti had left, Jeanne helped Madame off with her mourning clothes and gloves, unwrapping the long black veil and then sponging away the marks that the fresh dye had left on the baronne's face and neck, with a basin of warm water and a cake of soap. The dye streaks looked like long bruises running down from behind her ears, in all the places where her sweat had dampened the fabric and made it bleed. Her hair, tucked away under the fitted veil, was no longer in its usual elaborate style. Jeanne brushed it out, as she did on the days before Monsieur Paget came to style her coiffure. Her hair was the colour of new wood and fell down to her hips, thinning out at the ends into wispy strands that crinkled and puffed up when they were combed, individual hairs rising up and questing after the teeth of the comb as if they were animated by some living impulse of their own, separate from their owner.

Madame's body should have contained no mysteries for Jeanne, who dressed her and bathed her and trimmed her fingernails as she held her hands out pliantly like a child, who emptied the night soil out of her chamberpot and carried her menstrual clothes down to the laundress. But occasionally still it did, when she combed out Madame's long, long hair and plaited it, or when she unlaced her dress and saw the pink marks the stays had pressed into her flesh, the way her skin moved with her breath.

Jeanne was never sure what the baronne and Mademoiselle de Conti did together – what *could* two women do, in that way? she wondered sometimes, idly, while she was pressing dresses or taking Anne's place with the children or reading one of Madame's fashion circulars. Surely they didn't have all the requisite parts, and it wasn't the sort of mystery that one could enquire of the chambermaids. Once Laure had spoken disparagingly of a magic ritual that required a priest to get down on his knees and kiss a woman's cunt, so Jeanne supposed there were all kinds of permutations of sex that one couldn't have guessed at, from being a farmer's daughter and knowing what bulls did with cows, but she wasn't sure which were common, and the thought pricked her with anxiety as much as it tantalised her curiosity.

Once, she might have condemned them. Now she thought of La Chapelle, with her clyster and her spirits and her enchanted wafer, who had told her that anything could be forgiven. She wondered at that sometimes. She was not sure she believed it. Still, when she'd opened a door to find Madame and her woman lover kissing, believing Jeanne safely away on some errand, she'd stepped back as silently as she could and eased the door closed behind her.

Tonight there was a quiet, repressed energy in Madame's demeanour, as if her skin, as well as the little waving fronds of her hair, were sending off sparks that might catch on anything in the room and burn it down. She and Mademoiselle de Conti had been plotting, certainly, and whatever accord they had come to had shaken her out of her lassitude. Jeanne lay down in her alcove and tossed and turned for a long time, feeling the energy pouring off her mistress, hearing the quick, unsteady sound of her breathing.

Her mind kept turning the same problem over and over, without reaching any solution. She had to get out of this house, she had to get as far away as possible, she had to get some more money so that she could get out. The police would take her if she didn't. She'd been such a fool. She had nearly lulled herself to sleep that way when she heard the baronne throw her covers back and step lightly down onto the floor. Jeanne lay still and listened, pretending that sleep had already pulled her away.

Marie Catherine heard the floor creak under her feet and paused at her bedroom door, easing it open so that the hinges made no sound. It was not illicit, what she was doing, but still the terror of her husband's death gripped her, and she expected to find his bloody corpse in the hallway as much as she expected a curious servant. No, his corpse was beneath the ground. But the image tugged at the back of her mind as if it were a baby that cuddled at her shoulder and mouthed her hair. She took the lamp from her bedside, but she did not strike a light – not in her bedroom, where it might have woken Jeanne, or in the hallway, although the passage was empty and so dark that she had to hold one hand in front of her face and grope her way along the wall, moving the way a mole must move, deep underground. She found the door to her husband's cabinet and felt her way to the lock with her fingers, feeling almost as if the polished wood was breathing under her hand. The door opened into a less suffocating darkness, relieved by the greyed-out silhouette of the window, and she was able to close it behind her and strike a light.

Marie Catherine cupped the lamp's flame with her hand, nursing it to make sure it caught, and her movement seemed to send things flying into every corner of the room. The flame flickered and then burned steady. She set the lamp down on her husband's desk.

The drawer he had taken from her writing table lay on the floor by his desk, the letters inside it pawed through and scattered across the floor. He must have knelt there, beside his chair, searching for evidence of her guilt. When she bent down by the drawer to shuffle her papers back together, Marie Catherine felt as if she had stepped through his ghost.

She had not come for her own letters. Once she had heaped them back into the drawer and neatened their edges, she sat down in the leather chair drawn up by his desk. The desk came with its own ring of keys, each one fitting a different drawer or pigeonhole, each keyhole edged in figured brass and looking like a little open mouth. The keys had been in her husband's pocket when he died, and now they were in hers. The wood rippled like water in the lamplight.

She chose a key and tried drawers until she found the one that opened to its kiss. The lower-left drawer, on a level with her knee. Inside, the papers were jumbled – a broken pen, several sheaves of letters tied together with ribbon. On the shelves around her the baron's library, the account books of the Cardonnoy estates, gave off the dry, petrified smell of old leather, and any of those books might have a letter or a bill or some vital piece of paperwork slipped casually inside, to mark a page.

There, that was the ghost. Not behind her, but unfolding itself from the drawer with a sound of paper rustling. He was standing before her, white and blood-red, adjusting his cravat over the black hole that had taken his throat and most of his jaw. He opened his mouth to condemn her and she heard the sound of pen against paper, imagined a pen wet with ink like a slick tongue.

'Stand aside, please.' She had summoned him by imagining him. This room contained the record of his life and so he was there, and he stood in judgement of her, and in the language of death he found her false, wicked, murderous.

He reached out for her. His touch was a cold draught.

'I'm done with you,' she told him. 'You're in *my* house.'

She put her hand out and reached through him, for the topmost bundle of papers, the red ribbon, closing her eyes and groping for the drawer, so that she wouldn't see when he caught her wrist and dripped blood onto her face. There was a chill on her face, there was a sound of rustling, the crisp noise of someone skimming through an old book.

When she opened her eyes, the apparition was gone. Eventually her heartbeat quieted.

She untied the ribbon that bound the papers. She began to read.

Marie Catherine ate her breakfast with the children in the nursery. She was yawning, exhausted and glitteringly bright-eyed from her work the night before, and her mind seemed to move in strange circles, like an eel underwater, making shapes that she couldn't quite predict. She didn't yet know if she'd found anything that might save her. Before breakfast she lined up Jeanne, Anne and the children in front of the cross on the nursery wall and made them kneel, and then she knelt before them and read from her prayer book with her widow's veil pulled piously over her head. She could see Nicolas and Sophie eyeing each other across the breakfast table after the prayer was done and the food was set out. Jeanne, too, fidgeted in her place by the door. She seemed animated by incredible nerves this past day, jumping when Marie Catherine called her name or moved behind her. When Marie Catherine had come back from the baron's study in the morning, the keys clinking in her hand, Jeanne had been awake, making up the bed that the baronne hadn't slept in, and she had stayed calmly bent over her work as if determined not to acknowledge Marie Catherine's absence in any way.

'Is Papa in heaven?' Nicolas blurted out. He had a spoonful of porridge in his mouth that he hadn't finished swallowing.

'Be quiet!' Sophie hissed at him, and her hand darted out to pinch him. Marie Catherine straightened up, her attention turning back from Jeanne, her head swimming with the beginning pressure of a headache.

'That's enough!' She caught Sophie's wrist as her hand snaked back from Nicolas's ear. There were big tears starting in his eyes, a little leak of porridge dribbling down his mouth. Marie Catherine wished his unhappiness moved her more, but she was exhausted. 'Don't pinch your brother.'

She took her napkin and wiped Nicolas's eyes with it, and then his mouth.

'We hope very much that your father is in heaven. That's why we pray to God for his soul.' This didn't stop Nicolas from crying, and she wasn't sure what else she should say.

She felt a sudden eruption of rage towards the baron. If only he had managed to die of flux last year when he had been ill, before anyone had been suspicious of poison or other dark deeds. If only he had been a little older, in worse health, the victim of an unfortunate hunting accident. There were a thousand ways a man could die before his time without foul play, and he'd somehow avoided all of them and was now going to carry on killing her by degrees from beyond the grave. She remembered the apparition that her fear had summoned the night before, sighing and bleeding on the carpet. If she'd had his body in front of her, she would have kicked it. She tried to smile comfortingly.

'You must be very good, and keep him in your thoughts and prayers,' she said. She wiped her eyes with her veil, for Jeanne's benefit. 'We are all sinners, but it only requires God's mercy to intervene and save us.'

'Sophie hasn't been good,' Nicolas whispered. He was theatrically rubbing his ear where she'd pinched him. 'She broke her doll.'

Before he had finished speaking, Sophie let out a shriek of frustration and cracked her spoon down on the edge of her plate. 'I *didn't* break her! And you're a tattletale!'

'Sophie, eat your food and stop screaming!' Marie Catherine was also yelling now. Sophie's shriek had gone through her ear like a needle. She put her hands over her ears, then took a deep breath and lowered them. 'Wait, no. Put your spoon down and bring me the doll.'

She didn't know where this animosity between the children had come from. Since the night of their father's death, they'd been almost uncannily close, whispering together, Sophie holding Nicolas's hand and shepherding him around the house. Minutes before breakfast they'd been playing an elaborate game that had left toy soldiers tied up in bits of ribbon scattered all over the nursery floor.

Sophie put her spoon down by her plate, painfully slowly, wiping it clean with her napkin and checking it for any remaining smear of porridge and then pausing to glare at Nicolas before she scraped her chair out, to make it clear what she thought of her brother's accusation and her mother's orders. The doll was hidden in the space between the head of her bed and the wall, wrapped up lovingly in a handkerchief. When Sophie brought her to Marie Catherine, she cradled her as if she was holding a live baby.

It was a little porcelain fashion doll. Originally she had been sent from Marie Catherine's dressmaker, in a doll-dress embroidered with lilies and trimmed with lace ruffles, an example of the year's styles. Once the full-sized dresses had been commissioned and paid for, the doll and her finery had been passed on to Sophie. Her white porcelain cheeks were made up with big circles of rouge. Her hair was horsehair, a little coarse, but Sophie must have stolen a pinch of her mother's argentine and powdered it, for it was tinted silver. She held out the doll to her mother, still swaddled in the handkerchief.

'She's not broken,' she insisted, as Marie Catherine unwrapped her.

The doll's right hand was missing, severed jaggedly from her wrist. Marie Catherine touched the broken piece and the rough edge of the porcelain sliced a bloodlessly stinging nick on the tip of her finger. Sophie now looked as if she might cry, but rebelliously, her chin tucked into her collarbone in frustrated pride. Nicolas was squirming guiltily in his chair, ignoring his breakfast.

'Sophie, you can't treat your toys this way,' Marie Catherine said.

Sophie's fists were clenched at her sides, her face full of the strain of explaining herself. She huffed out a breath with the anger of a child unjustly punished.

'I wanted her to be like the stone bride from your story.' Another of those long, miserable breaths. 'Please don't take her away.'

Marie Catherine put the doll down on the table by her porridge. She was too tired, and she could feel Nicolas and Jeanne watching her as Sophie hung her head miserably and glared at the floor.

'It's all right, darling. Don't break any more dolls.' She pulled Sophie forward into the nest of her skirts and tucked her head under her chin. Sophie squirmed for a minute, then raised her arms and returned the embrace.

'Now that Papa's dead, we only ever say prayers together,' she sniffed, into the crinkling folds of the widow's veil. 'You didn't even come to the nursery last night.'

'I'm sorry, Sophie,' Marie Catherine said. 'I'll be there tonight. And tomorrow night.'

She stroked Sophie's back.

'Nicolas, why don't you come over here, too.'

He slipped down from his seat and joined the embrace. Marie Catherine ran her fingers through his hair. Sophie squirmed away from her brother's touch, but after a moment she relaxed and sniffled into her mother's shoulder. They stayed like that for a while, Marie Catherine feeling the little warm bodies radiating heat through her clothes and making her neck sweat under the veil.

'I'll be there tonight,' Marie Catherine said. 'I promise.'

Henri appeared in the doorway beside Jeanne, who leaned away from him as if in a breeze. Madame de Cardonnoy stood up.

'Madame.' The baron's valet bowed. 'Monsieur de la Reynie is waiting for you below.'

'Thank you, Henri. Tell him I'm coming.' She tugged her veil straighter, keeping her voice level.

She found La Reynie waiting in the salon, his back turned to the door. The winter sunlight streaming in through the window made the tight, dark curls of his hair look something like an abandoned bird's nest, an impression Madame de Cardonnoy tried to quash as soon as she'd thought of it. Plenty of men wore wigs with those curls, which the king had made stylish, but only La Reynie looked so windswept. He was the sort of man who couldn't resist running his fingers through his hair when he was thinking.

He was tapping his foot on the carpet, and the soft, muted impact of his shoe sounded, to Marie Catherine's ears, disproportionately ominous. Henri held the door open for her, and she felt that something in his face expressed a malignant glee when she walked through it.

'Good morning, Monsieur,' she said to La Reynie. 'I'm pleased to see you again so soon. Do you have any news about my husband?'

La Reynie turned. As he did so, Madame de Cardonnoy heard a footstep behind her, and when she jumped and turned, she saw that there were two policemen standing on either side of the door, like lackeys, but stationed against the wall so that one couldn't see them on entering the room. She felt Jeanne, beside her, recoil.

'My servant did not tell me that you had brought your men with you,' Madame de Cardonnoy said coolly. She was furious at Jeanne for her obvious dismay. She had thought the girl was steadier than that. But if she was already frightened, she couldn't be trusted to keep secret the letter that Madame de Cardonnoy had sent to Victoire. 'Jeanne, please leave us alone.'

Jeanne hesitated at the door, between the two policemen.

'Go on,' Marie Catherine said. 'This is private business.'

'I'm afraid I have more information to share with you,' La Reynie said, once the door had closed behind her. When he bowed, the movement was stiff. 'A man submitted a complaint yesterday claiming that on the night of your husband's death, two men came to the house of a painter named Alain Lavoie. The painter identified the men as your husband's valet and the man who guards your door. His neighbour, who filed the complaint, said that Lavoie was badly beaten, and that their reason for attacking him was that your husband claimed to have discovered an ... attachment between the two of you.'

Marie Catherine took a breath. He hadn't learned of Victoire then. Still, tears started in her eyes and she had to swallow, trying to step back from the edge of the chasm that was opening up before her.

'He accused the servants alone? They should have been with my husband. They left with him that afternoon.'

'Have you nothing to say about the painter?'

'Of course not – it's entirely absurd,' she said. Monsieur de la Reynie's foot was still tapping its eager beat on the carpet. She realised, to her despair, that he was not interested in her reply. 'My husband was jealous, it's true. He spent a great deal of his time at court, where I hear the ladies are very free, and we were often apart. But he himself engaged Monsieur Lavoie to paint my portrait, and I've met him only once, at a sitting where my children and my maid were present. I have no idea how he could have believed such a thing, and still less how you can suggest it to me as though it were credible.'

She spoke quickly, trying not to look as though she was considering her words, even as all her attention was focused on what she could say now.

'So you've had no conversation with this painter? No meetings outside of the portrait sittings, no correspondence? He's never visited here?'

Madame de Cardonnoy could feel her pulse fluttering away in her throat. To be caught out for the sake of a moment of vanity, a man whose hand she'd never so much as touched. La Reynie was staring at her with the face of a solemn statue. At least he was looking at her.

'I wrote him one letter, a children's story,' she said finally. 'I told my children a fairy story, to keep them still during the sitting, and afterwards he wrote me to express his curiosity about the end. There was nothing in it that I couldn't have said in front of my own children. My son could tell you the whole tale now, if you asked him.' She saw that something in La Reynie's posture softened when she mentioned her son, and for a moment she allowed herself to breathe.

Then the bolt on the door clicked open. It was Henri, the valet, the gold braid of his uniform looking dusty against the fabric's fresh black dye. He'd drawn himself up pompously straight.

'I wish to speak, Monsieur,' he said to Monsieur de la Reynie. Through the open door, Madame de Cardonnoy could see Jeanne, too, caught almost exactly in the pose of a woman listening at a doorframe. She shook her skirts out and took two faltering steps backwards into the hallway. Madame de Cardonnoy could feel the atmosphere of the room slipping out of her control, with the same sense of inevitability that came from knowing one was going to fall off a horse. Henri had chosen his entrance as if he were the star of an opera, and however mean and conniving he was, it would be impossible, now, to send him away.

'Speak then,' she said. 'Say whatever nonsense it is that's making you listen at doors.'

La Reynie gestured encouragingly at Henri, but Madame de Cardonnoy saw that his eyes slid back to her face, puzzled, watching her reaction.

'The painter did visit here,' said Henri, and he held one hand tucked into his coat-tails as he spoke, as if he were at a grand gathering and not a meeting with the police. Madame de Cardonnoy felt her jaw clench. 'He came to the gate, asking for Madame when Monsieur was out, and Caspar, the guard, admitted him, thinking that he had come to see about the painting. But after Monsieur arrived home, Arnaud said that he had looked up at a window and spied a gentleman he didn't know going into Madame's cabinet, and then kissing her in the hallway.'

'And what say you, Madame?' asked La Reynie.

'That did not happen,' said Marie Catherine. 'Monsieur Lavoie never visited here, except to begin his portrait.'

She was trying to keep her voice level, but still she could hear her words trembling with anger. Would the anger make her more credible, or less? She didn't know. She'd spent all night imagining the angles from which La Reynie might come at her, the strands he might pull to make her confess, the ways she might deflect him. She hadn't thought of this – the dull invention of a servant who hated her and had loved her husband, and knew only enough to blame her for his death.

'Monsieur Lavoie did visit the hôtel.'

Jeanne, who had been dithering about on the other side of the open door, stepped up now and stood in the doorway, her hands clasped demurely before her – very demurely, Madame de Cardonnoy thought, for someone who was about to invent lies on top of lies. She raised her chin and tried to hide the trembling of her hands under her long veil.

'Excuse me for speaking out of turn,' Jeanne said, looking at her feet. Her heart was hammering somewhere at the back of her mouth, as if it wanted to jump out from between her lips. Maybe the policemen would only think she was too modest to want to speak in front of them.

'Go on,' La Reynie said.

He frightened her. More than she'd thought he would. When Jeanne Gagnier, the farmer's daughter, whose family name she had discarded, had fallen pregnant, she'd been sent to the police and sobbed her way through a confession, to discourage her from doing away with the baby once it was born. Or perhaps just to humiliate her for her fault. But if they took Madame they would learn that Jeanne had carried the letter, and Henri would call her the murderer's accomplice. They would find out her friendship with La Chapelle.

'He did come here,' Jeanne said again, before her nerve could fail her. 'But although he asked for Madame at the door, he was here to see me. The cook can tell you that, or any of the boys who work in the kitchen. He drew my portrait. I have it here.'

She was rushing through her words to get the story out. Although Jeanne knew herself to be skilled at dissembling, had learned to walk and talk like a lady, she could feel the farmer's uncouth daughter rushing in and taking back the hands, the voice that had once been hers. When she tried to fish the painter's portrait out of the pocket tucked into her skirt, her fingers slipped on the coin that Mademoiselle de Conti had given her and nearly dropped it on the floor.

'Here,' she said, 'look, he drew it of me.'

The Lieutenant General of Police took the edge of the paper without touching her hand and studied it. At last he nodded.

'It is a fair likeness. The man in the corridor?'

Jeanne's eyes slid up and met Madame de Cardonnoy's, where she stood in the square of light cast by the window. Madame had made her face very blank, in the way she did when she was bored, or at dinner with her husband and waiting while he spoke, or trying to suppress her annoyance with one of the children. It was an expression that meant she did not want to show what she felt, and so it might mean anything. Jeanne saw it only briefly before she looked back at La Reynie, then down at her hands.

'I shouldn't – I didn't do anything indecent. Only I had tried on one of Madame's dresses, and used some of her powder in my hair. Arnaud saw that, perhaps, and mistook me, in the window.'

'I see.' La Reynie looked back at the drawing in his hands.

'Was Monsieur Lavoie badly hurt?' Jeanne asked, after a moment of silence. Her face was flushing. She had just remembered that she was supposed to be enamoured of the painter and should be upset at hearing that he'd been beaten. 'If I'd thought—' she stumbled on. 'I mean, I knew Monsieur le Baron was very jealous, but if I had ever thought he would suspect Monsieur Lavoie of indecency, I would have confessed at once!'

Her voice squeaked on the last words, and she blushed. So much the better, she supposed, if they thought her head was full of wind and feathers, but she stung all over with embarrassment. She didn't wish ill on the painter. She hoped he hadn't broken any bones. Henri was looking at her with hatred.

'I wish you had told me this earlier, Jeanne,' said Madame de Cardonnoy with beautiful condescension, crossing the room on a rustle of black silk. 'It would have spared some difficulty. Does that satisfy your doubt, Monsieur de la Reynie?'

'It seems to,' the lieutenant general said.

Jeanne curtseyed. The conversation was now once more between the masters, and she had become almost invisible.

'I'm going through my husband's papers,' Madame de Cardonnoy said. 'I hope to discuss them with you soon. Perhaps without the servants.'

'Until then, I'll take my leave. My men will speak more with the painter. It's strange that he should be beaten by the baron's servants on the same day as the baron's death.'

'Perhaps,' said Madame de Cardonnoy.

When the lieutenant general and his men were in the hallway, she turned to Henri.

'Get your things. You're dismissed. I never want to see you in this house again.'

The valet's face reddened. For a moment she thought he would come at her with his fists, but instead he turned and ran from the room. In the hall there was a howl and a crash, and when Madame de Cardonnoy rushed to the door, she saw that, in the entrance-way, Henri had heaved a mahogany table across the space, shattering the painted vase that stood on it. La Reynie and his men stood, stunned, in the door, and the valet paused there defiantly for a minute before the two policemen came back down the hall and tried to catch hold of his arms. The three of them were a single animal moving across the entranceway, drunk and struggling, and when Marie Catherine looked past them, she saw La Reynie's bear-like eyes gleaming, as if at the end of a hunt.

'Please, gentlemen, don't hurt him, let him go in peace,' said Madame de Cardonnoy. 'As you can see, my husband's death has touched him very deeply.'

Chapter Nine

———

A traiteur, packing up the last late order of sweetmeats to please the guests at a high house's card table, had seen a horse and rider on the rue du Four, galloping at speed, the rider's hat pulled down over his face, his black hair streaming behind him like night clouds. The traiteur viewed him as a kind of apparition, a gust of wind that had slipped by and nearly knocked his tray out of his hands as he went to load it onto his push-cart, tangible only by the foul-smelling mud the horse's hooves kicked up and the way the rain parted around him, like a shower of glass beads. His coat was the colourless shade of wet cloth, the traiteur admitted, but he was riding fast through the night street, like a man pursued.

That, so far, was the Baron de Cardonnoy's murderer – a phantom whose face was obscured by the night and the rain, his hair and his horse's flanks turned dark by water, the blood on his clothes soaking down to his skin as the winter rain did its best to wash him clean. He seemed, to Gabriel Nicolas de la Reynie, a symbol for everything that was wrong in Paris – faceless, cowardly, a creature moved by such unknowable appetites that it was impossible to count him as a human.

When he was a child, La Reynie had seen the monsters from his nurse's ghost stories in his dreams, until she'd stopped telling them entirely, making vague references to his cowardice when she tucked him into bed. He'd long since ceased to fear the shadows, putting his faith in God, whose approving eye lit the street lamps at night and saw each husband home with his wife and children, each sparrow bedded down in its nest, the king himself in his palace surrounded by a blaze of candles. God's strong hand made the earth turn in order, and men's faith allowed the full completion of their creator's intention.

But the city denied him. La Reynie's coach jostled on the cobblestone streets of Saint-Germain-des-Prés. When had that faith been shaken?

He had questioned the Duchesse de Bouillon at the Châtelet after her arrest, with a jeering crowd outside the gates. The husband she had attempted to poison stood at her right hand, her lover at her left. Together they made a mockery of the law, and still the crowd cheered the trio as they came and departed.

After the questioning La Reynie had ridden to Versailles and spent two hours closeted with the king, standing before him, the king's hand even, once, reaching out to touch his shoulder, his raised arm wafting the scent of the king's sweat to his nose. The king wore no perfume. The king had seemed to be enclosed in a halo – the lines on his face, the creases in his clothing, the yellow mark on a front tooth seemed, in the royal atmosphere, something more than human, merely the external trappings of a presence that obliterated with its divine force.

And yet, as the hours passed, La Reynie became almost ecstatic. The king, in his golden halo, talked of poison, of assassination attempts, of the unnatural relations between men that flourished in the back staircases and the stables and salons of his court. More than the illicit gambling or the vast sums expended on dress, the city of Paris, the court at Versailles like a vast, swollen head feeding on its own body, or the impoverished countryside, the king was afraid of this corruption of nature. And it was he, La Reynie, who would see it all and root it out.

La Reynie had entered the palace at Versailles with awe at the gold, the carvings, the vastness of the structure itself, which towered more like a cliff dropping off into the sea than like a building made by men – all this opulence and, beneath it, the secret dealings in poison, in witchcraft, the men and women who had summoned devils, who had given in to pleasures that no one should name. The ladies of the court went to La Chapelle and La Voisin for their abortions, and La Reynie thought that he could see the sin on them, in their powdered faces and in the lovely dresses that bared too much of their throats. The Minister of Finance's son had been accused of attacking a young man who refused his advances with a sword. The king's own brother was known to pick his favourites among the gentlemen of the court, and these men, too, came and went in the same rooms as the king. It was as if he had bitten into a red, ripe apple and found it teeming with worms.

The city was not whole.

In the breast pocket of his coat he carried a letter from the Minister of War, Louvois, talking of demonic rites and treason against the king. Where had this darkness come from? In his city, on the streets over which he had jurisdiction? When he ate, now, La Reynie thought of poison, and of spells that robbed their victims of strength. When he questioned his prisoners, their confessions were written on loose sheets, not in the record books of the Grand Châtelet. So that the pages could be removed from the record more easily, if they accused anyone too near the king.

But it was La Reynie they said looked like the devil.

It had rained again, early in the morning, and his coach, bound for the Châtelet, seemed to be travelling in its own envelope of foul smell that bubbled its way out of the winter mud. He wished for cold weather again, to freeze it over.

The Châtelet, when he reached it, loomed over the carriage, its towers like a series of squat thumbs pointing up towards the sky. The air in the street smelled like blood from the butchers' stalls at Les Halles, which lay just to the north of the fortress. The river, too, wafted its stink up to surround the towers, and a solitary swan – the muddy remnant of a flock that the king had imported to beautify the river – had wandered up from the quay and was picking at bits of bruised cabbage with its snake's neck.

Louis Bazin de Bezons was already waiting for him inside the Châtelet, his body slouched heavily against one of the Châtelet's cold-breathing stone walls. Bezons was the commissioner of the Chambre Ardente, the council that had been summoned to review accusations of poisoning. He moved ponderously, his weight falling into each footstep as if he carried justice like a heavy load around his neck. When he spoke, too, it was often after a long pause, which might make his interlocutor feel that he was not being listened to at all.

'Shall we be requesting a warrant for the arrest of Madame de Cardonnoy?' Bezons asked when La Reynie entered.

La Reynie shook his head. He was already starting up the hallway, towards the cells and the interrogation room. He hated to be still when there was work at hand. Behind him, Bezons sighed and hurried to match La Reynie's stride.

'But what about the painter? Wasn't the baronne putting horns on her husband?'

La Reynie shook his head at the enclosing stone walls, although he wasn't sure if Bezons could see him. The corridors of the Châtelet were dim, built for defence of the river, and they exhaled cold air that seemed to seep up from deep in the earth. Their rafters skimmed low over La Reynie's head, like the inside of a honeycomb. He found the closeness comforting. It gave him a sense of order.

'The husband was wrong,' he said. 'The painter was courting her maid. The baronne knew nothing of it.'

'And you believe her?' Bezons's shortness of breath gave his voice a laughing quality. 'A lady's maid will take on all kinds of sins for the sake of her mistress.'

'She had tokens from him. A portrait he'd made of her. It could have been intended for no one else.' There had been just a moment when he had believed the valet's testimony, and his rage that the baronne had lied to him so brazenly and with such sincerity had almost overwhelmed him. La Reynie felt guilty for that now. He had been so quick to credit a servant's word.

'Hmph.' Bezons took a few jogging steps to catch up him. 'It would be best if we could solve this quickly. It's the talk of every salon. In a week or two they're going to start claiming that *we* murdered the man.'

'It wasn't the painter,' he said again.

The failure of his own police work secretly pleased him. In the sordid dealings of poison and enchantment that had become his daily life, he had been relieved to find Madame de Cardonnoy as she seemed to be: proud but honest, clear-eyed, mourning a husband to whom she had performed her duties, even if they were not reciprocated with his love. In her drawing room, proud and incorruptible, she had reminded him very faintly of his own wife, who had died thirty years before and had faded in his memory so that now only her tender outline remained. Should there not still be some such women in Paris?

He passed his hand over his face as he and Bezons approached the cell that was their destination. Sometimes thought came to him in such rapid streams that he needed the physical movement of his hands to dispel it. He had outpaced Bezons. The commissioner of the Chambre Ardente caught him up, panting.

Two of the prison guards approached from the other end of the corridor. Between them shuffled a figure whose limbs were wasted like knotted rope. He walked bent over, like an old man perhaps, although to La Reynie's eyes the movement was more like that of a monkey, a swinging, cringing gait. But when he raised his head and looked at La Reynie, his green eyes, which had once bewitched noblemen and criminals alike, priests and witches, men and women, still had a haunted force behind them. He was losing his hair in handfuls.

From another chamber, a woman's voice cried out. Bezons wrinkled his nose.

'Do you know who that is?'

When the magician Lesage laughed, it was a raw laugh.

'I think you're torturing my lover, that old bitch. I hear she's sentenced to die.'

'So she is.' La Reynie did not ask how Lesage had heard this news. The prisoners were housed three to a cell, and guards talked, prisoners talked – sometimes they shouted to each other down hallways and turned the fortress into a reverberating hive of angry voices. The Minister of War had written to him, too, suggesting that someone was carrying messages in from outside the prison. And yet as easy as it was to explain Lesage's knowledge, the certainty with which he said the words made La Reynie shiver.

This wasted man had once claimed to have, at his beck and call, an army of spirits who did his bidding, unseen angels who whispered secrets in his ear, delivered letters with his clients' innermost wishes written in their own hands, guided him to where treasure was buried in the ground and communicated with Satan himself. He had done spells by passing a pigeon's bloody heart under the chalice during Mass, and by desecrating human bones.

He and his lover, the crone La Voisin, had been king and queen of the underworld.

Bezons unlocked the door of the interrogation room and the guards entered first, with Lesage. A clerk came with a lamp to supplement the light of the narrow window. La Reynie waited in the doorway until Bezons and the prisoner were seated. He did not like to turn his back on the sorcerer, although after his outburst about La Voisin, Lesage seemed to have grown contrite and now sat with his hands folded meekly in front of him.

The clerk sat down on his stool. He had the ledger of the case before him, but he wrote the date on a loose sheet of paper inserted into the book, rather than on the bound pages.

Bezons took a chair behind the bureau near the window. La Reynie preferred to stand, as it gave him freedom to walk back and forth across the room while he thought. He could feel the commissioner's irritated glance following him, wishing that he would be still. But La Reynie hated hearing the sounds of torture, however well deserved. He needed the freedom to turn his back to Lesage, so that the sorcerer wouldn't see the discomfort written on his face when La Voisin's screams came through the wall.

'Shall we resume with the case of the Maréchal de Luxembourg?'

'Wait a moment,' La Reynie said. 'Lesage. Did you ever meet the Baron de Cardonnoy?'

The magician looked up at him, his eyes clear and confident. He didn't seem to find the question surprising. La Reynie saw the baronne in his mind's eye. *I am afraid of what I might discover about my own husband if I look at him too closely*, she had said.

'I never met him,' Lesage said. But just as La Reynie was letting out the breath he'd been holding, Lesage leaned forward, with an expression almost of pleasure. 'But I … heard of him.'

'What did you hear?'

Lesage shook his head sadly. 'Isn't this baron a small fish, Monsieur? I thought you intended to catch a general.'

The Maréchal de Luxembourg had once been a celebrated general and now occupied a prison cell at Vincennes.

'What did you know of the baron?'

Lesage was tapping one finger against the knuckles of the other hand, a disconcerting, noiseless rhythm.

'Let me think. Cardonnoy, Cardonnoy, a little baron – you know he wouldn't have been one of my greatest customers, when I served such *illustrious* people, but I do know his name. Of course! Was he not a member of Madame de Fontet's salon? I did the paper trick for him, one night.'

This was a trick Lesage had explained in detail. A curious patron wrote a letter addressed to Lesage's attendant spirits, enumerating the wishes that he or she desired to be granted. The letter was then crumpled and coated in wax, for which Lesage substituted, through prestidigitation, a similar wax ball, this one filled with gunpowder, which he threw into a fire and made explode. Later he read the requests and returned them to their authors, saying that the spirits had received the message they had believed destroyed.

'I thought you said you hadn't met Monsieur de Cardonnoy?'

'Oh no, Monsieur,' said Lesage, with a smug smile. 'I've met everyone.'

'What did he write, in his letter to the spirits?' La Reynie asked. The lamp's wick hadn't been trimmed properly and it was guttering and smoking, casting unsettling shadows across the strip of daylight that lanced in through the narrow window. He took a deep breath. Lesage was lying. 'God damn you, I know you never met him,' La Reynie said. 'His wife was a member of Madame de Fontet's salon, not him.'

'I didn't say I knew him well,' Lesage replied, unwinding from his slouch until he was looking La Reynie straight in the eye. 'But I met him. Once. He's a little lord, like many others, I didn't pay him close attention. I need a moment to remember.'

'What was in the letter?' said Reynie.

A scream echoed down the hall. The torturers were applying their art once more. La Voisin wailed, without words. The torturers would be tightening the brodequins around her legs until her flesh was crushed, to see if her testimony withstood the trial of pain. Lesage seemed to perk up and lean towards the sound of her cries, like a dog scenting a rat.

'You didn't want to witness her last confession for yourself, Monsieur?' he asked.

La Reynie said nothing.

'She's the worst of them, you know,' Lesage continued, after a pause. 'A wicked, wicked woman. It's lucky that so many of the court trusted me, that they came to me instead of her, because she would have sold them true poison to solve their troubles, and I only sold them a few child's tricks with balled-up papers and talk of spirits, and so lulled them quite innocently into believing that all of their worst wishes would be granted. The king himself has me to thank for that – that I only did a little false magic, and never turned to poison.'

'What do you know of the Baron de Cardonnoy?' La Reynie asked. The more Lesage put him off and misdirected him, the more certain he became that the magician did know something, that what he had thought was a wild guess was really a stroke of luck. It was Lesage's habit to delay like this, to drag his feet and insist he had forgotten the details, when he was on the verge of some explosive revelation.

Lesage closed his eyes. 'The Baron de Cardonnoy was unhappy with his choice of wife. You know, the husband's often unhappy when his wife goes about in society without him. It gives her too many opportunities to sin. Cardonnoy, Cardonnoy – I remember! La Bosse or La Chapelle had an agent in that house, a little servant who sent news back from the salons so that they could fake their fortunes better. That's why I think I know so much about this baron, though we only met the once. He wouldn't pay me, you see. I promised him all his heart's desires would be fulfilled, if he would only give me two thousand livres, but the man thought that was too high a price for happiness.'

La Reynie tapped his foot. There was no point in reminding Lesage that he'd just claimed his spells were all fakery and could fulfil no one's desires. 'Who was the spy in Hôtel Cardonnoy?'

Lesage shook his head, as if his ears were ringing.

'How could I remember? La Bosse and La Voisin and La Chapelle shared their little spider's web. Their servants were in every noble house – why should I remember the names of such people? They all hated each other in secret.'

La Voisin's screams were increasing in volume, and La Reynie, who had been shamefully ill the last time he had watched the brodequins applied, began to fear that her cries would discomfit him more than they did Lesage.

'Who was the spy? Was it the man's valet? Did *he* visit fortune-tellers?' No wonder the baron's valet had wanted to cast suspicion on his mistress, if he had any connection with La Voisin.

'You'll have to ask La Bosse about that. Or maybe *her* in the next room,' Lesage said, jerking his head towards the sound of La Voisin's torture with an indecent grin.

'La Bosse is dead, so we can hardly question her,' La Reynie said. La Bosse had been one of the first women the police had arrested, after she had bragged to a dinner guest about her skill with poisons. She had been executed almost a year earlier.

'Then perhaps you must ask La Chapelle.'

'Why would she have a spy there?'

It was clear Lesage didn't remember the name of La Bosse's go-between or had exaggerated something that he knew only from hearsay. But still La Reynie hoped he might squeeze something useful out of him.

'This baron was ambitious,' Lesage said. 'He visited fortune-tellers, he wanted all the news from Versailles, who to support and who to importune for favours, and who might be about to fall out of favour. He was a rich man, wasn't he, not some little backwater baron after all, and every man like that hopes he'll make his name at court and die a marquis. I remember there was some Breton priest who mentioned his name more than once, a friend of La Voisin and La Grange. I can't remember his name, but I know the Breton used to send his mistress to La Chapelle for abortions, poor woman.'

Bezons, seated behind the bureau, brought his hand down on the table. 'God damn you, can't you do better than *some Breton*? Give us a name!'

Lesage nodded, and went on nodding long after the gesture had become meaningless. He rubbed his hands together to warm them. He seemed to be savouring La Reynie's frustration.

'Oh, I couldn't say,' said Lesage. 'You understand, I am not like these people. I'm just a charlatan. I did a public service, because all of these corrupt lords and ladies, they wanted poisons, black magic, the desecration of the host – there was truly nothing they thought too evil to do, once it was offered to them, and La Voisin and those others, they would do it all. La Bosse once had a client take a heart impaled with iron nails into a church, to bring about the death of the man he thought had cheated him. I was always the lesser sin, Monsieur. When people came to me for divine help, I cheated them, yes, but I didn't damn them. No, I saved many from the likes of La Bosse.'

'Tell us something useful, Lesage,' said La Reynie. 'This is all hearsay, and I have to solve a murder.'

'A murder?' Lesage leaned forward. 'This baron's the suspect? No, no, he's dead. Of course.' Lesage's ability to read the small changes in the air of a room made it seem as if he really was attended by spirits. 'I'd look at this baron's wife, who goes visiting without her husband. There are many unhappy wives in Paris. They'll bring the whole city down.'

'Is that all you have?' La Reynie snapped. 'He visited fortune-tellers, his wife was unhappy? You don't remember anything.'

'I do!' Lesage gasped, bent forward at the waist, wrung his hands. The ropy sinews of his neck stood out through the collar of his shirt. La Reynie noticed again how inhuman he looked, how monkeyish. 'I have – I have knowledge such as would make your hair stand on end, Messieurs. You must hear me out. You *must*.'

And in fact the desperate conviction with which Lesage spoke did make the hairs on the back of La Reynie's neck prickle into gooseflesh. He could see the look of unease that passed over Bezons's face and then resolved itself into a stony scowl.

'That Breton priest, he lived near Les Invalides. He was the same one who used to travel to sell love potions to Madame de Montespan and her ladies. Cardonnoy was another of his clients – I heard a little of their dealings.'

La Reynie had noticed that Lesage often brought up the king's mistress's name when he was becoming frightened, as if it were a kind of protective spell in itself. All of his testimony circled around that woman. He feared to give a clear account of her and yet he couldn't stop repeating her name. Still, there were proofs of Lesage's sincerity, although in his testimony he rambled and stammered and contradicted himself. The magician had been arrested once before, twelve years ago, at which trial he had been condemned for blasphemy and sentenced to life as an oarsman in the fleet of French galleys that plied the Mediterranean, skirmishing with the Spanish, the Turks, the Venetians and the Genovese. Men did not return from that sentence. They died, or they eked out their lives chained to the oars. And yet, five years later, Lesage had reappeared in Paris, still green-eyed, his beard a little wild, walking stooped and hungry, but plying his sleight-of-hand tricks once again.

Some power, human or inhuman, had freed him.

Lesage had not named his benefactor at court, if he had ever had one. But the records of his first arrest included the claim – unsubstantiated – that one of the clients who had purchased his frog oils and love spells had been Madame de Montespan, in the days before she became the king's mistress.

And if Lesage had sold her love potions, and she had used those potions on the king? La Reynie was not sure that he believed it. But he knew there were others who did. Lesage was cautious about what he claimed against her, but La Reynie had heard it said that she had paid for black Masses where infants were sacrificed in order to convince the devil to grant her wishes, and that there was a network of fallen priests in Paris willing to perform such requests.

With or without the aid of magic, Madame de Montespan certainly had the influence required to save her former magician from the galleys. But if she had done so, then it must be supposed that Lesage's influence reached as far as Louis himself, and that the king was caught in a magic web that tied him to a woman who had pledged herself to the devil. No one must ever hear that the king's mistress had trafficked in black magic. Lesage himself, for all the force and conviction with which he testified against his former colleagues, the other sorcerers and poisoners and witches, was tongue-tied on the subject. But when pressed, he admitted that he knew things he was afraid to say. He knew terrible things.

'You must listen to me, I've hardly told you anything yet,' Lesage whispered.

The magician's mind was like a sucking wave, pulling him under and into a world of salt water and whispers. Lesage was hungry. Ever since he had returned to Paris he'd found he could barely tolerate hunger, although it had been as constant as the ocean on board the galleys and in the off-season when the convicts and enslaved Turks performed forced labour in the seaside towns. Every meal set in front of him he ate as if someone might steal it, or the angry comite who oversaw the prisoners might knock it out of his hand as punishment for laziness. In the salons where he performed his magic he often inadvertently found himself staring past the fascinated faces of his audience and towards the invisible aura of whatever tray of delicacies the servants were carrying – the fruit pies, the islands of meringue floating in custard. The high ladies fainted for fresh peas and truffles boiled in champagne, but Lesage would have eaten anything sweet, although his teeth were weak. In the prison he ate his ration of beans and then curled around the hole in his stomach, the empty sack from which stories emerged.

'I think it must have been about two years ago that I met this baron,' he said. 'He was a courtier at Versailles? Yes, it would have been about the time that La Voisin and La Chapelle went to Saint-Germain to perform auguries for – what was her name? De Montespan's lady's maid. Around the time that the king began to be interested in Mademoiselle de Fontanges. I heard that Madame de Montespan threw tantrums at the thought that she might be replaced by another woman, and one so much younger. I doubt she shed a tear when Mademoiselle de Fontanges died, and so slowly, so that she'd lost all her beauty by the end.'

Flap, flap, flap, went the empty sack where his hunger was. He watched La Reynie's reaction as he mentioned the king's mistress. The man wanted de Montespan jailed, but was too cowardly to bring his accusations to the king, and usually the mention of her name distracted him so much that he lost his train of thought. Now La Reynie said, merely, 'And the Baron de Cardonnoy?'

So he must want this murderer badly. The lieutenant general's fear gave him away. Some men frequented fortune-tellers because they wanted to hear that they were strong and all would be well. Some came because they wanted to hear that what they feared was true.

'Even I couldn't say everything that goes on at court,' Lesage said. 'But this Breton priest – I'm sorry, I can't give you the details, I never wanted to know the man. I've been burned by such people before. As for the spy in Monsieur de Cardonnoy's house, you'll want someone who could read and write. Like the servant of the maréchal who signed his master's name to the devil's paperwork. La Voisin would know who it was, I'm sure. It's a pity her execution is so near. If you'd let me confront her again, I'd have it out of her in a moment, that liar. It's been a moment since she's screamed now, hasn't it? They must be giving her a rest, with her confessor.'

Lesage could have licked his lips, to see the way La Reynie flinched. The hypocrite was afraid of his own torturers.

He would have said anything. He had told so many lies, and now La Reynie had given him a new name, Cardonnoy, and just enough thread to spin out a web of story. The man didn't share the same circles as his wife, and so his marriage was unhappy. He'd heard his name on the lips of fortune-tellers, and so he was a schemer at Versailles. There had been a spy in his house – that much he was sure of. The rest of the story would come. La Reynie believed him best when he had to drag every word out of him, and he needed La Reynie's belief.

At night in his cell Lesage sometimes felt the earth tilt underneath him, as if he were still on the slave galley. Then he would feel the stagnant summer air of a becalmed ocean or the unending drip and seep of rain beneath the tent pitched over the oars, where the oarsmen slept in their chains, packed in like fish in a net, his scrawny, flea-bitten back touching his neighbour's bony knees, cold biting through his clothes. The Huguenots murmured prayers of patience to their god and the Turks prayed in their own language, almost silently, spinning out their laments in a voice low enough that the drowsy guards wouldn't hear and give them a kick. Others drank deep of the comite's sour, watered wine and then fouled themselves in their sleep. He had been one of them, often enough, trading his handful of bread for wine and then dragging himself to the railing in the night to vomit. So quickly they had reduced him to a little candle flame of intellect burning at the back of his neck, its only goal to keep the scraps of his flesh together, to go on breathing, to escape from pain.

Once upon a time he had been a man who had ambitions other than to continue living.

By daylight, the flies landed on his eyelids and drank his sweat as he pulled with both hands on the oar, the ache of the work travelling all the way up his spine.

His mind was a wave. It kept taking him back to the boat. From the benches, the oars were the haphazard pikes of an advancing army, rising and then falling to cut the water. One felt the resistance of the waves against the oar's blade, the blistering twist against calloused hands when the oar pulled free, raining down salt droplets. They drank the sweat that rolled down their lips.

The Turks called to each other in their own language, back and forth across the aisle of the coursier. All of the officers believed that the Turks were the strongest oarsmen, better than the Huguenots and the criminals, taller and, besides, more resigned to having been kidnapped and brought to a bad life in a country far from their own. They spoke pidgin French and abstained from the comite's wine. At night on the water, each oarsman bedded down chest-to-knees, the deck too cramped to lie flat. The officers slept on trestles laid over the forest of chained bodies. How many days Lesage had woken up that way, parched, starving, the knobs of his spine digging a groove against the bench, his head fallen slack against the bearded head of a Turk, a Huguenot, some desperate man who, for his religion, had been stripped of all but the barest threads of his life.

He, Lesage, had stripped religion from itself. He had profaned the host. He had performed miracles and petty, childish tricks. He had been a magician who commanded an army of spirits, like Solomon, and now he was hungry and his back was burned from the sun. He held a crust of bread under his shirt. He ate it, mouthful by mouthful, throughout the day, rolling each bite around his tongue until it softened with spit and became porridge. He was trying to make it last and, besides, his teeth hurt when he chewed. He was trying to perform a miracle and turn one loaf into a thousand loaves. The chains that locked him to his oar had worn blisters into his skin and proved the worthlessness of all of his miracles.

When they set him free, he had returned to Paris. He'd remembered La Voisin a thousand times on the water, and then, when he'd grown too hungry, forgotten her entirely. He'd left the boat and bundled up his oarsman's cloak and gone back to Paris, and stood at her doorstep, and eaten turnip soup and mutton at her table, and felt a new kind of rage rising in his throat along with the old lust and the old resentment. So the witch's husband beat her. Should he give a fuck? She still drank her fill of wine, slept in a warm bed, earned enough coins with her spells and poisons to buy bread. She was nothing to him. Inside his stomach there was an ocean with a beetle-oared ship crawling across it, slowly, staffed by groans, never advancing.

I'm hungry, the ocean said. *The rest of you can get fucked.*

'Was there anyone in Paris who might have held something against the Baron de Cardonnoy?' Lieutenant General La Reynie asked.

And the ocean said, *Throw them all in. La-Voison-La-Filastre-La-Chapelle-Soissons-Luxembourg-Montespan-Jesus-The-Pope-The-King. I will tell you a story that never ends, I will feed you a mountain of bodies, but I will not go back to the oar.*

And the magician Lesage said, 'Oh yes, he had enemies. That renegade priest, I heard he passed a consecrated wafer with the baron's name written on it under the communion chalice during Masses for a month, to bring about the downfall of a rival. Now I can barely remember if the matter was love or business, but – yes, both, perhaps, because didn't he court the same woman for his mistress as the Marquis de Feuquières? I heard he visited La Chapelle, and she gave him a jar with the blood of pigeon in it, and told him to piss in it and then hide it in the lady's carriage, to ensure that she'd be able to think of nothing but him. Perhaps his wife heard that story, too.'

'Which priest was it?'

'Mariette. Or – what was his name, Roberges? The one who always needed La Chapelle's services.'

Lesage laughed. He could put names together all day. He knew the citizens of the underworld, who they'd kissed and who they'd stolen from. He would catch La Reynie in a net of a thousand names and it would not be enough to buy him his freedom, but it would purchase his life. Because they would not put him to death or to the oar until he had told them everything he knew, and the story of what he knew was never-ending.

'Who was the spy that La Voisin and the fortune-tellers had in Hôtel Cardonnoy?'

'I never met him, Monsieur, I don't know his name. But it would have been some little thug, dressed up like a good servant. The valet, or the coachman, or the wife's maid, someone close enough to the baron to know all of his affairs.'

Once he had prestidigitated secret messages, trafficked in

communion wafers, sold love potions, provided maps to hidden treasures, been paid for each marriage he brought about. Once he had spoken to a marquis with such magic in his voice that the beguiled man had buried a purse of gold by the river, believing it would sprout like an onion and produce more little coins. And Lesage had found the place and harvested his own payment. It was easy, now, to see La Reynie working his way through his questions, trying not to lead Lesage too much by the nose, lest he invent more lies. He lied anyway. He told him things he only half remembered, things he'd forgotten, things that he knew quite well had never been true. Just tell me how the baron died, Monsieur de la Reynie, Lesage thought. I'll help you even more if I know. And aren't you being a little solicitous of this dead man's wife?

The secretary took careful notes of all he said. The magic in his voice still worked, he knew. He saw Bezons shiver, and the lieutenant general tapped his desk with a close-pared fingernail, frowned, looked at the shadows on the ceiling, at the locked door, at Lesage's hands as they twisted in front of him, but never at Lesage's green eyes.

God save us, La Reynie thought, when he had finally exhausted his line of questioning. He barely knew more about the Baron de Cardonnoy than when he started, he had so much chaff to sift away from the truth.

Facing the magician Lesage in close quarters filled him with black exhaustion, as if he had spent the hours of questioning wrestling a shadow summoned from the abyss of the magician's conscience. The man was half mad. He confused dates and names, stumbled, corrected himself, until his explanations criss-crossed like the ugly reverse of a tapestry. But for all the faults in his testimony, the stories he told rang true. There had been poison, black magic, renegade priests, and all playing right at the feet of the king, ignored.

On La Reynie's desk were papers that needed attending to. It was the whole mundane business of Paris, whose care he had been charged with: the cleaning of her streets, the upkeep of her buildings, the price of her bread, her street lights, her granaries, her tradesmen, her rich, her poor, her criminals. He began the mental work of composing himself, tapping his pen against the pigeonhole drawers of his desk as he let the day's events fall into a shape that felt right. He had not got as much from Lesage as he had hoped. Perhaps La Voisin, having been questioned, at last, under torture, would name some new accomplice whose power at court had so far been a shield. When the secretary brought him the transcript of her confession he opened it immediately, hoping for a name, an accomplice, a thread on which he could pull to unravel the ghastly knot.

But the pages told him nothing new. It was the same story, the same names that he had already heard a thousand times.

He spread the papers out in front of him, trying to make notes, looking for some revealing turn of phrase he'd missed the first time he'd read them. Didn't the torturers know their work? Hadn't he heard her wailing?

But what could her screams mean, when she was already so accomplished in lies? His men had wasted their last chance to question her. Tomorrow she would be burned alive.

In her cell, Catherine La Voisin was singing. Her legs ached, but the wine the guards had brought with her last supper coursed through her body, turning the pain into a kind of pulsing drum. Her head spun. Her teeth were numb. Her voice was as raw as ever, and hoarse from crying during the torturers' last interrogation, but she had drunk her final bottle and she wanted to sing:

> *Madame wants a fu—*
> *A fuck – a forget-me-not flower*
> *To hang above her bed*
> *And dream of her lover's bower.*

If she had been able to stand, she would have gone to the door and bellowed the words into the hallway. As it was, between the verses she collapsed into giggles, snorting back her own tears, remembering that tomorrow she would die. The song quavered – she sucked in a hissing breath and went on:

> *Monsieur wants a cunt –*
> *A cunt – a country estate*

To profit from as he desires
And fill it with silver plate.

Down the hallway she heard another prisoner's voice join in, booming through the chorus, as if they were in a drinking hall in Paris, or sitting around her own little table in her home, sharing a bottle, two bottles, three. *Dance, dance the branle!*

The voice of her invisible companion made her laugh. Oh my friend, she thought, you have done yourself in, like me. Once they might have sung like this in her home, arms slung over each other's shoulders, while her daughter uncorked bottles of sour wine and her husband eyed her across the table. She would have drunk until she was gay enough to kick up her heels in the kitchen, to kiss her lover in front of the whole company, to pull up her skirt and show the street her bare arse.

It was true that she was afraid of the fire. Even after the torturers' visit, she could not imagine the pain. But if she was sure of her fate on earth, she was not yet sure of the afterlife. She had poisoned some men, she had played some clever tricks with the scriptures, but what about them – the men and women who came to her, and then sat in confession on Sundays? Would they burn, too? The whole world?

She would laugh in the face of any who pretended to be righteous.

Madame has such a great cunt –
Such a great, such great control
Over her husband's purse
She buys silk in bolts and rolls.

They sang together, still. La Voisin's voice cracked. The guards, now, were coming down the row of cells and banging doors as they went. *Dance, dance the branle!* Her legs were ruined. She would never dance again. She heard her unseen friend fall silent and thanked him, just as silently, for keeping her company, for however short a time. She went on with the chorus, drunkenly, until the guards were outside her cell, banging on the door, calling, 'Shut up, you old bag! Shouldn't your thoughts be on repentance?'

Chapter Ten

——

'So she broke the hand off her doll?'

'Sometimes I don't know what to do with her.'

'She believes in the story.'

'There was a tale my nurse used to tell me when I was small. In it, the heroine is courted by her brother. When he asks for her hand, she orders her servant to cut both of them off and send them to him in a silver casket. It frightened me so much, I used to be afraid to have my hands outside the quilt when I was sleeping. I was very young. It made all talk of asking for someone's hand seem ghastly.'

'Are you saying it *isn't* ghastly?'

Victoire was sitting on a stool watching as Madame de Cardonnoy's seamstress, dressed in plain grisette, put pins into the bodice of a new mourning gown. The dress was made of heavy brocade, dull black – a lustrous fabric would have been inappropriately gay – with white at the throat and the sleeves. It was both sombre enough for her state as a recent widow and rich enough to wear to Versailles. Victoire had convinced her that she must go to the palace. Her husband had spent many of his days there, was recognised at court, had been the recipient of a handful of offices. It would be right for her to pay her respects to the king upon the baron's death and, while she was there, she might speak with some of the courtiers he had been close to.

Victoire's offhand remark about the ghastliness of marriage made Marie Catherine's elbow twitch a little, so that the grisette's pin stuck her. She had no idea what the seamstress might think about Victoire's opinions on marriage, directed as they were to a recent widow. She made her face severe, and Victoire tilted her head back against the edge of her chair and fell silent.

Marie Catherine had, for the most part, avoided the court since her marriage and her early pregnancies. She could remember the enchantment of her first visits to Versailles: the old grounds of the last king's hunting lodge, the immensity of the building that seemed to have been dredged up out of the forest and the farmland, as if one had discovered an ancient and terrible temple in the wilderness. The last time she had attended the court had been to celebrate the wedding of the king's natural daughter and the Prince de Conti, Victoire's brother. It had been January, but the paths of the gardens were lined with orange trees bearing fruit, and between the banquet dishes every table was heaped with fresh flowers – tulips, hyacinths, jasmine, a thousand blooms out of season. They might have been taken for silk, if their heady fragrance hadn't risen into the air and combined with the scent of butter pastry, nutmeg, roast partridge and sweetbreads. Workmen had built two curved golden staircases up to the enormous windows of the ballroom, to make sure that the guests could enter easily, and the women climbing in and out of the windows were blue-lipped in their glimmering silk, the skin of their décolletage milk-white and puckering up into gooseflesh from the biting cold. Marie Catherine had worn a silk dress the colour of an unripe orange, embroidered from sleeve to skirt with little golden knights and ladies, each swain kneeling to take his beloved's hand.

But the dress was too airy and light for the weather. She had felt as if she'd been cast into the hell of Tantalus – here were the orange trees, the sweet flowers of spring, the head of lamb roasted in green sauce and garnished with its own feet, the blancmange in the shape of a dancing woman, her dress striped pink and white, the nightingales stewed with cardoons. But nowhere, as she climbed the enchanted stairway up to the ballroom windows on her husband the baron's arm, was there any warmth. They might all have been dancing corpses. The groom's family considered a marriage with one of the king's bastards to be a misalliance and were glum, except for Victoire, who thought marriage was a farce, and hid with the bride among the flowers when she bolted in terror from her husband's bed later that night.

Madame de Conti, Victoire's mother, herself rebellious in her youth, was in no hurry to marry off her youngest daughter and provide her with a fitting dowry. Everyone else could accept Victoire's eccentricities as the rightful inheritance of her house. So Victoire dressed scandalously, kidnapped her brother's bride and pretended to be an Amazon. Her father, before his death, had been known to practise alchemy and beat himself with a spoon.

Perhaps this was why Victoire never quite understood the things Marie Catherine hated about the court. Yes, the courtiers were snobs, they were two-faced, they ruined themselves at cards to win the momentary favour of their patrons, they lived in a warren of windowless rooms like an underground maze, but all this excited her. Victoire observed, flirted and saw no risk of her own ruin. Marie Catherine was a peasant wandering in a giant's castle.

'Will you raise your arms so that I can pin your waist, Madame?' said the grisette in the shop, and Marie Catherine complied. She'd taken off her widow's veil for the fitting. In the course of a few days she'd grown so used to wearing it that her naked head felt weightless and cold.

'How soon will it be ready?' asked Victoire.

'In two days, I think,' said the seamstress. 'It only needs some final adjustments. I'll need to fix the trim on the bodice, here, where I'm taking it in.'

'Good. We should make the trip to court soon.'

Jeanne came in, carrying a pair of cups from the itinerant coffee-seller who had set up his stand on the corner. The bittersweet smell of the coffee followed her. She gave Victoire her cup with a curtsey. Marie Catherine's glass she placed on a step-stool, for the moment when she could drop her arms again. Then Jeanne retreated and stood by the door, reaching out occasionally, absent-mindedly, to touch the trailing ends of the bolts of cloth heaped on the shelves to her left.

She had been very meek in the days since her magic trick with Monsieur Lavoie's drawing. Madame de Cardonnoy could not tell what Jeanne was thinking, although her fingers, as she helped the seamstress unlace the black court dress without disturbing the lie of the pins, were as quick and gentle as ever. Marie Catherine raised her arms, let Jeanne lift her hair off her neck and the dress over her head, watched Victoire watching her from her seat in the corner, as Marie Catherine stood in her shift and let the two women dress her, like a doll.

When they were back in the carriage, Marie Catherine once more enveloped in her old black dress and veil, Jeanne cleared her throat delicately.

'Madame, if you don't mind ...'

'What's the matter?'

'I have some bad news from my sister, outside Paris. Her little son is very sick. My uncle sent me a message yesterday, and I wondered if I could take the afternoon off and go and see him.'

'Of course, Jeanne.' Madame de Cardonnoy felt a ripple of relief at the request. It would be an easy way to have the girl out of the house, and would buy her some privacy with Victoire. She was too distracted to feel much genuine sympathy for the sick boy. Most children fell sick at some time. Many lived. 'You can leave as soon as you like.'

Jeanne, however, did not look up from her lap, where her hands were twisted around a handkerchief.

'Thank you, Madame. Only ... my family are country people. They don't have the money to treat the boy, or to feed him well. Since I am in service in a great house they've asked me for help, and if I could have my wages in advance, I could send something back with my uncle, to pay for the doctor.'

Marie Catherine paused and her eyes darted to Victoire, who sat next to her on the carriage bench. Jeanne's wages were paid yearly, like all the Cardonnoy servants', and the baron was dilatory enough about payment that the servants were sometimes owed several years of back wages and collected them only when they left Hôtel Cardonnoy permanently. Marie Catherine paid Jeanne's wages herself, kept her well dressed in clothes fit for a lady's maid and occasionally gave her a gift of ribbon or lace trim or a little money, for diligent service, but Jeanne rarely asked for anything above this sort of token, and the timing was deeply suspicious. Jeanne had been steady in her loyalty so far – she had carried the letter to Victoire, she had produced Lavoie's drawing for Monsieur de la Reynie. But the early payment of her wages would give her the freedom to run, and she might run to the police.

Jeanne had been loyal. She could have asked for much more money, knowing what she did. Marie Catherine needed her loyalty too much to deny her. When she reached for her purse, Victoire put a hand on her wrist.

Marie Catherine watched Jeanne's face change at Victoire's gesture. It was a quiet transformation – a slight hardening of the line of her mouth, a downward tilt of her head. But her disappointment was plain. Madame de Cardonnoy had never been stingy with her before.

She shook Victoire's hand off and took an écu from her pocket. 'Of course, Jeanne. Tell your family I will ask our priest to pray for the boy's health.' Although she didn't quite believe in the sick child, after all.

'Thank you, Madame.'

But Jeanne was quiet and pensive for the rest of the ride back to Saint-Germain-des-Prés, and Marie Catherine could see the way she held her hands balled up in her skirt.

'Why did you do that?' she asked Victoire, once they were safely in her cabinet in Hôtel Cardonnoy and Jeanne had been sent with the Swiss guard to find a rented fiacre that would take her to her uncle's lodging. 'Do you want her to think she's being punished for her loyalty?'

'I gave her a silver coin when she came with your letter.' Victoire crossed her arms over her chest. 'Has she spent it already? How could she have? Whatever she wants that money for, it's not a sick nephew.'

'She's been trustworthy so far. Henri might have ruined me, without her help.'

'We'll have to hope you continue to be lucky then. I wish I'd brought my girl to send after her and find out where on earth she's going.'

Victoire turned away from her then, sorting papers with brisk, choppy movements. Marie Catherine tried to catch her eye and failed. All day the air between them had been tense. Victoire had kissed her cheek when they first were alone in the study, but it was a quick kiss, more of custom than of passion, and she had pulled away afterwards as if disappointed. Marie Catherine was afraid that the murder had brought out something hard in Victoire.

She seemed jealous of Marie Catherine's attention, in a way that she had never been. When the baronne turned away from her – towards the baron's papers, towards Jeanne – when she rebuffed her quips at the seamstress's shop, Victoire's posture tightened with disappointment. Or was it guilt? If so, it came to her differently than to Marie Catherine.

'She's more likely to betray us if you mistreat her,' Marie Catherine said, touching Victoire's sleeve.

'You don't know that,' Victoire snapped. 'Your husband used to beat his valet, and the man's still defending him after his death.'

Marie Catherine took her hand away. 'I suppose my husband must not have treated me poorly enough then.' She had tried to say the words lightly. It wasn't a success.

'All right,' said Victoire. She smoothed her hands over her face. 'You're right. I shouldn't have done that. I'm ashamed.'

Marie Catherine stepped close behind her and, bending down, put her forehead in the curve of Victoire's shoulder. She smelled like powder and irises, and like the perfume she wore in the city. It was comforting to stand there, with her chest pressed against Victoire's back, but Victoire remained tense in her arms.

'What is it?'

'Nothing.' Like a child without the words to describe what's gone wrong. 'We should get to work.'

She peeled Marie Catherine's hands off her waist and sat down at the desk, taking deep, unsteady breaths. Marie Catherine watched her, but Victoire didn't glance up.

The écu might have bought a piece of fringe off the sleeve of the elaborate brocaded mourning dress that her seamstress was now sewing. It was nothing. But in the servant girl's hands it acquired the power to unsettle her. She kept seeing the passage of the silver into Jeanne's hands, her fingers closing over it.

Jeanne stopped the fiacre near Les Halles, half a mile away from the address Laure had given her. She had a superstitious fear that the driver might return to Hôtel Cardonnoy and give Madame her destination, so she ducked down a little alley and hid in a doorway to try and catch her bearings. The street was overhung by a sign for a cobbler's shop and a windowbox, out of which some wife was selling winter potatoes and shrunken cabbages from her garden. When Jeanne pulled her skirts up, she saw that in her haste she'd put one of her pretty embroidered shoes into mud or horse shit. She tried to scrape her sole clean on the doorstep.

The vegetable woman hissed at her. 'Get on your way! We're decent people, we don't want you here!'

'I'm sure your husband likes to see your face every night, cow!' Jeanne called back, trembling. But the insult gave her the courage she needed to brush down her skirts and step back out into the street instead of lingering.

Her own outburst embarrassed her a little. Would it have been better to have held up her head and pretended she couldn't hear the insult, as a lady might have? She could certainly have thought of a wittier reply. It wasn't until she had gone three blocks and passed a couple standing on a corner – she powder-pale and dressed in ragged silk, he in servants' braid with his arm around her waist – that she realised the vegetable-seller must have seen Jeanne's own cast-off lady's dress, with its lavender ruffles and faint, indelible stains of wear along the hem, and assumed she was one of the prostitutes who frequented the gardens at the nearby Tuileries, trawling for noblemen or at least their servants. The man looked up from his temporary lover and whistled at her. Jeanne hurried past, watching, from the corner of her eye, as the man's partner put her hand on his cheek to turn his eyes back towards her.

Jeanne pulled her winter mantle tighter over her chest. She was used to running errands for Madame, but it made her uneasy to be away from the streets she knew well. Part of it was the way that men like that whistled or followed her, even when they knew she was just someone's servant girl, but there was something else in it, too. Sometimes she felt as if she was uneasily sharing her eyes with the country girl she'd once been. She could go into a fashionable coffee house with its crystal chandeliers and the waiters would see her dress and serve her as if she were a lady – as if anyone could become anything in Paris. But it was an illusion. Her dress was only half as fine as a lady's. The waiters condescended to the house in which she served, not to her, and the men who whistled at her served as a reminder that, even if she could transform herself into a princess in the eyes of the crowd, she could also be transformed into other things, many of which she wouldn't like. Even those like La Chapelle, who understood the magic by which people remade themselves better than anyone else Jeanne knew – even she could be cast down.

Jeanne didn't know which building was Madame Camille's, and so she stopped on the street that Laure had indicated and looked for someone to ask. It was the kind of street where one could rent a furnished room, dirty but cheap enough – although Jeanne had heard that the landlords charged single women double. The gutters were clogged with household filth. Jeanne didn't like to approach any of the men waiting on the street or going in and out of houses, and the women were just as frightening. As she watched, a fraying bureaucratic creature with stains on his white cuffs tumbled out of a doorway, buttoning his coat, and after him came a woman dressed only in her shift and stays, her hair tumbling down her back in a cloud of powder, screaming insults into the cold air.

'And take your blistered cock to someone who's more of a fool! Foutu! I wasn't born yesterday!' She wrapped her arms around herself, then shivered. She was barefoot. She paused for only a moment on the doorstep before slamming the door.

No one else on the street seemed to find this exchange particularly noteworthy. An old woman hissed at the man as he hurried away.

After La Chapelle had found her a place at Hôtel Cardonnoy, Jeanne had often looked out of the window of Madame's coach and begun the sentence, *If La Chapelle hadn't helped me, I would have been condemned* ... But the thought usually remained unfinished.

Finally she screwed up her courage and walked over to an older woman who held the hand of a small child dressed in a sexless long wool shirt. 'Can you tell me which of these buildings is the one run by Madame Camille?'

'Ah, you're new here.' She pointed at a door. 'The rents are high, and the room is bad. I have a friend a few streets away who might give you a better offer.'

'No, I'm – visiting a friend.' Jeanne stumbled over the sentence. She'd almost said, *I'm not one of those women, I'm not staying*, but then she'd thought that this woman might well be one of *those women*, changed out of her working clothes.

'As you like.' The woman nodded, curtly, and took her child away.

Jeanne approached the door of the house where Laure was staying, found it unlocked and went upstairs.

'I should visit the painter.'

'You can't! That's incredibly foolish. Think how it will look.'

'A widow can't want to know how her husband spent his last night?'

'I thought you had enough trouble making La Reynie believe he wasn't your lover the first time. That man's a wolf – he'll take the faintest trace of impropriety for blood.'

Marie Catherine sighed. 'I wish Henri hadn't had that outburst. He was my husband's confidant. He knew more about his doings than I ever did.'

She and Victoire were sitting together in her husband's office, going through his papers. She'd filed documents according to their type – personal letters, documents asking for favours or loans or court appointments, letters asking for the repayment of debts. Separate from the rest of the papers were the ledger books containing her husband's finances. These detailed the income from the estates at Cardonnoy, from his royal offices, from the sale or rental of lands and goods. When the baron's father had died, the estate had been in decay, but between Marie Catherine's money and his own keen financial instincts he had reversed the slow seepage of the Cardonnoy fortune.

The ledgers, however, were a disaster. Marie Catherine had been taught to manage a household's income, both in the convent and by her mother' s example. But high ladies didn't do such work, whatever the nuns taught. Marie Catherine's father had bitterly mocked her mother whenever she revealed her knowledge of money – the proof that she was only a shopkeeper's daughter. After her own marriage, Marie Catherine had been shut out of the management of the estate. Her husband kept the details of his finances to himself.

He had not kept clear accounts. Some of the entries were written in the baron's hand, and others in the hand of the intendant who managed the baron's estates at Cardonnoy. Sometimes he had slipped letters promising or requesting money into the books, perhaps in lieu of entering expenditures, or perhaps simply as a reminder to himself to decide what to do about them.

'Can you read this? I can't make sense of the handwriting.' Marie Catherine passed a letter to Victoire. 'As for Monsieur Lavoie, surely going to see him will give us a better sense of whether the Lieutenant General of Police considers him a serious suspect. And if he doesn't, I owe him some kind of recompense for my husband's behaviour.'

Victoire dropped the letter on her lap. 'Do you *like* this painter?'

Marie Catherine shrugged. 'He was charming. And I'm sorry that any harm came to him because of his interest in my fairy tale.'

Victoire, surely, heard the undertone of guilt in her voice. It was Victoire's custom to be frank when she found another lady beautiful, but Marie Catherine was private about her own inclinations, and she felt sick knowing that her encouragement of the painter, however gentle, had made him fall foul of her husband.

'You haven't told *me* that tale yet.'

'I didn't tell him the ending, either,' she said. 'I upset the children with it instead. I lost my head when I thought my husband might send me away, and I frightened them.'

'A little adversity makes the ending happier,' Victoire said with a smile, as if she had forgotten their earlier disagreement. Marie Catherine felt herself flushing.

'Will you take a look at that letter?'

'Don't be angry with me, Marie.' She bent her head as if she were reading the paper Marie Catherine had handed her, but her eyes remained fixed on the salutation. 'The children will be all right. It's just a story.'

'I'm not angry.' If she were honest with herself, Marie Catherine knew that she was trying to pick a fight. But Victoire's light-heartedness frightened her. She didn't know what lay underneath it.

It was the worst possible time to argue. How many days like this could they have, alone in the privacy of the baron's study? And yet she didn't seem to be in control of herself, although she could see that Victoire was trying to soothe her, with her jokes and the sad way she bent her head over her sheaf of papers.

'"To Monseigneur the Baron de Cardonnoy,"' Victoire read, softly, '"best wishes, et cetera" – this is chicken scratch, it's illegible – "enclosed is the talisman you requested, which, being wrapped in a piece of cloth worn by Monsieur so-and-so, and buried in consecrated ground, will have a salutary influence on the proceedings that concern you."' Victoire looked up from the paper. 'This is a magic charm! Did Monsieur de Cardonnoy see fortune-tellers?'

Marie Catherine shook her head. 'Not since the time when everyone at court was obsessed with that man who could tell a man's fortune by looking at his writing.'

'The queen herself patronised him, so that's hardly damning.' Victoire fanned herself with the letter.

'This letter still might be, though,' said Marie Catherine. 'Who is the man whose clothes he was supposed to get?'

'The name's left out.'

'And the name of the letter writer?'

Victoire paused. 'He's a priest. Père Roblin.'

Marie Catherine reached for the letter. Her eyes met Victoire's for a moment, and then they both looked away at the same time. A priest selling spells was explosive – it would mean black magic, devil worship, the profanation of his holy calling. It would mean that her husband had had dealings with men who might very easily commit murder.

That morning she had had a letter from Monsieur de la Reynie. A man on the rue du Four had seen a swift rider, who he thought wore bloodstains on his coat, about the time of her husband's murder. The horseman had been well dressed, he said, the horse a colour he couldn't identify in the rain. Monsieur de la Reynie asked her to look, particularly, for men of some means with whom her husband might have quarrelled.

Marie Catherine's hands trembled.

'It's not dated. But if he put the priest's letter in the account book around the time it was received, and not later, it was sent about two years ago, before any of these rumours about poison became public. It's too old.'

It might be nothing, after all.

'It might not be,' said Victoire. 'What would he have wanted a sorcerer for?'

'It wasn't a love charm. That would have mentioned a lady's name.' She was afraid to look too closely at the letter. She imagined it might grow legs and try to run away.

'Unless it was intended to harm the lady's husband,' said Victoire.

'Is that something you know much about?' she snapped. She was ashamed the moment she'd said it. It was something she might have said to the baron, in anger, and she was sure she'd finally said the thing that would ignite Victoire's own temper. Instead Victoire took a deep, unsteady breath and looked back at the letter.

'Be serious. It's a rumour they toss around at court. The Princesse de Tingry wants to remove her sister so that she can enjoy her sister's husband.'

'I've always doubted that. I've met the Marquis de Luxembourg. The man's hideous.' Her hands were shaking a little in her lap. Surely now they'd fight.

'I know that, but so is Mademoiselle de Tingry,' Victoire said. 'I think people believe that rumour just because there's an awful fascination in imagining them in bed together. It's not true, anyway. They say she cried when Monsieur de la Reynie questioned her about it. She's taken a vow of celibacy.'

At court, Victoire had learned to disguise her feelings, but Marie Catherine could see that she was upset. Her voice sounded almost carefree, but her eyes were focused intently on some point in the room to the left of Marie Catherine's shoulder.

Marie Catherine held the letter up again.

'So it's more court gossip then.'

'I thought we were looking for a scandalous story?'

'I know. It's just ugly.'

'So it is.'

Marie Catherine could see the muscles of Victoire's throat working as she tried to master herself. She swallowed, twisted her hands in her lap and finally leaned forward until her knee was pressed against Marie Catherine's through the many layers of her skirts, and looked into her eyes. Marie Catherine found it hard to hold her gaze. She wondered, if she crumbled and put her head in the girl's lap, whether Victoire would find some way to rescue her on her own, while Marie Catherine herself was busy being paralysed by fear.

'Are you all right?' Victoire asked.

'I'm well enough,' she said, fidgeting with the pile of letters on her lap.

'You aren't.' Victoire put a hand on her wrist. 'I'm sorry I interfered with your maid earlier.'

'That's not it.' Her skin was uncomfortably sensitised where Victoire was touching her, as if pins and needles were travelling up her arm. But she'd hurt Victoire's feelings when she'd sniped about love spells. It would hurt her again if she drew her hand away.

'I'm sorry,' said Victoire again.

'I'm frightened. That's all it is.'

The truth was that once she would have turned to Victoire instinctively with her fear, and now she didn't know what she should do. It was as if some eruption from the earth had shifted the landscape between them, so that she no longer knew where the old boundary lines lay. She had lain awake, some nights, imagining what might have happened if she had not refused Victoire's offer to take the blame – how safe she might have felt then, in her household, surrounded by her children and her servants and the protection of her good name. And then she had frozen over with the horror of imagining that dear body enclosed in a lightless cell, or led to the axemen at the place de Grève. Would she really risk not only herself, but her children, for Victoire's sake?

It appeared she would.

'Marie, I'm so sorry,' Victoire said, after they'd sat in silence for a while, Marie Catherine idly flipping the letter over in her hands. Now she looked up and saw that Victoire was biting her lower lip as if to ward off tears. 'I've made myself a burden to you,' she said and swiped a hand over her eyes. She had always been proud. She hated anyone to see her embarrassed, or weeping, or weak. When something touched her too deeply she made a joke of it, or she disappeared inside herself and returned only when she had transformed her sadness into some feeling that was more acceptable to her. The first time Marie Catherine had seen her cry, she had been enchanted. With Victoire there was no greater mark of trust.

Marie Catherine caught her hand and kissed her fingers.

'You aren't a burden to me.'

Victoire shook her head, as if she were shooing away a bee.

'I will take the blame if you need me to. I meant that when I promised it.'

'Why are you despairing now? This is the best thing we've found so far.' She held Victoire's hand against her cheek, and the girl let out a breath and put her head on Marie Catherine's shoulder. When Marie Catherine put her arms around her, she could feel her shoulders shaking. But she cried almost silently.

After a little while Victoire straightened up and wiped her face with her handkerchief.

'I'm sorry I said that thing, earlier,' Marie Catherine said.

But Victoire wouldn't speak about her feelings. She put on a smile, only a little shaky, and reached out for the letter again. 'What could Monsieur de Cardonnoy have wanted that spell for, do you think?'

Marie Catherine looked at the ledger, still open on her lap. Expenditures. She recognised the name of the baron's lawyer. 'Two years ago Monsieur de Cardonnoy was involved in a law suit that went badly for him,' she said. 'He was so angry that he sent away his old intendant, who'd managed his affairs for years, and whose father had managed *his* father's affairs.'

The old baron had, before his death, been a sieve of debts and unwise expenditures. He had sided against the king in the Fronde, the rebellion that had blighted Louis's early years as a monarch and turned Paris itself against its ruler, and while many men had successfully regained their status at court and proved their loyalty, old Monsieur de Cardonnoy never quite recovered either his fortune or his reputation. The old baron had dragged along in noble near-poverty, but the new one, once his father had died, had successfully gambled with his inheritance, selling off some part of his ancestral lands to finance his life at court, leasing away the rights to the monopolies that his father had held in Paris and, finally, sweeping up Marie Catherine, the financier's only daughter, who came to his house carrying ten times her weight in gold, in exchange for the noble history of his name. With his capital assured, he had set about regaining the old Cardonnoy rights and privileges, ensuring with as much assiduousness as any bourgeois tax-farmer that his money would, like spring seeds planted in fertile ground, continue to grow.

The baron had, for the most part, been successful. His chief regret had been a piece of good farmland that he had sold in a hurry, early in his career, in order to make good on a gambling debt to no less a person than the king's brother. The best one might have said for the debt was that the baron had perhaps been overwhelmed by his proximity to royalty, for at the time he had been new at court and had wagered far more than he was capable of paying. The land, therefore, had been sold in a hurry, at a loss, and his intendant's management of the sale had seen some fault in the paperwork, for in the years that followed he and the buyer would bitterly dispute whether the surveyed land included in the sale encompassed the farmland only or also an adjacent woodland, rich in timber, and worth far more, the baron felt, than the money he had received.

The case went against the baron. He blamed first the dishonesty of the financier he had sold to, and then the servant who had managed the affair, and finally Marie Catherine, whose dowry had come too late, and who, despite the long seasons spent at her father's country house, did not understand what it was to know that the land was your birthright, the soil your bones, to walk on the land that your fathers had walked on for far more than four generations, only to have it snatched away by lawyers.

She had conceded that she did not understand. Privately she had thought that if a contract made carelessly and under duress were not legally binding, then she ought also to be released from her marriage and regain what she had brought as a dowry. But she had kept that opinion to herself.

Now she laughed. 'I supposed he asked the devil to intervene in his lawsuit.'

Victoire, too, was smiling now. Her fingers found a curl escaping from under the widow's veil and tugged it until it hung loose across Marie Catherine's face, which made Marie Catherine laugh more, with a strength that felt like a prelude to hysteria. She leaned forward and kissed Victoire, quickly, on the corner of her smiling mouth, and Victoire caught her by her veil and held her there when she would have pulled away.

Behind them, the door to the baron's study creaked. Marie Catherine jumped away from Victoire's hand on her neck. At first it appeared that no one was there and the door had swung open of its own accord. After a moment she saw Sophie's face peering around the doorframe. She'd got down on her knees, as if she hoped to creep in unnoticed.

'You ought to be in the nursery,' Marie Catherine told her, breathlessly.

Sophie rolled her eyes up to the ceiling, as if she was supplicating the angels. 'It's not *fair*.'

The sound of footsteps echoed in the hallway, and Anne appeared at the door.

'I'm sorry, Madame. She slipped away when she should have been doing her lessons.'

The nursemaid tried to take Sophie by the hand, but she ran forward and wrapped her arms around Madame de Cardonnoy's waist. Victoire reached out and ruffled Sophie's hair, so that her shiny curls were mussed, and Sophie looked up at her in surprise.

'Let her stay,' Marie Catherine said. 'Bring down her books, she can do her lesson here. As long as she's *quiet* and well behaved.'

The last line she delivered with a little press of her hand on Sophie's shoulder. Sophie nodded. Victoire raised her eyebrows at her.

'Will you tell us a new story?' Sophie asked.

'Tonight. If you're good.'

'I'd like to hear it too,' Victoire said, and she looked towards Sophie with a tentative smile, as if they were playing a game and she were waiting for the girl's approval.

Marie Catherine took Victoire's hand in one of hers and Sophie's in the other and squeezed.

'Wait. Both of you. There's work to do.'

She picked up the papers.

There was a little window in Laure's room that overlooked the alley, casting a thin stripe of light across the grimy floor. Jeanne found herself staring at the light instead of Laure's face. Laure held the coin Jeanne had given her and flipped it back and forth between her fingers. Jeanne had kept half her money for herself, the écu Mademoiselle de Conti had given her burning a shameful hole in the pocket of her dress.

'They say La Voisin's execution will be today,' Laure said. 'I don't dare go.'

She touched the red birthmark on her face, a silent explanation. The mark was too distinctive – she'd be recognised.

'Would you want to see it?' Jeanne asked.

'I would. It would be good if there was someone there at her death who bore her no ill will.'

'I thought she and your mother didn't get along?' Jeanne felt herself trapped in a parody of a social visit. Her voice sounded high and artificial to her own ears. It was her accent – the words that Laure herself had trained her to pronounce like a lady. She remembered holding hands with Laure in La Chapelle's garden, walking back and forth among the cabbages, reading aloud from *Le Mercure galant*, about poetry, the theatre, the styles of the season, and how the reading had felt like a process of enchantment, from the girl who took away the soiled bedclothes to a fine lady. Now she felt like a block of wood. Laure's eyes were red-rimmed and her face was drawn. She seemed infinitely far away.

'They didn't like each other, it's true. But I forgive her. It was a small quarrel.'

There was a long pause. Jeanne looked out the window. There were pigeons roosting on the roof and they cooed and rustled. The sheets on the bed were dirty. Jeanne thought she saw a stain the colour of menstrual blood, indelible even after long scrubbing.

'There's no hope for Mother, you know. I don't dare visit her. Even La Voisin's daughter is imprisoned. I heard she turned herself in.' Laure was looking at her hands, picking at the skin around her nails.

'Did she really sell poisons?' Jeanne blurted out.

'I don't know. She said that she didn't and La Voisin did. I think La Voisin probably says that *she* didn't and Maman did.' Laure sounded so uncertain that Jeanne decided she didn't want to hear any more.

'Will you leave Paris?'

Laure sighed. 'I don't know how to start again without her. And I don't know how far my money will take me.'

She looked up at Jeanne, shaking her head as if she were shaking her thoughts away.

'I'm sorry. I must sound so ungrateful.'

'Don't,' Jeanne said. 'I'm the one who owes you.'

But Mademoiselle de Conti's money was a cold bruise on her leg. She wanted it, in case she had to run herself. She felt as if Laure had asked her to give away her dress and go out onto the street naked.

'She's so close, La Voisin. The execution will be at the place de Grève. Some of the women who stay here have gone to watch.' Laure's eyes were focused on the windowsill.

The silence settled back on the room.

'Did you know, my mistress's husband was murdered,' Jeanne said.

'What? How?' Laure looked up at her. 'Are you saying *he* was poisoned?'

'He was shot.'

Jeanne tugged at the trim on her bodice, trying to readjust her dress so that the boning in her underclothes didn't pinch. The bloodstains on Laure's sheets, the general air of squalor, the sounds of creaking stairs, slamming doors and fucking emanating from furnished rooms above and below, all were making her squirm with second-hand humiliation for Laure.

'I think Madame planned it.' The words fell out of her mouth like a pebble, surprisingly light and small. 'I think she had me carry a letter, explaining how it was to be done.' As soon as she'd spoken, she was horrified at herself. If the police ever caught Laure, how could Jeanne expect her to keep her secrets, when she couldn't keep them herself?

Laure sat on her bed perfectly quietly, waiting for Jeanne to go on. It was a look Jeanne remembered well from her fortune-telling: the strange calm of her marked face, the way her eyes seemed to film over and regard some invisible presence. If one sat in silence long enough, one could watch Laure's eyes dart upwards and then follow her gaze around the room, as it observed something that left no visible impression on the air.

Jeanne believed in what Laure saw. And yet that power hadn't stopped the police from finding La Chapelle.

'So you see,' Jeanne said, 'I may need to find some way to flee Paris, too, if Madame is arrested. Because the police will believe that I assisted her.' She twisted her hands uneasily behind her back. Jeanne didn't believe that Laure kept her own record of the debt between them. Perhaps she thought that Jeanne had already repaid her. But what Laure and her mother had given Jeanne was a new life, and what Jeanne had returned was less than that.

'What was in the letter?' Laure had been watching the dust move in the dark corner beneath the window, but now she looked up and met Jeanne's eyes.

'I'm an idiot. I didn't read it. I was afraid to break the seal.' She glanced at the corner where Laure had been staring, then swallowed. 'What did you see?'

Laure shook her head. '*I don't like to describe them*,' she'd said, long ago, when Jeanne first asked, shivering, what she saw when she spoke to the spirits. '*They're strange*.' Her darting gaze had made Jeanne feel intimately acquainted with the beings of the other world, how they moved, how they tiptoed and glided on the ceiling, or hung in the drying linen and watched her while she washed her face in the morning. Now, again, she had the feeling of a supernatural watcher. Did it look into her heart and see what Laure couldn't?

Why didn't you warn me that I ought to have read that letter before I delivered it? she wondered silently, and then felt blasphemous. Why shouldn't it choose Laure instead of her? Laure was kind, and holy in the way that Jeanne imagined the virgin saints.

'You're not an idiot,' said Laure.

Jeanne put her hands over her face.

'I didn't give you all of my money,' she said. She fumbled in her skirt until she found Mademoiselle de Conti's écu at the bottom of the pocket. 'Here's the rest. Take it.'

She held the coin out flat in the palm of her hand. At first she felt embarrassed, as she had when she stepped forward in front of Henri and lied to the police. But there was something else underneath the embarrassment, a kind of elation – not because she'd stopped being afraid, but because she'd decided her fear didn't matter. Laure was the kind of person who gave what she had when it was needed, without reckoning what it cost her. Jeanne knew she wasn't like Laure. But she would be, today.

'Oh, Jeanne.' Laure shook her head. 'You'll need it as much as I do, if you're right about your mistress.'

'No.' Jeanne could feel her resolve hardening as she spoke. 'I'll manage. I can get more money. I can steal it if I have to.'

What she did not say was, *You once took on a great risk in order to help me. Allow me to do so in return.* La Chapelle had never spoken of the danger or the expenses she had incurred by taking in Jeanne. She had simply asked, kindly, whether Jeanne would remember her, at her new post in the baron's house. Noble words were for those who couldn't communicate through the invisible signs written in the outer world, in a gesture, in a friend's face.

Jeanne smiled. 'Take it. After all, you promised me once I'll yet live to be old.'

Laure frowned at her. She didn't stretch out her hand. Jeanne put the coin down on the blanket beside her. Her face was burning.

'Take it, please. And write to let me know where you've gone, if you can.'

Impulsively she got down on her knees and embraced Laure's skirts, pressing her forehead into the other girl's knees. The silk hem of her skirt swept up a ratted tangle of dust from under the bed, which gusted along in her wake as she scrambled up and bolted from the room. She heard Laure's footsteps follow her to the door, Laure calling, 'Jeanne! Your mistress ...' But she was as light as a seedpod blown on the wind. She had to leave, or else she would end up regretting the money, which she had only risked her life to get. She turned for a last look at Laure's face and waved gaily, then smiled as her feet in their delicate heeled slippers tap-tapped down the squalid stairwell. Tap-tap, she spun out on the last step as if she were dancing at a ball, then opened the door to the outside world and floated into the street. She felt as if, along with that piece of silver, she'd thrown away her past one more time and had become Jeanne-of-no-particular-name, nineteen years old, who lived by her wits and owned a silk dress and one true portrait of herself in black charcoal, drawn by a man who did not love her, but wanted her favour.

The cold air hit her face and shocked her back to herself. She was a fool who'd given away the money for her own escape. She pulled her mantle tight around herself and laughed. She barely had the pocket change to take her back to the hôtel. When she'd run out of laughter, she left the alley on light steps, looking at none of the men, and flagged down a rented carriage.

What had possessed her? At least Laure would be all right.

The coachman shook his head at Jeanne sadly.

'Oh no, Mademoiselle, it will be difficult to cross the river now. All the crowds have gathered to watch the execution of that poisoner, La Voisin. The streets are crowded with traffic. It will be a long drive for me indeed.'

Jeanne bit her tongue over a sharp reply.

'Just take me to the edge of the crowd then, and I'll get out and walk.'

The driver grinned at her. 'Going to watch with the others as she burns then?'

'Maybe so.' She opened the door and sat down on the musty upholstery, which breathed out a sigh of dust as she settled in. The air inside the carriage was cold and close.

The crowd was indeed thick on the rue Saint-Antoine, whatever the coachman might have said to drive up his fare. When he pulled in behind a line of coaches, Jeanne got out and paid him, and pushed her way into the street. She looked at the gold braid the waiting drivers were wearing, at the crests on the carriage doors, and counted the members of the nobility, customers of La Voisin's or strangers, who'd come to watch the spectacle of her death.

There was one more thing that she could do, while she was pretending to be fearless. There would be one soul at La Voisin's death who didn't wish her ill, as Laure had wanted.

She shoved her way between two tall men, one of whom slapped at her and nearly caught her on the ear, and then she pushed farther into the crowd, the press of bodies turning the winter day warm. There was a woman on the corner selling roasted chestnuts. Their smoke hung in the air, over the smell of horse sweat and cabbage, like a lady's perfume.

'Chestnuts!' the woman was calling over the noise of the crowd. 'Hot chestnuts!'

La Voisin's cart must have passed already. The crowd was moving towards the place de Grève like a snail, never seeming to consciously step forward, but slowly, undulatingly changing place. Men and women called the poisoner's name and jeered. Jeanne ducked low to slide under a man's waving arm, sidled a woman out of her way, felt some unseen person grab at her skirt and try to squeeze – shoved off the bulk of an immense man in lawyerly dress – and finally washed up under a shop window facing the place de Grève, with its gallows and its single stone cross, mounted high on a column. She climbed up on an empty crate to look over the crowd and tried to shake off the feeling that all those bodies were trying to seize her and push her up towards the executioners.

There was a clear space in the centre of the square, and by it stood the convict's wagon. Little figures were heaping straw around the stake, which was blowing away in the cold wind as they piled it up. Jeanne held her hand up to shade her eyes against the winter sun. Two ragged children climbed up on the crate beside her, jostling each other for a better view.

Far away, two guards dragged a struggling figure out of the cart. She was wearing white. Her legs were bound with fetters – she kicked them together, like a fish. She lay limp on the ground and made them drag her. Through it all, her mouth was open, a black hole in her pink face, chafed with cold. It was impossible to hear what she was shouting, over the low rumbling of the crowd assembled to watch her death. It looked, more than anything, like a ghastly and inexpert puppet show. Her confessor ran forward, a black mouse in a white collar, offering her the cross, and the little poisoner-puppet shoved it away and turned her face to the ground.

Jeanne felt as if the crate on which she was standing had risen into the air and was hovering somewhere far above the crowd, so that she had the same view as a passing crow, and felt as far removed from the proceedings. She thought she ought to have flinched when they lit the straw, and the smoke began to curl up around La Voisin's feet, but instead she felt as if she was a kite flying away from herself on a long string. La Voisin kicked at the burning straw, in defiance of the chains binding her to the stake. A heap of smouldering straw tumbled off the platform, and the executioner piled it back up with a long pitchfork. La Voisin kicked the pitchfork. She kicked, again, the straw. The smoke rose so thickly that it became hard to see the movements of the little imprisoned figure at the foot of the stake. The flames were very bright.

What Jeanne hadn't been prepared for was how long it took. She'd half expected La Voisin to go up like a slip of paper held to a candle flame, her soul escaping into the air as soon as the fire touched her. But of course the pyre didn't burn that way, and it wasn't possible to pretend that she was only a marionette woman while she was in the flames. When she first screamed, in real pain and not the helpless fury at her impending death, there was a moment when the audience went silent and listened to the high, wavering sound. Then they called out again, heckling her, promising hell.

Jeanne made the sign of the cross over her chest. Her lips seemed to have frozen together with cold. When she opened her mouth to whisper, there was a sort of gummy film clinging to them, cold as the air and tasting of smoke. She murmured, *Our Father*, but stopped herself, the words of the prayer ringing inside her head, sounding less merciful than she had hoped. She pictured La Chapelle, in her dark cell, waiting to be sentenced to death, and then she imagined the smoke parting so that the tiny burning woman could fly away into the night on the wings of – what, the holy ghost? Her demon familiar? Her guardian fairy's chariot? The smoke did not open, but it drifted out over the crowd and stung Jeanne's eyes.

Maybe they would burn Jeanne too, if they knew her.

'Hail Mary,' she whispered. 'Pray for us sinners, now and at the hour of our death.'

And on her breast, where she'd first made the sign of the cross, she traced the letters *AGLA*, which La Chapelle, who had not been able to save herself, had sworn were magic, and which she had given to Jeanne to eat when she woke up from her long sickness.

She closed her eyes against the sun and the smoke. Maybe the prayer had some power even in her mouth. Maybe the burned woman's soul would ascend to heaven, and stand outside the golden gates and cry, *Open the door, for I, too, am going to come in.*

Chapter Eleven

———

Dear Monsieur Lavoie,

By now you have certainly learned the news of my husband's murder, and so I hope you will pardon me for not having written to you sooner. I am afraid that my grief at my husband's passing has eclipsed my distress at his conduct towards you. I know that you must surely bear some ill will towards him – and perhaps towards me – for his unwarranted visit to your house, and perhaps even for the untimeliness of his death, which has left you in the eyes of the police. For this I could not blame you, for, as short as our acquaintance has been, I am convinced that you are innocent in the matter of my husband's murder, and it must be a double blow to lose a patron and at the same moment have your reputation tarnished by suspicion. I hope, for this reason, that you will not think I am being too insistent when I ask you to tell me what occurred on the night of my husband's death, during the time that he visited your house. It is my greatest desire (as, I imagine, it must be yours) to find the man responsible for my husband's murder and bring him to justice.

Marie Catherine de Cardonnoy

'You shouldn't have sent that letter, Madame.'

Victoire was sitting across from her in the carriage, her sharp fox's face haloed by a hood trimmed with grey fur. The heat of close-packed bodies – hers and Victoire's, Jeanne's, the two children's – warmed the inside of the carriage slightly, enough that a veil of steam formed on the windows, but still the outside air crept in through the floorboards and reminded them all of winter. Marie Catherine had packed the children in with hot bricks wrapped in blankets to keep them from catching cold on the long ride to the palace at Versailles. Still the ride was uncomfortable. At the beginning of the journey Sophie and Nicolas had sat together by the window and played a hand-clapping game, but now they were bored and sulky. Madame de Cardonnoy's neck sweated under her mourning mantle of black brocade, while the cold draught had turned Victoire's nose a shade of pink that her powder did not quite conceal. The carriage itself jostled over every pothole, sometimes so violently that Marie Catherine had to cling to the seat to avoid sliding onto the floor, and every time Nicolas might have drifted off into a nap, some bump in the road woke him.

She was unhappy with the tone Victoire had taken about the letter, and more upset that she'd raised the topic in front of Jeanne and the children. Since her husband's death, Victoire had been at her house daily, whenever her presence was not required at Versailles. There was privacy to read her husband's papers, and even sometimes, barely, to kiss. Whenever a third person was in the room, Marie Catherine found that she and Victoire almost recoiled from each other, as if even the silence of their closeness might give them away.

'I don't see anything untoward about writing to him to ask for details of my husband's last night,' she said primly. 'I believe he is an honourable man – he, too, must want to find my husband's murderer, even if he held a grudge against him.'

What was truer was that she was terrified of the questions that La Reynie's men might have put to the painter. The lieutenant general's communications with her had been terse. He gave no more news of the rider that some witnesses had described. He asked for a summary of her husband's papers, and she had sent along a list of men who owed him gambling debts, but received no reply.

And what had Lavoie told him? She imagined ordering the

carriage to his house and shaking it out of him. It was an impulsive desire, but she couldn't banish it entirely.

'Why would he be angry with Papa?' Nicolas asked.

Marie Catherine put her hand on his head. 'They'd had a quarrel. That's all.'

'If they'd quarrelled, how do you know he isn't the murderer?' said Sophie.

'Because he was ill that night, chérie.'

Sophie hung her head, unsatisfied. She was old enough, Marie Catherine thought, to know that something was wrong, but not to know what quarter the danger came from – only that those around her felt it and would not let her into the secret.

After Jeanne had produced Lavoie's drawing of her for the Lieutenant General of Police, after her mysterious visit to her ailing relative, Marie Catherine had spoken to the girl alone in her cabinet. What had the painter said to her when he came to Hôtel Cardonnoy? *Nothing,* said the girl, *only that he was curious if you would receive him.* And had the drawing been a love token? *I do not know.* And the kiss in the hallway?

Jeanne had looked at her from under her eyelashes.

That, she said, *I invented.*

There was no reason to believe that the painter would sustain that lie, and so Jeanne had only bought her a little time with her deception.

For two years the girl had lived as close to her as a third hand, combing out her hair, powdering her face and neck, lacing her dress. She knew the hour in the night that Madame de Cardonnoy got up to piss, and how often the baron came to her bedroom, and the day on which her menses were due. And yet the gulf of unknowing that lay between them had produced an intimacy that was entirely new. It was as if, after a long day of riding, during which she had barely glanced at Jeanne's face, they were now travelling together through the dark, forced to keep close, so that each could find the other by the rustle of a sleeve, although neither could see the other's face. Marie Catherine had wanted to ask some question that would let her know whether Jeanne, also, understood what she was feeling, but instead she watched the girl's face, the stray freckles that lasted on her skin even in winter, the fawn-coloured needles of her eyelashes. And Jeanne looked at her folded hands, sharing the moment of not knowing, like a rabbit lying still in long grass, waiting for a child's footsteps – or a hawk's, or a hunter's – to pass safely by.

And the écu that Mademoiselle de Conti had given her? And the money that she herself had given Jeanne, for her family?

Jeanne's brow creased a little.

Do you begrudge me, Madame?

In the carriage the children were fussing.

'Stop touching me, Nicolas!'

Nicolas was lying half across his sister with his arms around her neck – rather sweetly, Madame de Cardonnoy thought, even if it did look uncomfortable for Sophie. When Marie Catherine looked at him, he leaned his head back and beamed at her, and Sophie screwed up her face in frustration and scooted towards the carriage door, dragging her brother along.

'Make him stop it, Maman! He's heavy. He's going to wrinkle my dress.'

'I'm not *doing* anything!'

Victoire laughed, and Marie Catherine glared at her. It *was* funny. But Sophie was capable of sliding down onto the carriage floor and crying the whole way to Versailles. And while her tear-stained face might have been taken as a sign of grief at her father's death, Marie Catherine didn't want to ride in the carriage with a screaming child.

'Nicolas, don't hang on your sister. Go and sit next to Mademoiselle de Conti.'

'Yes, we'll be ruffians together. May I wear your little hat? I want to feel dashing.'

'It's mourning clothes,' said Nicolas seriously, as he slid over to sit by Victoire. He looked down at the periwinkle folds of her gown, a little bewildered. When Victoire was visiting his mother, she often talked over his head, an adult who didn't care for children. Now she was dressed in court clothes and she was noticing him. It gave Marie Catherine a little shock of alarm, for before the baron's death she had kept Victoire and the children apart, like flowers pressed between separate pages of a book. The idea that Victoire might love the children, or they her, was a pleasant fantasy that became unsettling as it became more real.

Sophie snuggled in next to Marie Catherine, tucked her warm brick more securely into her skirt and sniffled.

'Nicolas never gets in trouble when he's bad,' she whispered. Marie Catherine put her arm around her, feeling how small her shoulders were under her travelling cloak.

'Both of you must be on your best behaviour at the palace,' she told them. 'Mademoiselle de Conti has done a great deal of work to arrange our audience with the king.'

'Do you see the king all the time?' Nicolas craned his head to look up at Victoire's face.

'No, Monsieur Nicolas, this is a special privilege. But I am friendly with a woman who is very good friends with him, and she has done me a favour because of the sympathy she feels for your mother.'

The woman to whom Victoire referred was Madame de Montespan, the king's mistress. It was an honour to pay a mourning visit to the palace, and Marie Catherine knew that talk of the baron's murder was almost as much in vogue as gossip about poisons. There would be many curious eyes on her and the children. But even the briefest audience with the king, if it went well, might help deflect suspicion from her.

'You mustn't cry or make a scene,' Marie Catherine said. 'Be quiet and gentle, like I told you at home, and don't speak to anyone unless you're spoken to first.'

Nicolas nodded and gripped Victoire's sleeve. Sophie was still sulking.

'I'll tell a story to pass the time,' she offered. 'What do you say?'

'All right,' said Sophie, hesitantly.

'Where shall I start?' She was toying anxiously with the fingers of her gloves. She hadn't told the children a story since the baron's death. 'Victoire? Give me an idea.'

'Why don't you tell us about an enchanted palace, like the one we're going to?'

'All right.' Marie Catherine took a breath. 'Listen. Once, in a place far from any land you've ever heard of, there lived two sorceresses, one red and one white. They had been the closest of bosom friends, but now they were mortal enemies. The cause of their quarrel was a little foundling girl, who had been left on the doorstep of the white sorceress when she was just a baby, without a note or any sign of where she had come from. The red sorceress had stumbled over the child in her swaddling clothes one morning when she was paying a call on her friend and carried her over the white sorceress's threshold, and after that they had raised the child together, doting on her and dressing her in beautiful clothes and summoning phantoms from the air and enchanted toys for her to play with.'

Marie Catherine closed her eyes. She felt Sophie's head radiating heat as the girl leaned against her side. She heard the creak of the carriage wheels, and the sounds of the city outside.

'The sorceresses,' she said, 'lived in two enchanted palaces on two neighbouring mountain peaks, far above the world. The white sorceress's house was made entirely of glass, and whenever anyone walked down its hall or danced in its grand chambers, a thousand rainbows accompanied them, refracted from the crystal panes, and a thousand ghostly reflections shadowed their every movement. At night, the lights from the white sorceress's house lit up the whole mountain as brightly as day, and anyone who looked could have seen the sorceress and her adopted child inside, feasting and laughing together. The transparent walls of the palace meant that in that house there were no secrets and no double-dealing, for all was visible, and the house's inhabitants were reminded to behave with nobility and kindness.'

Nicolas kicked the seat across from him, with an expression of glee. 'So could they see when there's a rat in the wall?'

Victoire laughed. 'I don't think a sorceress's house would have rats, Monsieur.'

Marie Catherine smoothed her hands over her skirt and continued. 'The red sorceress's house, however, was made entirely of silk, and anyone who entered could not have failed to be seduced by the bright colours and sensuous patterns of its walls. There were tapestries worked with the embroidery of a thousand invisible hands, and sheer curtains painted with scenes from ancient myth, and rooms all of velvet whose walls were so soft they seemed to purr when you stroked them, like a contented cat. And sometimes, when a wind came up on the mountain, you might walk one of the palace's twisting corridors only for a wall to blow away and reveal a room or a courtyard that no one had ever seen before, which seemed to conceal untold marvels. All who entered the red sorceress's house could not help but be seduced by its beauty, could not help but lie down on its many silk pillows and trail their hands in the clear water of its fountains, for it was a palace of delight.'

On the street a man was roasting chestnuts and for a minute their warm smell filled the carriage, as they passed through the halo of smoke.

'So for the first years of her life the foundling girl travelled between one house and the other, and in each she was loved and cherished. But when she turned sixteen the sorceresses decided that it was time to find her a husband, and there they quarrelled.'

Marie Catherine paused. The carriage was enveloped in honking and rustling feathers. Someone had chased a goose into the road. Sophie pressed her nose to the window.

'The white sorceress, you see,' Marie Catherine continued, once the noise had subsided, 'thought that no match but a king was fit for her adopted daughter, and she had sent the girl's portrait to the sovereign of a neighbouring kingdom, with promises that she would have every gift that her guardian's magic could bestow upon her to ensure that she was a gentle and just queen. But the red sorceress thought more of love than of politics, and so she had chosen the most beautiful of the shepherds whose flocks grazed the mountain and, guiding him secretly through the paths of her realm, she had shown him to a meadow where her foster child picked flowers and there, while he was dumbstruck at the girl's beauty, she had promised that their lives together should remain like this moment, for ever, and they should always live in delight at each other's presence.'

'I like the red sorceress's choice better,' Victoire murmured.

'Isn't it better to be a queen, though?' asked Sophie sharply, and then she seemed to think better of her question and turned back to the window before Victoire could answer.

'Neither the white sorceress nor the red approved of the other's choice. And here they quarrelled, for the white sorceress believed that since the girl had been left on her doorstep, the child was hers alone, and she alone should decide her fate. But the red sorceress believed that because it was she who had first discovered the child, and because she had brought her into the white sorceress's house only after she had taken the child in her arms and kissed her cheeks, and rocked her against her breast, that the girl was her daughter, and she should have the final say when it came to her destiny.'

'Ah,' said Victoire. 'I think I've had the privilege of meeting these two distinguished ladies.'

'Really?' said Nicolas.

'*Victoire*,' said Marie Catherine. It was true that she had been thinking, in some capacity, of Athénaïs de Montespan, the king's mistress, and of Madame de Maintenon, a religious widow who had raised the king's illegitimate children with Madame de Montespan and was now rumoured to be the king's new favourite, despite her age and her piety. Once the two women had been friends, but now they vied for influence. Red and white, pleasure and rectitude. It wasn't a comparison that would be good to make in front of the children.

'We're about to take the children to see the king,' she said pointedly. Victoire looked contrite.

'I'm sorry, Nicolas, I'm a terrible liar,' said Victoire. 'And rude, also. I was raised in a cave by a tribe of bats – your mother will tell you the whole story.'

'Wait for the end of this one, please,' said Marie Catherine. But she felt herself softening. She had once told the children a story of a princess who fell in love with a wild man, who was covered in fur like a wolf's from his neck to his knees. She had told the story of Victoire's bloody coat in Madame de Fontet's salon, and then the blood had leaped out of the coat and killed her husband. It was difficult to go on imagining the harm they had caused, when what she wanted was the impossible dream that they might live together, Marie Catherine as the children's mother and Victoire as their governess, their aunt, their father.

She had made her sorceresses foolish and quarrelsome, so that she would not have to mourn that unlikely future too much.

'The foundling girl,' she said, 'who loved both of the sorceresses equally, did not know who to obey. She swore that she would not offend either of her caretakers by refusing their advice, which made the white sorceress so angry that she locked the girl up in the highest tower of her glass palace. But the red sorceress sent a bird to carry her a ladder made of gossamer thread, so that the girl could climb down from the window and escape.'

The children were quiet now. Sophie's eyes were focused on her lap, moving quickly back and forth as if she were watching the scene play out in miniature in the folds of her skirt.

'But the foundling girl was so unhappy to have been the cause of her mothers' quarrel that instead of going to the palace of silk, she ran away down the mountainside, weeping. And when she was exhausted, she lay down and slept in the wilderness and woke to discover that she was quite lost.'

Marie Catherine paused for breath. What story was she telling? A tale of two bad mothers, and the child caught up in their scheming. As if the fairy tale might atone for what she could not atone for.

This time, at least, she wouldn't let herself frighten them.

'The foundling girl,' she said, 'had nothing but the clothes on her back, and two little toys that she often carried with her in her pockets. One, a gift from the white sorceress, was a clear glass marble, inside which was an inexhaustible light. The other, from the red sorceress, was a golden whistle in the shape of a songbird, whose sound was a sweet lullaby.'

Jeanne, who had been silent, was sitting with her forehead pressed against the windowpane of the coach, her eyes closed in a way that suggested she was only pretending to sleep. Victoire leaned in and nudged Marie Catherine's ankle with the toe of her silk shoe.

'Go on, please.'

'All right. The foundling girl wandered until she came upon a swift mountain river. There the handsome shepherd who the red sorceress had intended for the girl's husband was bathing, while his sheep wandered freely in the meadow beyond. And he was indeed handsome, but the foundling girl cared nothing for that. So she blew into the whistle that the red sorceress had given her, and the shepherd heard the music on the wind as he left the river and was lulled, and he fell fast asleep in a bed of moss, naked as the day he was born. And the girl put on his cap and trousers and left him her dress to cover himself when he woke, and set out again along the mountain path.'

'He can't go about in *girl's* clothes, though,' said Sophie, grimacing.

'Well, he can if it's at the opera,' Victoire said. She had left her foot next to Marie Catherine's foot and now she ran it up her ankle, concealed by her long dress.

'What does that mean?' Sophie had managed to imitate the tone of a salon lady scandalised by someone else's lack of decorum.

'Nothing, Sophie,' said Marie Catherine, and Sophie scooted towards the window, hurt by the slight impatience in her mother's voice. 'Listen. The white sorceress had woken in the morning and discovered that her daughter had fled. Seeing the silken ladder, she had gone to the house of the red sorceress in a rage, intending to strike her with her ivory wand and kill her, but the red sorceress was sitting in her garden of mulberry trees, and weeping and weeping, because her little bird had returned, but it had not brought her daughter with it.

'And when the two sorceresses realised they had driven their child away, they embraced, and cried together.'

Perhaps, Marie Catherine thought, she might be willing to share Sophie's love, if her daughter could love Victoire, too.

'Meanwhile,' she said, 'the foundling girl was walking the path down the mountain. The way was pleasant, shaded by flowering myrtle and carpeted with bluebells. Then, all of a sudden, there was a sound of horns, and hounds baying, and a hunting party appeared out of the woods. At the head of hunters was the king who the white sorceress had intended for the girl's husband.'

The carriage had now left the outskirts of Paris and the road was clear. The coachman called to the horses, and the road outside began to slip by faster, green and jostling.

'"You," called the king, "boy. We are hunting a black stag, with horns and hooves of jet. He was wounded near the river, but our dogs have lost the trail. Has he passed this way?"

'The foundling girl pulled her shepherd's cap low over her face and said that she had not seen him.

'The king looked at her more closely. "Why," he said. "You look so like the child of the white sorceress that I could swear you were her brother. I believed that girl was a vanished princess or the child of fairies, and yet now it seems that she is merely the abandoned daughter of some peasant."'

Nicolas had overcome his shyness enough to lean sleepily against the rigid pannier that supported Mademoiselle de Conti's court skirt. Victoire patted the boy's head absent-mindedly.

'I suppose if this king married the sorceresses' daughter, he'd blame her for her origins,' Victoire said, seriously.

'Perhaps,' said Marie Catherine. 'In any case, he rode away, but his mind was troubled, and he missed the trail of his stag. But the sorceresses' child continued on her way, and soon she came across a trail of blood. She followed the stag's path until she reached a deep crevasse in the earth. From the crevasse came the sound of crying. Now the girl took the glowing marble, her gift from the white sorceress, and used it to light the way before her. She walked deep into the dark cave, and the shadows drew back. And so she found the black stag, weeping over the arrow lodged in his shoulder.

'"Who is there?" the stag called.'

Marie Catherine paused to collect her thoughts and rearrange her dress. She unwrapped one of the heated bricks, now cool enough to touch, and pressed her hands against it, trying to warm them.

'Here, let me help.' Victoire held out her own hands and chafed Marie Catherine's between them.

'What next, Maman?' asked Nicolas.

'Just a minute,' said Marie Catherine. 'I'm thinking.'

She was enjoying the feeling of Victoire's hands on hers. Even in public, there were secret ways that they could touch.

'Don't you know how it ends?' Sophie asked.

'Yes, but I'm not sure of everything that happens in the middle.'

'Do my hands next,' said Nicolas, holding them out to Victoire. 'They're cold, too.'

'The sorceresses' child thought that she had never seen such a lovely creature in all of her life,' Marie Catherine said. 'The stag's coat was as dark as the night sky, and so sleek that it seemed to be dappled with stars. His branching antlers were draped with new leaves, so that he seemed to wear the crown of spring on his head. Even his tears were like drops of crystal. But the strangest thing of all was that when she held her magic light up to see him better, his shadow was the shadow of a man, and not a stag at all. The sorceress's daughter jumped when she saw this, and then she asked him how he had come there.

'"Once," said the stag, "I was the prince of a far-away kingdom. For a long time my father ruled wisely and well, but when I was sixteen my mother died, and my father remarried a wicked fairy. The new queen was jealous and wished me ill, and so one day when I was out riding, she met me in the wood and asked me to sit down in the glade and dine with her, and no sooner had I drunk her wine and eaten her bread than she struck me across the face with a twig of oak, and I was transformed as you see me, into a beast of the forest. I have wandered for a long time, and now I think that I shall die before my father ever learns of my fate."'

Victoire was still holding Nicolas's hands between her own, with a look of deep seriousness, as if she were a doctor performing a delicate operation. Marie Catherine felt unreasonably grateful for her presence, for her dizzying swings between sorrow and laughter. The day before, she had come to Hôtel Cardonnoy and dismounted from her carriage almost in tears, and lain down on a chaise in inconsolable silence. *I don't feel guilty*, she'd said, finally. *I won't – he doesn't deserve it. But I could have stopped all this from happening if I hadn't kissed you in the hallway.*

And now? She was smiling again, and stroking Nicolas's hair.

"'Let me help you," the sorceresses' daughter said. And she took the arrow out of his shoulder, and took off her shepherd's cloth cap and sash and used them to stop the bleeding. "Come with me," she said then, "for I am the daughter of the sorceresses who live high on the mountain, and I know if we go to them, they will protect you and tend your wounds better than I can."'

Marie Catherine fumbled with the edge of her lace veil. They were near Versailles. Perhaps the carriage had creased her dress. Perhaps her veil was askew and would show too much of her hair. Victoire saw her fidgeting and slid her foot delicately up Marie Catherine's ankle.

'They had only gone a little way up the mountain, however, when they heard, once more, the sound of horns and dogs. The king's party was returning and, before they could hide away, the king, riding at the head of the hunt, saw the girl leading the wild stag as if he were a tame horse. Without her shepherd's cap, her long hair fell down around her shoulders, and the king realised that she was no peasant boy, but the girl who the white sorceress had promised as his bride, and he felt betrayed. He spurred his horse towards them, and he would quickly have overtaken them if the sorceresses' daughter had not flung her arms around the stag's neck and said, "Dear stag, are you strong enough to carry me a little way? For I cannot outrun the hunt alone."'

The carriage swerved in the road and sped up, and when Madame de Cardonnoy pulled the curtain back from the window, she saw that they were overtaking the public coach that carried curious travellers and petitioners to Versailles. The Cardonnoy coachman drew alongside the public coach for a minute, as if racing, although the other driver had made no attempt to whip up his horses – indeed, they did not look up to the task. Through the window Marie Catherine made eye contact, momentarily, with a man in a matted wig, and then they had left the carriage behind and were travelling alone, enveloped in the sound of rattling wheels.

Marie Catherine let her voice speed up to match the carriage's pace.

'The stag nodded his assent, so the girl leaped up on his back, and he bounded up the mountain path as fast as his wounds would allow. For a while they drew ahead of the hunt, but then the stag's strength faltered and he stumbled and nearly fell. And the king drew so close that his outstretched fingertips nearly touched the sorceresses' daughter's long hair.'

The children's breath turned to a mist that hung before their faces as they exhaled. Victoire was sitting with her hand on Nicolas's shoulder. Even Jeanne stirred, the whites of her eyes visible for a moment beneath her eyelids, as if the chase had followed her into a dream.

'But now the girl and stag were near the home of the sorceresses, and the white sorceress, watching from the highest tower of her glass palace, saw them running and sent down a bolt of lightning, so that the king had to veer away from the path, and he missed his chance to grab the girl and pull her off the stag's back. So the stag drew ahead of the hunting party once more, but his strength was nearly gone and soon he stumbled and fell again, and once again the king overtook them. But this time the red sorceress, watching from a tower of her palace of silk, saw them approaching and called down a thick fog, so that all was veiled in white, and the king didn't know which way to turn. The foundling girl and the stag, too, would have been lost, except that the girl took the white sorceress's marble in her right hand, and its light cut a swathe through the mist. In her left hand she took the red sorceress's whistle, and when she blew into it, her mother's birds came and flew beside her, keeping her on the right path. In that way she came to the space between the two palaces, and there the black stag collapsed from exhaustion, for he had run too far with his wounds and he was very near death.'

Marie Catherine paused, only for a moment, and the carriage struck a stone in the road and jarred the entire box, so that Sophie grabbed her mother's hand, and Jeanne jumped awake.

'The two sorceresses ran to meet their child. The red sorceress saw that the stag's dark coat was soaked with blood, and at once she sprinkled him with an enchanted draught, and his wounds closed and he was whole again. And the white sorceress saw the human shadow that followed him and knew his true nature, and she struck him on the forehead with her magic wand, and suddenly the sorceresses' daughter was embracing not a wild beast, but a prince, as handsome and gentle as the stag had been. And both of the girl's mothers knew that this prince would be her choice of husband, and they loved her so much that neither thought for even a moment of opposing her.'

'Were they happy after that?' Sophie asked.

'Yes.' Victoire spoke before Marie Catherine could. 'They all lived happily, for the rest of their lives.'

Victoire tugged the curtain back from the window of the carriage, reaching over Jeanne's shoulder. The servant girl rubbed her face, as if it had suddenly occurred to her that the other occupants of the carriage might have been watching her sleep.

'We're almost there,' Victoire murmured. 'You can see the gates.' And, leaning forward, she said very softly, to Madame de Cardonnoy alone, 'Look, it's the sorceress's silk palace.'

'Hush.' She squeezed Victoire's hand. 'You don't know what the children will repeat.' She had a sudden vision of Athénaïs de Montespan, fat with childbearing and wrapped in an enchanted halo. Rumour had it that she and the king quarrelled all the time now, that she screamed at him in her private chambers, and that last year she had been so enraged by the king's flirtation with a younger woman, Mademoiselle de Fontanges, that she'd stormed away from court and spent weeks at her residence in Paris.

'But I don't see how anyone could fall in love with a stag,' said Sophie, and instead of answering, Madame de Cardonnoy pulled on her daughter's black velvet sleeve and pointed to the curlicued golden gates that barred the way to the palace, crowned by the king's face, his hair blown back from his brow and transforming into the rays of the sun. Behind the gates, the palace rose like a mute cliff, so large it seemed to be some uncanny natural formation, rather than a man-made dwelling. The road smelled like horse manure.

The carriage made its way through the high gates, and then they climbed out and walked the path up to the palace on foot. Madame de Cardonnoy kept her hand on Nicolas's shoulder. Sophie was old enough to be subdued by the vast block of the palace, larger than the country house on the Cardonnoy estates and rising out of the emptiness of the formal gardens unnaturally, surrounded only by its own outer wings, without the comforting envelopment of Paris. She scanned the upper roof with wide, white eyes. Jeanne, walking close behind her, wore an expression that might have been exhaustion or the suppressed desire to stare upwards in dismay at the palace's silhouette. Victoire and the other courtiers liked to complain that the air at Versailles was poisoned by the marshy flat on which it had been constructed, but Marie Catherine always felt that the thickness in the air, the blanketing unease, was a result of the similarity the palace bore to all enchanted houses in which a lonely beast or sorcerer lived.

On this day the winter air was damp and cold, and the lawn was wreathed in a layer of ghostly mist. Servants in livery circulated through the gardens like spirit messengers, touching courtiers on their sleeves or holding the train of a glittering dress. The women wore their hair elaborately curled and powdered white with argentine, and Marie Catherine felt uneasily conscious of how dark and batlike she must look beside them, with her own hair shrouded in the widow's mantle. At the end of the gardens, one could see the newest wings of the palace, still under construction and braced with scaffolding, the workmen balancing in the skeleton of the construction like a flock of birds.

As they stepped under the shadow of the palace, Victoire drew close to Marie Catherine and leaned in to whisper in her ear. She could feel the weight of the heavy formal skirt pressing against her own dress, tugging at her black crepe mantle.

'I've asked Madame de Montespan if the king will see you directly. He will – but the audience may not last long. It's only so that he can see you, and then we'll go to her chambers afterwards and pay our respects to her.'

'All right,' said Marie Catherine. She was steeling her nerves. The palace set her on edge.

'Don't try to speak too much. I think it's better if the children stay by me, so they don't cause a fuss. Your lady's maid will wait with the other servants.'

'Of course.'

At the entrance they were handed off between lackeys, passing under a hundred crystal chandeliers that, even in daylight, cast a glitter of reflected light onto the walls and floor, like raindrops scattered over the frescoes or the silk wallpaper. In all the halls there was a faint but pervasive smell of piss and old meat, the smell of the streets of Paris in winter, so that Marie Catherine found herself holding her breath before each inhalation. The king, it was said, hated perfume more than anything and suffered from migraines if he touched it, so Marie Catherine didn't dare take out her handkerchief, which was scented with orange blossoms.

The ceiling opened up above her, farther and farther away, like the roof of a giant mouth, the chandelier glittering like teeth, and she smelled the breath of the beast. The walls pulsed, swallowed. This was a building that ate men.

Marie Catherine pushed the vision away and made herself admire the vast expense that had gone into the gently gleaming floors, the thick rugs with flowering designs worked into their silks, the tabletops made of red marble and green porphyry, topped with painted vases from China, or with hyacinths cultivated, miraculously, in the dead of winter. She took Nicolas's hand in one of her hands, and Sophie's in the other.

Finally they arrived at the door to the king's chambers. Their lackey conferred with the lackey at the door, and they were instructed to wait. Marie Catherine had expected to be led to a formal audience hall, but this room, she realised quickly – from the courtiers waiting in the bright hall windows, gossiping, eyeing her and Victoire – was a more private chamber. She felt her heart begin to beat erratically in her throat, like a panicked bird. And yet when the door opened for her, the room was crowded. She saw Monsieur, the king's brother, and his wife, and a young powdered man who must have been one of his favourites, and a rank of other faces, their expressions transforming from mirth to a studied sympathy and shock as she entered the room, leaving Jeanne and the children behind at the door. Louis was sitting in an armchair before a round table, one sculpted leg extended before him, a deck of cards in his hand. He laid the cards down on the marble table-top, and Madame de Cardonnoy sank into the lowest curtsey of which she was capable, so that the hem of her black veil pooled on the floor and the weight of her court skirt nearly pulled her down on one knee.

Then the king took her hand and made her rise, and she looked directly into his face. This close, she realised that he was growing old. The magnificent curled hair was not his own, the skin under his eyes had slackened into soft folds like fresh dough, his cheeks were thick and jowly. She held his eyes, which were piercing. He brought her gloved hand to his lips and kissed it, then released her.

'I knew your husband, Madame,' the king said. 'Rest assured that we will find his murderer.'

'Thank you,' she answered. 'Justice is in your hands.'

'I remember you came here once as a young girl, before the palace was built,' Louis said. 'You wore a pink dress and you rode out hunting with us. I remember that fondly.'

'I am glad to hear that, Your Majesty,' said Marie Catherine, although she had no memory of the day he described. He had confused her with another woman.

The king nodded, the curls of his wig tumbling forward on his shoulders. And then, like that, the audience was over. No one touched her, but the crowd in the chamber drew imperceptibly tighter around the man at its centre, a voice was raised in brief condolence, Marie Catherine curtseyed again, withdrew, saw the king's brother raise his hand to her, curtseyed again when she reached the door, found herself outside. Found that she was trembling uncontrollably. Found that she could not remember any detail of the appointments of the room, except the round marble tabletop on which the king's hand had rested, and the great precision with which she had observed the texture of his skin, his eyelashes, the gentle pressure of his hand on hers.

I knew your husband, Madame. Spoken in that gentle, slightly stiff old man's voice. The loose fold of flesh that hung from under his chin. It was as if her image of the king were superimposed over the king himself, the force of divine right giving the smallest details of his being an uncountable weight. He pulled everything towards him, the way the sun makes a deeply rooted plant turn to follow it.

She linked arms with Victoire, still shaking, let herself be stopped by a waiting courtier, a man whose name and face she did not know, and – 'The Baronne de Cardonnoy, I presume? Such a terrible story about your husband, the entire court is in shock, allow me to pay my respects' – another kiss on her hand, she wished he wouldn't touch her, even through her soft gloves. Victoire pulled her away down the corridor with the children in tow. She must look distraught, a distraught widow. She had stopped shaking, but her body felt unreal.

'Don't worry, everyone feels the way you do, after a first meeting,' Victoire murmured to her. She had painted a little rouge on her cheeks in the carriage, but Marie Catherine thought that under the paint she, too, looked pale. 'You did well.'

'Was that man behaving strangely?' Madame de Cardonnoy asked.

'It's just curiosity. They want to be close to whoever seems to have the king's favour.' Victoire's mouth was set in a wavering line.

'I don't remember that hunting party at all. I don't think it happened.'

'Your memory may be better than his,' said Victoire. 'But it was good of you not to tell him so.'

Marie Catherine squeezed her hand, and then they arrived at the chambers of Athénaïs de Montespan. Victoire's face was brimming over with a smile of sympathy and she pushed the children forward, saying the formulaic words of sorrow, Marie Catherine curtseying and rising to press Athénaïs's soft white hand, the smell of roses and musk wafting off her, in defiance of the king's hatred of scent. Her dress was the colour of new leaves, her mouth a round redcurrant in her soft face. Her smile at Marie Catherine seemed quite genuine. She offered her sympathy. A few moments later she was laughing with her companions, Marie Catherine hovering still in their circle, separated from them only by the barrier of the widow's veil, and the gaiety continued as ever, men and women exclaiming at the negligence of the police, reassuring her in the same breath of the imminent arrest of her husband's murderer.

She could not help becoming bored. Very little wit was required of a bereaved woman, and soon they were talking of other things. The smell of perfume and the draught from the window made her sleepy. The meeting, clearly, would go on for hours, perhaps far into the night. Victoire had no trouble keeping up with the flow of conversation, and watching her joke made Marie Catherine feel distant from her and sad. Sometimes she reached out and touched Marie Catherine's shoulder, a woman comforting her friend.

She could not help imagining a different carriage ride than the one ahead of her – not the potholed road back from Versailles, with the children at her side, but the long excursions that she and Victoire used to take around the Bois de Boulogne, with the curtains drawn so that the coach's dim interior became its own self-contained world, with only the two of them inhabiting it. How in the darkness, alone, she and Victoire might spin another story, one they'd tell together, as the carriage creaked and glided along the road towards the dawn.

Sometimes her thoughts went back to her husband, turning to dust in the long night under the earth. She could not maintain her sense of sin. Instead she felt the vast relief of the empty house, of her private chambers, alive with Victoire's image, and the annihilating fear of discovery. He, who had been alive a week ago, was dead. As good as by her hand. She remembered walking in the orchards with him one summer at Cardonnoy, during her first pregnancy, or perhaps her second, one of the children she had bled out onto the sheets of their marriage bed, her hands knotted into fists and blue-knuckled as she felt the blood seeping down her legs, as she grew terrified that the child's death would kill her. After it happened twice, it no longer frightened her so much. It was just a rebellion of the body.

Before that, in the orchard, she had been sixteen, and the baron, his greying hair dappled with the pattern of leaves, had pulled a pear down for her from a high branch. They could hear the song of peasants working in the adjacent field. The orchard itself was swarmed with speck-like flies, and fat bees attracted by the ripening fruit. She had swung her fan to ward them off, laughing at the way they hung in mid-air and fought against the breeze. As soon as the baron had put the pear in her hand, she knew it was unripe, the flesh hard and green. Still, she had eaten the whole thing, tannic and bitter, and smiled at her husband, and he had breathed in deeply and looked in satisfaction at everything that surrounded them. It was not a lover's memory – she did not love him, but she had wanted to please him the way that a child wants to please a strict tutor. She had not wanted to say that the pear was green, and the pregnancy anyway made her want to eat strange things, to dip a finger in a box of argentine and lick the powder off, or chew the gelatinous round of soap when she bathed. She ate the pear and liked it, and in Madame de Montespan's quarters she tasted it again, and she wondered what the baron had been thinking that afternoon, and why it was this ordinary memory that came back to her, and whether she could have changed herself in some way that would have made her marriage happier. If she had turned her face away from the pear's sticky, wooden flesh. If she had not miscarried that pregnancy.

'And I hear that you, Madame, are known for the stories you tell in Madame de Fontet's salon.' The voice, and Victoire's hand on her wrist, brought Madame de Cardonnoy back to her surroundings. The speaker was a young woman, a girl whose name Marie Catherine did not know, but her face expressed a kind of pity for her silence, a desire to pull her back into the circle of light.

'Oh.' Marie Catherine shook her head. 'They're only fairy stories. The kind of tales a nurse might tell.' The denial was entirely by rote now, but she had said it so quietly that she saw the girl lean forward a little to catch the words off her lips.

'Madame de Cardonnoy is being modest,' said Victoire. 'She knows that all praise is truer when it comes from someone else's tongue.'

'You should return and tell us a story of the court,' said the girl, with a glance at Madame de Montespan. Athénaïs nodded approvingly. 'I'm sure we'd all like to see ourselves reflected in such a mirror, and you would have ample inspiration from your surroundings.'

'Certainly.' She tugged the edge of her black mantle a little. 'But I shouldn't like to appear to compete with the true poets here.'

Sophie's hand tugged at her sleeve. Looking at her daughter, Marie Catherine could read on the little pinched face that she was bored and desperate to leave, but was too intimidated to say so. Marie Catherine touched her neck above the collar, let the conversation turn from her own tales to Racine and the theatre, the criminal passions of Phèdre, the nobility of tragedy, whether there was anything playing in Paris that was worth the journey, or whether the women attended merely to have an excuse to let the world see them in their most beautiful clothes, an attraction that had paled somewhat, now that every bourgeois fishwife owned a silk gown embroidered with pearls, overturning all distinction between high and low. A girl's convent school had enacted a performance of Racine recently and that had been a truly noble spectacle, attended by ministers and performed with the most graceful innocence imaginable. Marie Catherine didn't dare let her mind wander again, in case Athénaïs saw her boredom.

Finally Madame de Cardonnoy judged that she could leave without impropriety. The children, anyway, were squirming, despite all instructions to be good. Marie Catherine put a hand on the back of each little head and pushed them towards Madame de Montespan, and first Sophie, then Nicolas bowed deeply and kissed the king's mistress's plump, dimpled hand.

Victoire did not accompany them back to Paris. She had her own apartment at Versailles, where she would stay for the next several days, obeying the rhythms of the court, far from the man's jacket folded up in the bottom of a trunk in her family's hôtel at the place Royale, the red cloth stained with darker blood. It was impossible to say goodbye to her properly. She left Madame de Montespan's chambers with only a glance at the girl, which she hoped communicated what she would have said to Victoire alone, away from the courtiers' eyes. A lackey was sent to call Jeanne from the servants' table. Then, crossing the flat expanse of the gardens, whose air seemed much colder after the fug of perfume in Madame de Montespan's rooms, Madame de Cardonnoy turned back to watch the palace and saw the way the afternoon light caught the thousand windowpanes and turned them into reflecting mirrors, and wondered which of those carpeted halls the king was striding down in his silk-soft high-heeled boots, and whether behind any of those windows some anonymous stranger was watching her, unseen.

III

—

The Water of Life and Death

Chapter Twelve

———

The bruises had faded. Lavoie was left with a blotchy green stain over his right eye, a swollen finger and a deep, cutting pain in his ribs when he changed positions or breathed in deeply. The first two days he had pissed blood. Now that had stopped.

The police had questioned him, in a closed room in the Grand Châtelet, as to his relationship with the Baron de Cardonnoy, as to his correspondence with the baron's wife, as to the events of the night the baron had come to his house. Lavoie had directed them to observe the painting he had made of the baron, which hung in the man's own salon, and the baronne's letter, which consisted of a chaste fairy tale.

They had asked him about his visit to Hôtel Cardonnoy in the baronne's absence. And there he had stumbled. In fact he no longer had any clear sense of what his intentions had been, as if the violence of the baron's men had dislodged them from his brain. Another narrative, in which he had written to the baronne in the most perfunctory curiosity over the end of a fairy tale, in which he had listened only because it was a distraction for the baronne's restive children, in which the private visit to Hôtel Cardonnoy had never occurred was growing over the real events like ivy.

What had he been thinking? That the worst he would face for his visit was some gossip from the baron's household. That the two or three brawls he had participated in as a student had left him equipped to fend off another man's servants. That Madame de Cardonnoy had been so charmed by his wit and his skill with paint that she would defend him from her husband's suspicions. That

Madame de Cardonnoy had been so charmed after that meeting that she was still thinking of him.

The police asked: had he paid court to the baronne's servant girl? Had he drawn her? Had he kissed her? Lavoie gaped at them.

No, he said. He had not.

He was reminded, none too gently, that he was being questioned in connection with the Baron de Cardonnoy's murder and should tell the truth to its fullest extent, before God and the law.

And how, he asked them, was he supposed to have murdered the Baron de Cardonnoy in the night, when his neighbours had found him bleeding on his own floor some time after?

Only then did he realise, with a shock of shame, that the baronne's servant girl had extended her credit to protect him. That he had flirted with Madame and asked her lady's maid to arrange a meeting would be damning. But a dalliance with a pretty servant could only reflect badly on the girl herself, and so, by compromising her own reputation, she had protected Lavoie's and that of her mistress. He, meanwhile, was a fool who had denied everything.

And so he had hurried to make himself loathsome. He had courted the baronne's maid, he avowed, only because he was interested in gaining admission to Madame de Fontet's salon, where the beauties and the wits of Paris gathered, and where he might gain the means to build his reputation, and with it his fortune. His interest in Madame de Cardonnoy's fairy tales were of a similar flavour. He had wanted only his own gain, he had never imagined the baron might misunderstand, he was horrified that the police were questioning him, upright man that he was.

It was clear that he himself could not be the baron's assassin, injured as he had been. And he owned no horse on which he could have fled the scene of the murder.

Did he have friends, though, who might have avenged the baron's treatment of him?

He did not. They let him leave.

A loutish adolescent boy took up residence on his street, where he picked things out of his teeth under the sign for Monsieur Peret's bakery, and annoyed the women by hissing at them like a goose, and stared intently at Lavoie's door every time someone seemed poised to go in or out.

At home, Lavoie wrapped his swollen finger tightly in a hand-kerchief, which helped with the pain of gripping a brush, and began to draw.

By lamplight, at first, late at the night, which was a waste of tallow and paper, because the shadows as he drew them by the lamp's flame turned eerie and distorted in daylight. But when he lay down in bed the images assaulted him, and he had to pick up his pen in order to transfer them outside himself, because if he lay still with them and tried to sleep, it was as if he was looking through the cracks in God's work and peering directly into a bright and noisy hell.

So he put off the moment of sleep. He drew, first, Aeneas car-rying Anchises out of a burning Troy, a silhouette of their shape, the young man carrying the old one as if they had been welded together by pain. Then Aeneas' face, in detail, framed by Anchises' arthritic hands. Anchises' head was bent, his face half hidden in the wasted arm that gripped his son's neck, his one visible eye staring backwards in fear towards the burning city that he had been too weak even to flee. Lavoie drew him from half a dozen angles, until he had found the face he'd pictured and, as he drew, he felt that he was setting down a kind of organising blueprint for his misery. Next was Troy itself. He drew the boiling clouds through which Mars in his chariot looked down, a parody of an angel. He drew the coachman who had beaten his screaming horse on the rue Saint-Sulpice, and dressed him in a flowing Greek robe, and put a spear in his hand. He drew Helen, but he put her hands over her lovely eyes, so that he was required to draw only a mouth tight with fear, that might have been beautiful, or not. He did not know where on the ground Helen would stand, or the driver with his horse, or any of the other figures of war. He pictured them like a boiling mass, tumbling out of the smoke of Troy head over heels, chasing the bent figure whose steps, far out on the sands bordering the ocean, were heavy with the weight of the old man he carried on his back.

It would not be a noble painting. It had no composition, no structure to the scene, only a broken net of swords, faces, blood. It ought to have been full of shadows that would hide the gruesome details, but Lavoie had never painted darkness, and the scene in his mind was drenched in poppy reds, golden sunlight and the clear green of the ocean's waves as they retreated along the sand. No chiaroscuro, just a terrible and engulfing light.

When he did manage to sleep, he dreamed that he had found a secret staircase that led off his studio, which, when he walked down it, was full of cold blue light and thousands of buzzing flies, which landed on his face and hands and were impossible to shake off. When he killed them, their corpses piled under his feet. It did not, however, occur to him in the dream to turn back and lock the door. Or not until he had gone what seemed like many miles. Then he found that the way back was blocked by the same black cloud that he had already walked through, and the stairs had become so steep that he had to crawl on his hands and knees to make any headway.

On subsequent nights he could no longer find the secret door, but the flies of his nightmare had leaked out and now inhabited every room of his house. This was a worse dream, because when he woke it was never clear to him how real it had been, and he would take a bite of his morning bread and butter and find himself, as he chewed, imagining the dead corpse of an insect baked into the dough. By daylight he ignored these visions, worked on a portrait of a comte for which he had been paid and which had not yet been completed, and attempted not to jump so violently as to upset his paints when Berthe or a neighbour knocked on his door. He cooked and ground vermilion, a delicate operation, watching as the mixture of sulphur and quicksilver changed colour under his grindstone, from black to liver to crimson. He avoided going outside, disgusted by the idea that passers-by in the street might stare at his battered face (and this was before he accounted for his dread of the teenaged police spy he believed had been assigned to watch his movements), and as a result the house seemed to close in around him, like a clenched fist, and leave him no room to breathe.

When he received Madame de Cardonnoy's letter, he paced back and forth in his hallway and cursed her name. If she had not written to him with the continuation of that foolish tale. If she had responded to his interest with coldness, as a good wife should. If she had taken more care with her correspondence, and had not let Lavoie's letter fall into her husband's hands.

So *now* she wanted information about her husband – in the

216

interest, naturally, of clearing Lavoie's good name. Now she dared to write to him as if she were any good, grieving wife, as if she hadn't – but then he wasn't sure what he thought she had done. In his first moment of rage Lavoie had imagined her handing Monsieur de Cardonnoy the letter he'd written, incriminating him in place of whoever her real lover was. But in truth, he didn't know if she had had a lover or not. Perhaps Jeanne's lie about the kiss was meant to conceal one of the maid's own indiscretions, or perhaps it had been an invention. And though he knew the baron only slightly, he realised that Cardonnoy was old and his wife was still young, that he was strict and controlling and she was a wit in the salons, that he spent many of his days at court and left his wife alone in that grand hôtel in Paris. And perhaps the baron also had a predisposition for the kind of brutality he had visited on Lavoie. What wife wouldn't stray?

Neither had Lavoie been entirely innocent. His interest in the baronne had been only a thought, but he knew himself well enough to realise that, while he admired the young maidens whose parents took them to his studio to be painted, and paid, occasionally, for the attentions of the women who walked the Tuileries alone in fine clothes, the kind of woman that he liked best was the one who was another man's wife. It wasn't a mercenary impulse, but the fact that adultery made love doomed and heroic, a game of wits in which the opponents were good sense, reputation and the many eyes of the outer world. An affair with the baronne could never have gone very far. But it would have had a weight out of proportion to its substance, as now Lavoie knew that his anger was out of proportion with Madame de Cardonnoy's treatment of him.

On their first meeting he had admired her subtlety, her indirection, the sly message of her story and her poise as she told it. All those things had charmed him, and if they offended him now, he admitted to himself, it was not because he was disgusted by adultery, but rather because he had believed that she felt an inclination for him, and now he felt that he had been toyed with and discarded. He should have been angry with her husband. But he had cared only for her husband's business, and not for his regard.

He returned to the story of the sculptor and his living statue. Had it just been flattery? He wanted to believe that she had seen some quality in his work that inspired the tale, the same thing he felt sometimes, that the canvas was a window that he could open to let its contents into the world.

He rehearsed these ideas for a little while after he received the letter and for a time he felt invigorated by anger, by his own courtesy at excusing the baronne for her husband's behaviour, by the idea that she might still come to him and ask for his forgiveness, and feel pity and remorse when she saw his bruises, and the way he'd wrapped his sprained fingers so that he could go on painting. But eventually his imagination wore him out, and the scenes he'd pictured seemed small and embarrassing. She was under scrutiny after her husband's death, as he was. There was nothing he could do to help her. He was not sure that he would have cared to, if he could have.

To Marie Catherine, Baronne de Cardonnoy:

Madame,

You will not believe the encounter I have had while walking the gardens of Versailles. It is cold yet for taking the air, but in such close walls one must find some way of being under the sky. In this way, I walked past some icy fountains and wandered through a grotto much wilted by snow, when I came upon the young Duc de Maine and she who is his governess, and who is sometimes named, at court, Madame de Maintenant, after the very great favour the king shows her (without regard for the feelings of Madame de Montespan, whose children by the king she has the care of). The Duc de Maine, I shall say, though he is a frail child, was delighted by this late snow, and took advantage of his governess's pensive mood to run ahead and, scooping up handfuls of snow from the ground, make a show as if he were bombarding the battlements of a besieged city. I tucked up my skirts and joined him in the game, and was quite warm in my fur cape, although I will admit that court dress is very awkward to run in, so that by the end of the game my skirts were wet with the melted snow from the young duc's cannonballs.

It is good to see children at court.

Once Madame his governess had caught up to us, she asked

me to walk a while with her, arm in arm. This would ordinarily be a mark of favour, for all know that she is much admired by the king. But I fear I have again outdone myself, for, once my arm was securely linked with hers and I could not escape, she remarked, quite casually, that one must leave the running and fighting to the men, for it is not our lot. 'A woman who cross-dresses, in thought or deed, usurps the place of the other sex and makes herself a monster!'

It is also said that this lady was once a great wit, but now makes herself dull and prudish in company, on the instructions of her confessor, who would have her mortify her pride.

As for my fine coat and trousers, I have long since bowed to the will of the times and put them away. And may they soon disappear, also, from memory, and leave me in good credit with all gentle people.

I miss you.

Yours always,

Victoire de Conti

Marie Catherine put the letter down on her writing table and then laid her head down on top of it, cradling her face in the folds of her black sleeve. Behind her, she heard Jeanne's foot pause in the gentle rhythm it was tapping as she sewed, and then begin again, deliberately.

It had been just over a week since her visit to Versailles, and not yet three since her husband's death. A late snow had closed the road to Versailles, then melted, leaving a sea of sucking mud that broke carriage wheels and mired horses. Finally the weather had turned cold again, the road had frozen hard and now tiny, glittering flakes of snow were falling outside and leaving a pattern like a lace shawl on the cobblestones in the courtyard.

It was the first letter she had received from Victoire since the weather had made the roads impassable. While she waited she had driven herself to desperation wondering what was happening at court, what was happening in the Grand Châtelet, when Victoire would come back to Paris. Now Victoire sent her this confection of gossip, as if her life was once again simple. And if anyone were reading her correspondence, they'd know that the girl couldn't write a civil line about Madame de Maintenon, who had care of the king's children and also, it was said, a great influence on his actions. Who was sometimes mockingly called Madame de *Maintenant* – Madame *Right-Now* – which Marie Catherine thought showed remarkable optimism about her staying power. The king had had plenty of dalliances with young beauties, forgotten in six weeks or six months, but Madame de Maintenon had captivated him as a woman of forty-five. Many at court might wish her out of favour, but it was clear enough that her relationship with the king was more than a dalliance.

Gossip and wit. Marie Catherine couldn't help but wonder whether Victoire felt some relief to be absent at Versailles, away from the black-draped windows of Hôtel Cardonnoy and from Marie Catherine's desperation and secrecy and confused reproaches. She folded the letter and put it away in her drawer and, as she did so, she tried to tell herself that the best thing Victoire could do for both of them was carry on as if everything was ordinary and she had no fear of anyone watching her.

The enforced boredom of early mourning was wearing on her. The image of Victoire at Versailles, laughing and chasing snowballs, only made her jealous. Marie Catherine wished she could summon her into the room through imagination. She might have begged Victoire to say again that she still loved her, that she regretted nothing, or she might have simply thrown her down on the bed.

Marie Catherine would have thought that fear and guilt would have made the desires of the flesh wither away, but instead she kept finding that in quiet moments she had an intense awareness of her skin under her respectable dress. As if her body had simply grown used to wringing pleasure out of secrecy and fear. Sometimes it took all her self-control not to send Jeanne out of the room on a pretend errand, so that she could hike up her skirt and do with her hands what she and Victoire might have done together.

If Victoire were here, instead of busy at Versailles, offending Madame de Maintenon, the woman who was very likely to be the king's next mistress.

Marie Catherine wished she had some distraction. Enforced

solitude made her walk back along the paths of earlier memories. She remembered a dinner her father had hosted for a group of lords from the parliament, before his ennoblement, and how she, a child, had sneaked down in her nightgown to catch a glimpse of the lords and ladies dressed in silk and velvet. Her mother had presided over the table in utter silence, picking at the slivers of truffle on her sweetbreads, her mouth pulled into a servile smile. Marie Catherine knew now that her father would have enjoined her to speak as little as possible, for her accent betrayed her bourgeois roots. When a lady caught sight of Marie Catherine peeping through the door, her father had taken her by the hand and made her recite some pretty verses, for which she was rewarded with applause and a thimbleful of wine spirits flavoured with lemon oil and musk.

The next morning her father had woken her up early, hungover and stern, and whipped her with a willow switch from the garden. She was not to interrupt his business unless she was called on to do so.

But he could also be kind, when it was not a matter of business. He bought her silk dresses, a singing canary in a wicker cage, every volume of *Artamène*, which he might reasonably have denied her on the grounds that it did not do to let young girls read novels containing the opinion that marriage amounted to slavery. Instead he had lent her the books from his own library, verse and drama and science, which he so rarely opened himself, and had told her, 'You may think whatever you want in private, my dear, but do your duty and keep those beliefs that might upset decorum to yourself. Your spirit is free, but your speech and your conduct must be ruled by custom.'

She missed him, now. He had died when she was twenty-five, outliving her mother, but encumbered, as he grew older, by a tumour that swelled out of the skin of his neck and made his face painful to look at. No medicinal bleeding or draught of mercury had helped contain it – instead it festered from repeated, failed bleedings. At the end, he had seemed to Marie Catherine exhausted, barely recognising her face or the face of the doctor who attended him.

Sometimes she wondered what might have happened if it had been her mother who survived him. Would she have turned her face away when Marie Catherine came to her and begged for her help in escaping her marriage, as her father had? Perhaps she would have resigned herself too long ago to her own fate, to have much pity for Marie Catherine's.

But perhaps things might have ended differently. She was sorry, now, that she had never tried to know her mother. She had been only sixteen when she died, and pregnant with her own child.

The mourning dress Marie Catherine had worn for her husband's funeral was the same as that she had worn for her father's, lifted out from the chest where it lay and hastily re-trimmed, the sleeves altered to hide the work of moths. Mourning fashions did not change quickly, but the dress had grown tight across her breasts and waist, and it smelled of lavender and mould.

Now she had a chest full of such dresses.

A knock sounded on the door to her bedroom, and Arnaud opened the door without waiting for her response and said, 'There is a Mademoiselle in the hall waiting to see you, Madame.'

'Send her in.' Marie Catherine folded Victoire's letter up and tucked it into her sleeve. So the girl had made it back to Paris on the same weather that had brought her letter. Marie Catherine was full of excitement and nerves. She had wanted to see Victoire, and here she was, as if her imagination had called out to her and speeded her along the road. She hoped the news she had brought was no worse than before. She feared she had detected something mocking in Arnaud's smile as he declared her.

Maybe he would see Victoire in and then listen at the door, as Henri had done with Monsieur de la Reynie. In the past days she had often entered a room to find Caspar and Arnaud talking together, and when they stood up at attention she had been overcome with the belief that they were discussing her, and had forgotten what she had entered the room to do.

But when her visitor came to the door, it was not Victoire, but Mademoiselle de Scudéry. The old woman walked stiffly, with one arm supported by Arnaud and the other gripping an ivory-topped cane. A pearl brooch fastened her dress high on her throat, and her grey hair frizzed out of its simple arrangement at the nape of her neck, all of which made her look as if she had undertaken a long journey.

Marie Catherine leaped up from her seat.

'Forgive me, Mademoiselle. My servant did not adequately announce you. If I had known it was you, I would have come down to meet you.' She gestured to Jeanne, and the servant girl jumped off the claw-footed chair in which she was sitting and beckoned Mademoiselle de Scudéry over to it. Marie Catherine hoped that her disappointment at seeing the old writer, in place of Victoire, didn't show too clearly on her face.

Mademoiselle de Scudéry lifted her cane from the floor by a few inches and wagged it back and forth sternly. 'Please don't mind the decorum. I have come to pay a visit to a friend' – here she paused to catch her breath and lowered herself, with Jeanne's help, into the chair that the servant girl had just vacated – 'to a friend, I hope I may say, in grief. I would have come earlier, but your husband's death has attracted such attention that I feared you might feel overcrowded by mourners whose interest was more in observing a scandal than in offering comfort. Besides, I have been confined to my bed with a great pain in my ear. You will have to speak loudly.'

'Thank you,' said Madame de Cardonnoy.

She stood for a minute in front of Mademoiselle de Scudéry, her hand braced on the chair in front of her writing table, caught awkwardly between standing and sitting. Mademoiselle de Scudéry's speech had flowed out of her mouth as if she had rehearsed it, and Marie Catherine was uncertain how to respond. Some part of her was still prepared only for Victoire, and found the writer as awkward as Cendrillon must have found her fairy godmother, when that woman first appeared to lift her out of the kitchen ash.

Mademoiselle de Scudéry raised an eyebrow, not unkindly, and Marie Catherine realised she must look silly, standing with one hand half outstretched as if she was afraid that her guest might fall out of her chair. She sat.

Jeanne, standing by the door, gave a discomfited little curtsey and stepped outside, the door clicking shut behind her.

'I'm very sorry to have missed your gathering on Saturday. Since my husband's death there is little of polite society that I regret, but I truly did want to meet your friends,' Madame de Cardonnoy said, loudly.

'You missed very little,' Mademoiselle de Scudéry told her. 'My house is humble, and many of my friends are as old as I am.'

'All the better,' Marie Catherine said. 'One could avoid hearing about every fashionable gentleman's latest lovers.'

She felt a deep gratitude for Mademoiselle de Scudéry's impeccable manners. Already she was falling back into the rhythm of play-modesty and glowing praise that reigned in Madame de Fontet's salon. It was as if Mademoiselle de Scudéry had momentarily swept aside all the dumb silence and piety that mourning required and allowed her to breathe a little.

'Do you imagine, then, that the old do not love?' Mademoiselle de Scudéry asked, archly. 'I see you have not read your Plato.' But then she bowed her head. 'Forgive me, I did not come here to scold you.'

'Never mind.' Madame de Cardonnoy spoke quietly, and then realised that Mademoiselle de Scudéry could not have heard her. But the old woman nodded as if she had understood.

'You know I never married,' Madeleine de Scudéry said after a few moments of silence. 'Nor do I particularly regret the husband I might have had, and so perhaps what comfort I have to offer may seem unkind.'

'I will forgive you, as long as you are more circumspect than the Lieutenant General of Police, who wished to accuse me of his murder.'

She was surprised at the relief she felt, saying the words aloud. She had been accused of her husband's murder. Perhaps that was what they said about her, in the salons she had frequented.

'Very well.' Mademoiselle de Scudéry looked up from her hands and met Marie Catherine's gaze, with a look that was kind and also deeply weary. 'Your husband's death is, without doubt, an atrocity. It is right that you should wish to see his killer brought to justice, and it is right that you should pray for his soul, and mourn him as custom and duty demand. But remember that you are not the first lady to be mismatched in her family's choice of husband, or to conduct your life to a great extent apart from him. There you are joined by many worthy women, whose aspirations were greater than to be a man's servant. If the bond between you and your husband was more one of duty than of love, do not allow yourself to think that you are guilty in his death for this reason. One can respect a man, and behave honourably towards him, and not love him, and there is no crime in that.'

Throughout this speech Mademoiselle de Scudéry had spoken with the calm, clear projection of an orator. It was as if she had stepped through a doorway, into the world of her work, where the course of history was decided through speech, where heroic men and women lived and died by their words.

A better world, Marie Catherine had thought when she was a girl who still believed that she might find a place like the courts of *Artamène*. Now she pulled the edge of her widow's veil across her face and used it to dab at the water seeping from her eyes. She could have told the old Sappho a tale, but she could not match her forthrightness.

She was more guilty, she knew, than Mademoiselle de Scudéry believed.

'Oh, I beg your pardon.' Mademoiselle de Scudéry scraped her chair across the floor and put a hand on Marie Catherine's knee. 'I am afraid I have overstepped myself. Or perhaps your situation is not what I understood it to be.'

Madame de Cardonnoy dropped the corner of her veil, put her hand over Mademoiselle de Scudéry's bony one, swallowed. Her voice came out just above a whisper.

'I feel … I am not free to speak as I would wish to.'

Mademoiselle de Scudéry inclined her head closer, so that Marie Catherine could smell the faint scent of musk that clung to her neck, the soft scent of her powder, and the frizzed ends of her hair were nearly touching Marie Catherine's cheek. Her mother, if she had lived, would not have aged this way. But she felt for a moment that she could reach back through time and make this woman into her mother.

'Speak louder, child,' Mademoiselle de Scudéry said gently. 'I cannot hear you.'

Madame de Cardonnoy leaned in, closer still, until her nose was nearly brushing Madeleine de Scudéry's ear and she could picture her words falling into that curved shell, as if down a well.

I am afraid, she might have whispered then. If she had dared.

But in the end she wiped her eyes and turned her face away.

'I am sorry,' she said. 'I was overcome, for a moment.'

'Forgive me. I was given to understand that your marriage was not a love match, and so I thought perhaps I should speak frankly.'

Her voice had lost its strength, and now she sounded uncertain and old.

'Is that what Madame de Fontet told you?'

'It is.'

Madame de Cardonnoy shook her head. 'It isn't a lie. That isn't what upset me.' She found herself looking at the window. Mademoiselle de Scudéry's face pushed her gaze away as if it were the repelling pole of a magnet. 'It's true that I was married very young, according to my father's wishes and not my own. Now I imagine the rumour is that I took the example of Madame de Poulaillon or the Comtesse de Soissons and attempted to do away with my husband. But if my marriage was unhappy, it doesn't mean that I was willing to murder to escape it.'

It was as close to a confession as she could come. Her throat felt as if it were closing up.

'I see.' Mademoiselle de Scudéry sighed and sat back in her chair. 'You know, in my youth I often imagined the kingdom of Sauromates, where the Amazons reigned by their own customs, surrounded by the desert that protected them from encroachment by the armies of men.'

'I remember.' Marie Catherine wiped her eyes with the edge of her veil. 'I read of it in *Artamène*, when I was a girl.'

'What one does not think of, in daydreams, is the enormity of the task. How many men and women must have fallen in battle, to carve out that country for the Amazons. How much good farmland must have been razed, to make that encircling wasteland. And yet, nevertheless, one wishes to be free.'

'It has always seemed to me that you are.' Marie Catherine held herself very still. She could imagine herself, easily, falling at Mademoiselle de Scudéry's knees, begging for her advice, her help, her forgiveness. As if the novelist were her own mother. And yet she knew that she would not do so. Likewise, she felt the great circumspection of Mademoiselle de Scudéry's sympathy – veiled in metaphor, expressed as a long-ago dream.

How did one ever cross that gap, into the mystery of another human? When she and Victoire had first kissed, in a cabinet at Madame de Fontet's, where Marie Catherine had been drunk on rossoly. How terrified she had been, how the terror didn't matter, she opened her mouth and found the girl's teeth, and Victoire put her hands against her face and asked her, *Are you all right? Have I hurt you?* while she closed her eyes and trembled from the fear and the sudden flame of desire that she had thought would be cold inside her forever. How had Victoire been brave enough? Marie Catherine had laughed with her in the salons and held her hand in her carriage for a month, and she had never been brave enough to do anything more.

And yet she would not have consented to the murder of her husband, and Victoire, in her eagerness to rescue her, had not asked. *A woman who cross-dresses makes herself a monster.* Marie Catherine did not believe it. But she couldn't escape the fear that what lay between Victoire and her had been poisoned by the careless violence of her own desire.

'I do enjoy a great degree of freedom,' said Mademoiselle de Scudéry. 'And yet I would have wished the same for many others who do not.' She took her hand back from Marie Catherine's shoulder and rested it on the head of her cane. 'It is unfortunate, that we live in such times. But it is the way of things that each attends to his own affairs, and fears to overextend his power in the aid of his friends.'

'There are still those who protect their friends, at their own expense.'

'So there are.' Mademoiselle de Scudéry sat back in her chair, as if something had been decided. 'And I have tried to do so, when I'm called upon.'

Marie Catherine couldn't think how to respond to that. 'Can I have the servants bring you something? Coffee, or something to eat?'

'No coffee, thank you, it upsets my digestion. If you had a glass of brandy ...'

'Of course. I'll have Jeanne bring in some sweets as well.'

She went to the door of her cabinet and called, then came back to her seat.

'Do you ever believe,' she began, 'that your life would have been happier if you had not imagined that land, and had it to compare with this one?'

'No,' said Mademoiselle de Scudéry very solemnly. 'No, I think that my life would have been a worse one.'

They watched each other for a moment. Then the door opened and Jeanne came in with a tray and, like that, the enchanted moment was broken, and they sat together and talked of the weather, and the court, and the tales of Herodotus, as if neither had spoken any word that verged on a confession.

Jeanne was in the entrance hall when Caspar and Arnaud escorted the baron's old valet, Henri, through the front door of Hôtel Cardonnoy. The valet was stumbling between them, looking quite drunk, his greying shirt – for he had not kept the Cardonnoy servants' uniform when he left – splashed down the front with mud, and his shoes tracking something unpleasantly slick and noxious-looking onto the carpet. Jeanne held her handkerchief over her nose, and for a moment she considered escaping up the stairs and out of the old valet's sight, but then his bleary eyes focused on her, and he took two wavering steps away from the servants escorting him and fell down at her feet.

'Slut,' he muttered.

Jeanne lifted her skirts out of the way and used the tip of her slipper to nudge him, and the mud he was wearing, away from her.

'Where did you find this creature?' she asked Caspar, in the most impeccable accent she was capable of.

The guard shrugged. 'Tavern. Madame wants to question him.' He also looked somewhat the worse for drink.

'In *this* condition?' Jeanne made a face at the valet, who was struggling to rise, cursing the while.

Another shrug. 'Took a while to talk him into leaving.'

Arnaud came forward and hoisted Henri up by the armpits. The old valet stuck his arm out and pointed at Jeanne. His eyes took a moment to focus on her face.

'You'll pay for what you did,' he stuttered. 'You lied.'

'Clean the vomit off your shoes before you begin accusing me,' said Jeanne. 'If you call me any more names, I'll beat you with the poker.' She thought she would have done it, too, and damn Arnaud and Caspar if they tried to stop her. It was not the first time any of them had returned to the hôtel drunk together. Jeanne had long suspected that they funded their outings by skimming the cream from the household expenses, and that Henri even put his hand directly into the baron's purse occasionally, to make up for the baron's stinginess. She loathed him for it, not because the stealing offended her, but because she couldn't believe he had the courage. But God knew he hadn't been sent out of the household with the money for two weeks' worth of drinking.

Arnaud leaned the valet against Caspar and took a long step towards her.

'Give your tongue a rest, Jeanne. He loved Monsieur.'

Henri had always filled her with a kind of revulsion, and not merely because he lorded it over the other servants, or deigned to give her orders, or called her dog-faced when she wouldn't flirt with him. He had served the baron since he was a boy, and he was proud of it – proud of his loyalty, of his uniform, of the baron's trust. She might have been like him, she thought, in another life, a man whose whole self revolved around his master.

'He's a pig,' said Jeanne. 'What does Madame want him for?'

'I'm not privileged to know,' said Arnaud, putting on a mockery of a gentleman's accent.

'She wants to talk about what he said to the police, Jeanne,' said Caspar, more calmly. 'What else could he be for?'

'He's good for nothing, as far as I know,' Jeanne snapped.

Caspar shrugged, as if to say there was nothing further he could offer, and steered Henri down the hall and towards the kitchens.

Madame de Cardonnoy was waiting in the large salon. She had gone, at first, to the kitchen, to see Henri where he was bedded down by the warm stove, but he was incoherent and only half able to rouse himself to answer questions. The lackeys who had brought him in were themselves unsteady on their feet, good for little other than sitting around the kitchen table and toasting bread and cheese on the end of a long fork.

She left them to it, with instructions that they were to bring her husband's valet to her once he had slept it off, and in the meantime they should at all costs prevent him from leaving. The cook sighed in her direction as she left, and informed Madame de Cardonnoy that she should expect supper to be delayed, for the kitchen boy was not yet back from the market. She could tell that he resented having a trio of drunk men taking up space around his table, especially so early in the afternoon. She waved him away. Let supper come when it was ready, let the boy take as long as he liked at the market – only make sure that the valet Henri harmed no one and did not leave without speaking to her. The cook shook his head and turned out his bowl of bread dough next to Caspar's elbow. The two lackeys performed half-hearted bows, still seated.

She left with the distinct feeling that they would begin talking about her as soon as she was gone.

In contrast with the steaming warmth and activity of the kitchens, the salon was cold, and for a while Marie Catherine stretched out on the chaise longue and closed her eyes, her veil pulled tightly around her in lieu of a blanket. She didn't want to call Agnès, the chambermaid, to have her make up the fire. After a while the door opened and Jeanne came and looked over the back of the chaise.

'Did you tell Caspar to bring that man here, Madame?'

'I did.'

Jeanne curtseyed. 'Very well then.' She sounded even more disappointed than the cook.

'You wish he was gone?'

'He cursed me in the hallway.'

'I hope he may be able to tell me some things that relate to the circumstances of my husband's death.' Finally Marie Catherine sat up and tugged her veil back into place. Jeanne had turned her face away, but she could see the girl's sceptical look. If Jeanne, too, turned against her, it would be worse than anything the cook or Arnaud could manufacture.

'He means you ill, Madame,' said Jeanne. 'He will try to find another way to get his revenge, even if he ruins himself to do it.'

'Perhaps,' said Marie Catherine. 'But my husband had dealings with a renegade priest before he died, and I think Henri can tell me who it was.'

Jeanne bit her lip. 'If I were you, I would think it unwise to have dealings with such people.'

'Thank you, Jeanne. You may go.'

Jeanne left with all courtesy, but her unhappiness hung in the room after she had gone, like thick air before a rainfall. Madame de Cardonnoy felt stretched thin with waiting, ready to lie back and fall asleep again on the stiff cushions of the chaise.

I have just a few questions to ask you, she thought, rehearsing the scene in her head. *I am ready to forgive our previous misunderstanding, and I hope that you can do the same.* And she smiled, for a visitor who was not present, and held out her hand graciously to be clasped or kissed.

Chapter Thirteen

——

A little way past Les Invalides, not so far from the river and out of the noise of traffic from the main road, there was a church, not grand, with a belltower barely higher than the roofs of the houses around it, a pitiful weedy graveyard the size of a lady's handkerchief laid on the ground, and a priest's residence behind it. Madame de Cardonnoy bade her coachman stop the horses on the main road and wait there. She could see at a glance that the narrow alley would pose problems for the passage of the carriage, and she was torn between her impulse to keep the lackey within easy shouting distance and her desire to run this errand without an audience.

Jeanne, too, she asked to wait.

That morning she had also sent Caspar and Arnaud out of the room while she spoke with Henri, asking them to wait by the door to her salon and to enter only if she called. Her husband's valet had stood in front of her for a moment and then, once the doors were closed, he threw himself down in an armchair across the room and clutched his head, ignoring all rules of etiquette. She could have counted on one hand the times she had seen the valet sit down in her presence. But she knew that her husband entrusted him with his secrets, for they were rarely ever apart.

Now, as she opened the gate to the churchyard, there was a light, cool rain falling, and the mud sucked at her satin shoes. The alley wasn't as foul as the main road, and from the long grass and the gnarled tree whose bare branches overhung the entrance rose up a smell of green, wet growing things, a spring smell almost, although the weather was still biting and it was some weeks, she thought, until the first buds would appear on the branches of that old apple tree.

A strange joke, to plant an apple in a churchyard. But it made her feel certain that she had come to the right place.

She wished Victoire were there with her. Perhaps she should have told her where she was going – but she couldn't put this information in a letter, and she didn't dare wait after talking to Henri. It was the sort of adventure the girl might have enjoyed once, a secret visit to the home of a renegade priest. Perhaps the churchyard would be haunted by his familiar spirits. Perhaps anything at all could happen.

She tried to call up the girl's presence beside her, to keep her company as she walked through the churchyard, and for a moment it felt as if she was there, a transparent column of warmth that moved just outside the edges of her vision. She was dressed in her man's coat and she was neither a man nor a woman.

Then Marie Catherine passed under the apple tree and a strange feeling crept up the back of her neck, as if some creature had reached out from its branches to twitch its fingers under her veil. Her sense of an invisible companion dissolved. Her shoes squelched in the mud. Perhaps she should simply have sent the priest's letter to Monsieur de la Reynie, when she found it. But it had been written so long ago.

Henri had not wanted to speak to her, after she had called him. But he had been chastened by the encounter with the police. The smell of drink wafted off him. She had no idea when her husband had last paid his wages.

She had spoken to him calmly, sadly, of the friendship that she knew he had had with her husband. With such clarity in her intention that she had actually, for a moment, felt herself beginning to weep, and then she had dried her tears hastily on her sleeve and felt ashamed, because she was weeping for something that she did not really feel – for the servant boy with the beardless chin who had attended her husband on her wedding night, and not for her husband, and not for this grieving man who no longer wore the gold braid of her household.

The rain in the churchyard made a whispering sound. She

reached the little blackened oak door that marked the entrance to the priest's residence and knocked, first gently, then louder, the hammer end of her fist ringing an echo from the wood. For some time no one answered, and in those few minutes the rain slackened off into a chilly mist, which dampened the widow's veil and made it stick to Marie Catherine's cheeks. She knocked again.

Finally the door opened a sliver, and a woman of about forty with flyaway yellow hair peeked out into the cold. She would have been handsome, Marie Catherine thought, if her face had not been so gaunt, and if she did not crouch a little in the doorway, as if she might be about to get down on her knees and press her forehead into the doorstep to atone for some offence.

'I'm looking for Père Roblin,' Madame de Cardonnoy said.

'Oh no.' The housekeeper began to edge the door shut, as if that was all the reply needed, and Marie Catherine leaned into the doorway and put her elbow in the crack, in case she should decide to close the door entirely. 'He's not here, Madame.'

'Where can I find him?'

'No, no.' The blonde woman shook her head. 'I really could not say.'

'Then let me come in, at least.' She had a sudden, ridiculous vision of the priest couching in a corner of the hallway, with a bread knife in his hand or perhaps a chalice used to perform Mass, waiting to brain her for intruding. Perhaps she should have had the coachman accompany her, or at least Jeanne.

'I don't know, Madame,' said the housekeeper.

'Please, it's raining. My cloak's wet through. At least let me come in for a moment to dry it. I just want to speak to your master.'

She had almost wedged herself in to the open doorway, and now the housekeeper gave one last weak shove in an attempt to close it, then softened and held the door open for her.

'Only I cannot help you at all, Madame. Père Roblin is out on business, seeing to his flock, and I could not say when he will return. I cannot help you with what you want.'

Marie Catherine stepped inside. The hallway was dark, laid with big, uneven flagstones that seemed to breathe cold up into the room. The housekeeper led her into the kitchen, which had only one narrow window, but where the embers of a fire glowed cheerfully. Marie Catherine felt her face touched, in turn, by the fire's warmth and the draught from the hallway. The housekeeper came up behind her and took her cloak from her hands.

'I wanted to ask—' she began, but the housekeeper interrupted her.

'We can't do anything for you now, Madame. If there is something you desire, I think it is best that you should pray.'

Marie Catherine crossed her arms over her chest and looked the housekeeper up and down. She was small, frail, with a little caved-in pigeon's chest, and beautiful hands with perfectly oval nails, although her skin was chapped with cold and kitchen work. Under Marie Catherine's gaze, she folded in on herself, lowered her head and covered her mouth to conceal a wet, hacking cough.

'That's not the kind of assistance I require,' Marie Catherine said softly, and the housekeeper raised her head and shot her a look full of concern. Perhaps she heard the secret triumph in Marie Catherine's voice – because, yes, here was something she could use. She hadn't been wrong.

'Then what, Madame? I swear, I do not know where he is.'

'My husband—' Marie Catherine began, and the housekeeper put her hand over her mouth and then, as quickly as a startled bird, took Marie Catherine's cloak from where it had hung by the fire and touched her on her shoulder, and began to try and dress her, to steer her out and away.

'Please, Madame, no husbands. I can't help you.'

'Stop,' Marie Catherine protested and, when the woman's light hands had finished clasping the cloak and gripped her more firmly to push her away, she raised her voice and twisted her shoulders to escape her grasp. 'Stop!'

The housekeeper, startled, came back at Marie Catherine and shoved her towards the door and they struggled briefly, Marie Catherine snagging her mantle on the poker and then trying to hang on, absurdly, to the mantel of the fireplace as the housekeeper pushed her away. She was taller than the other woman, but her shoes were slippery with mud. There was a tearing sound as Marie Catherine's cloak ripped, and then she stumbled backwards and the housekeeper, exhausting her strength, lost her grip on Marie Catherine's arm and doubled over in a fit of coughing.

'Forgive me, Madame,' she mumbled, when she had her breath back.

'No, forgive me. I swear I am not looking for what you think I am. My husband – I believe he was a – a friend, we'll say, of Père Roblin. I would like to speak to him. That is all. I think my husband may have come here, before, to speak with the priest. And I'd like to know whether he did.' She was babbling, she knew.

The housekeeper shook her head. 'I couldn't say.'

Henri, too, had refused to answer her questions at first, when she summoned him back to Hôtel Cardonnoy. With blank incomprehension, and then with nastiness. *Why don't you look for Père what's-his-name up your skirt, Madame?* And she had told him that she would call in Caspar and Arnaud and tell the two lackeys that Henri had made such comments about her person. They were his friends, but they would have beaten him if she had ordered it, in the spirit of correction. When Monsieur de la Reynie's men had thrown him out of the hôtel, they had willingly helped.

I forgive you, she'd said. And then, *I found his letters to the priest. Can you tell me, at least, whether they were love potions, whether he was involved with some other lady?* Henri had idolised the baron, she knew. He had loved him. She knew him. And so she had received an address, an account of the baron's visits, and Henri had received a place to sleep in the kitchen, good food, what was due to him of the salary that the baron had long left unpaid, or had debited against the cost of the cloth for his gold-braided uniform. The valet knew he was betraying his old master, she thought. But he was dirty, and hungry, and he had run out of money for drink, so she had only to do what she could to make it easy for him to accept the shelter she was offering. He knew how it stood, she thought. But his master was dead, and he was exhausted and had no proof against her.

The priest's housekeeper, however, she did not know how to play.

'When did he leave?' Marie Catherine leaned forward, gripping the housekeeper's forearms. The woman sighed, shook her head.

'It was four days ago, Madame. I don't know when he will be back. He travels sometimes, he has a benefactor outside Paris who requires him, who he gives spiritual advice to.'

'And if I described my husband, could you tell me if he'd been here?'

'I don't know, Madame. I'm only in the kitchen, and I answer the door when the father isn't available, but I don't know anything about people who come to seek his advice. There are many people who come to hear about God or to ask for absolution – the priest doesn't reject anyone, he has a good heart. I don't ask any man or woman for a name. I haven't asked for yours, just the same. I know nothing, truly.'

'Of course,' Marie Catherine said, 'a good servant doesn't pry into her master's affairs. But surely you've served in this house, you must have some idea of who comes and goes, even if the father's business is a mystery to you. What I want is only an idea of what my husband might have discussed with Père Roblin, even to know for sure whether he came here. Even the address of some friend of his, who might know more, that would help me immensely.'

Marie Catherine could see that the woman was near tears, but it didn't change what she needed. She pulled up the chair that stood by the kitchen table and sat her down in it, as if she were a doll.

'It must be very difficult to be alone in this house, in the winter. Do you come from Paris? Or is your family outside the city?'

The housekeeper sniffed. She was taking advantage of the reprieve in questions to wipe her eyes, as surreptitiously as she could, with the edge of her sleeve.

'I've only a brother and his wife, Madame, and they and their children are ...' She caught herself, coughed again, made a gesture that encompassed a vague idea of *elsewhere, not in Paris*.

'You must miss them.'

'Oh, it's been a long time.' The housekeeper nodded at the table, her hands tucked primly in her lap, not meeting Madame de Cardonnoy's eyes, neither trusting her nor brave enough to tell her to leave.

'I hope,' Marie Catherine said, leaning against the table, trying to make her voice warm, almost conspiratorial, 'that Père Roblin pays your wages regularly enough that you can go to visit them sometimes. Holy men often forget things of the material world, and I imagine that might make it very difficult to serve them.'

She had bought Henri, although he might hate her for it. She thought she could buy this woman, too.

'In truth, it's been some years since I have seen them, Madame,' said the housekeeper.

'Perhaps I could give you a gift,' Marie Catherine suggested. 'The priest certainly doesn't need you, if he's travelling to see a patron. Close up the house, pack up a little money or linen to bring to your family and leave the city for a while.'

'I couldn't, Madame.' The housekeeper's expression was unreadable – it might have been gratitude, terror or resignation.

'Listen to me,' Marie Catherine said. She put her hands on the table and leaned towards her. 'You know that something wrong was happening in this house, or else you would not be so frightened.'

Her words came out harsher than she had intended, and again the housekeeper was lifting her hands, as if to shield her face, as she'd done when Marie Catherine had struck her. She felt the guilt again, at her cruelty, but it was weak. She thought she would even kill this woman, if she had to, if it ensured her survival, and that of Victoire, and that of her children.

At that moment the door to the kitchen creaked open and Marie Catherine jumped back, picturing the priest returned, or else some other purchaser of his services, slipping through the front door to demand a spell or an augury. Or La Reynie himself, his face freezing over into grim satisfaction at having caught her in this place.

Instead the person who stood at the doorway was a boy of about twelve, his chin jutting out stubbornly as he met Marie Catherine's eyes. He had the housekeeper's snub nose, but his face, even in winter, was red with running about in the cold sun, and he carried himself like a little cat, both timid and angry.

'You must go, Madame,' he said. His voice was still a child's voice.

Madame de Cardonnoy could feel her pulse thrumming in her temples from her moment of shock.

The housekeeper's chair scraped across the flagstones as she stood up.

'Michel, you are to wait upstairs and out of sight while there are visitors.'

The boy shook his head, his chin jutting out a little more, mulishly.

'We don't need noble ladies here, and this one is upsetting you!'

Madame de Cardonnoy took a few steps towards the door. The boy Michel was still small, and as she approached him he had to tilt his head up to look into her face, which he did gracelessly, his lips pressed into a tight line.

'This child is the priest's son, isn't he?' she asked quietly.

'I'm *not* that man's son,' Michel exclaimed, but the housekeeper put her hands on the table and began to cry.

Marie Catherine slipped her hand into the pocket of her dress, pulled out a handkerchief embroidered with a border of blooming violets, and a purse full of money. She gave the handkerchief to the housekeeper and kept the purse in her left hand, weighing it awkwardly in her palm. Finally she counted out a few écus and put them on the table.

'Here is what I would like to know,' she said. 'My husband visited Père Roblin about two years ago. At the time he was having legal difficulty over a piece of land. I believe he asked for some spiritual intervention, either to influence the court that ruled on his case or to persuade the buyer to abandon his lawsuit. I want to know whether you remember him, and I want to know whether he continued to visit the priest after the matter was resolved.'

Michel stepped towards the table, reaching for the coins she'd laid there. His mother made a peremptory gesture, but it was Marie Catherine's hand on his shoulder that stopped him. He looked up at her and flushed, but his hand stilled before he could push the purse away.

She could see that he was a proud child. It must pain him to be the priest's illegitimate son, never acknowledged by his father, hidden away from guests. It must pain him to understand that he and his mother needed the money that Marie Catherine was offering.

'My husband was about so tall,' she said, gesturing at the height she intended. As she spoke, the baron's figure took shape in the air before her, solid, tall, expressionless. 'He was in his forties, he still had all his hair, but it was turning silver, and he wore it cropped close under a wig. He had dark eyes, his eyebrows grew very wild and he did not trim them, he had one rotten molar and a brown stain on his front tooth. His nose was shaped – like so. Bigger than mine, with thin nostrils. His carriage was drawn by a pair of bay horses, the crest on the carriage door was a wild pig and the name under it was Cardonnoy.'

'He was here,' said the boy, very quickly. 'He took charms from the priest.'

239

He did not say, *from my father*. The housekeeper crossed the room and pinched him by the ear.

'He was not here,' she said. 'I do not know him.'

'He was here and he paid for spells and he talked a long time with the priest,' insisted Michel, twisting free of her. 'He wanted the favour of a lady at court who was close to the king. He wanted paying offices, and the friendship of the royal family, and to purchase an estate near Versailles. And he wanted protection from theft by his servants and his wife. He came many times.'

'Michel,' said his mother. 'That man is dead. He was murdered.' She shook her head and looked at Marie Catherine. 'The boy doesn't know anything. He invents things. Will you bring the police here for that?'

'I don't want to soil my husband's name needlessly.' She spoke sharply. The realisation that, finally, she'd found something to give La Reynie had caught her so tightly that her hands were shaking. She could take this and make it better. She could make the whole thing so clear that La Reynie would never look at her with a moment's suspicion. He would never see through her to Victoire.

'I *do* know,' Michel cut in. 'The priest never knew when I was listening in, and I heard his dealings.'

'When did he leave and where did he go?' Marie Catherine asked.

'He did not leave an address,' said the housekeeper.

'He didn't even leave a note or some money,' said the boy. 'He's been gone more than two weeks. We simply woke up and he had packed a travelling bag with his clothes and the contents of his strongbox during the night. We're nearly out of credit at the market.'

The housekeeper slapped him. Michel rubbed his pink cheek with an expression of quiet surprise, then of acceptance.

'You always take his side,' he murmured.

'My husband was killed not three weeks ago,' Marie Catherine said softly. 'You should not protect this priest. But you should leave Paris. If your boy knows what he says, the police may not take it lightly, even though he is a child.'

The housekeeper shook her head. 'You don't understand at all.'

Marie Catherine took the embroidered handkerchief from her

slack fingers and folded it into a square. Then, after a moment, she tossed it into the fire. She could feel the boy's eyes following her movement, and when she looked at him, he frowned at her, wondering, she thought, why she had thrown away such a delicate thing.

She had remembered the priest's letter, which instructed that her husband should find some cloth touched by the man he wanted to bewitch. She did not want anything of hers to stay in this house.

'Thank you,' she said, 'for your help.'

And she walked past the woman and her son to the door. The housekeeper did not try to see her out. She had left the money on the table. The bolt in the old oak door squealed as she pulled it open, and then she heard footsteps behind her in the corridor.

It was the boy Michel, red-cheeked and panting.

'If they catch Roblin, will they burn him like they did La Voisin the poisoner?'

Marie Catherine shook her head.

'I don't know. Only if he's guilty, I hope.' For a moment she nearly choked on the words. He was not guilty of the thing that she required him to be guilty of. Whatever else he had done.

'I hope they do,' Michel said coldly. 'I hope they burn him. He's a wicked man.'

Marie Catherine took a few steps back towards him, leaving the door ajar. The anger in his voice had shocked her. There was something terribly wrong with this child. She put her hands on his shoulders and the boy seemed to realise what he had said, for he bowed his head and coughed, twice, swiping the back of his hand across his face to try and hide his tears. A cold wind blew in from the outside, and for a moment she believed in the priest's spirits and knew that she had meddled in something she shouldn't have touched.

'Listen,' Marie Catherine said, 'your mother is trying to protect you. If you tell the police what you told me, if you say you knew of dealings in spells, they may blame you for knowing and having done nothing. If they come to ask you questions, you must tell them that you said nothing because you were afraid for your life, and your mother was afraid for hers. Do you understand?'

The boy was now crying quite openly. His nose and the tips of his ears had turned bright red. Marie Catherine pulled him into an embrace, and he hiccupped and flinched away when she touched him. She ran a hand over the back of his head and let him go.

One day Nicolas would be this big, she thought, and probably this headstrong and proud, but perhaps if she was lucky he would not be so badly hurt by life.

'If I'd known that speaking to the police would do anything, I would have done it as soon as I could find my way there,' Michel said. 'I would have betrayed him years ago. I wish someone had.'

Marie Catherine put her hand on his shoulder.

'Think of your mother,' she said. 'Remember what I told you.'

Outside, the rain had quickened. At first Marie Catherine pulled her cloak tightly around her, but then, as the shower wetted down her veil and pulled strands of her hair across her forehead, she let go of the cloak, pulled her skirts up above the ankle and ran through the churchyard, like a young girl.

'Home,' she called, rapping on the ceiling of the carriage, and the horses shifted restively and then pulled forward, their hooves echoing on the cobbled street.

It took her a long time to catch her breath, and all the while in the carriage her clothes breathed out that wet wool smell and, with it, the scent of smoke from the priest's kitchen, and of new mud.

That night she had no patience for the children. Her head ached, she felt soft and woozy, so she left Sophie and Nicolas with her supper half eaten and called for Jeanne to fill her a bath. Jeanne and Anne wrestled the enormous copper tub up the stairs and into her bedroom, moving bent-backed and bow-legged, like a pair of old washerwomen dressed incongruously in their hand-me-down silks. Jeanne carried two steaming pails of water up from the cauldron boiling in the kitchen, splashed her wrist painfully on the second trip and leaned against the wall at the top of the stairs to rest. Madame was sitting in her straight-backed chair at her writing table, combing out her long hair tangled from days under the stifling veil. Jeanne left her bucket and opened the doors along the hall on the ground floor until she found Arnaud and Caspar and the coachman playing cards around one of the baron's delicate gilt salon tables.

'Can't you bring water for Madame's bath?' she snapped. 'You're useless. She's been calling for you. I had to do half of your work myself.'

She left while they were still reluctantly unfolding themselves out of their chairs.

The burn on her wrist was turning brilliantly pink. She rubbed it a little, trying to make the pain fade, to no avail, and then she went back to Madame's room and took the comb from her hand and began untangling the baronne's hair, starting at the very ends, which fell nearly to her hips, working the comb up carefully towards the nape of her neck, which was hot to the touch.

When the lackeys came to the bedroom with their pails, Jeanne took them at the entrance and carried them to the tub, protecting Madame in her loose shift from the eyes of the men. She was pink and pensive by the lamplight, and her eyes had hollowed out in a way that made Jeanne think of pressing a finger into fresh bread dough. When she stripped down entirely and climbed into the bath, she hissed at the heat.

'Shall I add some water from the pitcher to cool it?'

'No, no. I want it hot. I've been cold all day.'

Jeanne could see the flush of heat moving across Madame de Cardonnoy's skin, from her breasts floating on the water up to her neck, her cheeks, the fleshy lobes of her ears. Jeanne took a damp cloth and began to scrub at the streaks of dye on her mistress's shoulders, working her cloth into a lather and then rubbing circles on Madame's skin, pulling her hair out of the way and looping it over her shoulder in a long rope, which floated and unravelled like golden pond weed. Her pubic hair, too, breathed and undulated slightly in the cloudy water. Jeanne poured a few drops of carnation oil into the bath, and the flower's spicy scent rose up with the steam. She ran the cloth across Madame's forehead and wasn't sure whether the droplets left behind were bathwater or fever sweat.

When Jeanne had helped her out of the high-backed tub, Madame de Cardonnoy groped her way to the bed and lay damp on the coverlet, curled up like a bean flower and shivering. Her face was very red. Her breasts left damp marks on her shift.

'Come up, Madame, sit by the fire, your hair needs to dry,' Jeanne said, but the baronne shook her head and curled her knees into her chest.

'I'm tired,' she said. 'It's so cold.'

Later Anne brought the children in to say goodnight, and she kissed their foreheads and then let her head roll limply into the pillow. Madame's fever was worse than it had been. Jeanne fetched hot bricks from the kitchen, wrapped them and packed them in around her. She wasn't sure if she should call for the doctor. Her mistress was half sleeping, not delirious, only much too warm. Jeanne could see her eyes moving rapidly under her papery closed lids, as if she were chasing some unobtainable object in her dreams. She sponged her forehead with a cloth, and Madame's eyes fluttered open. She made a swimming movement against the bed as if she were ready to flee.

'Give me—' she stuttered, and retched. Jeanne ducked and pulled the chamberpot from under the bed, while Madame de Cardonnoy gagged into her hair and then vomited a stream of clear bile into the pot. She'd barely touched her dinner. Jeanne looked to the door, wanting to call for Anne or for help, but she was afraid that one of the footmen would come instead, and she wouldn't let Caspar or Arnaud see Madame de Cardonnoy in this state. She put the pot in Madame's lap and began looping her hair into a thick rope over her neck, dampening a towel and sponging at the place where she'd soiled her shift. Madame flinched at the cold cloth, retched again, caught her breath and lay back. The room was full of the sharp smell of bile, of Madame's cloying sweat.

'Hush now, it's all right,' Jeanne said, uncertainly. She put the reeking pot back under the bed and brushed Madame's hair back from her face, watched as her eyes closed with a sigh, then blinked open again.

'If something happens to me,' Madame de Cardonnoy said.

'You should close your eyes,' said Jeanne. 'You've overtaxed yourself today.'

But it was true that men and women in the prime of health sometimes died like this. Jeanne didn't want to hear of it.

'Listen.' She gripped Jeanne's wrist with its limp, cold cloth. 'If something happens, take the children and the carriage and the trunk with my old shifts in it, and go to Mademoiselle de Conti. She is my closest friend. I want her to be in charge of the children's education.'

'Yes, Madame.' Jeanne bowed her head. She didn't want to think that what Madame was telling her was a genuine premonition. She didn't want to look at her face and maybe see her conviction written there. She didn't want to be entrusted with getting Madame's children to Mademoiselle de Conti.

'Get me a paper – I'm going to write it down. I want no other guardian appointed for them.'

Jeanne went to the writing table, rifled through the things inside it. Behind her, the door creaked on its hinges. She turned and saw Sophie's face peering through the gap.

'Oh, for heaven's sake,' said Jeanne, crossing to the door. 'Your mother's ill, you ought to be in bed.'

She took the girl by her shoulder and tried to steer her out into the hallway, but Sophie slipped away and climbed up into the big bed on which her mother was lying.

'Maman's sick.' Nicolas was behind her in the doorway, holding a tin soldier clutched in his fist. Jeanne tried to push him back towards the nursery, but he leaned into her skirt and wrapped his arms around her legs.

Sometimes Jeanne thought Sophie had a kind of instinct for chaos and disorder. Where there was broken china, where there was sickness, there she wanted to be. Now she lay down with her head on Madame's shoulder and knotted a fist in her mother's shift, which was still damp from Jeanne's careful dabbing with the cloth. Jeanne gripped her by the armpits and began to prise her up. Nicolas shadowed her steps like a kid goat.

'Darling, I want to sleep,' said Madame.

'I'll sleep with you!'

'You can't sleep next to your mother while she's sick. It's unhealthy,' said Jeanne. Sophie writhed in her grasp and turned until she was looking Jeanne in the eyes, furiously, as if she could burn through her skull with the force of her gaze.

'It's all right, Jeanne,' said Madame de Cardonnoy. 'Just until she falls asleep, then Anne can carry her up to the nursery.'

Her eyes were already fluttering shut. Sophie curled up against her side and clung there, sleepily, and they were stuck together so tightly that Jeanne sighed and picked Nicolas up, balancing his weight on her hip and humming as she carried him back to the nursery. He was pliant, sticky, beginning already to fall asleep when she tucked him in. Then she went to the yard to empty the chamberpot, and took a piece of the pheasant that Madame had not eaten from a tray in the kitchen, then lay down on her own pallet with her fingers still shiny with grease.

Madame wouldn't die. But if she did? Would anything stop La Reynie asking the servants about their master's death? Caspar or Arnaud would certainly tell him that Jeanne knew all of her mistress's deeds, whatever they were.

Jeanne woke sometime later in the night, with her skin running with sweat and her stomach heaving. She kicked off her blankets and wadded them up in a ball at her feet, and then the room became cold and she shivered with fever. It was a long way to the chamberpot tucked once more under the bed, and her legs shook as she squatted over it, humiliated, hearing the sounds of Madame asleep in the bed beside her and afraid that her sobbing breaths or the foul smell of diarrhoea would wake her up and let her see Jeanne's misery. Her legs were so weak she was afraid she would knock over the pot, or fall into it. She steadied herself against the bed, worked her way down onto her hands and knees once the nausea had released her, then crawled back to her pallet.

She woke up and it was already light. Sophie was gone from the bed. Someone had pulled Jeanne's blanket back up to her chin, and she felt dizzy and sweaty under it. She staggered up. Madame was at her writing table. When Jeanne went to her and touched her forehead, it was blessedly cool against her own hot, shivering hands. She felt the bile coming up her throat, swallowed, forced it back down.

'Ah, you're awake,' Madame de Cardonnoy said. 'I had Anne bring an extra blanket for you. Arnaud is to call a doctor if things take a turn for the worse, but as I'm recovered, I hope you will be too.'

Jeanne lay back down on her pallet, and Madame left the room. The ceiling tilted appallingly when she moved her head, and little dizzying pieces of dreams or memories played at the edge of her vision whenever she tried to grope her way back into sleep. Finally she dragged herself up, stumbling, and knelt down in front of the chest that held Madame's underclothes, packed away with lavender to keep them smelling fresh. She lifted the clothes out in a pile and looked at the empty bottom of the trunk, finding nothing, and so she began to refold everything, putting each shift back away neatly, that she might not be caught prying. Near the end her fingers caught on a waistband that was stiff, where the linen should have been soft and pliable. There was a hard knot in the fabric. She turned the shift inside out, found places where something heavy had been sewn into the seams with neat, small stitches. She closed her eyes, and her fingers counted out the smooth intervals of a strand of pearls, the loop and stone of a ring.

She did not think Madame had worn many of her jewels lately. But then they were not appropriate for a woman in deep mourning. She put the shift away with its sisters, then, on second thoughts, buried it deeper in the chest, where it would not be one of the first things a chambermaid might take out.

When she'd finished, she pulled the chamberpot back out from under the bed and immediately the lingering smell of shit made her sick. She retched and brought up nothing. Finally, in exhaustion, she stuck her fingers deep into her mouth and succeeded in spitting up a few spoonfuls of bile, which burned her throat and made a foamy scum on the bottom of the pot.

Her stomach had settled a little. She thought she'd never get the taste of it out of her mouth. After gathering her strength, she climbed into Madame's enormous bed and pulled the covers up over her. There was a line of sweat from her hairline down to the end of her spine. The feather mattress was so soft that, as she closed her eyes, she thought she might drown in it.

Chapter Fourteen

———

Madame de Cardonnoy had woken up all at once in the bright sunlight, hearing the noise of the day filtering in from the courtyard. The cook was back from the butcher's and was unloading baskets of meat with the help of the kitchen boys. Somewhere on the street a dog was yelping. The man who sharpened the knives was walking down the boulevard, calling for customers. She felt as if she had taken off her fever like an old, dirty dress.

She left Jeanne sleeping, sweaty and feverish on her pallet, and took her breakfast upstairs, with the children. Anne waited inexpertly at the table, pouring bittersweet coffee into Marie Catherine's patterned cup and cutting Nicolas's omelette into small pieces. Even the children seemed softer and better-behaved today, Nicolas looking up from his lap to ask, 'Are you better, Maman?' with an expression of sweet and childish worry. She'd left off her veil and wore only the black mourning dress, with a piece of lilac ribbon tied in bows around her wrists. She felt only the smallest traces of illness in her body. That she was thirsty. That the breeze from the open window in the children's room touched her face like cool relief. That everything in her vision seemed soft-edged and vaporous, as if she were looking at the world through a veil of steam.

'I'm much better, thank you. I feel entirely well.'

She led the children in their morning prayers, kneeling down on the nursery floor before the cross on the wall. Nicolas bent his head and mumbled fervently through the words he knew by rote, his eyes focused on some piece of the carpet in front of him, as if he was looking through it and into an invisible world. Sophie closed her eyes when she prayed, and her face became fiercely concentrated on some vision inside herself. Marie Catherine got up when she was finished and touched her children's hair.

'Be good today, please,' she said. 'I have some things to do.'

'Where are you going?' Sophie asked.

'I'll be back soon, sweetheart.'

She left the children and climbed into the carriage and wished that she could turn her desperation into something outside her. She must have a tale for Monsieur de la Reynie, and she believed she knew now how the pieces would come together. The renegade priest who had fled the city. The years-old letter. The thread that she would use to stitch them to her husband's murder. Once she had finished, it would look more real than the truth.

In the carriage she stroked the fur fringe on her cloak and imagined the weight of a marble figure beside her, as if the fairy of her creation was a friend, or a mother of whom she could ask advice. Help me, she thought. Give me some help outside myself.

Lavoie was in his studio when someone knocked on the door. For a while he ignored the sound. He was in his shirt sleeves, and his fingers were daubed with paint where he'd touched his palette carelessly. His boots were standing by the door. He'd have to clean his hands if he didn't want to get paint on his shoes, and he was absorbed in the painting that he'd finally begun – in the line of colour and light where the sea's waves met the edge of the sky. It was dawn over the burning city and smelled like the acrid, clean scent of oil and pigment.

He left his caller standing on the doorstep for some time, and for a while he thought the man must have left, but then after a few minutes of silence there was a renewed knocking. The pounding sent an unpleasant memory running up his spine. It was not, at least, night. In the street someone shouted his name, and he heard it dimly through the windowpane.

'Monsieur Lavoie! Your neighbour says that you are at home!'

Finally he washed off his hands and pulled the boots on, in no particular hurry. He chose the plain coat. The brocade one he wore to call on clients needed to have the cuffs washed. He thought his hair was probably mussed, but he didn't look at himself in the distorting mirror of polished metal that hung over his shaving basin.

The man at the door wore the Cardonnoy livery. Not one of the men who had beaten him. Or was he? It was as if Lavoie's vision shimmered when he looked at him, and he didn't know if he had seen him before. He had nearly slammed the door in the man's face, but the lackey stuck his foot in the gap and wrestled with him, panting, 'Excuse me, Monsieur Painter, Madame desires to speak with you, if you would kindly forgive this intrusion.'

Lavoie looked up across the street and saw the carriage waiting, the Cardonnoy seal on its door, a dark curtain drawn across the window, like a sealed coffin in which the lady was folded up for safe keeping.

The little police spy who Lavoie was fairly certain had been assigned to watch him was lounging across the street, his arms crossed, doing nothing to disguise his expression of interest. Lavoie met the boy's eyes, and the spy shrugged and pursed his lips to begin whistling.

'Madame sends her deepest regrets for your trials at the hands of her former servants and desires to do what she can to atone for their errors. If you would consent to let her in.' The lackey drawled out the words slightly mockingly, in a voice that made it clear he did not think Lavoie had the right to deny a baronne entrance to his house, and he was merely reciting a polite message that his mistress had impressed on him.

Lavoie stepped aside, making his face match the other man's mocking expression. This wasn't one of the men who had forced his way into Lavoie's house and beaten him. He was certain now, or nearly certain.

'Tell Madame she may make herself welcome,' he said.

The lackey went to the carriage and conferred with its occupant through the window while Lavoie watched from his doorstep. Then the man held the door open and a black-gloved hand emerged from the recesses of the carriage and braced itself on his arm, and a dress and veil and dainty black satin shoes climbed down from the running board and stepped across the muddy gutter. Madame de Cardonnoy released the servant's hand, and he followed at her heels as far as the painter's door. Lavoie wondered where her lady's maid was. Then Madame de Cardonnoy and the servant had reached him and she held out her gloved hand and said, 'Monsieur Lavoie, good morning,' and he had no choice but to take her hand and bow, which he did stiffly, his eyes on the police informer. When he looked accidentally at Madame de Cardonnoy's face, he saw that her blue eyes were a little hollow, feverishly bright, and a bronze-coloured curl had worked its way out from under her veil.

He was alarmed to realise that he still found her lovely. She was his own age, but she seemed older, like a kind of wicked fairy godmother. He had spent so much time rehearsing the words they had exchanged at their last meeting, trying to decide whether he forgave her for giving her husband the letter he'd written to her, that the woman before him now seemed like an allegory of herself, a figure in which he'd invested all his desire and anger. Had she read his thoughts from across the city and appeared on the morning breeze? He could almost have believed it.

'How can I help you, Madame?' Lavoie held the door open. She passed through it, stood in his hallway, brushed down her voluminous black skirts as if checking for mud, then looked up at him. Her lackey was hovering by the doorway.

'I want first of all to apologise for my husband's behaviour towards you. It was unconscionable and base of him, and although I could say that such behaviour does not reflect the kind of man he was, I know that saying so would do nothing to soothe your injury. If you will let me, I am here to make what amends I can.' She half turned towards the door, while Lavoie was still struggling to formulate a reply, and spoke to the lackey. 'Arnaud, will you go out and see that the coach isn't blocking traffic? The coachman may need to take it out to the boulevard.'

The servant bowed and left. Lavoie gaped at her.

'Get him back in here, Madame,' he said, once he'd recovered his faculties. 'There's a police informant on my front doorstep. It's bad enough that you came to my home *with* your servant. Do you have any idea of the kind of questions the police have asked me about you?'

It did not help his sense of irreality that he had been privately imagining this kind of meeting with her, and she wasn't reading her lines quite as he would have written them.

'He'll be gone for ten minutes moving the carriage,' the baronne replied, as if she hadn't heard his question. 'Even if I were here for an amorous meeting, that's not nearly enough time to get all this off and then on again, and I don't have my lady's maid to help me.'

At *all this*, she made an impish gesture that moved from the veiled crown of her head to the black hem of her dress, her black-gloved hands skimming past and dismissing the whole paraphernalia of mourning. Her expression and that quick movement of her hand had as much effect on Lavoie as if she'd stripped off all her clothes in his hall. Not because it made him picture her naked skin, although it did, but because she seemed so delicately confident that no one would touch her, that she wouldn't be harmed, and Lavoie himself was so afraid.

'You're mad,' he said. 'Did you kill your husband?'

'No.' She shook her head. 'How can you ask that? I was in the nursery with my children the entire night. Every servant in the house can vouch for me.'

She didn't seem taken aback by the question. Perhaps the police had been at her already and she was expecting it. Or perhaps she assumed that she did not have to answer for herself in front of Lavoie, that it didn't matter what he asked or whether he believed her answer.

'Madame, no one's accusing you of holding the gun. They seem to have picked *me* for that role, and I assure you I was quite as incapable that night as you were.'

'I didn't kill him, nor did I conspire to kill him,' she said. Very seriously, as though they were equals.

'And I'm sure it was a coincidence that he was out in Paris trying to find and murder your lover on the night of his death.' Lavoie planted himself by the door, watching the tiny movements of her face as she heard him out. Her glassy eyes might have expressed surprise or pity. His hands were unsteady, so he balled them into fists and crossed his arms over his chest. 'Your girl may have lied to the police, but I know I never set foot in your bedroom or had her there.'

'Don't be vulgar, please. You tried to visit me, my husband took

it the wrong way. That's all. Servants start rumours sometimes.'
She'd turned her back on Lavoie and walked to the edge of the
staircase. Her husband had tried that trick also, of not looking at
him when he spoke. The memory was, for a moment, uncanny.

'Yes, I'm sure that's all,' Lavoie spat. He was no longer trying to
adhere to the rules of politeness. A police informer listening at the
door would have been delighted. 'And what do you need now? A
little vial of orpiment to poison rats at Hôtel Cardonnoy? Don't act
like I'm a fool – I'm not one.'

He would have liked to imagine that she had come to his house
because she thought of him as he had been thinking of her. But he
wasn't going to permit himself to imagine that.

'Truly, Monsieur, I've never thought you were a fool.'

It would have been pleasant to be able to break the baronne's
calm, but she was still speaking as if they had met, by chance, in
Madame de Fontet's salon, and Lavoie's outburst was too minor to
be acknowledged.

'I came to apologise, for myself and for my husband, and to pay
you the money he owed you. For the portrait, which I will understand if you do not wish to complete. I don't expect to restore your
goodwill, but I owe you a debt.'

She took a purse out of her pocket and held it out to him. Lavoie
could see that it was heavy, but he felt a repugnance towards the
money. He waved her off.

'Don't try to buy me off, it's insulting. I'll keep your secret. I don't
know enough about you to betray you.'

'Take it,' she said. 'It's only what's owed to you – and something
for the harm my husband caused you.'

'Why don't you answer a question instead, Madame? It's one I've
been longing to know the answer to. Did you give Monsieur de
Cardonnoy my letter of your own free will? Did you know that
he would come here?' Lavoie's voice, he was ashamed to realise,
was shaking. He couldn't meet the baronne's eyes, so he turned and
looked at the wall, feeling again the humiliation of her husband's
visit, the knowledge that he would only ever be, to their kind, a
small man, as expendable as a loyal horse or hound.

The baronne's power had been her attraction. She had smiled at
him, and he had felt as if he could take her hand and let her draw

him through a door and into another world. Now she was standing in his own bare whitewashed hallway, and he was like any other creature who couldn't refuse her money.

He was already regretting how quickly he'd waved away her purse. There was less satisfaction in the knowledge that he couldn't be bought than there would have been in paying off his bill at the apothecary.

'I didn't give him your letter,' Madame de Cardonnoy said. She spoke hesitantly. He still couldn't bring himself to look at her. He was shocked when her voice cracked. 'He was in a rage and he broke down the door to my room and took my writing case. I thought he might kill me in front of my children.'

'Is that what happened?' Lavoie looked back at her. Her face was pink. She wiped her eyes with her thumb, as if she was alone. He might have tried to comfort her, but it felt indecent to acknowledge her distress, after the way he'd spoken.

'No,' she said. Already she looked almost recovered. The tears had dried up as quickly as they had appeared. 'I don't believe he would have killed me. But I did think he'd beat me. Perhaps if he had, he might have left you alone.'

'Why did you come here?' Lavoie asked her. He was realising that he really didn't know. He had the ideas presented by his inclination and by his resentment, which described to him two different versions of the same woman. Neither of whom was the baronne as she stood before him.

'What do you want, Monsieur Lavoie?'

She said it so archly, and with the same solicitous tone of courtesy, that Lavoie found himself wanting to play along, as if the game of polite compliments and subterranean meaning was a dance whose steps she was offering to teach him. She wasn't weeping. He wasn't injured. They were merely playing a game together, in which the distance between them was its own uneasy form of intimacy.

'Perhaps you could dig up your husband and kick him for me,' he said.

As an attempt to shock her out of her salon mannerisms, it was not quite successful, but it did momentarily wipe the sorrow off her face. Madame de Cardonnoy put a hand over her mouth to disguise her laugh.

254

'Sometimes I wish I could do that, too,' she admitted.

'What a strange coincidence.' Lavoie felt his anger loosening, almost against his will, as if he were a knot that the baronne had untied by laughing. This, also, was why he'd liked her, at first.

'I'm sorry for the part I had in what happened to you,' she said, and her words seemed very genuine.

'I'll recover.'

They stood in silence for moment, during which Madame de Cardonnoy tugged her gloves off, used them to fan her face limply and then put them back on. She seemed to be casting about for something to say.

'I wanted to ask,' she said finally, 'a moment ago – orpiment?'

'I spoke without thinking,' Lavoie said. 'It's used as a pigment, in painting.'

'I thought I'd heard it was used that way. I know you may think I am a kind of Madame de Poullaillon for asking.'

Lavoie smiled at her, although she had not been wrong to suggest that he thought her very like one of the ladies who had been brought to trial by La Reynie for trying to poison their husbands.

'It makes a yellow that doesn't fade with the passage of time. The clearest yellows – for a bird's wing, or a bolt of silk, or a tulip in bloom – all come from orpiment. And if you burn it, it turns into a kind of earthy red, such as you might use to enliven a lady's blush, or her lips, if mixed properly.' His hand, as he spoke, described a shape with an imaginary brush, which might have been a loose curl of hair or the bow of a woman's mouth. 'The brightest yellows are all painted with poison. Other yellows – saffron, Avignon berries, Dutch earth – they're duller, or they don't mix well with oil, or they fade after they're applied to the canvas.'

'How strange.'

The door creaked open and the lackey Arnaud reappeared.

'The carriage is moved, Madame. I'll go and fetch it when you're ready to leave.'

'Thank you, Arnaud,' she said briskly and then, without pausing, she continued a conversation that she and Lavoie had not been having. 'Monsieur Lavoie, if you are so hesitant to take payment for a portrait that can't be completed while my children and I are in mourning, perhaps you'd be willing to show me around your workshop? I'll look for a landscape, or some small piece there, and leave the portrait for another time.'

'Of course, Madame.' Lavoie bowed his way up the stairs. The lackey's presence had an effect on him such that he felt the continual need to bow, so as to avoid the impression of impropriety. Just as certainly, however, his excessive deference seemed to him flirtatious, the kind of deliberate and exaggerated courtesy that a man paid only to a woman he admired.

The baronne, as far as he could tell, suffered from no such embarrassment. Lavoie suspected this was because she was a much more accomplished liar than he was. Which ought to have put him back on guard, but instead he was drawn in her wake like a piece of wood eddying on a current. Perhaps the light of her charm would hide his defects.

'Arnaud, you may wait in the hall,' Madame de Cardonnoy said, before following Lavoie up the stairs.

In the workshop she paused at the door, drew in a deep breath and then pulled out her handkerchief to shield herself from the smell of sizing and paint that hung in the air. It was a smell that Lavoie rarely noticed any more, being so used to the tools of his trade: the rancid smell of oil, the tinny scent of cooking verdigris prepared for green pigment, smells of earth, distemper, the smoke of Roman vitriol or of blue ash, for the preparation of which one melted salt, ammonia, nitre and copper together in a crucible. He should have aired the room out more recently, but he hated the cold more than the smell. Madame de Cardonnoy herself trailed a faint breeze of orange flower and bergamot.

'Why are we continuing this charade, Madame?' he asked quietly, stepping close enough to her elbow that he could speak into her ear.

'What did you tell the police when they questioned you?' Madame de Cardonnoy whispered back to him.

'You do know how to get the servants out of a room, don't you?' His words came out biting, and somewhat louder than he'd intended. He hoped his tone didn't carry down the stairs.

'Please, Monsieur Lavoie. I don't know what happened after my husband left the hôtel and I've had a great deal of anxiety, wondering what the police may think.'

'They asked me why your husband came to my house. How he left me. What he said. Whether I had had an affair with his wife, which I'm sure the police are going to wonder about again, after today.' He looked over his shoulder involuntarily. He'd left the door to the workshop open, to avoid any appearance of secrecy – if the servant heard voices, if he wondered, if he came up the stairs. There was something perversely thrilling in the danger, which clipped his voice and made the skin on the back of his neck prickle.

Lavoie had no sooner noticed the thrill of bravery creeping up his shoulders than he cursed himself for it. He'd been a coward with the baron, when bravery might have saved him some pain, and now he'd suddenly discovered a taste for adventure, when it could only ruin him. Any idiot would have had the sense to throw Madame de Cardonnoy out on her ear.

'And when they asked you about your visit to my maid?' She was still speaking quite close to his ear, which gave the whole encounter an air of demented flirtation.

Lavoie sighed. 'Forgive me, Madame, if I had been let in on that story I might have been a better liar.'

'Jeanne never informed me that you had paid her a call,' the baronne said coolly.

'And she didn't tell me that I'd made love to her while she was dressed up in your clothes, so I suppose we were all surprised in our own way by that news.' His consciousness of her breath, close enough almost to stir his hair, was discomfiting, so he went to the table where some of his brushes were soaking and rattled them around in the jar.

'Was there anything else you had to lie about?' She reached out a hand towards him, admonishingly, the tiniest gesture, and with the heavy folds of her veil she looked once more like a statue that had come to life and was turning from stone into flesh. Again it was impossible to offend her.

'My neighbours found me that night. I was in no state to have killed a man.'

'Of course not.'

The truth was that that night had become a kind of closed room inside his head. He wasn't entirely sure what he would find if he opened the door, and he had the feeling that things inside it might have moved and slid into disturbing shapes. He didn't want to look.

'Did you come here to buy me off?' he asked. He might not be above being paid for his silence, in the end, but he wasn't sure that his cooperation would do her much good.

'I came here to buy a painting,' she said sweetly. 'By way of apology for my husband.'

The baronne began to walk along the edge of the room, past the portrait of a rich textile merchant on which Lavoie was finishing the design of a fabulous brocade jacket, to the painting that he'd been working on when her servant knocked on his door.

'What's this?' Madame de Cardonnoy raised her gloved hand, reaching towards the foaming edge of a wave, and Lavoie caught her by the wrist.

'Don't. It's still wet.'

She smiled at him. 'Monsieur Lavoie, I know better than to touch such a work.'

He let go of her hand very quickly.

'Forgive me, it is a new painting. I would not normally show it to visitors so early. Here, on the horizon' – and he gestured towards the shape of a rising cliff and a city wall – 'is Troy, and these figures are Aeneas and Anchises, escaping to their ships.'

'The water runs red, under the cliffs.'

'It isn't finished. It will look more natural, once I've worked it more. What you're seeing now is only the ground of the painting, and the beginning of the shadows of figures. Helen will stand here, on the clifftop. I thought to paint her covering her eyes with her veil.'

She leaned in close to look at the place he'd indicated, as if she could already see Helen's figure.

'Hmm. Do you think a woman like Helen would be afraid to look at her own handiwork?'

Lavoie shrugged. '*I* am afraid. Would you like to be the painter who tried to capture the most beautiful woman in the world?'

If she had looked at his sketches, she might have left with the impression that there was a specific woman he was thinking of, to stand in for Helen's beauty and her duplicity. He was glad he hadn't painted her figure yet.

'Oh, but beauty fades. If the Trojan War lasted for ten years, she'd no longer be a girl by its end.' She looked sidelong at him and then back to the painting. It was an eerily comfortable moment. For a moment he could have forgotten both her dead husband and the police informant on his doorstep.

'I'd like to think, though, that even if she aged, the power that she had to move the world might be preserved,' he said. 'So that even if her hair turned white with sorrow, one might look at her and catch a glimmer of why the war was fought.'

The baronne frowned but held her tongue, bending forward in silence to look at the brushstrokes with which he'd delineated the walls of Troy, the red and gold rays of the rising sun. Lavoie stepped back and watched her look at his work.

'How much would you sell it for?' she asked, as if it were the simplest question in the world.

'It's not finished,' said Lavoie. Silently he was calculating what price he might put on it if any other patron had asked, and how much more he could reasonably charge the baronne for the danger she was putting him in. 'It's going to take me months, at the very least. I don't have an assistant.'

'Of course,' she said. 'You could consider it a commission. I could give you five hundred livres now, and we'd call that, say, one-third of the final payment?'

That might have been merely a generous fee, if Lavoie had previously won the Prix de Rome and painted King Louis's own portrait. As it was, he'd never been paid so much for anything. He could buy a dozen coats with lace cuffs. He wondered, with a stupid pang, whether she even liked the painting.

'You're generous, Madame.' Lavoie swallowed. 'But … you realise that my silence won't save you? I doubt the police put much stock in my word, even before you paid me this visit.'

Madame de Cardonnoy sighed. She raised a hand and tucked the curl that had escaped from her veil back into place.

'There's one other favour I want to ask of you, but I'm afraid that in doing so I will compromise us both.'

Lavoie, who had already started back towards the door of the workshop, froze near the window. His stomach lurched unpleasantly with the realisation that she was about to tell him something he didn't want to hear. Of course she wasn't going to pay him just to mind his own business.

'What are you hoping for, Madame?'

'There's something I'd like to know, but I'm afraid it's a very foolish question.' She was speaking to the painting of Troy, not to him. 'If it came about that you found a vial of orpiment, without any label signifying what it was, would it be easy to identify?'

'If it were pure orpiment, its colour would betray it.' He was trying to keep his voice steady, but he could feel himself being drawn into a place he didn't want to visit. As if the door to the night he didn't want to think about had opened and he was frozen, again, in front of his powerful visitor, hoping that this time he could make the conversation play out differently. 'If it were mixed with some other preparation, the colour might be dimmed and then it would be difficult to know, unless one tested its effect somehow. Then, of course, there are other yellow substances, so a vial of yellow might not be a vial of poison.'

He was trying to treat her question as a theoretical one, as if she had asked him about pigments or what each figure represented in an allegorical scene. *Don't tell me this*, he wanted to say to her. *When I asked, it wasn't because I wanted the truth.* Once again she was slipping out from behind the image he'd made of her, no longer the foolish, over-generous rich woman, but something else.

'And do you know how it's mixed when it's mixed as a poison?' The baronne was twisting her handkerchief in her fingers, and Lavoie could see that her hands were shaking.

'Madame, do you mean to poison someone?'

'No, of course not.' She shook her head, twice, sharply.

'Then what?'

Don't tell me. No, tell me. She paused for a very long time, and Lavoie wanted to grab her by the shoulders and shake her. *I know I'm not the man your servants saw you kiss, so why pretend with me that you had no lover, that he had nothing to do with your husband's death? Why pretend you came here for some reason other than to buy me off?* But still he wanted not to know the thing that he knew.

Madame de Cardonnoy cleared her throat.

'There is ... someone I know, who saw my husband on the night of his death, but cannot come forward without causing a scandal.

If it happened, however, that I could discover a vial of poison in among my husband's things, I might be able to point the police in the right direction. Without implicating my friend.'

He didn't believe her. The disbelief was so immediate that he struggled even to hear the details of the story she was offering him. A friend, of course. Why didn't she ask her lover to get her the poison?

'Forgive me, Madame, you are very convincing when you swear you didn't kill your husband, but not for one moment do I believe that story is true. Send your servant to the chemist's and say you need it to kill rats, I will not get involved in this.' His voice was clipped and precise, but he could feel his heartbeat pounding in his ears. He wasn't brave, after all.

'I see.' Lavoie could see the movement of her throat as she swallowed. 'Then I will leave you.'

Possibly what was wrong with him was not the visit that her husband had paid him in the night, or the cracked rib that still hurt him when he breathed too deep, but the possibility that he was in love with her – a stupid inclination for a woman he didn't know and had every reason to distrust. Would a hopeless love be better than knowing that it was the charm worked by her money? He didn't really believe it, even as he was formulating the thought, but something drew him towards her, whether it was his useless hatred of her husband or the desire he'd first felt when he painted her portrait, the scent of her perfume, the feeling he still had that she might, like the enchantress of her stories, take his hand and work some transformation whose substance he couldn't predict.

He wanted to help her. But he didn't want to risk his life.

'Wait.' She was halfway to the door when Lavoie grabbed awkwardly at her veil, then her arm. 'Tell me why. The real reason.'

She brushed him off. 'Surely you see why that would be impossible, Monsieur.'

'I'm not inclined to betray your trust. Unless ...' He gestured at the ceiling, helplessly. He would be entirely capable of betraying her, if she told him too much. He could be mercenary. He was afraid of prison, and of death.

'Unless it's something truly damning? What kind of matter do you think this is, Monsieur Lavoie?' She was staring at him very intently as he blocked her way to the door with his outstretched arm, his other hand still clenched in the fabric of her sleeve. He could feel the tension in her arm as she shifted weight; and she, likewise, could feel his grip slacken on her clothes, as if he'd thought better of grabbing her, and then tighten again as he regained his resolve.

'Did you kill him?'

It would have been possible then for her to scream, calling her servant Arnaud from the hall downstairs, saying (it was true) that the painter had grabbed at her, pulled her arm, almost torn her veil, blocked her exit, that she was frightened for her life. Instead she held Lavoie's gaze as he looked at her.

He was not a bad man, Madame de Cardonnoy thought. But she should not have trusted him.

'I did not kill him,' she said. 'Now I'd like to leave.'

'Did you know he would be killed?'

'I did not,' she said. 'And that is the truth.'

'If you want me to involve myself in this,' Lavoie said, 'then I must know what is it I am agreeing to.'

'And if I said I conspired in his murder – which I did not, but it seems to be the only answer you will accept – what would you do, Monsieur?'

'I don't know.' He didn't drop the arm that was barring her way. His face was creased so that he might have been one of the figures in his own painting, looking back towards Troy. Madame de Cardonnoy touched his wrist with her glove and, at the pressure of her hand, he took his away from the door jamb and let it fall to his side.

'I'll leave this purse for you,' she said. 'If you don't want to associate with me any more, you may pick another painting to send me. If you send me a message, I will have a servant pick it up, so that you need not trouble yourself to arrange its transportation to my hôtel. Or keep the money as a gift.'

'And that's to be all then?'

'I think so. And, truly, I regret the extent to which I have involved you in a matter that has nothing to do with you.' She nodded to him, gave a small, slight curtsey that was still deeper than politeness required, began to turn away.

Again Lavoie caught her sleeve at the door.

'If I were to buy the thing that you've asked of me,' he began, rushing the words so that they tripped over each other on the way past his lips, 'it would take me a few days. But if I bought it, along with some other tools of my trade, I would draw far less notice than you would, if you tried to obtain it directly.'

Marie Catherine drew her spine up a little straighter, shook her head. There was a kind of fear that existed in the possibility of success, hand in hand with it, the shock one might feel on jumping off a high cliff and finding oneself suspended in an invisible net, instead of broken on the rocks below. She had paid Lavoie a visit on such a tenuous thread because she could not stop thinking about whether he had upheld Jeanne's story. Because what she had to give La Reynie was too vague and uncertain. Because she had remembered hearing that a painter must use poison to mix his colours.

'That is why I asked you,' she said. 'But it was an unreasonable request, and we won't speak of it further.'

For a moment she hoped that Lavoie would nod, and the moment where he might have helped her in defiance of reason would pass in silence. Instead he looked into her eyes as intently as if he were trying to read her thoughts. As he looked, Marie Catherine saw that he had very thick, feminine eyelashes, and a greyish spot in the green of his left eye, and the frivolity of this observation comforted her. Perhaps if the judges found her guilty, she would go to the place de Grève and have a last moment to admire the white of the executioner's teeth, or the charming curls of her confessor's hair.

'Tell me this, Madame. *Who* do you want it for? It is to keep someone silent?'

'No.' She shook her head. 'My husband wrote – there are letters, in his office, written to a man, a rogue priest, that talk about spells. I persuaded one of this man's servants to speak to me, a young boy, but he's afraid to go to the police. He's only a child. The priest himself has already fled Paris – if the police want to bring him in for questioning, they will have to hunt him down. And without the servant boy's testimony, I doubt there is enough in the letters to persuade them to seek out this man. But if I could give them the letters, and a vial of poison that I found enclosed with them in my husband's study, and the news that he fled Paris in the days since my husband's death, I think that would be enough to make them credit even the theories of a woman.'

That was as much of the truth as she could tell him. He already knew enough to condemn her, if he wanted to.

'And suspicion would be directed away from you,' Lavoie said.

'And from you,' Marie Catherine replied.

The painter gave her a brisk nod.

'What else do you know about this priest?' he asked.

'Only a little. He sold spells, perhaps other things. The servant boy – the one I spoke to – is the man's natural son. His mother was keeping him hidden in a cupboard, or nearly. And he loathes the priest and wishes him dead. Whatever the man is, he isn't a good priest or a kind father.'

Lavoie looked at her face as if he believed he could read the truth in her eyes. She wasn't sure what he found there, or what he might want to find. Perhaps it had been a mistake to offer him the money so blatantly. But she didn't think she could have carried off a seduction.

'I'll think on it,' he said finally. 'You'll have an answer soon.'

'Don't put it in writing,' Marie Catherine said quickly.

'Of course not. I'll have to send you a painting. Something smaller than the historical one, that I can finish quickly. If you still want that one ...' He let the sentence trail off, and she could see how much he hoped that she had liked it, genuinely, and his fear that she had only complimented it to flatter him.

'I haven't seen anything like it,' she said. 'It's beautiful.'

'Perhaps you'll still think that when it's finished.' He gestured to lead her out of the door, then paused. 'One other thing.'

'Oh?'

'Your friend. The one who you are protecting.'

'I thought we agreed that was an invention,' Marie Catherine said. 'I must apologise for imposing on your trust.'

Lavoie sighed, and for a moment she thought he would press her further, but instead he brushed off his shabby coat and stepped through the door.

'And we've truly talked too long,' he said. Then, raising his voice, he bowed her down the stairs, saying, 'I hope you've enjoyed the tour of my workshop, Madame, and I am glad you have found a piece you like. Please do not worry about sending payment immediately – a week or two after you've received the finished piece will do, and until then you still have credit with me.'

Marie Catherine laughed. 'You do not drive a hard enough bargain, Monsieur Lavoie. But I look forward to the painting.'

Arnaud was still waiting in the hall, looking bored.

'I'm sorry, Arnaud, I forgot to tell you to bring the carriage back round. Can you run and tell the coachman to hurry?'

The servant bowed, and left.

'Thank you,' she said to Lavoie.

'I haven't agreed yet,' the painter said. 'I can imagine this is how your rogue priest began his career, and I certainly don't want to end up like him.'

'Escaped, you mean?' she asked, as lightly as she could. 'It would be sad indeed to leave Paris.'

'You are a very disturbing person.' Lavoie shook his head at her, which made her laugh. She would have liked to be this man's friend, she thought, in another world. She could have introduced him to Madame de Fontet, and hung one of his paintings in her own salon and watched his star rise.

'Thank you for your help. Really.'

They stood in silence for a minute or two, during which Madame de Cardonnoy felt the painter watching her, an expression of slight sadness on his face.

'You did much better with business conversation coming down the stairs than going up them,' she said, finally. 'I was surprised. I thought you were going to be tongue-tied again.'

'Well, your footman had scared me half to death when he appeared on my doorstep,' Lavoie said. 'I haven't learned to love the men who wear the Cardonnoy uniform.'

The sound of carriage wheels filtered in from the street.

'Goodbye,' Lavoie said. 'Good luck. I suppose we won't see each other again. It will be better if I manage the delivery without coming to your hôtel.'

'Would you want to see me again?' She turned towards him. 'I thought you found me disturbing.'

Lavoie frowned at her. 'Do you think I agreed to this just because I hate your husband?'

But the door creaked open and he cut himself off, arranged his face back into an expression approaching neutrality, bowed to her.

'Good day, Madame. Travel safely.'

'Good day, Monsieur Lavoie.'

Arnaud handed her up into the carriage. When the door had closed on her and left her alone, she had a sudden feeling of vertigo, which rushed from her toes up to her ribcage and left her nauseous. Perhaps she couldn't trust the painter. Perhaps she could, and what she and Victoire had done would be wiped clean. She could feel her chest tightening, and she gasped and gasped but couldn't catch her breath. She pressed her forehead against the carriage window. The streets rolled by as if she were dreaming them, shabby fiacres and sedan chairs and men and women on foot, hurrying through the mud in clothes that might once have been fine. A crier on the street called, 'Oranges, oranges, ladies, take your pleasure!' If Victoire had been with her, Marie Catherine might have put her head in the girl's lap and been comforted, but Victoire was at Versailles and might as well have been on the moon. Nothing seemed solid. She couldn't breathe.

Gradually the cool glass against her skin calmed her, and she left fear behind and went to a place without past or future or punishment, but only the shadow and noise of the city, through which she passed like a kind of ghost.

When she dismounted from the carriage at Hôtel Cardonnoy the courtyard was nearly empty, unusual at this hour of the afternoon. The stable boy alone peeked out of the carriage house at the sound of her arrival, slinging the piece of tack he'd been polishing over his shoulder and running to help the coachman. Besides him, only the kitchen boys Philippe and Albert hovered in a knot by the kitchen entrance and, on seeing Arnaud hand her down from the carriage, Philippe ran into the house, leaving Albert to shake the potato peelings out of his bowl and follow. A battle-scarred white cat sat alone on the steps to the house cleaning itself, and when it saw the carriage it directed a blue-eyed glare at Marie Catherine through the window and leaped away into the bushes.

Still no one had appeared in the courtyard, until Anne burst out of the front door, running. She was wringing a sodden cloth in her hands, too distressed to curtsey.

'Madame, I've called the doctor,' she said in a rush, stopping short just in front of Madame de Cardonnoy, her hands seeking her mistress's, a familiarity she had never before taken. 'It's the children. They both took ill after you left.'

Chapter Fifteen

———

In the nursery Nicolas was crying. The air was warm and heavy with the smell of fever sweat, and his hair was matted to his head and stuck up damply when he rubbed his eyes or his pink face. Anne had built up the fire, so that as soon as Marie Catherine stepped into the children's room she could feel the band of her veil adhering to her forehead, the heavy crepe of her dress turning sticky under her arms and down her ribs. She tore the veil off and shook the pins out of her plait. Sophie was sleeping limply in the bed beside Nicolas, her face flushed feverish pink.

'Nicolas, darling.' She kissed his forehead, and he cried louder.

'He's been like that the past half-hour,' Anne said. 'He cries, I can't do anything – he's vomited his whole stomach up.'

'Maman, it's too warm.' Nicolas squirmed in her embrace and whined pitifully.

'Where's the doctor? Someone get him.'

'Madame, we called when Sophie fell ill. At once. He hasn't come yet.'

'Then tell the coachman he's to go back out and fetch him.'

'He should be—' Anne began, but Marie Catherine cut her off with a gesture.

'Now! And where's Jeanne?'

Anne crumpled under her gaze, as she did when anyone spoke to her sharply. Madame de Cardonnoy barely noticed. She was smoothing Nicolas's hair back over his forehead, then passing to Sophie, who stirred miserably in her sleep when her mother touched her face. Anne hung in the doorway, waiting to be dismissed. There were nervous tears starting in her eyes.

'Well, go! What are you waiting for? And send Jeanne.'

Marie Catherine had already forgotten that Jeanne had been sick when she left that morning. Anne was gentle with the children, but it was Jeanne's sense that Marie Catherine trusted. Once, when Sophie had had an attack of stomach sickness, Jeanne had visited some wise woman she knew in Paris and returned with a powder that, mixed into a little broth, helped her hold down her food. And, unlike Anne, she wouldn't be afraid.

Marie Catherine pulled Sophie's bedclothes tighter under her chin, checked the window to make sure it was securely latched and then drew the curtains over it, which made the room dim but reduced the chill that emanated from the windowpanes. The fire cast long fingers of shadow up the walls and made the silhouettes of Sophie's dolls move and whisper to each other.

The baron had lain bloody in the salon downstairs, and now, Marie Catherine thought, his ghost was here to claim his right to his children. She wished she could reject that thought, but it had occurred too suddenly and vividly.

'Maman, it's so warm.' Nicolas's crying had subsided, and now he just sniffled, twisting in his bed until the sheet made a rope around him. Marie Catherine found a basin of water that Anne had left on the dressing table, dipped a cloth in it, lit a candle to chase away the shadows and began to sponge off his forehead.

'Hush, Nicolas, sleep.'

'Everything hurts.'

'What's happening?' In the next bed, Sophie sat up on her pillow and then collapsed backwards as if she couldn't support her own weight. 'Where did the cat go?'

She had pulled the covers around her head as if to hide in them.

'What's wrong?' Marie Catherine asked, wondering wildly where the servants were.

'I'm so thirsty, my throat hurts so much,' Sophie whispered and then, squeezing her eyes shut, 'I had bad dreams.'

Marie Catherine brought her a cup of water, and Sophie took a small sip and then pushed it away.

'I can't.'

'Don't be afraid, it will be all right. Here, take your doll.' The doll with the broken hand, Sophie's favourite, was lying halfway under the bed. Marie Catherine tucked her in next to Sophie's pillow, and the girl curled around her and clenched the edge of the broken porcelain in her fist. Marie Catherine wanted to peel her fingers back, in case she cut herself. But she hoped the doll might be a talisman that could keep Sophie tethered to the world of the living. She put her hand on Sophie's hot forehead, took it away, rushed to the door to look for the servants, found the hallway empty and closed the door tightly to keep out the draught that she imagined she felt. She went and sat down on the floor, in the space between the children's beds, and reached out a hand on each side to hold the children's small hands.

'It's been a long time since I told you a story, hasn't it?' she said, trying to make her voice cheerful. 'How would you like that?'

'All right,' said Sophie, very weakly.

'Good. Just take a little sip of water first, yes?'

Sophie let her bring the cup to her lips, then turned her head away. 'It tastes bad. It's cold.'

'Drink a little.'

Sophie drank, reluctantly, coughed, let a foamy line of water trickle down her chin.

Where were the servants? Where was Jeanne? Marie Catherine finally remembered that the maid, when she had last seen her, had been asleep in her alcove and was tossing under the weight of a fever. It had seemed like nothing. Marie Catherine had recovered so quickly. Now it was as if the entire household had fled, leaving her here with the two sick children and no one to help.

'Once, far from Paris, there was a widow who lived alone with her daughter.' She tried to keep her voice steady as she began the tale. 'One day the girl's mother took sick. For days she tossed and turned, and it seemed that no medicine would cure her. So the girl went out into the forest to weep, and there the devil appeared to her. "Why do you cry, my child?" the devil asked, and he had a sweet voice, although he was very ugly to look at.'

Sophie lay with her cheek on her pillow, watching her mother with heavy eyelids.

'Sophie? Nicolas? Are you listening?' She needed to hear their voices, even as she hoped that the tale would lull them to sleep and bring them relief from the fever.

'Yes, Maman.'

'Good.' Marie Catherine cleared her throat. 'The girl told the devil that she was weeping for her mother, who was ill. "I can sell you a draught that cures all ills," said the devil, "but the price is high. For you will have to come with me to hell and serve me there for seven years, and if during that time you disobey me, it will be for eternity that your soul is forfeit."'

It was not the first time the children had been ill. But Marie Catherine was already trying to keep herself from picturing the worst, as if imagining it would summon it. She felt that she was calling the devil himself to come in and bargain. She would trade her health for theirs. The children shouldn't suffer for their mother's fault.

'The girl shivered, but she accepted the bargain, and the devil gave her a little vial of clear water and told her to wet her mother's lips with it and she would be healed. And truly, she had no sooner opened the bottle than the air of her mother's cottage smelled sweeter, as if spring had come in the middle of winter, and just as soon as the old woman had taken a drink, she opened her eyes and sprang up from her sickbed, and danced around the room with her child in her arms, laughing.

'But the girl was downcast, for now she had to pack her bonnet and her extra shift, and a bit of dried apple to eat on the road, and prepare to meet the devil and go with him to hell. And when she told her mother how she had bargained for her life, the old woman, too, was sad and sat at her table and wept.'

The children were quiet. Sophie nodded, fitfully, and closed her eyes.

'Are you listening?'

Sophie nodded. She was falling asleep, sinking back down into the fever.

'"No," the old woman said, "I will not allow you to go to hell in my place." And she hid the girl in the chest at the foot of the bed and told her to be quiet as a mouse. So the next day, when the devil grew tired of waiting in the wood and came to see where his vassal was, the mother opened the door a sliver and, when he asked why her daughter was tarrying, she told him that the girl was dead.'

At this point, the door creaked. Madame de Cardonnoy jumped, hoping to see the face of the doctor – but it was Jeanne, half dressed, with two burning roses in each cheek.

'Madame,' she said and curtseyed.

'I thought you were ill.'

'Anne said you had called for me.' She leaned unsteadily against the doorframe. 'It took me some time to dress. Anne's in distress. The cook's sick too, and some of the kitchen staff, and the man she sent out to fetch the doctor hasn't returned.'

'God preserve us,' said Marie Catherine. Jeanne leaned in the doorway and watched her, wavering like a man returned from a night of drinking. Marie Catherine caught a flicker of movement out of the corner of her eye and jumped, believing in ghosts, and saw that it was nothing and the room was empty.

'What do you need, Madame?' the servant girl asked.

'Nothing.' Marie Catherine hesitated. 'Only – wait with me, please. For the doctor to come.'

'Madame.' Jeanne's curtsey dipped dangerously low, and she caught herself and felt her way over to Nicolas's bed, where she sank to the floor and rested her head against the mattress. 'Tell me if you require anything and I'll get up.'

Marie Catherine shook her head. Jeanne did not look well. 'I'd forgotten you were feverish when I told Anne to fetch you. Lie down. There's an extra blanket in the trunk.'

She stood to fetch the blanket, and Jeanne lay down with her head on the floor, curled around the foot of Nicolas's bed like a spring caterpillar wrapped around a branch. Marie Catherine put the blanket over her, and Jeanne raised her head and looked up at her.

'Forgive me. I'm so tired.'

'I was telling the children a story. But they're sleeping now.'

Jeanne let her head fall back on the floor and lay on her side, facing Marie Catherine, her eyes gleaming in the flickering light of the candle.

'I'll listen, if you go on.' Illness gave her a directness of speech that she rarely showed before her mistress. Marie Catherine took a deep breath.

'The old woman told the devil that her daughter had died that morning of fright, so terrified had she been of the journey to hell, and that if her soul was not already among his servants, then he could have no further claim on her. But the devil did not believe her, and he demanded proof. So the mother closed the door on him and went to the oak chest where her daughter was hidden, and then, with tears in her eyes, she cut off the girl's left hand and carried it out to him. And the girl bit her tongue and did not cry out.

"'There is your proof," the old woman said to the devil. Still the devil was suspicious.'

Sophie had dropped her doll and now held her two clenched fists close to her mouth, as if there was something that she was determined not to let go of, even in sleep. Marie Catherine reached across and tucked the blanket more firmly under her chin, hiding her two knotted hands. She was grateful for Jeanne, whose presence allowed her to go on telling the tale that was only just keeping her real fears at bay.

"'Listen," said the old woman. "I understand that I owe you a debt, and I am happy to repay it. My daughter may be dead, but I will go in her place, and I swear you will have nothing to complain of in my work." Then the devil relented, for he liked the idea that this old woman, still mourning her daughter, must go and be his servant. And the old woman went inside and put some bread and apples in a basket, and bandaged her daughter's wound, and then she took the devil's hand and set off with him on the road to hell.'

She had to stop or her voice would crack. She looked at her hands folded in her lap. They were swimming behind a curtain of water.

'Madame?' Jeanne asked softly.

'It's nothing.' She took deep breaths until the tears began to dry. 'For seven years her daughter stayed alone in their cottage. When she planted peas in the garden, they grew to the size of apples, and the apple tree bowed to the ground with the weight of its fruit. Her cow gave her cream instead of milk, and her beehives overflowed with honey. It was as if the mere scent of the magic water that the devil had given her breathed new life into everything. But she missed her mother, and at night she would look into the fire and think of the old woman, working in hell to pay off her debt. The girl let her hair grow until it reached her ankles, then trailed on the floor behind her. She let her face go unwashed, and her nails grew into claws, and her clothes turned into rags. She didn't plant or hoe, but the garden grew up around her and fed her, and when people passed by the way to her cottage they told each other that there was the house of the wild woman, who was mourning the death of her mother.'

Nicolas stirred in his bed and whimpered. 'Maman, I'm going to be sick.'

Someone had moved the chamberpot. Marie Catherine leaned under the bed and searched for a handle, for the cold of the porcelain, and found nothing. Finally she took the washbasin from the dressing table, still half full of cool water, and held it out next to Nicolas's bed. She had to help him sit up, bracing his head in the crook of her arm while he vomited, the bile floating in thick strands through the washing water. His hair was matted to his skull with sweat, and when he had finished and squirmed back down under the covers she could still feel the damp impression of his head against her breast.

'Shall I take that, Madame?' Jeanne had risen to her knees and was holding out her hands for the bowl.

'Leave it, please,' Marie Catherine said. 'Someone's already whisked away the chamberpot. We may need it again.'

Jeanne nodded, sank down to the floor and pulled her blankets tighter around her. She was not so delirious now as she had been in the morning, but still her head and her hands felt heavy, as if she were swimming through some substance that was thicker than air and resisted her at every turn. Odd details struck her – the rabbitlike movement of Sophie's feet under the covers, the way Madame kept wiping her palms on her dress after touching Nicolas's sweaty hair. So Madame de Cardonnoy was afraid for the children. Strange to see this woman who had power over her livelihood, over even her life, held fast in the hand of God and unable to peer out of his fist. Jeanne wondered if Madame felt it too, the presence of divine judgement, if she considered it a punishment for her sins.

Jeanne's own sins were jumbled together – the letter she'd carried, the pregnancy she'd ended, the man she had allowed to take her to bed, not even for pleasure, but only because she'd believed that he would marry her and buy her a pretty dress and then her life would be solved. She had lied – to her mistress, to the police. She had carried money and secrets for Laure, she had carried a deep sympathy in her heart for La Chapelle, the witch, and for La Voisin, the poisoner. Even for Madame she felt a kind of protective compassion that was not love, exactly, or loyalty, or envy of the privileges of her station, but the knowledge necessary for close service. Always Jeanne was splitting into two selves – one loyal, humble, obedient to God, the law and her mistress, and the other a secret stranger, who lived under the skin of the good servant girl and did as she pleased. The stranger who knew that her fever was breaking, that her body was strong, that God, whatever he thought of her, was not yet ready to kill her.

'Will you go on telling the story?' Jeanne asked, after Madame had sat for a while in silence. Her stomach was heaving and her head still felt as heavy as if someone had filled her skull with old washing water, but she could see that her mistress was lost in dark thoughts.

Madame de Cardonnoy shook her head. 'They're sleeping. They can't hear it.'

'I will.' At La Chapelle's, and in the house in which she'd served before, she had been taught not to assert herself like this. It should not matter what Jeanne wanted to hear. Although Madame was not the kind of employer who might have mocked her or punished her for speaking in this way, she would have been puzzled by it.

'Very well, I'll go on.' Madame spoke so quietly it was impossible to know whether she had noticed that Jeanne had spoken out of turn. Jeanne lay down with her head on the floor, cradled in her arms, and watched Madame de Cardonnoy as she turned her hands over in her lap, inventing the next part of the story. She could feel the cold seeping up through the rug, touching her ribs with an icy cat's tongue. She watched the dust moving in the fibres of the carpet with the current of her breath, and when she looked up she met Madame's eyes, watching her as she so rarely did, looking closely at her face instead of letting her eyes glide politely away from Jeanne's eyes.

'Meanwhile the girl's mother was working off her debt in hell.

The devil gave her a set of keys to his palace, and every morning the old woman would sweep out the ashes from his hundred fireplaces, where the sad souls of the damned burned to light the devil's house at night, and then she would chop and carry great cords of wood to stoke the hearth in the kitchen, where the sad souls of the damned were boiled during the day. And in the evening, when she was tired to her bones, the devil would call her in to eat supper with him, and she would sit across from him at a long table, wearing her dirty clothes, and the devil would eat white bread with butter, roast meat, candied oranges, cakes soaked in honey, cinnamon and mace. And when he was done, he would pass his plates to the old woman, who ate only the crusts of his bread because she was afraid to eat the fruits of hell.'

Jeanne closed her eyes. What did Madame de Cardonnoy know about eating the crusts from a great table? She was a woman who ate white bread and fresh asparagus. But there was something in the story that made Jeanne think, just for a moment, that Madame had seen her – that she had seen the way Jeanne looked at her world. As if she should care whether Madame saw her at all.

Would Madame really go down to the devil for her children, if it came to it? La Chapelle would have gone, for Laure. Would anyone go down that way for Jeanne? She didn't think her own mother would have.

'Where is Anne?' Madame de Cardonnoy asked, speaking to no one. Certainly not, exactly, to Jeanne. 'Where is the doctor?'

'He will come soon, Madame. The coachman has gone to fetch him, and soon he will find him and bring him here.' She spoke soothingly, the way she would to a child, without regard for whether the words were true.

'My father never trusted doctors,' Madame de Cardonnoy said. 'He'd say that any illness that couldn't be cured by rest and the grace of God could not be cured either by some bearded creature with a bag full of powders. He still summoned them when he was dying. I suppose he lost his nerve.'

'Do you remember him, Madame?' Jeanne asked. Her stomach churned, and she tried to summon back the image that the baronne's words had conjured for her, of the brave old woman carrying her bundle of apples through the lonely rooms of hell.

'Of course. In my prayers, with my mother. He did not have an easy death. Is your father … ?' She trailed off, suggestively. Not asking, *alive?*

Jeanne shook her head. She had not seen her father since he had put her on the back of the cart that would take her to Paris, to the house where her aunt worked. She had not been able to write, nor he to read. She had watched him recede into the distance down the road, feeling something dull coming loose inside her chest and streaming out as the creaking wheels took her farther and farther from home. Who could say if he was still alive?

'No,' she said. 'God rest him.' And with that, she erased the farm, and her family, and made herself the daughter of the cart driver who'd taken her to Paris and left her on her aunt's doorstep, guiding her there with a hand on her shoulder to make certain she didn't lose her way and find herself in some house of ill repute. She imagined that man, with his beard going to white, older than her father and softer, and she said, again, 'God rest him.'

'I'm sorry,' said Madame de Cardonnoy.

'The doctor will come soon, Madame.'

'Do you remember when Sophie was sick?' Madame asked. 'There was a wise woman, who you went to for a remedy.'

'I remember. But she too is dead now.' Jeanne sniffed. Poor La Chapelle would burn, like La Voisin.

'Oh.' Marie Catherine pulled at her skirts, so that they were spread out more neatly on the floor, darkness making the black cloth fade into the red of the carpet. She no longer quite believed in the doctor, or in any part of the world outside this room, the sleeping children like statues themselves, who might wake or might not. Her body itself felt cold and heavy, as if there were some thicker substance where her blood had once circulated.

'The old woman had a key to every room in the devil's palace but one,' she said, after a while. 'The last key was a little golden one that the devil wore on a ribbon around his neck, and it unlocked a plain iron door at the very centre of the palace, which was so low that the old woman would have had to stoop to enter it. Sometimes she would stop in her work and listen at this door, and when she did, she would hear birdsong, and the sound of rushing water, and a cool breeze rustling the leaves of the trees of the forest, and even a sound like her daughter's laughter. And for a moment she would feel the heat of hell recede and she would be happy.

'But when the devil came across her listening at this little door, he laughed, and said, "Leave that door to me, little mother, for if I catch you inside, it will be eternity you spend with me and not seven short years."'

Marie Catherine ran her hand over Nicolas's hair as he slept, and then over Sophie's hands.

'So for a while the old woman left the door alone, but as time passed, she found herself drawn there once again. And when she listened with her ear pressed to the keyhole, she thought she could hear her daughter singing.'

At the foot of Nicolas's bed, Jeanne sat up and pressed her hand over her throat.

'Madame, I feel sick.'

Madame de Cardonnoy pushed the reeking basin she'd held for Nicolas towards the servant girl, who crouched over it on her hands and knees, trying to turn her face away from the smell even as she dry-retched. Her hair was falling into her face – she'd done it up badly, in haste and, Marie Catherine thought, with trembling hands. Marie Catherine inched forward, across the floor, pulled the loose skein of Jeanne's hair back from her forehead, twisted it securely at her neck. Jeanne was having trouble bringing up whatever was in her stomach. She choked for a long time and then caught her breath, on the point of weeping. Marie Catherine was still holding her hair back from her face, smoothing the little tendrils of it that clung to her damp forehead.

'Darling.' She spoke, without thinking, as if she were talking to a dear friend or a child, rather than to a servant. 'You're not doing any good here. Go down and sleep.'

Jeanne shook her head.

'I'm all right.' She put her head down on the carpet, by Madame de Cardonnoy's knee, looking miserable. Sickness had pulled her face back into childhood, washing away the mute knowingness that she had worn so often in the past weeks and leaving a look of determination that was strangely bright and innocent in its purity. Marie Catherine reached out and put the back of her hand against the girl's forehead, feeling the fever beating under her skin.

'I found your jewels,' Jeanne said.

'What?' She didn't remove her hand. She thought for a moment that the girl might be speaking out of a fever dream.

'The ones you hid in your clothing chest. The chambermaid could have come across them, easily.' There was a fierceness to her expression that Marie Catherine had never seen before, or rarely, in moments when Jeanne did not know she was being looked at.

'So you found them instead?' She might have been afraid, but fear for the children had rinsed her clean. She might have held Jeanne down by the wrists and said, *What will you do with what you know?* But the desire wasn't in her. She took her hand away from Jeanne's forehead. They might have been clinging together to a raft in the wake of the wreck of some ship, far out at sea.

The silence was broken by a knock on the door and, ignoring protocol, Arnaud burst into the room, bowed, pulled himself up straight.

'The doctor, Madame.'

'Thank heaven.' She struggled up under the heavy weight of her petticoats, bracing herself on Nicolas's bed. This Doctor Girondeau, who she had met before, was a tall, delicate man, who always became taller and thinner in her imagination, dressed in a white curling wig and lace cuffs. He had a high tenor voice that sometimes had a birdlike whistle of asthma in it. He was obsequious, too, with his little 'Forgive me, Madame, for the delay, you understand about the weather, this Parisian mud is simply too much for my carriage.' Always, she remembered from other visits, he had one thousand similar soft-spoken complaints. But she liked the gentleness with which his manicured hands felt his patient's pulse, taking Sophie's transparent green-veined wrist off the bed and inclining his head as if he were listening to something that the rhythm of her heartbeats might tell him.

He was gentle, too, with the scalpel, if a bleeding was necessary. He did not take too much.

'Please look at them, Monsieur. Let me know whatever you need. And my maid is ill as well.'

Girondeau was already by the bedside, still talking without especially expecting an answer, about how his carriage mare had thrown a shoe just the other week, leaving him stranded on his expedition to visit a venerable gentleman with an attack of gout, whose name Madame de Cardonnoy would surely know. Marie Catherine found herself tapping her foot.

But there was something soothing about the doctor's continual stream of inanities, as if they revealed a professional instinct that said that this, too, was no emergency – a difficult case perhaps, but not so much as to put a stop to the necessary ebb and flow of polite conversation. The doctor perfumed his cuffs with orange-blossom water, to dispel the foul air of the sickroom. Madame de Cardonnoy was overcome with such relief and gratitude that she put a hand over her mouth and, behind it, let out a deep sigh.

'And the kitchen staff, Madame.' Arnaud bowed again, backing out of the doorway, as if he were embarrassed by his interruption, or afraid that the miasma of sickness would seize him as well if he ventured too far into the room.

'The whole household has it,' Marie Catherine said.

'Stomach sickness?' asked Girondeau.

'Yes, badly.'

'Hmm. Have you changed your cook?'

'Not at all.'

'Other kitchen staff? Visitors?'

'Not since my husband's death. My mind has been away from the household affairs.'

Girondeau nodded. 'Servants can make mistakes, under such circumstances. Something spoiled, perhaps. When it's only one member of the household, people get all kinds of ideas these days. Such fear of poison. The truth is that such illnesses often occur in spring and summer, as the warming of the air causes the miasma from the sewers to circulate. Now I will just open this vein to relieve the fever.'

And already he had his scalpel at hand, already the basin, and he was turning to Arnaud at the door and asking for *a little egg from the kitchen, with the white nicely separated from the yolk*, and then there was the cleanness of the cut, Sophie's eyelids fluttering open, heavy with sleep and pain, and the slow drip of blood into the basin. Sophie tried to twitch her arm back out of his grasp, and the doctor pressed the meat of her thumb between his fingers and soothed her, 'There now, it's only a little blood, be an obedient child.'

The cloth that he held against her wrist to stop the flow was stained with old blood, but he managed to keep the red off his cuffs. When the egg came, he mixed it, in the cup Arnaud had carried it in, with the contents of a blue bottle that, uncorked, filled the room with the smell of roses and turpentine, sharp as if he had opened a window and let in a gust of bracingly cold air. Madame de Cardonnoy breathed deeply and watched him as he applied the potion to the long, straight cut, as he folded Sophie's free hand under the blanket to prevent her from touching the wound with her fingers.

'Ah, Madame,' the doctor said, looking back at Madame de Cardonnoy. 'I should have asked you to leave the room. But then you do not faint at the sight of blood?'

'No, Monsieur. Not since giving birth to my children.'

Certainly a shiver went through her when the scalpel passed down Nicolas's pale arm, when he cried, fighting the doctor with weak arms, so that the blade slipped and zigzagged on his skin. She held him by the shoulders, saying, *Hush now, it's all right.* Only a little blood to cool the fever. Girondeau had a tonic, too, which he prescribed to relieve such ailments. The worst of it was not Nicolas's disconsolate crying, but the way, beneath the turpentine smell of the doctor's ointment, the room was full of the scent of butchery. One didn't want to imagine a child cut open, spread out on a plate like a witch's meal. It would be easier not to look when he cried. To go out of the room and let the doctor work, surrounded by his own meaningless bedside chatter, dropping *pit-pit* like rain off a roof. When he'd finished with the scalpel, Nicolas was pale and fretful. He seemed, mostly, exhausted by the ordeal.

'You haven't taken too much?' she asked, watching the red slosh up the sides of the bowl as the doctor put it down on the table.

'No, he's a strong boy. He'll sleep now – it will be better. Open your mouth for this spoon now, little gentleman.' And Nicolas turned his face away and had to have his lips prised open by his mother. Gently.

'I can leave some of the same mixture for the servants?' Girondeau suggested, graciously.

'I'd like you to look at my maid specially.'

And Jeanne curtseyed, swaying, sat down on the edge of the bed to be examined.

'Certainly, certainly.' He took her hand. 'Not a high fever. A little blood, perhaps.'

'Monsieur, I believe I will be well without it,' said Jeanne. 'The children are more fragile.'

He smiled. 'Of course. But you city girls too are delicate. The children, Madame la Baronne' – and he turned back to Marie Catherine as seamlessly as if Jeanne had never spoken – 'the children might do better if you remove to the country a little early this year. Paris is an unhealthy city.'

His hands with the scalpel were gentle still, but Madame de Cardonnoy thought the precise movements of his small fingers did not quite conceal a kind of benign indifference to the girl he was handling, as if the baronne had ordered him from caprice to administer his cures to a lapdog or the children's favourite cat. Jeanne bore the bloodletting without complaint. When it was finished, she held the cloth against her arm and looked at the blood seeping up through it.

'A day of rest,' said the doctor. 'No work, young lady, you may tell your mistress I have ordered it.'

'Thank you, Monsieur,' said Jeanne.

Madame de Cardonnoy did not come with him to the servants' quarters, where the kitchen staff were sleeping away the fever and the fires were banked and cold. She sent Arnaud to the traiteur, to bring soup for the children, when they woke. The doctor insisted that it should be a thin broth, not too hot, a little bread moistened in it and easy to chew.

'Will you come back tomorrow, Doctor?' she asked.

'Of course, Madame, if you desire it,' he said. 'I believe they are in no grave danger, but perhaps when they are stronger you might take them from Paris. When the whole household is afflicted, a change of air can work wonders.'

He bowed, one hand supporting his tightly curled wig.

'Thank you.' She turned to Jeanne as he left and pushed her towards the door with a gentle hand. 'You should go downstairs and rest. I'll fetch Anne.'

'I'll sit up with you,' Jeanne said. 'If you please.' She was wavering upright, but her face was determined. Marie Catherine retrieved her blanket from the floor and draped it around her shoulders.

Nicolas had already fallen back asleep. The flush of fever had faded away and left his face pale. Sophie was awake, running her fingers over the residue of the ointment that the doctor had applied to her cut.

'You should close your eyes, chérie.'

Sophie shook her head, mutely. The bloodletting had drained the flush from her cheeks.

'Shall I go on with the story? Do you remember where we left off?'

Again the child said nothing, but she slid down in the bed and let her cheek rest on the white pillow, looking up at Marie Catherine expectantly.

'Listen,' Marie Catherine said, and she reached out and touched Sophie's forehead, still warm, she thought, but not so feverish as before. 'One night when the seven years were nearly over, it happened that the devil sat down to dinner and from his pocket he brought out the old woman's daughter's left hand, which was as soft and white as the day she had given it to him. And he said, "Little mother, I have kept this hand next to my heart, and although the years have passed, it has not withered. And I think your daughter, too, is not dead, but is alive and well, and when your seven years with me are over, I will come and bring her down to hell for another seven years, and seven after that, until all her days are gone, because you have been untruthful with me."'

She looked between Sophie and Jeanne, who had crept in close and was resting her head against the foot of Sophie's bed.

'The old woman wept,' she said, 'and insisted that her daughter was dead. But the devil only laughed, and drank glass after glass of wine until he fell asleep at the table, and snored with his head thrown back. And then the old woman steeled her nerves and crept up close to him, and she put her hand in the pocket of his fine silk coat and took out her daughter's hand. And then she took the golden key from around his neck and put it around her own, and went to the forbidden door. For she thought that if the devil learned of her disobedience, he would keep her in hell, instead of her daughter.

'When she opened the door, the air that surrounded her was like the first cool breath of spring and she stepped inside quickly, but she left the door open, so that the devil would feel how the heat of hell had dimmed and would find her and punish her, and forget her child.'

Sophie's eyes blinked shut, then moved to watch Madame de Cardonnoy's hands as she described the movement of the old woman's hands with her own, turning the key in the lock.

'On the other side of the door was a garden, surrounded by stone walls that went up beyond the old woman's sight. White roses grew up the stones, and honeysuckle, and canes of blackberry, and birds flew between the close walls. At the centre of the garden was a straight white tree, from whose branches hung a heavy weight of golden apples, and from the tree's roots there came a spring, and the old woman had no sooner touched her fingertips to its water than she knew it was the water of life, for which her daughter had bargained with the devil. And the old woman sat down by the spring, and kissed her daughter's hand and cried.

'She cried for a long time, and then she heard a voice from above, calling, "Mother! Mother, is that really you?" It was her daughter's voice.'

Marie Catherine had started crying again, to her shame. She would have liked to pretend there was nothing she feared. Jeanne reached out and put a warm hand on her elbow, in silence. Sophie was watching her with an expression of exhausted fierceness. Her blood had left a stain on the sheets.

'Now,' she said, and her voice was only a little unsteady, 'the daughter had left her cottage, and as she made her way sadly through the woods, she heard the sound of weeping coming from an old dry well. And when she went to the well's edge and looked down, she saw all the way through the crust of the earth and into hell, where her mother was sitting by the spring of the water of life, crying. And as her mother looked up and saw her, too, there was a roar that shook the earth, for the devil had woken and discovered that his key and his little white hand were gone. And the old woman raised her arms, as if to embrace her daughter, and called farewell to her, because she knew that the devil was coming to take her away.

'"Wait," said the daughter. "Climb the tree, as high as you can, and I will pull you out."

'So the mother wrapped up her daughter's hand in her handkerchief, and dipped the bundle in the water of life and began to climb. But although she had grown so thin in hell that even the highest, most slender branches of the tree barely bent under her weight, the edge of the well was still too far away and she could not reach her daughter's outstretched hand. Below, in the garden, there was a puff of smoke, for the devil had put on his coat of eternal fire and was nearly at the door to the garden. "It's no use," called the old woman to her daughter. "Farewell!"'

Sophie coughed, miserably, and Marie Catherine stopped the tale and put a hand on her daughter's chest, feeling her ribs heave.

'I feel better now, Maman,' Sophie murmured. 'I'm all right.'

Marie Catherine pulled the stained sheets up to her daughter's neck, tucking her in against the draught. Jeanne reached out from her seat on the floor and took Sophie's hand in hers, to keep her from picking at her scab.

'Then,' said Marie Catherine, 'the daughter leaned over the well and threw down her hair, which had grown so long while she was alone that it made a rope that stretched all the way to her mother's hands and below, as far as the spring where the water of life bubbled up into hell. And the old woman took hold of her hair and climbed up to the lip of the well, to safety. And the two of them embraced, and laughed at their good fortune.

'But their happiness lasted only a moment. Because the devil had seen the old woman climbing up her daughter's long hair and he, too, had grabbed the end of her tangled plait and begun to climb. And soon a column of black smoke emerged from the well, and the daughter cried out in fear. But the old woman was not afraid, and she ran to the wood pile and took the axe that lay there and then hurried back to her daughter and, just as the devil's clawed hand was reaching for the lip of the well, she chopped off her daughter's long plait, and the devil's littlest finger with it. And the devil fell back down the well, and whether it was the shock of having fallen from grace a second time or the insult of his missing finger, he never dared to come for either the old woman or her daughter again.'

Let it come true, she thought. *Let it come true.*

'As for the two women, they prospered. That night the old woman sat down with her daughter to dinner and, when the meal was done, she combed the knots from her hair, and washed the dirt from the girl's face, and cut her long nails. Then she unwrapped the little severed hand that she had taken from the devil and laid it against her daughter's wrist, where, bathed in the water of life, it grew back whole.'

Sophie's eyes were closed again. Her slow breath sucked in a strand of hair that lay across her mouth and then blew it out like a banner. Madame de Cardonnoy kissed her forehead. It was warm, but she thought finally that the worst was over, and she might wake from the dream she was dreaming and live.

Chapter Sixteen

———

It was four days before the children were out of bed, still shaky from fever, but walking now, tripping up and down the stairs and then sitting exhausted on the top step. They were not to go outside, to avoid the poisonous air of the thawing city. Still, Nicolas's weak stomach had been joined by a hacking cough that left him breathless and out of sorts, lying on the floor and weeping like a younger child. He had trouble forgiving Marie Catherine for having let the doctor cut him, and sometimes when she wanted to kiss his cheeks, he shoved her away.

In the kitchen and the servants' quarters, too, the sickness had taken its toll. The cesspit behind the hôtel was a stinking morass that, even covered over with straw, wafted the scent of contagion through the house whenever the wind was unfriendly. One by one the servants had taken ill, then healed, except for the youngest kitchen boy, Philippe, who had been so ill that the cook had sent for a Parisian uncle to come and bear him away on a stretcher, and no one in the house had since received any indication of whether he was well or dead.

Jeanne, like Madame de Cardonnoy herself, had been quite well after only a day. Anne was impervious to all evil airs and vapours, and fetched water and helped cook and cleaned the children's dirty bed sheets without any sign of succumbing to the disease.

Meanwhile, preparations were under way to take the children to the Cardonnoy estates. Dresses and toys were packed and waiting in the hall, and the children's tutor had been engaged to travel to the country for the spring and instruct them. In the country manor, servants were cleaning, uncovering the furniture, killing spiders and airing out sheets that had lain packed in old chests with sprigs of lavender to keep the moths away. The baron's intendant was readying the accounting books for the eyes of Madame de Cardonnoy, who had written of her intention to oversee her husband's property with her own eyes, for the benefit of her young son.

She would send the children first, with Anne and the tutor. Marie Catherine felt a kind of anguish about following them. She was afraid that the house at Cardonnoy might be as haunted by the baron's ghost as Paris was, and even lonelier. She and the baron had gone to Cardonnoy every summer for years. There she had been pregnant, there she had miscarried: the child before Sophie, the child after her. The summer she had been twenty they had been trying to conceive again, and she had walked out every evening for weeks to the edge of the pear orchard and sobbed through the golden hour, then taken the long walk back to the baron in the grey of dusk. Since then the beauty of the orchards had been dimmed for her.

But perhaps Victoire would visit her. Then the estate at Cardonnoy might become something different. She and Victoire might be prisoners in the same fortress, or religious women sworn into the service of God. Together with the children, she might even believe that Victoire was a man and her husband, or they might simply be two women together, as if that were the natural order of things. Perhaps none of the country servants would think it strange if a woman friend from the city slept in her bed. She could move Jeanne down the hall to sleep with the children.

And then Victoire's mother would call her back to her duties at court, and to her family. Perhaps her visit could last a month or two, if they were lucky.

She and Victoire had spent just one night together since her visit to Versailles. The girl had come in the evening, fresh and cold in a riding habit, carrying a tonic that her mother's doctor swore by, for relief from flux. Marie Catherine had Jeanne bring their supper to the table in her bedroom, where they ate, together, and whispered to each other.

'Did you read my letter?' she asked, as Victoire picked

mushrooms off her plate and ate them. The note she'd sent telling Victoire about the children's illness had contained another of her secret messages, written in milk and describing her visit to the painter.

'I read it.' Victoire shook her head. 'I couldn't think what to write back. I told you before – it's a mistake to trust him.'

'He hasn't gone to La Reynie yet.' But it was true that Marie Catherine wondered what actions the painter might be turning over, in the privacy of his house. She could not visit him again.

Victoire sighed. 'I think the poison's too dangerous, Marie. The priest is suspicious enough. Send La Reynie the letter, be done with it.'

'The letter's too old by itself. If this man had any other clients, then why kill my husband for a matter that's years past, that no one seemed likely to discover until after his death? Only a desperate person would have done something like this. So he has to look desperate.' She was twisting her napkin in her lap, avoiding Victoire's eyes. She could feel the rightness of her words, but she wasn't sure that she could persuade Victoire. 'Do you trust me?'

'Of course.' Victoire took a deep breath. 'But I'm afraid for you.'

After their supper they kissed each other on the cheek, which might have seemed natural, and Victoire stayed the night in a spare room freshly made up, which might also have seemed natural if, exhausted by the effort of holding her at a polite arm's length, Marie Catherine had not drunk a glass of brandy in her room, then got up once she was sure Jeanne was asleep and crept down the hallway, without lighting a candle.

When she touched Victoire's shoulder, the girl started up in bed and scrambled away as if Marie Catherine were a murderer come in the night. The cloth wrap had unwound itself from her hair, as if she had tossed and turned in her sleep. The moon lit up only a little slice of her cheek.

'I'm sorry,' Victoire said, 'I was dreaming.' But when she pulled Marie Catherine down on top of her, moving like a swimmer in a slow current, Marie Catherine could not shake the memory of her fear. So that she began to feel that she was hovering somewhere above her body, waiting for the steps that had followed her steps. As she put a twist of sheet in Victoire's mouth to keep her from gasping. As her skin broke out in gooseflesh from the cold of the room, and Victoire's arms locked around her waist as if she were caught underwater, and Marie Catherine would pull her out. Dark water like moonlight. She couldn't breathe. Victoire's hands snaked under her shift, between her legs, and for once the touch she knew so well felt alien. Marie Catherine pulled away, sat up with her feet hanging off the bed.

'I frightened you.'

'It's all right. It was just a dream.' Victoire crawled over the sheets and wrapped her arms around Marie Catherine's waist from behind, her chin on her shoulder. 'My maid says I wake her with them.'

'Are you all right?'

'Of course.' Victoire paused. It was clear that she was trying not to reproach Marie Catherine for pushing her away. 'I love you.'

Marie Catherine put her head on Victoire's stomach and lay like that for a while, listening to her breath, feeling, outside, the prison of eyes that was closing around their room, the footsteps coming down the hall to find them. There was a place in the hollow of Victoire's hip that always made her gasp: she kissed it. Victoire propped herself up on one elbow, looking at her. How many times had they kissed, had they fucked, under the fear of discovery, of the eyes that might be watching? This time didn't have to be any different. Marie Catherine would find the fire that kept her fear at bay. She would make this room in her husband's house their enchanted palace, her nakedness her armour. She pushed Victoire's legs apart and knelt between them, and then she kissed the triangle of hair that hid her sex.

Afterwards she lay beside Victoire without speaking, delaying the moment when she would have to go back to her own bed. She was living, already, the moment of separation, when she would leave for Cardonnoy, and Victoire would wait with her mother in Paris. Or when La Reynie himself would come to take her away.

The next day there was a letter from La Reynie. He was impatient to see Monsieur de Cardonnoy's papers. She had had time to look through them. But Lavoie had not yet sent her what he had promised to, and she put off the lieutenant general. *Soon*, she wrote. *Very soon*. She was acutely aware of how long she had delayed sending him anything of import about her husband. Lavoie had said that his preparations would take him a few days. So it must come soon, if he had not changed his mind. Perhaps he had.

When the painting finally arrived a day later, she watched Arnaud from the window of her bedroom, carrying the wrapped package under one arm. There was a knock on her bedroom door, which opened before she could call the lackey in. A tiny piece of presumptuousness, excused by his low bow. Excused by the fact that she had asked that he bring her the painting immediately.

Marie Catherine wondered whether she imagined the presumptuousness. Arnaud had always been a little proud. There was scarcely anything different, now, in his bearing.

'Madame.' He laid his package on the bed.

'Was there a note with it?'

'Here, Madame.' He put it into her hands.

Madame de Cardonnoy took the letter opener from her desk and cracked the seal, opened the letter in front of him:

Madame,

I hope the painting pleases you. It is a small work, and I hope that gazing on it will be a comfort in your sorrow. I have taken the liberty of framing it myself, as I fear you may be too distracted for such things, but if the frame does not suit you, the back can easily be unhooked and the painting removed.

The remainder of my bill, too, is enclosed, which you may pay as time permits.

Your servant,

Alain Lavoie

She put the letter down on her writing table, casually, and began untying the strings that held the painting in its paper wrapping. Still Arnaud was standing in the door, watching her with the politely bored demeanour of a servant who doesn't know when his services will next be required. When the paper fell away, she was glad that she had been so conscious of the lackey's presence, because while she did put a hand over her mouth in surprise, she did not think that the servant could tell that she had been very close to bursting out into scandalised laughter.

She had assumed that Monsieur Lavoie would send her some cast-off still life from his workshop. But what he had given her was a composition that she knew, immediately, was meant for her alone. Because the first impression she had was an exuberant burst of yellow, the profuse scrolled petals of a drift of freshly picked marigolds, laid on leaves of so drab a green that it seemed like all colours must fade into gold. King of yellows. A softer yellow, too, was the skull that formed the centre of the composition, a memento mori, bright flowers blooming around the image of death, a funeral wreath, and on an edge of paper peeking out from beneath the flowers (this too a white that was caressed with blue and yellow, a tiny daub of yellow so bright it seemed absurd that the paper could be so clearly, purely white) – on the paper the letters *In Memoriam*. And her husband's name. And in the background a candle burned with a yellow flame.

Absurd joke, this blazing monument to death, with its candle flame struggling upwards, strong and bright despite the certainty that it would be extinguished, its cut flowers that still bloomed with all of their colour and did not wilt. And all this stubborn resurgent life was painted, she knew, with orpiment.

Marie Catherine supposed that such colours, at least, gave Lavoie an easy excuse to buy what she had asked of him.

'Are you well, Madame?' Arnaud was still standing in the doorway. She took her hand away from her mouth.

'Yes, thank you. I had asked for something that might remind me of eternal life, in the face of death. You may go.'

And when he'd closed the door, she turned the painting over on the bed and unhooked the back of the frame, lifted the back board off and found, wrapped in an old piece of rag (*Monsieur Lavoie, you should have used a rag that didn't smell of turpentine*) – there, a vial the length of her longest finger, filled with a greasy-looking ointment that, like the flowers, the skull, the candle's flame, was as yellow as the king of all poisons.

The painter had kept their agreement.

A frisson of fear rose through her, like a flight of beating wings moving from her feet to the crown of her head. She sat down at her writing table and, with the vial at her right hand, she took a sheet of new paper and began, *Dear Monsieur de la Reynie ...*

What poisons were circulating in Paris? La Reynie wondered, even as he remembered the fires burning down to ash on La Voisin's pyre. It was said that she, now dead, had washed the shirt of young Madame de Poulaillon's husband in arsenic and thus contracted in him sores that ate away at his skin and caused his death. It was said that she'd sold another woman ground diamonds that, sprinkled into food, would tear the intestines of the one who ate them and provoke an agonising death. It was said that she could treat a bouquet of flowers with such substances that the one who inhaled their perfume would be dead by the next morning. It was said that she had worked with a renegade priest, and had sold poisoned cloth in the court itself, perhaps even to the king's own mistress, Madame de Montespan. But there was no profit in thinking of much that was said about Madame de Montespan. La Voisin was dead, and half of her colleagues were dead, and the rest would be put on trial, Lesage and La Chapelle and La Filastre and La Voisin's daughter – all that cabal of poisoners, abortionists and sorceresses.

And which of the men and women who had employed their services were in prison? Some had fled France. Some there was too little evidence to arrest. Some waited in prison, but what evidence was there against them that could be substantiated by confrontation? La Reynie had brought the Comtesse de Roure before La Voisin, a few days before her death, and the old witch had not even recognised the woman she claimed had been her client. She was the devil's servant to the last. She had confessed, and confessed, and confessed, and still left La Reynie grasping only air when it was time to put the noose around her accomplices' necks.

La Reynie was in his office, preparing the documents that would be used in the trial of La Chapelle. He still hadn't found her daughter. Rumour had it that the fortune-teller with the birthmark had fled Paris, perhaps on the back of a winged devil.

La Reynie told himself that the sin, the murder, the corruption of the bond of marriage, was the same whether it lived among the high or the low, that it deserved the same attention and the same punishment. But he did not believe it. Let the eternal fire take La Voisin, Lesage and La Chapelle, as it inevitably would. They had written no laws, influenced no policy, corrupted no officials, commanded no armies. Meanwhile the criminals at the fortress of Vincennes whispered that Madame de Montespan had purchased poison, that she had conducted black Masses, that she had bought potions that would bind the king's affections to her and make him do as she willed. In the court she bought and sold favours as if she herself were the king's true wife. When the Maréchal de Luxembourg, that famed general, had been summoned to the Châtelet to answer for his dealings in poison, she had stopped her carriage on the street and allowed him to kiss her hand, had comforted him when he wept.

And yet the king protected her. And yet La Reynie still could not build a case against Luxembourg, although he was imprisoned and the magician Lesage swore that he could implicate him in the blackest of crimes. And La Reynie felt, but feared to say, that it was all the doing of this bedevilled woman, who sat at the king's right hand, wearing the face of an angel.

Sometimes La Reynie felt as if it were he himself who was under a spell, who could not see what was in front of his nose, as if the devil himself had stepped in to protect his own and covered the eyes of the law with his clawed hands. He had not proven these claims of poison. He had not even caught the murderer of the Baron de Cardonnoy, who seemed to have dissolved in mid-air on the night of his crime. Nor had he discovered the name of the servant who Lesage had claimed spied for the poisoners, although he suspected the baron's valet, who had returned to the hôtel escorted by the baronne's servants after La Reynie had thrown him out.

He knew how his name was spoken in the city of Paris. He knew his reputation. And he attended confession regularly, where he detailed his sins: pride, doubt, vanity. He did not list anger among them, although at times he was consumed by it. Anger at the salonnières, at the Princes and Princesses of the Blood, who simpered when he called them in for questioning and then retired and maligned him in their dens of hypocrisy. They would never burn, not as La Voisin had burned, but at times he would have laughed to see it.

He had a letter from the Baronne de Cardonnoy on his desk, which he knew he ought to read instead of brooding. In the salons they said that he had not found the baron's murderer because he had made no attempt to do so, that his enmity against the court was so great that he would refuse justice to a murdered man. He could have arrested the painter, Lavoie, and gained himself some time in the investigation, but the man had been beaten too bloody to be the murderer. Rumour gave the baronne no other lovers. She attended salons, she was witty, she was beautiful, and she received no men alone and was said to spend long days taking the place of the nursemaid with her children. She had been a loyal wife.

Which was not to say that the baron had had no enemies. He had enriched himself at court, had had dealings in business that left both his debtors and his creditors dissatisfied. But his murder in front of his own house must have been an act of either great passion or great desperation, and La Reynie saw no man in Paris whose hatred and fear could have so overwhelmed all reason. The brazen daring of the act had become its own concealment, and La Reynie knew only that he was looking for a man with long dark hair.

Then there were Lesage's muddled insinuations, impossible to unwind.

The baronne's letter was still in front of him. He had the feeling it would contain some difficult matter. He took out his paper knife.

Dear Monsieur de la Reynie,

It is with hesitation that I write to you. I am loath to examine my husband's papers with an eye to his errors, and had hoped to find only the evidence of some perhaps undeserved grudge. What I have found disturbs me greatly, so that as much as I wish it to provide some clue to my husband's murderer, some other part of me hopes that it may be a false trail, easily resolved by wiser heads than mine.

In my husband's correspondence I have found two items that make reference to a Père Roblin. I have enclosed both here. The first was in a book of accounts, forgotten, or so it seemed to me, after being used to mark a page. It is undated, but I believe it to be about two years old.

The second item is written in a different hand and is unsigned. You will see that it commends this Père Roblin to my husband, and thanks him for arranging their meeting. With it was the vial that I have also sent to you. Both the letter and the vial were concealed behind a row of books as if to protect them from prying eyes (it is for this reason that I was so long in finding these things, although I confess I have spent some nights wondering whether to send them to you). With the rumours gripping the city, I have only the darkest guesses about what the vial might contain. I pray you will test it for me. Perhaps (I am afraid to say I hope) my apprehensions are wrong, and I have worried myself and delayed your investigation for a trifle.

If that is the case, I suppose we must speak again about my husband's papers. My enquiries have only left me dismayed, and now I wonder whether I should have consigned them to you all along.

With all due respect,

Marie Catherine la Jumelle, Baronne de Cardonnoy

La Reynie folded the letter back along its creases, then folded it again until it was a neat square in the palm of his hand. He opened the pouch that had come with the letter and plucked the vial out of it, eyed the evil-looking yellowish liquid inside it. Perhaps it seemed poisonous only because every other waking thought he had was already about poison.

He went to the door and called for a clerk.

'Monsieur?' He was a new man, young, with a thick head of sand-coloured hair, thin sparrowish shoulders.

'Do you know the stray cats nearby?'

'No, Monsieur.'

'I need – no, never mind. Get someone to bring me a bowl of milk. I'll do the other thing myself.'

The clerk nodded, confused by La Reynie's abruptness. Now the lieutenant general cut himself off with a gesture of irritation and made for the door, without stopping to take his overcoat off its hook.

'Milk, yes?' he said to the clerk. 'In a bowl.'

'Of course, Monsieur.'

There was a family of stray cats that lived behind the prison. Bezons was fond of them. When he had a chance, he would bring a dish of milk or a stinking fish head wrapped in paper, and set it out and then pet the cats when they came to eat. If any person crouched by the door and made a chirping noise, they would come, expecting food. La Reynie went down on one knee, pressing the embroidered edge of his coat into the mud, and the heaviness of his heart was mixed with some other emotion that he couldn't quite name. It was something like the sickness he felt after watching a prisoner tortured, when the thrill of his own power curdled and left him weak and ashamed.

The cat that came first was female. When he curled his hand under her belly to lift her up, he felt the hard knots of her breasts swollen with milk. She had kittens. She hissed at him, and he pushed her away.

The other cats were still friendly with him, still hungry. Three came and rubbed their faces against his knee, and he rubbed their ears, and finally chose the grey one, which yowled when La Reynie lifted him up, and dug his claws into La Reynie's coat, protesting. He did not want to go inside the prison. He was a taut wire with ears pressed flat against his skull, squirming around to get out of La Reynie's grip. The policemen the lieutenant general met on the way back to his office eyed him and the cat with concern – the cat yelling protest, and La Reynie with one arm locked firmly around it, squeezing. He let go with relief once he'd reached his office, and the cat sprang out of his arms and landed on its feet, content suddenly to sniff around his desk on padded feet, its ears pricked forward.

A knock on the door.

'Milk, Monsieur. In a bowl.'

'Don't let the cat out.' He could see how the cat froze at the sound of the creaking hinges.

'Of course, Monsieur.' The young man backed out, leaving La Reynie with the bowl of milk in his hand.

At his desk he opened the vial and dripped a spoon's worth into the milk. He wondered how to mix it, remembering the rumours of poisons that worked merely through contact with skin. Finally he picked up his paper knife and swirled it around the bowl for a long time.

'Here now. Come drink.'

The cat took a long time to approach the bowl on the floor, sniffing suspiciously, belly low to the ground. La Reynie pushed the milk towards him, and the cat took fright and darted off to hide in the shadow of the curtains. Picking him up and putting him down near the bowl only made him scratch La Reynie's hands. He resigned himself to waiting, while the cat crouched and sniffed and finally tasted the milk with his tongue and found it sweet and much to his liking.

Then La Reynie slid down to the floor and stroked him while he drank. The soft, warm body shivered under his hand, and the cat paused his meal to rub his face against La Reynie's cuff and purr trustingly. It was only an animal. It had no soul.

'Good cat,' he said. 'Drink up.'

'It is poison.'

He was in the black-draped salon at Hôtel Cardonnoy. The baronne was there, surprised with a woman friend, a lady with a slightly horsey face whose dark hair loaned a shadow to the powdering of argentine that she had combed through it. Madame de Cardonnoy was gripping her hand on the sofa.

'Mademoiselle de Conti ... perhaps you should wait in my cabinet.'

La Reynie could see her knuckles white through her skin where she held her friend's hand, the way the other hand fumbled with the edge of her veil. Conti was an old family, related to the king himself. The baronne had influential friends.

'It's too terrible,' Mademoiselle de Conti offered, in a low, fluting voice, which was prettier than her face.

'Please.' The baronne made a shooing motion, and Mademoiselle de Conti stood and curtseyed.

'Monsieur de la Reynie.' The younger woman lifted her chin when she addressed him, looking directly into his eyes.

Was there something a little hard under her manners? La Reynie wondered. Something a little protective of her friend? She was the type who might have called him a devil in the salons, who might have wanted to sit next to the baronne to observe him, to make sure that he didn't try to devour her or drag her off to the prison at Vincennes.

'Forgive me,' he said, once Mademoiselle de Conti had gone. 'I feel I should have spoken to you more privately.'

'Mademoiselle de Conti is a true friend. She won't report what she heard. But ...' The baronne made a little helpless gesture, folded her hands in her lap, and La Reynie, strangely embarrassed, fell back on the manner in which he presented information to Bezons or to his policemen, pacing back and forth with his hand gliding along the back of one of the hôtel's winged silk chairs.

'We tested the vial on a stray cat and it promptly expired.' He clicked his teeth shut over a description of the poison's symptoms, which were not appropriate for a woman like the baronne. 'My chemist believes it contained orpiment. A very powerful poison.'

Madame de Cardonnoy nodded. 'I have heard of it.'

'Do you know who he might have wanted it for?'

'No.' She spoke quickly, but her face was pensive, as if she wanted to turn away from the question but couldn't.

He paused, reached the end of the length he was pacing, turned back. It might have presented the effect of a hawk wheeling in mid-air to dive, but what he felt was uncertainty in the face of the baronne's resigned acceptance. 'I have heard that your household was ill.'

'Indeed.' She looked up at him and smiled. 'The doctor has advised that I send the children to Cardonnoy early this season, to escape the air of Paris. Tomorrow I will be alone in the house, to conclude my husband's affairs.'

Outside the sun must have emerged from behind a cloud, because the fragile grey light that filtered through the tall windows grew suddenly bright and suffused the black-shrouded room with gold. The light cut across Madame de Cardonnoy's dress like a reaching hand, leaving, in the black cloth, a stripe of brighter black.

'The manner of the sickness ...' La Reynie began.

Madame de Cardonnoy shifted in her seat, sighing, so that new folds of her dress moved in and out of the light. 'I am afraid the details are not fit for polite company. A disease of flux.'

'And do you trust your cook, Madame?'

Now she sat bolt upright and stared at him, eyes so wide there was a rim of white around her blue irises.

'I beg your pardon, Monsieur?'

La Reynie braced himself with both hands on the back of a chair, found a loose thread and pulled at it. Her dismay was clearly genuine, and he hoped she realised how much he regretted causing it. She had not looked so alarmed at anything he had said to her yet.

'It can be very difficult to distinguish symptoms of natural illness from poisoning, Madame. Arsenic poisoning looks very much like flux to a doctor, and often the only true answers come during an autopsy, if then. So I ask you: do you trust the servants in your kitchen? Is there anyone in the household who might wish you or your children harm?'

Madame de Cardonnoy shook her head. She had regained some control of her emotions – now she looked merely insulted. 'The cook himself was ill, Monsieur. The whole kitchen was ill, as was I, my children, my lady's maid. The youngest kitchen boy has been sent back to his family, he was so near death. Do you think that they would have knowingly taken poison?'

The expression of pride on her face made her look younger than she was, and almost naïve. La Reynie bowed his head.

'Of course, Madame. And I believe ... you had your servants bring your husband's valet back to Hôtel Cardonnoy one night, did you not?'

'Monsieur, I see you are very well informed about who has come and gone from my house.' She made a movement as if to stand, then sank back into the sofa, her lips compressed in a tight line.

La Reynie had almost regretted the necessity of having her house watched. He did believe that she was in mourning, that her sorrow was the kind of genuine, understated grief that requires retreat and solitude.

'It is my duty, Madame, to know who might have had reason to desire your husband's death.'

She shook her head. 'I knew your men were stationed outside the painter Lavoie's house, but I confess I did not notice them here.'

Very quickly, again, she had suppressed the note of anger in her voice and spoke once more like a woman too tired by the demands on her heart to be anything except direct, and plain, and gentle. She was running one hand over the silk upholstery of her sofa, as if she were petting a cat.

'I am not here because of that visit,' he said. 'I know you bought a painting from Monsieur Lavoie.'

'I felt I owed him some restitution for my husband's violence, if you must know.'

'That is not what I've come to discuss. Although I will tell you, frankly, that I think that visit shows a lapse in judgement, however charitably meant.'

The intensity of the afternoon sun was still hanging in the air of the salon, catching the spinning motes of dust that hung in the air. Syrupy. It should have been hard to move through. The baronne blinked and left her eyes closed for a moment before looking back at La Reynie.

'Do you have other complaints about my conduct, Monsieur?'

'When your husband's valet returned here, did he spend any time in the kitchens?'

Madame de Cardonnoy's gaze darted to the ceiling and then towards the window, as if she hoped there might be some other person in the room to whom La Reynie was addressing his questions.

'Monsieur, I summoned a doctor the moment my children fell ill, and he said nothing of poison.'

'Your husband's valet detests you,' La Reynie said. He could hear himself taking the tone of a lecturing tutor. 'He denounced you in my presence. Why did you bring him back after that? An unfaithful servant? There is no household in Paris that would find you unjust in dismissing him.' Most masters would have had the man beaten. It annoyed him, obscurely, that the baronne had not.

'He was not unfaithful. He served my husband since he was a boy. If he was unjust in blaming me for my husband's death, I can forgive him for being distracted by grief.' All this Madame de Cardonnoy said very crisply, as if she could hear the grim bent of La Reynie's private thoughts. 'When I found the first letter from this Père Roblin, this priest, I wanted to know what dealings my husband might have had with such a person, and I knew that Henri was loyal to him and attended him everywhere. When my servants found him, he was drunk and distraught. I gave him a place to sleep and some money.'

'And did he have access to the kitchen?'

'Yes, he slept there!' Madame de Cardonnoy punctuated her exclamation with a sharp movement of her hand. 'For one night. This is absurd.'

'I believe, Madame,' said La Reynie, 'that it was perhaps two days later that your children fell ill.'

'No. Monsieur, I will not believe that.' But she looked frightened, her brows drawing together to leave a crease at the centre of her forehead. 'Henri attended my husband on my wedding night. Since he was a boy of thirteen. He would not harm the children.'

'And if he knew this Père Roblin? If the poison was intended for you?'

'You think he would have poisoned his master's heirs to do that?'

'The Maréchal de Luxembourg's valet agreed to deal with the devil to secure his master's profit.'

'You think my husband wanted to poison me, and you have no difficulty telling me this to my face, while I am dressed in mourning for him.' She had drawn the mourning veil over her lap, perhaps unconsciously, and La Reynie found himself tongue-tied. It was impossible to tell this woman anything she didn't want to hear.

'I think your husband was an ambitious man,' he said finally, 'and such men often find marriage to be a means to an end. And I think that your sense of charity has left your household insecure, and your children in danger. If this valet sprinkled his poison in the flour or dripped it into the broth, it might have been days before the household consumed it, and the doctor who attended your deathbeds would have had no reason to suspect foul play.'

The baronne shook her head, one hand pressed to her temple as if she wished to cover her ears. 'You're wrong, Monsieur. I don't believe it. He spoke out of turn in front of you. But he was loyal. I remember when he was a boy he was rebellious sometimes, or careless. My husband used to beat him with a switch and he'd come back and cry at his feet and beg for forgiveness. He wouldn't have done what you say.'

'And yet he nearly beat Alain Lavoie to death when his master commanded it.'

Madame de Cardonnoy was silent, her hands folded in her lap.

'There is another reason I urge you to be cautious,' La Reynie said. 'When you first told me your fears about your husband's affairs, I asked some prisoners at the Châtelet, well connected with the criminal world, if they knew his name. I was told that La Voisin, who was so recently burned at the stake for her crimes, had placed one of her associates as a spy among the servants in this house. The man I spoke to did not know this agent's name, but he said that it would have been someone who was close to the lord or lady of the house. Such as a valet.'

Madame de Cardonnoy took a long breath. 'That cannot be true.'

'Do you know where Henri went after he left your hôtel?'

'No.'

'And what did he say about this Père Roblin?'

'Very little. He was reluctant to speak to me.'

'You should have sent me a message as soon as he was in your house, if you thought he knew something of these letters.'

'Yes, Monsieur. Perhaps.' She looked up from her hands and met La Reynie's eyes. 'I thought I could get the priest's address from him and send it to you.'

'You shouldn't have tried that.' La Reynie sighed. 'This priest is involved in some very wicked things, Madame. When I sent my men to his church after receiving your letter, it was empty. Your husband's murder occurred just after we began arresting members of the court for their dealings in poison. If this Père Roblin thought that your husband might be summoned – or if, perhaps, he knew that your husband had had a change of heart once the poison was in his hands – he might have become very desperate. A nobleman threatening to give evidence against him, with a letter written in the priest's own hand, with a vial of poison, would have doomed him before any tribunal.'

'Yes,' the baronne said. 'I suppose it would have.' She toyed with the edges of the veil in her lap, her face troubled.

La Reynie had thought all of this through, carefully, after his secretary had removed the cat's corpse from his office. The baronne, with her too-forgiving feminine generosity, had invited the murderer's accomplice back into her house. She had not seen the ill will her husband's servant bore towards her, even when he cursed her to her face. La Reynie could not help but admire her for it, even as he blamed her for the danger she had brought upon her children. For wasn't it for the sake of women like her – so innocent and so easily led astray – that he must root out the evil from Paris?

'If his man Henri was a spy for the priest or for La Voisin, he could have told them all your husband's movements. You remember that it was Henri who first accused you of involvement with the painter?'

'Yes, Monsieur. I remember.' Her gaze was fixed on her hands.

'May I ask you a favour, Madame?' La Reynie stretched out his hand towards her, although she was too far away to take it. Always the gestures of polite society came stiffly to him. If he had been in one of her salons, they would have laughed behind their hands, but the Baronne de Cardonnoy never seemed to be hiding mockery.

'What is it, Monsieur?'

'A woman like you isn't meant for police work. Go to your husband's estates, spend the days with your children, grieve in peace and quiet. These people are dangerous. You can do no good by hunting them down, and you risk your reputation and perhaps your life.'

She nodded. 'Thank you, Monsieur de la Reynie, for your advice.'

'Will you obey it?'

'I will try. I leave for Cardonnoy in a few days.' She rose, slowly, from her seat. 'Will you tell me if I can help you in any other way?'

'Of course, Madame.'

After he had gone, Victoire eased the door open and came and sat next to Marie Catherine where she was lying on the chaise, her ankles hanging off the end, looking like a woman from a painting or a dress that someone had discarded. Victoire lifted Marie Catherine's feet and put them in her lap, running her fingers over the knobby bone of her ankle.

'And have you seen the devil, Madame?' she asked. It was strange, coming face to face with La Reynie. Victoire was only now realising that some part of her had been expecting him to see through her.

'For God's sake, stop it.' Marie Catherine sat up and took her feet back. Slowly she began to unpin the widow's veil from her hair, letting the crepe puddle on the chaise and crease. 'You're not the one pretending to be the idiot pious widow for a man who thinks he ought to have the right to act in place of your father. But yes, repeat the joke that everyone in Paris has already heard.'

'I'm sorry. You're right, that joke's been everywhere.' Victoire had said those words often, recently. *I'm sorry. I'm sorry.* They never felt adequate to the situation, as if each apology was one cup scooped out of the ever-replenishing ocean. She would have apologised for something larger than her careless joke, if she had known how to formulate the words for it. 'Did he believe you?'

'I think so,' said Marie Catherine. 'For now. I only had to abase myself, because I'm just a stupid woman who doesn't know how to run her household. He thinks Henri poisoned the broth in the kitchen and made my children sick. And I had to nod and say, "Yes, Monsieur, yes, Monsieur, I'm a fool, Monsieur, of course it won't happen again."'

Victoire sat up and squeezed Marie Catherine's hand. She'd been pacing back and forth in the old baron's study the whole time Marie Catherine had remained closeted with La Reynie, wondering what the Lieutenant General of Police could be saying to her, whether there was something – anything – that they had overlooked, that would now give the game away. Could she bargain with the baron's ghost, as she had tried to, on many nights after his murder? Could she intervene in any way at all, if the police now blamed Marie Catherine?

Now her fear melted away.

'Marie, we could be celebrating! If he believes you, then it's nearly over. I'll pour you a toast.' She was already getting up, ready to call for Marie Catherine's man and a decanter. She danced an allemande across the floor. The light and Marie Catherine, too, were beautiful. Victoire could see the blue veins in her wrists as she counted the pins that had secured her veil to her hair.

'It's never going to be over,' Marie Catherine said, flatly.

Victoire turned back at the door. 'Do you believe that?'

'I know Henri loved my husband, but he didn't poison the children. I've tried my best to procure Monsieur de la Reynie a guilty man, but he only wants to eat innocents. And it's my fault. I hope the priest's little housekeeper has got away.'

The air in the room felt sharper than it had a moment ago. Victoire looked up at the ceiling. The truth was, she hadn't thought twice about the valet's fate. What part of her was made that way, so that a little cold voice in her heart insisted *that man does not matter*? As she had stood in the alley behind Hôtel Cardonnoy, the night she had done what she'd done, she had seen the baron in her mind's eye not as a man, but only as her lover's tormentor. She had barely realised that when she shot him, he would bleed blood, like any human.

Perhaps Marie Catherine was made with something that she lacked. She wanted to crawl towards it, the way a wolf in winter looks with fear and envy at the bright window of a peasant's house.

'You're not guilty,' Victoire said.

'Yes, I am.' She made a noise somewhere between a laugh and a sob. 'I'll never be able to disprove it, and it would be madness to try. For all I know, Henri did poison us all, and I brought a murderer into my house.'

'Marie, that's not your fault. And anyway it's me. I'm the one who caused all of this.'

Victoire didn't want to let those words hang in the air, so she opened the door and peeked out at the empty hallway. Her hands were shaking. She knotted her fingers together. If she could turn herself entirely to ice. *That man doesn't matter. Only we matter.* She wanted to believe it.

'I know, Victoire,' said Marie Catherine. 'It doesn't matter now.'

'Can you ever forgive me?'

She couldn't help remembering how Marie Catherine had pulled away the last time they had embraced, just at the moment when she had felt most ready to lose herself in her body. How she had come to Victoire's room, only to draw back from her, as if there was something in her that she no longer recognised. It didn't matter that she had already promised Victoire her forgiveness. Victoire could not forgive herself. For a moment she even wished that she could be harder, crueller, so that she wouldn't constantly have to turn to Marie Catherine and ask her, again, for the love she knew she didn't deserve.

Sometimes, before, she had exaggerated her other romances with Marie Catherine, to seem elegant and dangerous, to escape the loneliness she sometimes felt in her childhood room on the place Royale, where a rocking horse still stood in the corner by her toilette, or in her apartments at Versailles, which she shared with her mother. And because she was frightened. She could hold her lover but not possess her. She had wanted to live inside the way Marie Catherine looked at her. Now she was ashamed that she could not live up to that image of herself.

'I already have forgiven you.' Marie Catherine spoke very quickly, as if it were a promise that required no thought at all.

'Then what's wrong between us, Marie?'

Marie Catherine had her discarded veil in her hands and was twisting it back and forth, not looking at Victoire.

'I don't know.' She spoke quickly, shaking her head. 'It's not that I'm angry with you. It's just that at every moment I feel as though the entire city is watching us. I'm so tired of trying to be the person I'm expected to be. Maybe it will be better at Cardonnoy.'

Still Victoire felt sure that Marie Catherine had to be angry, in some corner of her heart. Not only because Victoire was angry with herself, with the way she'd thrilled with terror after the gun went off, how quickly her courage had failed, how she'd ridden home in the rain and shouted at her maid on the stairs, afraid that she'd see the darker spots of blood on her red coat. Sometimes, now, that night seemed unreal to her. There were days when she didn't think about it at all, when she sat with Marie Catherine talking through the ways they could put La Reynie off their trail as if the murder was just something that had happened, and wasn't her doing. Then at night she would remember.

She wasn't the hero she'd thought she was. If Marie Catherine saw her at all, she must see the way her weakness wrapped around her recklessness, like a vine choking a dying tree.

'I don't see how you can keep saying that you're not angry with me. I've brought all this trouble down on you, and there's no way I can help except to stay away from you. Every second that I'm at court I feel as if I've abandoned you. Don't you ever wish that I'd done what I said I would do and confessed?'

'No. I don't.' Finally Marie Catherine was looking at her, very squarely, as if Victoire were a servant girl who she was evaluating. There was something almost motherly in it. The tears were beginning again, however much she blinked.

'I'm the murderer you brought into your house.'

'You said that already. I don't care. I simply don't care what's right. You've sinned, I've sinned, I suppose we'll be judged before God, but I'll forgive you whatever you've done.' Marie Catherine's voice was calm, as if she had weighed the words and didn't have to think about them. As if she believed them, the way one might believe in a prayer one had repeated since childhood. She beckoned to Victoire. 'Come here?'

The few steps to the chaise felt very long, as if the room was expanding around her. She lay down on the cushions with her head in Marie Catherine's lap, smelling the scent of her powder, her jasmine perfume, the leather of her gloves, her sweat. Everything was swimming. Marie Catherine stroked her hair. She might have been a child again, Victoire thought, ashamed.

'I just wish that I could keep this from falling on Henri,' Marie Catherine murmured. 'If only he hadn't accused me in front of La Reynie.'

'I'm sorry.' She would be better, somehow.

'I know, my love.'

Chapter Seventeen

———

Recently at Hôtel Cardonnoy you could wonder whether there were voices in the walls. So it was when Jeanne woke up, with the first light of morning. She had heard, distinctly, the voice of a child, young and genderless, calling out as it ran down the hall outside Madame's chamber. But the children had been sent away to the Cardonnoy estates the day before. It wasn't, she thought, a dream. Long after she awoke, as she laid out Madame's dress for the day and fixed her own hair and fetched a basin of warm water for Madame's toilette, all with the utmost awareness of the small sounds of her work – long after, as the morning light strengthened and grew bright, she heard the sound of running footsteps outside the door, back and forth, racing, asking her without words to come out and catch the child, to feed it breakfast, take it back to bed, come down the staircase with its hand in hers.

She didn't know whose child it was. The Cardonnoy brother and sister would have called out to each other as they played their games, complaining or teasing each other. This apparition only laughed, sometimes. She wasn't sure whether the laugh sounded lonely or not, but she thought she might have liked to take the creature into Madame's cabinet and ask why it had come, and why only she heard it.

Of course when she opened the door, there was no one there.

Lavoie's face had healed, and now he could often step outside his house without that pervasive feeling of fear. He felt a lightness

that was not entirely the result of the fact that the police informant was no longer on his doorstep, but also came from the work
of his hands in his studio. The painting for Madame de Cardonnoy had been a quick piece. He had not cared for it, at first, but
once he had begun, it was like a clarifying fire. Perhaps it was
that the debt of violence he owed to the baron had been settled.
When he turned, now, to the painting of Troy, the work felt less
like descending into the muck of an evil dream, and instead the
vision flowed through his hands, however imperfectly, and left
him clean.

He was accepting portrait work again. He had bought a new
jacket cut from fine brocade. He thought, even, that Madame de
Cardonnoy might in some manner have put his name about in her
circles, because while the portrait of her and her children continued to languish in an attic in Hôtel Cardonnoy, unfinished and
unfinishable, he had received a note from a madame on the place
Royale, a Princess of the Blood with whom he had no connection,
who nevertheless enquired whether he was able to paint a small
portrait that she might send to a daughter who had taken religious
vows some years ago.

An old house, breathing with the noise of servants in the pas-
sageways. All was dim and hushed, the polished gold of the
furniture catching glints of winter sunlight, this Madame de Conti
dressed in a gown of ruffled purple-red silk, not the style of the
season, but rich. Another daughter, the youngest, her dark, curling
hair escaping from her hairdresser's style, reclined on a chaise and
read aloud while her mother sat straight-backed for the portrait. A
lady's maid brought tea and apple cakes and circled around Lavoie
like a nervous sparrow.

He studied Madame de Conti's face as he laid her shadow
down over the *imprimatura*. This woman, now in her sixties, was
famous enough that Lavoie knew something of her name. Her
mother had been Madame de Chevreuse, the famous intriguer,
her husband a rebel against the king who, it was said, went mad in
prison. Her son had married the king's natural daughter in January.
Her portrait was, perhaps, the largest commission Lavoie had ever
received.

'My daughter recommends you, Monsieur,' said Madame de

Conti. 'She says you painted some ladies of Madame de Fontet's salon.'

'Thank you, Madame,' said Lavoie, although he might have said, *Just one, and no one will ever see that portrait.* When he looked up, the daughter was watching him impassively. She had inherited her mother's rather striking brows and shadowed eyes, but not her ash-blonde hair or the gentle curve of her chin.

'Shall I go on reading, Maman?'

'Please, chérie.'

The novel she was reading seemed to be one long and beautiful conversation, and Lavoie only half listened to the arguments of Cloèlie asking her parents to let her marry according to her own inclination. He looked at the colours, the lined face of this woman as she would appear out of the shadows of the canvas, and only occasionally glanced at the daughter whose level voice filled the room. And more than once, at these moments, he found that although her reading had not faltered, she was also watching him, reciting the book, apparently, from memory.

'I should thank you,' he said at the end of the sitting, 'for your influence on your mother.'

'It is nothing, Monsieur,' said Mademoiselle de Conti. 'I am a friend of Madame de Cardonnoy. It was my pleasure to meet you.'

'My daughter has excellent taste, Monsieur Lavoie,' said Madame de Conti, stepping expertly between her child and Lavoie, as she might have done if he had presumed to take the girl's hand and kiss it. 'I trust her recommendation in all things.'

And he returned home wondering what transaction he had not been a party to. He did not think the look in Mademoiselle de Conti's eyes had been inclination. Rather it had been a kind of solemn curiosity, hard-edged in a way that he did not expect from the child of such a great house. Had it been suspicion? Or was it merely that the baronne had decided that the risk he had taken for her had earned more than their agreed-upon payment and had asked for other favours from other quarters?

He would make no more passionate mistakes, he told himself. He would see his paintings hang on the walls of Versailles.

*

Victoire was burning her gentleman's coat. She had promised herself that she would, many times, but each time her hands hesitated, not over the fire, but before she had even touched the clothes, which were hidden under the mattress of the high bed in her room on the place Royale. On the night of the day that the painter came to paint her mother, she sent her maid away and put on the trousers, then the shirt, then the coat. The sleeves were stained with blood. With her hair loose she looked like the ghost of herself, when she caught her reflection in the darkened window-panes. She barred the door. She imagined leaping down from the window, riding to Saint-Germain-des-Prés. She wished she hadn't schemed to bring the painter into her house. She had sat in the room with her mother, feeling invisible. Her long hair and her skirts were only another disguise, a costume that she had no native right to. If she had been a woman once, she had relinquished that claim when she spilled blood. Now who could say what she ought to be called.

How much better it would be if she could leave behind her skin and go out into the night like this, a ghost, dressed in another man's blood.

At times she felt the kick of the gun as it recoiled in her hands. The moment – the opening of the carriage door, the explosion – was so perfectly sealed away from the rest of her life that often it felt as if she'd done nothing at all. It was only that it came back at frightening moments, that she wondered why she couldn't rid herself of it, and then wondered, again, how she had ever believed that it was something she could be rid of. Sometimes she cursed herself, and sometimes she thought of Marie Catherine, locked away in some convent, deprived of her children, and knew that she could not regret what she had done. But why couldn't she hold on to her bravery? It guttered like a fire that burned its fuel too fast.

She imagined riding to Hôtel Cardonnoy in the night, to ask, again, *Can you love me still, although I've become the architect of your disaster?* Perhaps she would believe the answer, if she could ask just one more time.

Victoire fed the coat's bloody sleeves to the fire first. The gold buttons wouldn't burn, but they glowed red-hot among the coals. The trim singed and smoked. There was a knock on the door and she unbarred it to let her mother in. Victoire was dressed only in her shift.

She crossed the room on bare feet and put her arms around her mother's neck, breathing in the scent of her powder.

'What on earth are you doing?' Madame de Conti raised her thumb and smeared away the tear that was starting in her daughter's left eye.

'I'm burning the gentleman's suit I had made.'

Madame de Conti snorted. 'Good riddance. I thought that get-up was going to end with you in a convent, too. Give me the trousers, thank you, I'll feed them in as well.'

They passed the poker back and forth and watched the clothes burn. Madame de Conti did not remark on the stains. She had spent her own youth in the rebellion that shook France when Louis XIV inherited the throne. Her mother had fled France, returned and fled again. Her husband, Victoire's father, had been imprisoned and had, it was said, gone mad there. She rarely spoke of those times. One did not speak of rebellion against the king, not any more. And yet disgrace had also touched her with its hand, and she had learned how to step back out of its shadow.

'May I take it to mean that you're done with this business?' Madame de Conti asked her daughter.

'For a little while, at least.'

She had done what couldn't be undone, and the deed lived beside her like a shadow. Perhaps it always would. Victoire imagined her other self climbing the chimney with the smoke and sitting there, naked under the sky. Her mother passed her the poker, and Victoire nudged his sleeve back into the fire, watching him spark up, again, into incorporeal flames.

Tomorrow she would return to Versailles. To wait, once more, until disgrace found her, or gave some sign that it had passed her over.

At first Marie Catherine barely missed the children. It was easier, not to have one or the other of them showing up in a doorway when she was otherwise occupied, tugging at her skirts or asking for a sweet or tattling on the nursemaid. It was only after a day or two had passed that she began to worry. If the servants at Cardonnoy were feeding them well, if Sophie's new loose tooth was hurting her. Tiny, inconsequential questions. Would Anne let Nicolas go outside without his winter coat, sick as he'd been?

That morning she was sitting at the baron's old desk, in his office, clearing out the detritus of papers. That week she had found an unexpected peace in the monotony of numbers. She sat with Monsieur Viron, who kept her husband's books, and had him introduce her to the sums that filled her husband's coffers, now the inheritance of her son. She couldn't break herself of the habit of touching her quill to her lips when she was thinking, and so at night her mirror would greet her with a black mark over her mouth, as if she had sealed her lips with dark wax.

It was Jeanne who brought her the news of Henri. The girl, who had once seemed to Madame de Cardonnoy merely fastidious, had somehow drawn herself up in the weeks since the baron's death and become a sharp-faced person who observed everything and said nothing. Madame de Cardonnoy would notice, when Jeanne sat by her in the evening with her mending in her hands, or flitted about straightening the bottles on the cosmetics table, or scolded a chambermaid who had left the bedcovers messily creased, how carefully the servant girl observed her work, taking pains to conceal the many quick glances her eyes darted back at her mistress. Watching.

'Arnaud says that the police have arrested Henri,' she said, midcurtsey, as soon as she'd stepped into the baron's office. 'Madame.' With a very discreet nod of her head, as if to compensate for the abruptness of her words.

'However does he know that?' Madame de Cardonnoy put her pen down.

She had hoped that La Reynie, on leaving, would reconsider his theory of the valet's revenge on his mistress. That once he was alone, the idea that the baron's man might be desperate enough to poison children would seem hare-brained and stupid. She pitied Henri.

'Because Arnaud sneaks off to visit him and drink, when he's supposed to be doing errands for the hôtel,' Jeanne said.

'Hmm,' said Madame, and Jeanne felt a little frisson of shame for tattling. Even though she despised Arnaud.

'He says that he went to Henri's lodging house and that the widow living in the furnished room across from him said the police had come for that man and taken him away, and his friends had also better stop coming.'

'Thank you, Jeanne,' said Madame.

Jeanne let out her breath and then left the room with her face hot. She might have reminded Madame de Cardonnoy that she had served her faithfully, that she had lied in her service, scorned the police, carried a letter on the dark streets of Paris without asking what was in it. And so perhaps she deserved to know how her mistress stood with Monsieur de la Reynie. Instead she put her hands over her face. She could imagine Laure in front of her, in La Chapelle's garden, holding her hands, explaining in all gentleness. *Your employment was not to serve her faithfully, but to learn her affairs and know them as well as your own heart. If you let yourself believe that they are better than you, you will also believe the lies they tell themselves, and our job is to get at the truth.*

If only she hadn't spent those days ill. If only Mademoiselle de Conti hadn't been present when the lieutenant general appeared, peeking out of the baron's study every second heartbeat, she might have listened at the door while he talked to Madame. As it was, she didn't know what was going on, and she had given Laure all of her money, and she didn't know what to do about the jewels in the linen chest, and she had not done her duty. And Laure hadn't written to her. She went down the stairs cursing her own stupidity.

Thank you, Jeanne, she told herself at the bottom, having called herself a different kind of stupid cow for each of the thirty-two steps. *That will be all.*

Once again, she heard footsteps in the house, somewhere above her. It wasn't a servant. Not with that laughter.

The world might have moved sideways for a second. For a moment she thought that she might be seeing what Laure saw. Not a spirit, not a devil, just an intensification in the light and shadows that kissed each other in the hallway. Its image moved upside down across the ceiling, taking short steps like a child, running on all fours like a cat, bright as the after-image of the sun on her closed eyelids, a shape that was no creature she could have named, but that struck her down with the force of her recognition. Her hair stood on end.

'Who's there?'

No one. The spirit dissolved. Jeanne felt her heart beating in her palms and along her scalp. Then the maid Agnès came around the corner, and Jeanne was standing in the front hall of the Hôtel Cardonnoy that she knew, which had grown almost invisible to her from familiarity.

'Look at you, standing there as if there's no work to be done.' Agnès's voice might have sounded teasing, but it was a wonderstruck kind of teasing that suggested some people were getting above themselves.

Jeanne had to shake herself free of the reverie. Still, everything looked bright. When she went up to Madame's room, to pack the new black dresses into the trunks that would go to Cardonnoy and the vividly coloured silk gowns safely away until Madame needed them again, each dress seemed like the limp, insubstantial body of a ghost. The trunks, too, smelled of lavender, so that it might have been summer, somewhere far away.

The shift with the gold sewn into it was badly hidden. Jeanne found it with her fingers, balled up under the neatly folded skirts of Madame's mourning dress in her travelling trunk. Madame's folding was messy. It was unbelievable, the way she didn't bother to keep track of her movable fortune. The maids at Cardonnoy would have pulled it out, clucked over the creases, then wondered at its hidden cargo.

When she put it on under her own dress, it was for safe keeping. She had decided nothing, done nothing that could not still be reversed. If Madame didn't know how to hide her secrets, it was, after all, Jeanne's duty to hide them for her.

The weight of the gold settled over her shoulders like a shirt of chain mail.

There was no such thing as solitude at Versailles. Everywhere one went there were workmen, servants, courtiers at loose ends, trying to avoid the moment when they'd retire to their closet chambers, to be folded up for the night like unworn dresses. From her place in the chapel, Victoire could hear someone laughing, a slightly desperate and lonely sound. The laughter of someone whose companions won't join them in mirth. It moved down the corridor, away from her. She was kneeling towards the back of the chamber, with her hands clasped before her, looking not at the cross hung high on the wall, but at the stone floor before her.

The kneeling felt false and formal. She was trying to recapture the feeling, which she had stopped having a long time ago, of being a young girl in church, at her convent school, alone among the other students, with only the naked air hanging between her and the presence of the spirit. She had thought then, sometimes, that she would take holy orders as her sisters had, and live out her life behind the cloister walls. Perhaps if she could sit in stillness long enough, the dove would descend to her and explain why she was as she was, and to what purpose she had been made. Jeanne d'Arc had taken up a sword, Christine de Pizan had taken up her pen. Perhaps she too had a calling.

Slowly she had ceased to believe. Was it only that the world had come between her and that feeling – the opera, the lights of Paris, Madame Fontet's salon, the thousand distractions that were, in the end, her life? No, it had been a deeper rebellion. At night, in the convent, she had lain awake, looking up into the darkness, and she had said, *I will not bend*. She should have had a different life than this one. Instead she had thrown herself, fumbling, out of that alleyway with her gun, and when she had fallen she had let Marie Catherine pick her up and clean the blood off her.

She could still imagine the sacrifice, as she ought to have offered it. If she had killed him, she was willing to die for it. It was not the murder itself that froze her blood, but the fear that had come after it. What purpose did she have, if that violence, or that moment of courage, or that sin, didn't have the power to free her, or her lover? She would, she thought, have died for her. But it wasn't enough to die.

Someone had come into the chapel behind her. She heard footsteps, and the whisper of a lady's skirts. The woman walked up the aisle and stopped a little behind Victoire, who kept her head bent. Someone else was trying to be alone here. She felt the pressure of the other woman's eyes on her and she closed her own, listening to the rhythm of her own breath, neither praying nor thinking. After a while she gathered her skirts and got up, and found that the woman behind her was Madame de Maintenon, the king's confidante. She was middle-aged and meek-looking. Her eyes were soft, where La Montespan's glittered, and while they had been cast down in prayer when Victoire first recognised her, now she looked up and followed Victoire with her gaze. When Victoire would have passed by and left the chapel, Madame de Maintenon reached out and touched her sleeve, and Victoire paused.

'It's good to see you here, Mademoiselle de Conti.' Madame de Maintenon smiled. 'Will you sit with me a while?'

'Of course. If it would make you happy.' She was afraid that her tone sounded petulant. She sat by Madame de Maintenon and looked at her hands.

'You're a great deal like your mother, aren't you, Mademoiselle?'

'I haven't heard that said often,' Victoire replied. What most people observed about her mother was that she'd once been a beauty, and Victoire was not. She could tell that Madame de Maintenon was trying to work her way around to whatever topic she actually wanted to discuss, as delicately as she could manage. Victoire resented it, and resented her.

'I don't mean in appearance, but in spirit,' Madame de Maintenon said. 'Both of you share the same gifts from God – intelligence, loyalty, even the kind of bravery that's uncommon among women. But with those come dangers. It's easy to overstep one's station in the world.'

A cold rage was climbing up Victoire's back.

'As you did, Madame?' she asked, looking up into her companion's face. Madame de Maintenon had been the governess of the king's bastard children, before she was his confidante. Or his lover. She had been a woman from an impoverished noble family, the child of a despised Huguenot, who had married a man with no title and then outlived him. She had befriended Madame de Montespan, and then used the king's mistress to bring her closer to the king himself. Victoire was aware, as she looked into Madame de Maintenon's gentle eyes, that she had offered her a fairly mortal insult.

But Madame de Maintenon smiled.

'Yes, as I did.' She put her hand on Victoire's shoulder. 'When I was girl I went to a convent school, like you did, Mademoiselle de Conti. I was so very young, and clever, like you, and while I was there I found that my spirit rebelled against the discipline that the nuns imposed. Why should I sit silent and obedient in the chapel before dawn? Why should I ruin my hands scrubbing the floors, or mumble through a Latin verse that my convent teacher barely seemed to understand? I knew my talents were wasted there. And my family was so poor that I believed for a long time that my only choice would be to return and take holy orders, for no one will marry a girl without a dowry in these times. I was very proud. It is a vice I haven't overcome.'

Again, Victoire knew that Madame de Maintenon was circling around a point that she wanted to make. She spoke as if she simply did not understand that Victoire had been trying to offend her. But Victoire knew that she did understand. She felt helpless, rooted to the pew by anger and by the insipid weight of Madame de Maintenon's hand on her shoulder. She had never been able to conceal herself, and this woman was nothing but concealments.

'That must have been very difficult for you, Madame.' Her voice was stiff.

'Oh, a little,' said Madame de Maintenon. 'I think it was less of a trial than many are forced to bear. And I was lucky, because I found a dear friend, one of the nuns, who I loved so much that I thought I would happily die for her. It was through that friendship that I first came to love God, and I think if I had never formed that attachment, I would never have found my way to him.'

As she spoke, the walls of the chapel seemed to open out onto some flat and empty space. Victoire sat very still. She had not been this frightened when the king's companion scolded her for her gentleman's suit. If Madame de Maintenon knew her secret. Many women had bosom friends. But how many would die for them? It was as if she had looked into Victoire's heart and seen the writing there: *I will die for her.* Above everything else, she could not let it show on her face.

'What happened to your friend, Madame?' Victoire asked.

'She was a sister in the convent. I took my first communion with her by my side. And then I left those walls, and went out into the world.' Now she took her hand back from Victoire's shoulder. 'Will you look at me, child?'

Victoire turned and met her gaze.

'I know what power there is in friendship,' said Madame de Maintenon. 'But it can be turned to good or to evil.'

'Do you have cause for concern, in my case?' Victoire held Madame de Maintenon's gaze, feeling as if she had left herself behind. There was nothing to see in the other woman's eyes. It was like looking at the surface of a still lake, on which the sky is reflected.

'You know that I was friends with Madame de Montespan, once?'

'Yes, I know it,' Victoire said.

'Although she was involved in her adultery with the king, I thought her so charming and kind that I cared nothing for the sin. But you must know, surely, what they whisper of my old friend now?'

'I know what they say, but I don't know that it is believed.'

'Those who matter believe it.' Madame de Maintenon shook her head, a small gesture. 'It has taken a long time for the king to part with her, and I think for some years there has been little happiness between them. But he won't have it said that he was bewitched, and that he let a woman rule him.'

Victoire might have asked who would take Athénaïs's place in the king's affection. But she knew, as every member of the court knew. It was this woman, humble, old, no longer beautiful, who mortified her pride in company by pretending that she was stupid when she was not. If she had known, she would have brought Marie Catherine to her, and not to Madame de Montespan, when they had visited Versailles together.

'It's to your credit, that you've stood by your friend, Madame de Cardonnoy, and comforted her in her sorrow.' It was the first time that she had said the name that Victoire had been waiting for her to say. 'It's easy to forget a friend who's absent, or who has fallen on hard times. But I wonder, Mademoiselle de Conti, is this woman also a good friend to you? Does she lead you towards the right path, or away from it?'

'I know that I'm not what you consider a good woman, Madame,' said Victoire. She was trying to choose her words carefully, as she should have chosen them carefully earlier, in her letters, in the entire stretch of her life. 'But I hope you won't let that influence your opinion of my friend. She has done nothing wrong.'

'You seem very sure of it,' said Madame de Maintenon, 'but if that is the truth, I worry for her. Unlike you, she has no family left to protect her or her name. I fear you might be wise to step away from her now, before she falls.'

There was nothing ugly in her voice, which was as gentle as it had always been. Victoire felt the sudden unwanted prickling of tears in her eyes, and she forced herself to breathe slowly, to keep her gaze downcast until the urge to cry subsided. She was so shocked by the onset of the humiliating tears, by the intensity of her physical reaction, that it took her a moment to understand what Madame de Maintenon had said. When she understood, it was as if she had stumbled over a dark, hollow place inside herself.

'Do you have some reason to be concerned for the state of my soul, Madame?' Victoire had been looking at her hands, and now she looked up, into Madame de Maintenon's serene face.

'Only that I've heard a great deal of your adventures – your prince's outfit, your poetry, your role in Madame de Fontet's salon. Perhaps I have overstepped myself in speaking to you like this. But I have seen you downcast more than once this spring, and I have heard of what happened to your friend's husband, and I thought it would be kind to offer you some advice.'

'You read my poetry, Madame?' Victoire remembered, now, the poem that she had thoughtlessly given to Mademoiselle de Tavanne, thinking that she, too, might be a citizen of the secret country of women in which Victoire lived.

'I would leave such things to the gentlemen, Mademoiselle de Conti,' said Madame de Maintenon. 'Our glory isn't in poetry, but in obedience. I think that if you applied yourself there, you would find it challenge and adventure enough, even for a woman like you.'

'Thank you,' said Victoire. 'For your counsel.' She stood up and left the chapel, with her back straight. The feeling had left her body.

Was that to be her future, then? The king's new mistress denied that she would rule, but she would rule all the same, through piety and abnegation and those gentle reflections on her own sins. Could Victoire have learned to live that way, if she had never been in love? She was afraid that she might have. There was a heroism in self-denial that might, in the end, have pulled her in. She had felt it when she was kneeling in the chapel – that cold knowledge that she would relinquish anything if, in return, she could know for certain that Marie Catherine was safe.

Now she was afraid that she had made a mistake that would be impossible to undo. Madame de Maintenon knew her place in the world, and she would hesitate to accuse Victoire herself of any of her crimes. But Marie Catherine was no one, a little woman who had married up into the nobility as La Maintenon had married down. Victoire had brought Marie Catherine to Versailles, into the same room as Madame de Montespan. She had trusted the king's mistress to intercede for her. But Madame de Montespan's star was falling. Victoire had asked the wrong woman for help.

She wanted to saddle her horse and ride out from Versailles into the dusk, until she reached the gates of Hôtel Cardonnoy and could call up to Marie Catherine's window and ask her to run away with her and change her future. Instead she would write a letter, in their invisible ink, warning Marie to be on her guard. She would be a good daughter, for a little while. Perhaps she could still wait just long enough, bend just enough, that they would both be saved.

It was morning and La Reynie had not slept. He was half dozing in his carriage, his eyes closed against the early sun, his muscles tense against the inevitable jostling on Paris's cobbled streets. He'd woken in the night from a dream in which he observed La Voisin's torture and been unable to fall back asleep. Now he climbed down from his coach in a daze in front of the Châtelet, feeling the building looming over him like a living thing. It was an effect of his bad sleep.

He was so distracted that he barely saw the beggar child who uncurled from his post on the pavement until the boy was close enough to touch his sleeve. He raised a hand to ward him off instinctively, and behind him he heard his coachman crack the whip. But the boy's hands and face were clean, he saw, cleaner than he could have expected for a child who'd been sleeping curled up in the cold outside the prison. He clenched his hands on the sleeve of La Reynie's coat so fiercely that his knuckles turned white.

'Monsieur, you're the Lieutenant General of Police, are you not?'

La Reynie wrenched his arm back. 'I have nothing to give you.'

'I've been waiting for you, Monsieur. I want to talk to you about the crimes of Père Roblin. He's a priest, he's fled the city. My mother works for him, and I know everything he's done.'

How old was this boy? Twelve perhaps, with blond hair and light eyes and a short scar on his forehead, under his hair. His coat was worn out and he was shivering as he spoke, so that he stuttered on his words, and La Reynie almost did not hear the name of the priest, Roblin, who had occupied his thoughts since the day he'd received the letter from Madame de Cardonnoy containing his name. Since he had arrested the late baron's valet and asked him to tell him what he knew of this priest.

'What's your name, child?' he asked the boy.

'Michel.'

'And you're the priest's servant?'

'I'm his son.' The boy met his eyes, defiantly, and La Reynie found himself looking harder at the child, as if he would be able to read the signs of devilment in that young face.

'You'd better come inside.'

Michel followed him obediently, walking a few steps behind him like a hunting dog as La Reynie entered the fortress, called his clerk, unlocked the door to his office. He sat the boy on the low stool where prisoners under interrogation sat. His clerk took pen and paper and began to write the date.

'How long were you waiting outside?'

'I came yesterday, but I didn't know which carriage was yours, and I was afraid. So I went away and slept by Les Halles and came back.'

It was warmer within the Châtelet than without, but the boy seemed to have caught cold. He shivered and rubbed his hands together, drawing his knees up to his chest on the stool, the way a cat curls up to stay warm. He was not an ugly child, La Reynie thought, but there was something about him that seemed less than human, as if the sin of his conception was written into his features. The priest's child.

'And why have you come to me?'

'Because my father is a sorcerer,' said the boy. 'I've lived in his house for years and I heard everything he did, everything he promised to the people who came to see him. He—' Michel broke off, breathing hard, as if he was fighting some emotion he had not expected to feel. 'He promised he would kill me, if I told. He said he'd send his demons to drag me into hell. But I hate him, and I know I'm bound for hell anyway, because of what I've seen and told no one.'

The clerk's pen scratched away on his paper. La Reynie listened to it, exhaustion casting a grey pall over the edges of his vision, which seemed to him like a shroud that was now clearing. Not from Lesage or La Chapelle or some nobleman's servant, but from this forsaken child he would hear the truth. The things he had seen and never told.

'Did you live in the priest's own house?' La Reynie asked. He had sent his men there, after the Baron de Cardonnoy's valet gave him the address. They had found it empty, and the valet had raved that the baron's widow had gone to warn the man.

'We did,' said Michel. 'He kept me hidden. When he fled, my mother was so frightened. She wanted to go and find him, she thinks he has a patron in Rouen. But she doesn't know his name. We're staying in a room now – we had the money for that.'

'What were Père Roblin's crimes?' La Reynie asked. The boy startled and looked up at him. It was as if he had been lost in his own thoughts, as if he had only just now begun to notice the reality of the room he was in. He looked towards the narrow window, where a strip of pallid light was filtering in, and then towards the glass lamp that flickered on La Reynie's desk. La Reynie could see that he was afraid.

'He cast spells. I heard him say that if you gave the devil the body of an unbaptised child, he'd give you anything you wanted in return. When my mother was with child, he'd take her away and she'd come back sick.' Michel looked up, not at La Reynie but into the high corners of the room, where the dust hung from the ceiling. 'It wasn't her fault. She was afraid of him too.'

It was the same black magic that Lesage had hinted at, in his moments of greatest candour. The black Masses performed with the bodies of infants, the profits that could be turned from the most secret and disgusting sins. With this, he could hang up Madame de Montespan herself, perhaps. And others still.

'Did your master ...' La Reynie found that he couldn't quite bring himself to say *father*. 'Did he know a man named Cardonnoy?'

Michel nodded. 'His carriage had a crest with a wild boar on it. He came to the church, but not for some time.'

'What was he seeking there?'

The boy was silent for a while, and La Reynie thought that now it would begin – the things he did not know, or wouldn't speak of, despite the rush he'd been in to get out the worst of his father's sins when he sat down on the prisoner's stool. But finally Michel looked up, not at the shadows playing over the ceiling, but at La Reynie's face.

'My mother told me that the baron was murdered, in front of his house, before my father fled Paris. His widow came to us, my mother and I, and she brought us money to leave the city, and she said that if I told anyone of my father's crimes, I'd be blamed for them, too.'

La Reynie stood up. There was the veil – it had fallen away from his eyes at last. The salonnières said that La Reynie looked like the devil, but the truth was that the devil most resembled one of them. The devil was a figure so innocent that he could creep up behind a man and cover his eyes without his victim realising that there was anything amiss. A widow weeping over her husband. La Reynie had been so quick to dismiss the evidence against her. Because it was the valet's word against hers. Lesage's garbled stories against hers. Because he had wanted to believe that there was one good wife in Paris.

'Have someone take this boy to a cell,' he told his clerk. 'Then draft a letter for the arrest of Madame de Cardonnoy, before she leaves for her estate. We'll finish this interview later.'

La Reynie went to the door, called the jailor himself. The man, when he came, took the boy Michel by the collar of his coat, but Michel wouldn't rise from his seat. His eyes followed La Reynie and he hugged his knees to his chest, looking not quite frightened, but as if he had had some wild hope that he was now seeing dissolve in the air before him. It wasn't a child's face.

'Take him out,' said La Reynie. 'Take him away.'

Chapter Eighteen

With the authority of the police force of Paris, I issue this warrant for the arrest of Marie Catherine la Jumelle, Baronne de Cardonnoy. In connection with the death of this lady's husband, it is alleged by one Henri Jabot, valet to the late Charles Claude Germont, Baron de Cardonnoy, that this lady, having attempted to seduce him into an act of adultery against her husband, asked him to procure poison from a renegade priest who her husband had also frequented. That she and her maid, Jeanne Durand, carried on affairs with various noblemen, in pursuit of the advancement of her husband at court. That having been refused by the valet on account of his great loyalty to her husband, he believes she resorted to the aid of a renegade priest, one Père Roblin, who had previously performed black magic for her and her husband. That he frequently heard this lady, in her private moments, utter treasonous sayings, as that His Majesty the King was ruled by women and had no authority beyond what Madame de Montespan accorded him.

Henri Jabot presents these revelations along with a full confession of his own crimes, most saliently that he attempted to exact revenge for his master's death on this lady and her children by administering a poison to a broth that he hoped would be served to them. His testimony is supported by that of La Chapelle, the poisoner and abortionist, who claims that Madame de Cardonnoy's lady's maid, the same Jeanne Durand, was her secret accomplice and sent her news of all the affairs of the house. It is supported also by Michel Desvalles, the child of the priest's servant woman, who claims that after her husband's death, the Baronne de Cardonnoy visited the priest's servants bringing payment – for what services he does not know – and that she threatened them against going to the police.

According to the due course of the law, these accusations will be proved through confrontation between the accused and the witnesses, or refuted during the course of the same. In her dealings with society, this lady has presented herself as a very virtuous and honourable woman, and if this is indeed the truth it will, with God's will, prevail.

Signed,

Gabriel Nicolas de la Reynie, Lieutenant General of Police

It was afternoon when they came. The sun was coming in golden through the western windows and Madame de Cardonnoy was in her study, half dressed despite the late hour. The dove-coloured dressing gown that she wore over her shift wasn't really a mourning garment, but was subdued enough to wear in her own house without causing comment. Even her hair was fixed in the simplest style. Jeanne would walk past the door, see her bent over the baron's desk, or daydreaming about something beyond the window, or stretching her legs as she paced the long wall with the bookshelf. The bells of the Church of Saint-Sulpice had just tolled half past four.

'Jeanne,' Madame called. 'Go down and see what those policemen in the yard are here for.'

'Madame.' She curtseyed.

But when she reached the servants' entrance to the courtyard she saw that the two police had the gate guard, Caspar, and were each holding one of his arms. He quickly gave up struggling – they walked him to a bench by the stables and he sat down with his head in his hands. Jeanne hovered on the threshold. The other servants were beginning now to filter out of the kitchen, forming a loose curious circle well back from the police, as if getting too close might bring bad luck.

'They've come for Madame.' This was Albert the kitchen boy, slipping out the door to gawk. Jeanne stepped back from the doorway.

'They're saying Henri poisoned the household.'

'Do they want *her* for poisoning?' The other servants were crowding around now.

'I knew the baron's death came too close on the heels of that argument ...'

Jeanne wavered there for a moment, leaning against the open door. Then ran. Up the stairs, pausing at the top. Her hands were shaking. She could feel the weight of Madame's hidden jewels dragging at the hem of her shift. She had carried the message. Now she had the money on her. They might hang her for stealing, at best. It was a cold, clear day, the yard smelled of smoke, she saw again the place de Grève, as it had been at La Voisin's execution, as it had been in her dreams. *God forgives all*, La Chapelle had said when she baptised Jeanne's child. But La Chapelle was now doomed, and so was Madame. And so was Jeanne.

Madame was not in the study. The window was open. Her cabinet, too, was empty. The chest in which she kept her clothes was open and her dresses were strewn over the floor. A column of numbness was creeping up from Jeanne's fingertips, and when she touched the lid of the chest, it fell shut with a noise that shook the room. She went back to the study. The smell of smoke crept in from the open window. She was doomed. She had only to wait. She couldn't seem to breathe.

Then the spirit reached out and touched her. A humming pressure that moved from her forehead to her chin, as if some fluttering thing had lighted for a moment on her eyes in order to open them. Jeanne was sure she had felt it. Two burning hands pressed against her cheeks. A kiss on her forehead, saying that she must not despair, that some force she could not see still wished her well.

Perhaps Laure had sent one of her spirits, to watch over her. Perhaps La Voisin had heard Jeanne's prayer for her and had repaid it from beyond the grave. Her legs still weak, Jeanne went to her alcove and took down her winter cloak. She could feel her heart beating, nauseatingly, against the skin of her throat. She tied the cloak around her shoulders. She walked down the stairs.

In the courtyard the servants had dispersed a little. Jeanne

328

passed two policemen coming in through the doorway, stepped demurely aside to let them pass.

'Where's your mistress?'

'She was in Monsieur's study a moment ago.'

And they walked on.

Another policeman had taken Caspar the guard's position at the gate. Jeanne walked towards him as if in a dream, feeling the length of the courtyard stretch, horribly, the air grow thick as if it, too, was in league with the law and wanted to solidify into a prison of ice and keep her there. Laure's familiar spirit did not return to take her hand. It had done what was in its power to do.

'You there, servant girl! What's your name?'

Jeanne stopped. She was almost at the gate. She felt the weight of the gold dragging her shoulders down, making her stoop, cower. She thought her feet might sink six inches into the mud.

'My name is Anne,' she said. 'I'm the children's nursemaid.'

She thought Caspar, still seated slack as a bag of flour on the bench by the stable, must be close enough to hear her lie. But he didn't raise his head.

'What errand are you on? Don't you know your mistress is being arrested?'

'Of course, Monsieur, only I'm meant to go to the doctor. For the children.' That numbness again, as if her head was enveloped in a bubble of glass, through which it was impossible to breathe. 'They say – it's rumoured that their illness was the result of poison. The doctor didn't recognise it at first, and now the little ones have been sent to Cardonnoy. I have to fetch a remedy for them.'

'Jeanne Durand, the baronne's girl – where is she?'

Jeanne swallowed. 'I don't know, Monsieur. She was with the baronne a moment ago.'

Now the policeman raised his head and looked over her shoulder. When Jeanne turned, she saw that one of his companions was returning from the house.

'There's no sign of her,' he called towards the man guarding the gate. Jeanne's policeman wavered, waved her off, took a few steps away from his post to go and confer with his friend.

'May I go, Monsieur?' Her voice came from her throat like a frayed thread.

'Wait here.' And then he turned his back on her and bent his head close to his companion's, conferring.

She was three steps from the gate. On the road, carriages were passing with creaking wheels over the cobblestones. A man sat on the corner and sharpened knives. If the policemen didn't look up at her now. Jeanne swallowed. She walked out through the gate and onto the street.

Across the street, ducking between carriages. Some coachman cursed at her. If only he didn't shout too loudly, if only he didn't attract the attention of the men still talking together at Hôtel Cardonnoy, still expecting that she would be waiting obediently when they turned back. It was hard not to run down the street once she'd reached the other side. She held her back straight as if she had nothing to fear. She was carrying a small fortune in her dress, she could feel Madame's gold swinging with her skirts and bruising her shins. The thread that tied her to the hôtel spooled out longer and longer. Then she turned the corner, onto the boulevard near the church, and in the rush and call of traffic she knew that they hadn't caught her, that they wouldn't bring her back, that she was free.

If Madame had returned to see it, she might have told the story this way: once there was a servant girl whose family was too poor to keep her. They sent her to a grand house, where she raked the ashes and slept in the soot of the kitchen. It was hard work, but she earned enough to eat, and although she was poor, she was clever and prudent. It didn't matter whether she was beautiful. Girls like her were saved by their wits, not their beauty.

This girl also had a fairy godmother, who was sometimes a fine lady dressed in silk, but more often she was an old woman with wrinkled hands and a shop full of herbs and potions and other things that she kept in the dark and showed only to those she trusted with her secrets. When the owner of the grand house was cruel to the girl, her godmother gave her a silk dress and led her away in disguise, and found her a new place in a new house, where she could be safe while she waited for her fortune to find her.

Finally the time came when the godmother was on her death-bed. She called the girl to her, and kissed her forehead, and told her, 'Take the dress that I gave you and shake out the skirts.'

The girl obeyed and found that when she did so, gold and jewels fell from her petticoats.

'The time has come for me to leave you, my darling,' said the fairy godmother. 'Take my wand, and my magic dress, and go seek your own fortune.'

And she did.

Jeanne of no name, who owned one dress worth far more than its weight in gold. Who owned a prudent tongue and the power to walk in a crowd and become invisible. Who served no master. Who owned herself.

Madame de Cardonnoy had been at the window. She had seen Caspar shake his head and gesture at the police, she had seen the roughness with which they had taken him by the arm and she had known that everything was over. The letter Victoire had sent her, with its vague warning, still lay on her desk. She threw it into the fire. She threw off her dressing gown. She crossed the hallway in her shift and her stays, opened the chest of clothes that would be put away while she travelled to Cardonnoy. Her gowns were not made to be put on quickly, or by oneself. But there under her hands was the mantua of blue silk that she had worn, and loved, before her husband's death had dressed her in black. It was as loose and simple as air. It whispered down over her head like an embrace. Her jewels were – but the shift would be too difficult, and it was packed away with the chests for Cardonnoy. She put a string of pearls around her neck.

Down the stairs, down the hall to the servants' quarters. She careened into Agnès the chambermaid emerging from the kitchen, and the woman stepped back as if she'd seen a ghost, taking in Madame's dress, her shoes still unbuttoned on her feet.

'Madame, the police—'

'Quiet. I know. Stand back.' To her surprise, the words left her mouth with as much authority as if she knew nothing at all that was wrong.

And Agnès stayed and stared while Marie Catherine struggled with the window sash at the end of the hallway and forced it open, and then lowered herself, tumbling, out of it and into the alley at the back of the hôtel. She was among the blind backs of the grand houses whose courtyards faced out to the boulevard. Here was the refuse pile heaped and stinking with kitchen scraps; the spotted stray dog hunting for old bones or carrot peels, which started up and barked at her when she fell; the broken-down remains of an old carriage wheel leaning against the wall. Marie Catherine had sunk deep in the mud when she jumped, and now there was dirt caked on her stockings up to the ankles, and on her blue skirt where she'd stumbled and fallen down on one knee. She picked her way, leaning on the wall. She had to stop and button her shoes. The mud sucked at them as if it was trying to hold her back by the ankles, as if it wanted her to be barefoot as well as terrified.

She was hurrying as much as she could in the mud. When she reached the mouth of the alley she heard a call and there, leaning out of the back window, was the policeman. She gathered up her skirts to run and saw him tumble out of the window in a hurry, and then she saw nothing of him because her feet were under her and she was running along the crowded boulevard, hearing only his shout of frustration at the resisting mud, and the barking of the dog, and his order that she should turn round and surrender.

She barged past a tinker on the street, barely registered his silhouette hung with knives before she was past him. Pedestrians were turning to stare, but the policeman's shouts had not yet reached them and they had no reason to stop her. Once she had turned the corner of the boulevard she was a running woman in a fine dress stained with mud, a curiosity.

'Do you need help, Madame?' said a man in servants' livery, and she shook off his hands, looking around for a carriage, an open doorway, a break in the traffic of horses along the boulevard – anywhere that she could disappear.

In a moment they would find her.

She'd forgotten even to take a cloak against the cold, had not the least coin on her to step into a rented fiacre and hope to evade her pursuers that way. And, unused to running, she was out of breath. The cold air entered her lungs like the blow of a club.

She bent over, gasping, outside the Church of Saint-Sulpice, and as she paused her eyes fell on the guardian statue of Moses with his tablets and she ran up the stairs under his gaze. And entered through the church's open door. She could hear the shouting at the corner, coming towards her.

Once inside, the high arch of the ceiling stopped her for a moment. Her eyes travelled up to Christ on the cross, and beyond him the scaffolding rising above the unfinished north end. Afternoon light streamed through the windows, and the windows turned it blue and red and gold. She could see the patterns of the glass as they fell over her hands and arms.

She might have knelt down then before the image of Christ and allowed them to find her, repentant before God. And perhaps the law too would have forgiven her and allowed her to live out her sentence merely in a convent, with hard work and earnest remorse. But her feet took her not to the altar and the cross, but to the Lady Chapel, where the eyes of the Mother of God watched her from her solitude. And there at the front of the chapel, below Our Lady of the Old Tableware's sorrowful face, she wrapped the skirt of her mantua tightly around herself and crawled under a pew.

There were footsteps coming up the nave. She could see nothing except the flagstones and the hem of Mary's silver mantle on her pedestal. The chapel's windows cast a pattern of light like a rain of coloured spears on the floor.

'Is the lackey sure he saw her climb the steps?'

'What about the chapels?'

'No, look, son of a whore, the scaffolding at the north end is open. She's gone out through it.'

'We'll lose her!'

The voices echoed under the vaulted ceiling and reached her as if carried by the wind from far away. There was a fringe of dust clinging to the underside of the pew, and Marie Catherine covered her mouth and nose with her sleeve to try and keep from breathing. She could hear the soft sound of the policeman's shoes coming down the nave, not hurrying despite his companion's quick footsteps, pausing, searching. She was certain that he must be standing in the aisle of the Lady Chapel, that if she turned her head she would see his muddied shoes, that the best thing, after all, would be to crawl out from her hiding place and surrender, in order to avoid the long despair of waiting.

She heard no more footsteps. After some time had passed she

333

began to count, quickly, in time with her panicky breaths. Finally she reached a number high enough that she knew the policemen could no longer be searching the church. They must only have glanced into each chapel after all.

Still she felt powerless to rise or crawl out from under the pew. There was no more strength in her body. She was trembling, not only from the cold seeping up from the flagstones and through the diaphanous silk of her mantua, but from the knowledge that she had walked out of her own life and was travelling, now, through a future in which she was already doomed. That she was a fugitive must be as clear to any man or woman on the street as the colour of her dress, the mud on her shoes, her face streaked with dust from lying on the unswept floor in terror. She was certain. She drew her knees up to her chest. Her hands trembled. Now, if anyone came into the chapel, they'd see at once the blue edge of her skirt where it flowed out from under the pew.

Slowly the light changed. The setting sun sent a ray of green light reaching up the pedestal on which the image of the Virgin stood. It kissed the hem of her skirt and then began to retreat, slowly, like a lover who knows he must leave by sunset, but can't bear to hurry. Marie Catherine shifted, enough that she could rest her head on her arm. At Cardonnoy, Sophie and Nicolas would be having their supper. Plain food, the kind that was good for children: bread and butter and a little meat. Jam from the fruit of the Cardonnoy orchards. The sun would be going down over those fields, too, not yet ploughed for spring, and the story Anne told them before bed would be a simple one, something she'd heard from her grandmother, her real grandmother, with nothing in it that could frighten them, although Nicolas would plead for an ogre and then hide his face beneath the blankets if one appeared.

After a long time in that reverie, after she had climbed the stairs to the children's room and kissed each sleeping forehead, after she had sat by the side of the bed and listened to their sleeping breathing for what was, perhaps, the last time, she went out into the long, dark hallway of her imagination, towards a room in the house whose name she didn't know. She might have been walking back into her own childhood, crying out in the dark for someone to come and help her out of the bad dream from which she had only just awakened. She opened the door to her mother's room, and it led back into the church.

Now she could feel the eyes of the Virgin upon her, as she had at her husband's funeral. It had gone dark in the chapel. Our Lady of the Old Tableware was only an idea of a silhouette in the shadows. Marie Catherine's breath began to come quickly, as if she were running again. It was as if she had spent those hours beneath the pew as a dead woman and, waking, her body wanted to remember what it had been to be alive. She jumped, again, from the window, and her legs twitched as if she had asked them to run. She remembered lying naked in her marriage bed on the night of her wedding until the sunrise began to show at the window, wondering in almost the same way what was to become of her. Or the pleasure of dancing at Versailles, when she had seemed to float somewhere outside herself, a sprite beneath the heavy weight of her court dress. Or the danger in her blood, in the moment when she and Victoire had first kissed.

The Virgin did not move. She only watched, unbending. But her gaze was as real as if she had gathered up her silver skirts and stepped down from her column.

Slowly Marie Catherine's body grew warm again. She'd been crying into the sleeve of her dress, her free hand balled into a fist and pressed against her mouth to contain the sound of weeping. She dried her face. She was strong enough, then, to get up on her knees beneath the Virgin's gaze and crawl from under the pew. She was strong enough, also, to stand. The chapel and the church beyond it were dark. She could feel her heartbeat across her temples, as if her living blood was expanding beyond what her body could contain. The mud on her stockings and shoes had dried, and it flaked off as she walked down the nave. The Virgin's gaze on her back was not motherly, was not merciful or sad, was like a bolt of lightning running from the crown of her head to her heels, which told her that she was back from the dead. Beneath her mantua her skin was gooseflesh, the down between her breasts was standing on end with the cold.

Outside, the street lamps had been lit. She half expected someone to recognise her, but the men and women still on the road were busy about their own errands and didn't pause to look at her in the gloom, while she was walking and wondering at the bright haloes wavering around each lantern. She could not remember a time when she'd last been out like this, not in a carriage but out in the open, where the full strangeness of the night air could touch her. A traiteur wheeling a cart full of pastries, his path lit by one of the wandering lantern men, barked at her. She jumped out of his way and found herself laughing, a little hysterically. Her hair was coming loose, so she pulled it down and combed her fingers through it as she walked. A group of women in drab bonnets – were they washerwomen? – looked at her and then glanced quickly away. What must she look like, in her midnight-coloured silk, her lips turning blue with cold, her hair falling around her shoulders and wild and tangled as a wolf woman's? Like a public woman who'd had a misadventure, perhaps. Like a woman whose misfortune had made her invisible, who no honest person would want to look in the eye. Who was free to walk alone at night.

Though she had never travelled in Paris alone before, she knew the city well and she knew her path. Not to the grand houses where they might expect her, not to the house of Victoire, whose family might turn her away or hold her there; or Madame de Fontet, whose salon was already racked with scandal; or Mademoiselle de Scudéry, who might have known what it meant to die for love and yet knew nothing of Marie Catherine. It was a modest street. The lamps were shining like warm stars along the second storey. It was a long walk, and by the time she'd reached her destination the darkness was deep and quiet and menacing, and she was shaking with cold.

She had never seen the city in such a way. She had thought she lived in it, that it was her city, her theatres, her street signs, her men selling oranges and oysters on the corners, but she had been like a guest escorted by the lady of the house, who passes through and knows nothing about its secrets. She had never walked through the mud and heard the sound of a horse's hooves on the street, the crack of the coachman's whip as he passed her by.

She had felt no shame on her way, although some men huddled outside a public house whistled and laughed when she passed, but on this street she bowed her head, she tried to hide the wildness of her dress and her hair. Quickly she hurried to Lavoie's door, and sheltered herself in the doorway and knocked.

The door opened a crack, then all the way. She pushed the painter aside with the palm of her hand.

'Let me in quickly. I have to get off the street.'

'What on earth?' Lavoie stood back from her a bit, as if she were a wild animal that might harm him. 'Did you come here on foot?'

'Lock the door.'

'Your lips are blue.'

'Will you help me, Monsieur? I promise it will be the last favour I ask.'

She could not travel as she was. She would never make it the miles to Cardonnoy, to the children, the house with its stores, the carriage that could take her away across the border to freedom. She should have been afraid that the painter would refuse to help her, but she was beyond fear. The night itself would have to part to make her invisible. And she felt that he was, like her, one who had been very close to death and had escaped.

Lavoie bolted the door, as she'd asked, then put a hand over his eyes.

'You're lucky you weren't robbed on the way here.'

'The police came to my hôtel. I fled in such a hurry I've almost nothing to steal.'

'God have mercy. Will they come here?'

Marie Catherine shook her head.

'I don't think so. My plan worked too well, in fact – Monsieur de la Reynie became convinced that my household had already *been* poisoned, and he's arrested my husband's valet.' She pulled her hair into a loop over her shoulder, thinking. Lavoie was silent. 'I don't know what Henri told them. It can't have been very close to the truth.'

'What do you want, Madame?' the painter said.

'Different clothes. A man's costume, one I can ride in.'

'And in exchange?'

She took the string of pearls from her pocket.

'I am afraid you may need to wait a little while before selling them.'

Lavoie crossed his arms over his chest and didn't take the jewellery. 'Tell me this, Madame. How did your husband die?'

She looked at him. 'Something happened to me tonight,

337

Monsieur Lavoie. When I fled my house, I hid in the Lady Chapel at the Church of Saint-Sulpice and I was so frightened that I would have stayed there until the sun rose and the custodian discovered me. But the Virgin – she spoke to me, I think, with her eyes. And she gave me the strength to come here.'

There were tears starting in her eyes as she spoke. Lavoie thought that he could see her face glowing with a new power. If she had turned to stone and then back into flesh before him, he would have believed it. He would have believed that when she spoke, jewels fell from her mouth.

'The Lady helped you?'

'It's true. I'll forgive you if you laugh. I don't understand it, either.'

'I believe it,' he said. And he did.

'I have to ride to Cardonnoy tonight. My children are there. Will you help me?'

Lavoie stripped off the jacket he was wearing.

'I'll ask you to take this coat, if you would be so kind. I use the one with the gold buttons to see clients in. I'd rather not part with it.'

Madame de Cardonnoy laughed. 'Oh, but I'm going to leave you my dress. Or don't you think it would suit you?'

She lifted the mantua over her head by its hem and let it fall to the ground, where it drifted and released the scent of irises, powder and Parisian mud. Then Madame de Cardonnoy was standing in his hall in her white shift and her stays.

'Will you help me with my laces?'

She turned away from him, and he put his hands on her waist. She held her hair away from her back while he loosened her laces, and he could see the fine hairs standing up on the back of her neck, the beauty mark on her left shoulder. Her body was still cold from the wind outside. He could feel the chill in her laces, breathing off her skin, how she slowly became warm again as she stood there.

'I didn't kill him,' she said. 'I might have dreamed about it, sometimes, but I never knew until after it had happened. There is someone – someone I will not name. Who felt sympathy for my situation and decided, when I was in trouble with my husband, that night he came to your house, that his death might be the means to end that trouble.'

'Why didn't you go to this friend's house and ask for his help again, Madame?'

Madame de Cardonnoy looked over her shoulder at him. Lavoie was trying to touch her clothes without touching her. Her skin had the same smell as her dress – irises, sweat. Her hair seemed be to made up of minuscule strands of lightning. Her stays had left red marks on her shoulders and back, visible above the collar of her shift.

'Because she isn't the master of her own house, Monsieur, and so I might have been turned away.' Her stays dropped to the floor. She turned and met Lavoie's eyes. 'And because I can't bear to see her punished, even knowing that she is guilty.'

This time Lavoie thought she was telling the truth. But if she was lying, he found it no longer mattered to him.

'I'll get you a shirt.'

He took a shirt and trousers from his trunk and went back to help her into them. Holding the clothes out to her as she stood in her loose shift, with his own white shirt untucked and hanging down from his shoulders, he had the sudden impression of looking at a mirror image of himself, that she was transforming, as he watched her pull on his trousers, into a man, into Lavoie himself, into a kind of creature that he hadn't seen before. He could have kissed her, but the idea was more dangerous now than it had been when she was still a baronne. He turned away as she pulled the shift over her head.

'Does the coat hide my figure well enough?'

When he looked at her again, she was a clean-shaven man with wild long hair down to her hips, dressed in Lavoie's shabbiest coat.

'I think it does. Keep it buttoned. We'll have to cut your hair.'

She twisted a long strand between her fingers.

'What a shame. I haven't cut it since I was a girl.'

He took the scissors from his workshop and came back to her.

'Lean forward. You don't want it sticking to your coat.'

Long vines of hair fell around her face as she bent. He cut it just below her shoulders, and the trimmed strands fell to the floor in thick snakes. When she straightened, she was standing in a wheat-coloured circle that, in the lamplight, still looked alive.

'The soles are worn nearly through on my old boots. They'll be too large as well. We'll have to stuff them with rags.'

And he went about the business of finding them, wrapping her feet in old cloth, lacing the shoes up as she braced her foot on his knee.

'And maybe a scarf, to cover your face.'

'Thank you, Monsieur.' She spoke gravely, having left her bright silks and her bright hair in a pile on his floor and become a man. 'May I borrow enough to hire a horse?'

He laughed. 'It will come out of the purse that you paid me.'

'I'll owe you another debt.'

'Will you write to me, when you've gone where you're going? Without signing your name, perhaps. I want to know the end of the story.'

'Of course. Thank you, truly.' There was a passing shadow in the smile she gave him, and he knew that she wouldn't ask him why he had helped her.

Outside he hailed a passing fiacre, to take them to a place where she might hire a horse. He'd wanted to speak for her, to avoid the risk that her accent and the pitch of her voice might spoil her disguise, but she had him wait alone until she came out of the stables with the horse and saddle. He didn't know what she'd said inside. The night was lonely. He'd pulled his own scarf over his face so that the few passers-by would see only his eyes gleaming beneath the brim of his hat.

Perhaps he ought not to have promised himself that he would make no future mistakes.

Finally she came out leading a red mare, whose breath made clouds of fog in the cold air.

'Perhaps we'll meet again some day,' Madame de Cardonnoy said, once he'd held out his hands to help boost her into the horse's saddle. It was a restless creature, shifting back and forth inside its enveloping scent of hay and sweat and mud. He had to look up at her face now, and she could have been any rider out late on the street.

'Perhaps,' he said. 'God speed.'

'God keep you, Monsieur Lavoie.'

And horse and rider became, with a cry, one creature, which swiftly outpaced the circle of the street lamps and merged like a shadow with the night.

Epilogue

———

To Victoire Rose, Mademoiselle de Conti,

This letter is unsigned, but you will know who writes it. It may even be that several souls are ahead of you and me, and as it travels from a foreign country it may arrive to you with the seal broken, on the suspicion that it contains some unpleasantness, or else matters of great secrecy.

Alas, I can offer nothing of the kind! I am afraid there has been much foolishness in Paris of late. And while the news from home tells me that this scandal of poisons is much discredited, and many of those who were imprisoned have gone free, I can only confess that I was too faint-hearted to face those months in prison, even in the full confidence that the truth would, at last, come out and clear me of all wrongdoing. Perhaps some day I will be able to clear my name of the accusations against me and return to Paris, where my heart will always dwell. For now, my children are learning to speak Spanish. Perhaps you might, too, if one day you tire of life among the women of the court.

I do still receive my share of rumour here, and what they say is that there have been many changes there – that La Montespan, who I so admired, is out of favour and has been replaced by a stricter lady, who disapproves of the pastimes that were once in vogue. Perhaps you have adjusted to the new fashion, but somehow, my darling, I cannot picture you in that sombre company.

As you know, and must always know, I feel for you such bonds of friendship that I am incapable of putting them to paper. And I have so many adventures to relate that if I set them down here you might believe that they, too, were a tale of the kind I tell my children. One day I will tell them to you, in person. Perhaps you will sit across from me, at this table, and take an orange from this china bowl. It will be summer, as it is now, and the sound of the roaming bees will filter through from the garden, along with just this kind of golden sunlight, which is thicker and more like burnished metal than any light in Paris. I can feel your presence so clearly that I know, without a doubt, that it will come to pass.

Some day we will sit together, and I will ask you the fates of our common friends, and news from the salons, and how you have spent your days, on all the days that we have been apart. On that day you will also have the full story of my adventures, but that will have to wait. And so here is a fairy story, of the kind I tell my children. Forgive me – I know that such things are no longer the fashion in Paris, because they mislead the foolish, and disturb the natural order, and make the lowly into the kings of creation. Or so I've read, from pens wiser than mine. Nevertheless, I'm foolish. I find I don't want to give up my mother's stories, fashionable or no.

Once upon a time there was an ogre's wife. She lived with him for many years, and perhaps it was not such a bad marriage. The ogre was rich. He gave his wife silk embroidered by the hands of his hundred servant girls, and soft white gloves from Italy, and Chinese vases with painted birds so lifelike that the porcelain, when one touched it, was as soft as feathers. He gave her a grand house, servants, a bedroom that he only occasionally entered. He let her read what she liked, and didn't mind whose company she kept. He would, perhaps, have been a fine husband, if only he had not been an ogre.

Was she a good wife? She was, I think, a wife like many others. Sometimes she saw the monster to whom she was married sitting across from her at the dinner table and she wished that her life had been otherwise, that she had had the purity or the obstinacy to go to her death in her girlhood rather than accept her marriage, or to flee to the wilderness and live in rags, eating berries and the bark of trees.

There came a night when the ogre left, and when dawn broke,

his wife heard his carriage returning. Then instead of going to her mirror to dress for the day, she went to her window and opened it.

Before the window, she took off her silk shoes.

She took off her dress.

She cleaned the paint from her face.

She cut off her hair, and it fell to the floor in sheaves like ripe wheat.

She took off her skin of the ogre's wife, her breasts, her smile, her softness, until if anyone had been looking at her, they would not have known if she was a woman or a man.

She stepped up onto the windowsill.

And though sense and prior experience say that she should fall to her death, it does not happen that way. The air, alive, lifts her up. And she flies to her freedom.

And so, Victoire, I wish it for you.

A note on the text

―――

While this novel is a work of fiction, many of the events and people who inspired it are real. The story is set during the now-infamous Affair of the Poisons, which unrolled as follows:

In 1677 a woman named Marie Bosse was arrested after bragging at a dinner party that she had sold poison or 'inheritance powders' to people who wanted to rid themselves of relatives or spouses. After her arrest, she began to talk to police about the network of fortune-tellers who sold love potions, predicted the future and did various party tricks for prominent men and women in Paris and the royal court. Many of these fortune-tellers, La Bosse alleged, also sold poison. The police force, led by Gabriel Nicolas de la Reynie, began to make arrests of the fortune-tellers La Bosse had accused. In a move that was almost unprecedented, they also arrested two women from the nobility, Madame de Poulaillon and Madame de Léféron. Both were closely related to members of the French parliament, both accused of attempting to poison their husbands.

At this point it was widely believed that the women's connections in the parliament would protect them from punishment. Their proximity to the Nobility of the Robe (as parliament members were termed) raised serious concerns about parliament's ability to enforce the law equally. And while the police were gathering evidence for their trials, more and more fortune-tellers were being arrested, and soon Paris was embroiled in a full-blown panic about poison.

Perhaps the first fortune-tellers believed that the law would deal with them more lightly if they could help to arrest others who had committed worse crimes than they had. Under questioning, many of these women (and the occasional man) claimed that they had sold poisons or provided other illicit services, including abortions, black Masses and ritual sacrifice of infants, to very highly placed members of the nobility, including the Comtesse de Soissons, the Comtesse de Roure, the Duchesse de Bouillon, the Maréchal de Luxembourg and the king's own mistress, Madame de Montespan. The French legal system, at the time, relied on confrontations between witness and accused. Many of the fortune-tellers, when confronted with the men and women to whom they claimed to have sold poisons, failed to recognise them. There is little doubt that many of the accusations were inflated.

Nevertheless, Gabriel Nicolas de la Reynie, the Lieutenant General of Police, the Marquis de Louvois, Minister of War, and King Louis himself remained greatly concerned about the supposed epidemic of poisoners making a living in Paris. At this time there was no reliable way to test whether someone had died of poison, and as a result many recent deaths of prominent people that had originally been considered the product of natural illnesses began to look suspect. Many of the fortune-tellers alleged that they had served extremely powerful clients, and these stories – perhaps originally intended to persuade the police to tread warily – only fuelled the atmosphere of paranoia around the investigation.

Another circumstance that stoked the panic over poisons was the arrest of the man who styled himself the Magician Lesage. A former lover of La Voisin, another central figure in the poisoning cases, Lesage had many noble contacts, having been an occasional guest at Madame de Fontet's salon, where he performed magic tricks (and some occasional blackmail) on her guests. What was remarkable about Lesage's arrest was that he was discovered to have been previously sentenced, in 1668, to forced labour in perpetuity on a French war galley operating in the Mediterranean. Such galleys were run by slave labour, and were in general a sentence to a slow death. The fact that Lesage had been sent to one and had returned alive was so unheard of that it prompted investigators to believe he must have a powerful protector. Lesage himself encouraged this belief, suggesting that he had performed magic for the king's mistress, Madame de Montespan.

He was not the only person under investigation to believe that this claim might save him, but in practice his strategy backfired. As King Louis heard more and more about the allegations against his mistress (few of which were particularly persuasive – Lesage frequently confused dates and individuals, gave wildly contradictory testimony and argued with other key witnesses, and La Voisin recanted much of her testimony to her confessor shortly before her execution), he decided that to bring the investigation into the light of day would be to call into question his own judgement and reputation. He distanced himself from Madame de Montespan at court and ordered that the witnesses who had been most vocal in claiming to deal with her should not be brought to trial. Instead, Lesage, La Voisin's daughter and other key witnesses were imprisoned without trial in the fortress at Vincennes, where they were to be kept in solitary confinement for the rest of their lives.

This paranoia about poison, love potions and undue influence on the king also helped to fuel a backlash against the generation of salon women who had rejected the subordination of women in society, called for the participation of women in political life and argued that marriage for women, as it stood in France, was no better than slavery. Women like Mademoiselle de Scudéry and Mademoiselle de Montpensier, a cousin of King Louis XIV, wrote about utopian communities of women and also rejected marriage in their personal lives, often with the help of their great wealth. A younger generation of women followed them. While they were influential in shaping the French novel tradition, today many of them have fallen into obscurity.

Of these writers, the most direct influence on this novel is perhaps Madame d'Aulnoy, whose given name – like the hero of this book – was Marie Catherine. Married to a much older man at the age of fifteen, she fled France in 1669, after a plot to rid herself of her forced marriage by accusing her husband of treason backfired and left her wanted by the police. It's not known exactly where she spent the next decade, although she would later suggest that she had served her country as a spy in Spain, in return for which she won the right to return to Paris. At any rate, by the 1690s she had established her own salon in Paris, where she would become embroiled in a scandal over accusations that she had helped a younger friend, Madame Ticquet, pay a servant to shoot her own abusive husband with a pistol. These charges did not stick. Madame d'Aulnoy was never prosecuted, but after her friend's execution she retired from her social life for many years.

She published twelve books during her life, and was famous not only for her fairy tales (a term that she is said to have invented), but also for her historical novels and her (heavily fictionalised) memoirs.

A second source of inspiration is Henriette Julie de Castelnau Murat. Like Madame d'Aulnoy, she was a writer of fairy tales and memoir, whose life was embroiled in scandal. Her bestselling pseudo-memoir, *Mémoires de Madame la Comtesse de M—*, caused a stir in Paris for its depiction of marital abuse and for its narrator's frank depictions of sexual relationships with other women. Madame la Comtesse de M— was an occasional cross-dresser, who charmed women and shocked men by her skilled impersonation of the 'other' sex. The name 'Cardonnoy' is borrowed from a character in this book. Accusations of lesbianism followed Murat for years, forcing her to flee Paris and leading to her eventual exile in the Château de Loches, from which she made an unsuccessful escape attempt disguised as a man. It has been suggested that she is the inspiration for Perrault's fairy tale 'The Counterfeit Marquise', whose heroes are a pair of cross-dressed lovers who find, over the course of the story, a number of reasons to prefer living as a gender different from their assigned one, and end the tale happily united and living as they choose.

Much of the text that concerns real people and events is as close to accurate as I could make it. Reports of La Voisin's last hours depict her singing bawdy songs in her prison cell after her final meal, and that she fought her captors as they lifted her out of the prison cart to be tied to the stake where she would be burned. Her death was a public event in Paris, and writers such as Madame de Sévigné report lining up in the streets to watch her pass by on the way to her death.

In some places, however, I have taken liberties with the historical record. Our Lady of the Old Tableware was indeed the nickname of the Madonna at the Church of Saint-Sulpice (and she really was cast out of old spoons), but the statue was not installed there until sometime after 1680, when this novel takes place. Charlotte Marie de Lorraine, daughter of Madame de Chevreuse, the famous intriguer (and Victoire's mother in this text), in fact died young, without children (she had wanted to marry Armand de Bourbon, Prince de Conti – here Victoire's father – but Conti was dissuaded by his brother's disapproval). The fortune-teller La Chapelle and her daughter are inventions, as is the renegade priest Père Roblin, although many details are taken from reports about other people involved in the Affair of the Poisons. In particular the description of the baptism performed over a pre-term fetus is something that was originally said of La Voisin. As for the magic itself, the incantation *AGLA*, which Jeanne learns from La Chapelle and uses at La Voisin's execution, is a very old charm of obscure origin, said to offer protection against fire and fever.

The story of the symbolic 'hanging' of a naughty girl in a convent school, part of Madame de Cardonnoy's history here, is inspired by an incident in the life of the Maréchale de Beauvau, and the storytelling game played in Madame de Fontet's salon is based on a similar game described in Charlotte Rose de Caumont de La Force's novel *Jeux d'esprit* (Games of Wit). Mademoiselle de La Force is a writer of the same generation as Madame d'Aulnoy and the Comtesse de Murat. She wrote *Jeux d'esprit* while in exile from Paris, at the abbey of Gercy-en-Brie. And, of course, Madame d'Aulnoy herself is said, perhaps apocryphally, to have escaped the police who came to arrest her for treason by jumping out a back window of her house and taking refuge under the bier in a nearby church. I hope she would approve of this borrowing from her story, but I cannot guarantee it.

Authors whose works have been indispensable in the research for this book include Joan DeJean, Cissie Fairchilds, Carolyn Lougée, Anne Somerset, Lynn Wood Mollenauer and Marina Warner, among other scholarly writers. This book also could not exist without the work of Madame d'Aulnoy and her contemporaries, who served as both inspiration and guide.

Acknowledgements

——

Many people have been involved in the creation of this novel, and while I doubt that it's possible to thank them all thoroughly, I'm going to make some attempt here.

The seed that became *The Disenchantment* came to me during a graduate seminar on fairy tales taught by the wonderful Edward Carey, who briefly mentioned the work of Madame D'Aulnoy and inspired me to look up her life and work. It was because of this class that I realized that I had already read her fairy tales as a child, and the strange and sometimes disturbing stories that I had assumed were simply traditional tales that had been passed down through many tellers in fact had a particular author, who had her own particular life.

Many thanks to the faculty of the New Writers Project in Austin for their support as I began writing this book. In particular: Edward Carey was a generous and enthusiastic early reader, Elizabeth McCracken was a source of kindness and support, and Roger Reeves was very understanding about the fact that I kept missing assignments for his class because I was trying to write a novel. Thanks also to the New Writers Project itself, for giving me time outside of the real world to focus on my writing, and to my classmates at NWP and the Michener Center, for giving me a community of people equally invested in art.

My agent, Anna Stein, was a tireless advocate for this book through a long and rocky submission process. I want to thank her for believing in this novel and standing by it. Thanks also to Lucy

Morris and Sabhbh Curran, who enthusiastically represented the novel in the UK.

Thank you to Leonora Craig Cohen, my editor at Serpent's Tail, who took an early chance on this novel and whose insightful editorial advice made *The Disenchantment* a much better book. Thanks also to Shelley Wanger at Pantheon, and to everyone at Pantheon and Serpent's Tail who worked behind the scenes to make sure that this book came together in the real world.

Thank you to the booksellers at Malvern Books circa 2018–2020, in particular Stephanie Goehring, who helped me think of titles and let me cry on her balcony when things weren't going well. And thank you to Leti Bueno, Julie Poole, Fernando Flores, and Schandra Madha, for sharing your art and your encouragement and your book recommendations during the years we worked together.

Thank you to my parents, Elizabeth Spires and Madison Bell, for your advice and support, and for surrounding me with books.

Finally: thank you Valerie Stivers, brilliant and indispensable first reader, who stayed with this project from my first emails about the idea to the final draft. I couldn't ask for a more generous friend. And thank you Wade Redfearn, who saw me through the hard bits, and, I hope, will continue to share the good ones.